Lucy King spent her adolescence lost in the glamorous and exciting world of Mills & Boon when she really ought to have been paying attention to her teachers. But, as she couldn't live in a dream world for ever, she eventually acquired a degree in languages and an eclectic collection of jobs. After a decade in southwest Spain, Lucy now lives with her young family in Wiltshire, England. When not writing, or trying to think up new and innovative things to do with mince, she spends her time reading, failing to finish cryptic crosswords and dreaming of the golden beaches of Andalusia.

Melanie Milburne read her first Mills & Boon novel at the age of seventeen, in between studying for her final exams. After completing a master's degree in education she decided to write a novel, and thus her career as a romance author was born. Melanie is an ambassador for the Australian Childhood Foundation and a keen dog-lover and trainer. She enjoys long walks in the Tasmanian bush. In 2015 Melanie won the HOLT Medallion, a prestigious award honouring outstanding literary talent.

D0320476

Discover more at millsandboon.co.uk.

THE BILLIONAIRE WITHOUT RULES

LUCY KING

A CONTRACT FOR HIS RUNAWAY BRIDE

MELANIE MILBURNE

MILLS & BOON

First Published in Great Britain 2021
by Mills & Boon, an imprint of HarperCollins*Publishers* Ltd,
1 London Bridge Street, London, SE1 9GF

www.harpercollins.co.uk

HarperCollins*Publishers*
1st Floor, Watermarque Building,
Ringsend Road, Dublin 4, Ireland

The Billionaire without Rules © 2021 Lucy King

A Contract for His Runaway Bride © 2021 Melanie Milburne

ISBN: 978-0-263-28272-6

11/21

THE BILLIONAIRE
WITHOUT RULES

LUCY KING

MILLS & BOON

For the parents at my kids' school, who I shamelessly mined for info on many topics that pop up in this trilogy—from adoption to post-partum psychosis to how to get stranded in Venice to floating Caribbean bars to hacking into Times Square billboards. You know who you are!

CHAPTER ONE

'GREAT, ALEX, YOU'RE BACK. You'll never *guess* who's waiting for you in your office.'

Having shrugged off her jacket, Alexandra Osborne hung it and her bag on the coat stand and levelled her assistant and sometime associate, Becky, a look. She was in no mood for games. Or, right now, for Becky's perennially bubbly enthusiasm. She'd just ended yet another call informing her that a promising lead had gone absolutely nowhere and her gloom and anxiety were at an all-time high.

The absence of progress with regard to the case she'd been working on for the past eight months was both teeth-grindingly maddening and desperately worrying.

Last December, after discovering an adoption certificate while going through his late father's papers, billionaire hotelier Finn Calvert had hired her to look into the circumstances surrounding his birth.

Despite there being exceptionally little to go on, Alex had nevertheless eventually managed to trace the trail to a derelict orphanage on the Argentina-Bolivia border, where paperwork had been found in a battered filing cabinet that suggested her client was one of a set of triplets. Finn had immediately instructed her to locate

the others, and she'd poured considerable time and resources into it, to depressingly little avail.

One of Finn's long-lost brothers, Rico Rossi, had
turned up six weeks ago, in possession of a letter that
gave details of the agency his parents had used to adopt
him thirty-one years before and, with the injection of
new information, Alex had had high hopes. But the
agency no longer existed and so far no one had been
able to locate any archived records.

After a promising start she'd hit brick wall after brick
wall. Even the interview that Finn and Rico had recently
recorded, in which they'd entreated their third missing
brother to come forward, had produced no genuine leads.
It had been eight long months of precious little development and she desperately needed a breakthrough, because she could *not* allow this assignment to fail.

For one thing, she had a one hundred per cent success
rate that her pride would not have ruined. For another,
Finn Calvert was a hugely powerful and influential client
who, upon successful completion of the mission, would
be paying her not only the remaining half of her fee but
a staggeringly generous bonus. His recommendation
would open doors and his money would pay off debts
that were astronomical since London premises and the
kit required to do the job didn't come cheap.

Both, she'd realised when she'd accepted the case,
would accelerate her expansion plans by around four
years and all those people who should have supported
and encouraged her when young, but who'd instead believed she'd never amount to anything and hadn't hesitated to tell her so, would be laughing on the other side
of their face far sooner than she'd anticipated. Her success would be cemented and she'd have proved once and
for all that she'd conquered not only the environmen-

tal obstacles she'd encountered growing up but also the fear that with one false move she could end up like her deadbeat family.

There was no way she'd *ever* pass up the chance of that, so she'd thrown everything at it, even going so far as to turn down other lucrative work in order to devote all her time and resources to this one job, which would secure her future and realise her dreams.

She'd assumed it would be as straightforward as other similar cases had been, that she'd easily track down the adoption paperwork and from there find the answers Finn craved. She'd never expected to be in this position all these months later. Having to admit the possibility of defeat and being forced to move on to different assignments in order to stave off the threat of looming bankruptcy made her want to throw up.

'Who is it?' she asked, mustering up a smile while reminding herself that it wasn't Becky's fault progress was so slow and she had no right to take her worry or her bad mood out on her assistant.

'Only our missing triplet.'

Alex stopped in her tracks, the smile on her face freezing, the floor beneath her feet tilting for a second. All her churning thoughts skidded to a halt and her head spun. Seriously? The man she'd invested so much time and so many resources in looking for was here? Actually here? After so much disappointment and despair, it was hard to believe.

'You're joking.'

'I am *not*,' said Becky, practically bouncing on her seat. 'His name is Max Kentala and he arrived about five minutes ago.'

'Oh, my God.'

'I *know*. I was literally just about to text you.'

'I was beginning to give up hope of ever finding him,' said Alex, a rush of relief colliding with the shock still zinging around her system.

'Well, technically he found you,' her assistant pointed out in an unhelpful way that Alex decided to ignore.

'He must have seen the interview,' she said instead, her pulse racing as she tidied her shirt and smoothed her skirt.

'Ah, so that I *don't* know,' Becky admitted ruefully. 'I tried to find out how he came to be here but he was incredibly tight-lipped. Impossible to read. And, to be honest, it was kind of hard to concentrate. He's every bit as gorgeous as his brothers, maybe even more so, although I don't see how that's possible, given they're identical give or take a haircut and the odd scar or two. We're talking not just hot, but *scorchio*,' she added, her expression turning dreamy as she gazed into the distance. 'I think it's the eyes. That blue... They kind of make you forget your own name... I wonder if he's single...'

'Becky.'

Her assistant snapped back and pulled herself together. 'Yes, sorry,' she said with a grin as she fanned her face. 'Phew. Anyway, I showed him into your office and made him a coffee. I'll move around the appointments you have.'

'Thanks.'

'Brace yourself.'

Used to Becky's dramatic tendencies—not entirely helpful in a trainee private investigator, she had to acknowledge—Alex ignored the warning and headed for her office, the adrenaline powering along her veins kicking her heart rate up to a gallop.

Max Kentala's hotness was irrelevant, as was his marital status. That he was actually here was very definitely not. On the contrary, depending on what information he brought with him, it could be exactly the breakthrough she was so desperate for. It could be game-changing. If there was the remotest possibility her current predicament could be reversed, she'd grab it with both hands and never let go, so she needed all her wits about her.

Taking a deep breath to calm the shock, relief and anticipation crashing around inside her, Alex pulled her shoulders back, fixed a smile to her face and opened the door to her office.

'Good morning,' she said, her gaze instantly landing on the tall figure standing at her window with his back to her.

A broad back, she couldn't help noticing as her stomach clenched in a most peculiar way. Excellent shoulders. A trim waist, lean hips and long, long legs. Then he turned and his eyes met hers and it was as if time had stopped all over again. The air rushed from her lungs and goose bumps broke out all over her skin. And was it her imagination or had someone turned the heating on?

Well, Becky certainly hadn't been exaggerating, she thought dazedly as she struggled to get a grip on the extraordinarily intense impact of his gaze. *Scorchio* was an understatement. Max Kentala was quite possibly the best-looking man she'd ever come across in her thirty-three years. Not that she particularly went for the dishevelled surfer look. In fact, when she *did* date these days—which was rarely since firstly she tended to work unaccommodating hours and secondly, with a cheating ex-husband in her background, she had a whole host of issues to do with self-esteem and trust—her dates were generally clean-cut and tidy.

This man's unkempt dark hair was far too long for her liking and he was badly in need of a shave. His faded jeans had seen better days, although they did cling rather lovingly to his powerful thighs, and the untucked white shirt he wore so well had clearly never been introduced to an iron.

No. He wasn't her type. So why her stomach was flipping and her mouth had dried was a mystery. Maybe it was the eyes. They really were arrestingly compelling. Blue and deep and enigmatic, they looked as if they held a wealth of secrets—catnip to someone whose job it was to uncover hidden truths—and she wanted to dive right in.

And to do more than that, if she was being honest. She wanted to run her fingers through his hair while she pressed up against what looked like a very solid chest. She wanted to plaster her mouth to his and urge him to address the sudden throbbing ache between her thighs.

It was bizarre.

Alarming.

And deeply, horrifyingly inappropriate.

This man was part of her biggest, most important assignment. He might well hold key information about it. It wouldn't do to forget that. However attractive she found him—and there seemed little point in denying she did—she could not afford to get distracted. So what if he wore no wedding ring? That meant nothing. And as for the throbbing, what was that all about? It hadn't been that long since she'd had sex, had it? A year? Eighteen months at most? And why was she even thinking about sex?

Snapping free from the grip of the fierce, very unwelcome desire burning through her and putting an end to all thoughts of sex, Alex gave herself a mental shake and pulled herself together.

'Alex Osborne,' she said crisply, stepping forwards into the room and holding out her hand for him to shake.

He gave her a brief smile and took it. 'Max Kentala,' he replied, a faint American accent tingeing his deep voice which, to her irritation, sent shivers rippling up and down her spine despite her resolve to withstand his appeal.

'I'm very pleased to meet you, Mr Kentala.'

'Call me Max.'

'Alex,' she said, withdrawing her hand from his and resisting the urge to shake it free of the electricity the contact had sent zapping along her fingers and up her arm. 'Do take a seat.'

'Thank you.'

See, she told herself as she walked round to her side of the desk and smoothly lowered herself into her chair. Cool and professional. That was what she was. Not all hot and quivery and ridiculous. Still, it was good to be able to stop having to rely on her strangely wobbly knees and sit down.

'I take it you saw the interview,' she said, sounding remarkably composed considering she still felt as if she'd been thumped in the solar plexus with a flaming torch.

He gave a brief nod. 'I did.'

'When?'

'Yesterday.'

And now he was here. He hadn't wasted time. Finn was going to be thrilled. 'Can I also assume you'd like me to set up a meeting with your brothers?'

'I set up my own,' he drawled. 'I've just come from seeing them.'

Oh? That wasn't right. In the interview, Rico had told anyone with any information to contact *her*. He and his brother protected their privacy and she'd known the interview would generate more false leads than real ones, as had turned out to be the case. So what did Max think he was doing, bypassing her carefully laid plans like that?

'You were meant to go through me,' she said with a frown, not liking the idea of a potential loose cannon entering the arena one little bit. 'Those were the instructions.'

'But I don't follow instructions,' he said with an easy smile that, annoyingly, melted her stomach. 'I make my own arrangements.'

Not on this, he didn't, she thought darkly, pulling herself together and ignoring the dazzling effect of his smile. Uncovering the truth surrounding the triplets' birth and adoption was *her* assignment. Right from the start, Finn had given her total autonomy. She'd set the rules and established procedure. She was in charge. However glad she was that Max had shown up like this, he had no business meddling. She was not having her entire future potentially snatched away from her simply because he'd decided he was going to do things his way. Her blood chilled at the very thought of it.

Despite the laid-back look and the casual smile, the set of his jaw and the glint of steel in his eye suggested he wasn't to be underestimated, but she wasn't to be underestimated either. She'd given up a steady career in the police force to set up her own private investigating business. She'd taken a huge risk and she'd worked insanely hard. She'd come far but she had a lot further to go. Her dreams were of vital importance. They drove her every day to do more and be better. At one point, as a confused and miserable teenager, they'd been all she had. They were not going to be dashed by anyone or anything. Almost as bad, if everything went to pot and she lost her business, she could well find herself having to re-join the police, where she'd run the risk of bumping into her ex, who'd been a fellow officer and was still in the force, she'd last heard, and no one wanted that.

She needed Finn's good opinion and she needed his money, which meant *she* had to be the one to find the answers. So from here on in the man lounging so casually in the chair on the other side of her desk, looking as if he owned the place when he absolutely didn't, would be toeing *her* line.

'Why are you here, Max? What do you want?'

Sitting back and eyeing the coolly smiling woman in front of him with deceptive self-control, Max could think of a thing or two.

For a start he wanted her to carry on saying his name in that low husky voice, preferably breathing it right into his ear while he unbuttoned her silky-looking shirt and peeled it off her. Then she could shimmy out of the fitted skirt she had on, hop onto the desk and beckon him close. In an ideal world, she'd tug off the band tying her hair back and shake out the shiny dark brown mass while giving him a sultry encouraging smile. It was the lamest of clichés, he knew, but hey, this was his fantasy, albeit an unexpected one when he generally didn't go for the smart, tidy professional type.

But he had to admit she was stunning. Beneath the fringe she had wide light blue eyes surrounded by thick dark lashes, high defined cheekbones and a full, very kissable mouth he was finding it hard to keep his gaze off.

The minute he'd turned from the window and laid eyes on her the attraction had hit. He'd felt it in the instant tightening of his muscles, the savage kick of his pulse and the rush of blood south. The intensity of his response, striking with the force of a tsunami, had made him inwardly reel. He couldn't recall the last time he'd been so affected by a woman he'd only just met. Ever?

Not that any of that mattered. The startling impact of her clear blue gaze on him, which he'd felt like a blow to the gut and the effects of which still lingered, was irrelevant. As were her trim curves. He wasn't here for a quick, steamy office encounter, even if in an alternative universe Alex Osborne *had* decided to throw caution to the wind and do as he'd imagined.

He was here because of recent events.

Fifteen hours ago, all Max had known of family was a difficult, demanding mother who lived in New York with husband number four and a father who, after the bitterest of divorces, had abandoned him to move to Los Angeles, where he'd remained determinedly on his own for a decade until he'd suffered a fatal heart attack seven years ago.

To Max, up to the age of fourteen, family had meant endless disapproval and cold stony silences. It had meant constantly walking on eggshells in an environment devoid of true affection and respect, and bending over backwards to please yet failing every single time. It had meant a devastating awareness of not being good enough and living with the relentless guilt at never meeting expectations, all of which worsened after his mom had been granted sole custody of him in the wake of the divorce.

Since then it had involved coming to terms with having had a father who'd essentially abandoned him for good and managing a tricky, complex relationship with a woman who was needy, self-absorbed, hypersensitive and controlling. But he'd done it because she was his mother. Or so he'd always believed.

Then he'd seen the interview given by two men who were the spitting image of him apart from a few superficial differences, and what he'd understood of family had blown wide apart.

Max had been in his study at his home in the Caribbean when the video had been forwarded to him by his assistant with an instruction to click on it immediately. As a cyber security expert with global businesses and governments among his clients he never clicked on anything immediately, regardless of whence the recommendation came. When, at Audrey's insistence, he eventually had, yesterday afternoon, the shock had knocked the air from his lungs and drained the blood from his brain.

Pulse pounding, he'd watched the twenty-minute footage of Finn Calvert and Rico Rossi a further three times, pausing each time on the final frame in which Rico looked straight down the lens and urged their missing triplet to get in touch. He'd stared into the eyes that were identical to his own, the dizziness and chaos intensifying to the point he'd thought he was going to pass out, before gradually calming down enough to allow logic and process to take over.

In urgent need of answers to the myriad questions ricocheting around his head, he'd put in a quick, rare call to his mother, who'd confirmed that he had indeed been adopted from an orphanage in Argentina thirty-odd years ago and had then proceeded to try and make it all about her. Stunned and shaken to the core, Max had hung up before saying something he might regret, and had then hacked into the systems that would disclose as much information as there was about these men who could quite possibly be brothers he'd never known anything about.

Having established, among other things, that Finn and Rico shared his date of birth and were both currently in London, he'd booked himself onto the next flight. On landing this morning, he'd sent them each a message with details of where he'd be and when, should they be interested in meeting up.

Two hours later, the three of them were sitting in the bar of Finn's flagship central London hotel, swapping coffee for vintage champagne in celebration of having found each other after so long apart and firing questions back and forth, as if trying to cram half a lifetime into half a morning.

'Here's to long-lost brothers,' Finn said with a smile that could have been one of Max's own as he lifted his glass and tilted it towards his brothers.

'*Saluti,*' said Rico, following suit.

'Cheers.' Max tapped his glass against the other two and then knocked back half the contents, the fizz of the bubbles sliding down his throat adding fuel to the maelstrom of thoughts and emotions churning around inside him.

With the revelation that he was adopted, so many questions that had dogged him all his life had suddenly been answered. Such as how on earth he could ever be related to either of his parents, people who bore no re-semblance to him either physically or in temperament. Such as why he'd always felt an outsider. Why nothing he'd ever done was good enough. Why his father hadn't fought harder for him in the divorce. The strange yet deep-rooted sense that he wasn't where he was meant to be and he wasn't with the people he was meant to be with.

These were the people he was meant to be with, he knew with a certainty that he felt in his bones. His brothers. Who shared his dislike of milk and his skill with numbers, and who, like him, had had encounters of varying degrees with the law. Who he instantly got and who instantly got him. With whom he felt more of a connection in half an hour than he ever had with either of his so-called parents.

'Any idea how we ended up in an Argentinian orphanage or why we were separated?' Finn asked him and he snapped back.

'None,' he said with a quick frown.

'Nor me,' said Rico.

'Alex has hit a brick wall.'

Max raised his eyebrows. 'Alex?'

'Alex Osborne,' Finn clarified. 'The private investigator I hired. Progress has been virtually non-existent lately, which has been frustrating as hell, but then there isn't a whole lot to go on.'

'How about I look into it?'

'Could you?' asked Rico.

'Sure,' said Max.

Having just come to the end of one contract and the next starting in a month, he had time. He also had resources. But, more than that, he needed to get to the bottom of this. He'd spent the last decade believing he knew exactly who he was and where he was going. The news of his adoption had turned his world on its head. It might have answered many of the questions and cleared up much of the confusion he'd always had, but it had also thrown up even more. Who was he? Where had he come from? How had he ended up where he was? And that was just the start of it. The need for an explanation, for information, burned inside him like the hottest of fires.

'I have an extensive data network and know where to look, so that's a start.'

'It would be good to get to the truth,' Rico said. 'Whatever it may be. Anything you need, let me know.'

'Here are Alex's details,' said Finn, handing him a card.

'Leave it with me,' Max replied.

And now here he was, his pulse beating a fraction faster than usual and his senses oddly heightened as Alex continued to look at him while waiting expectantly and somewhat challengingly for him to tell her what he was doing here.

'I want everything you have on the case,' he said, ignoring the awareness and the buzz of desire firing his nerve-endings, and focusing on what was important.

Her eyebrows arched, her chin lifted and the temperature in the room seemed to drop thirty degrees. 'Why?'

Because he'd worked hard to get over the traumas of his childhood and as proof had spent the last decade living in at least some degree of peace. Because yesterday that peace had been shattered and he badly needed it back. Because he valued his brothers' kinship, wanted their approval and their acceptance—old habits died hard, clearly—and would do anything to get it. And, frankly, because she hadn't exactly got very far.

'Because I'll be taking things from here.'

CHAPTER TWO

WHAT? NO. NO WAY.

Alex stared at the man oozing arrogance from the other side of her desk, the outrage shooting through her doing a very good job of obliterating the inconvenient attraction still fizzing along her veins.

She'd been absolutely right to consider him a loose cannon with the potential to wreak havoc. He clearly posed a greater danger to her plans than she'd originally assumed. But if he thought he could swan in here and take over the investigation, he could think again. She was *not* meekly handing him what little she had just because he demanded it. This was *her* assignment, and her reputation and her *future* were at stake.

'I'm afraid that's not possible,' she said coolly.

He arched an eyebrow and languidly hooked the ankle of one leg over the knee of his other. 'Why not?'

'The information is confidential and Finn's my client,' she said, determinedly not glancing down and following the movement, 'not you.'

'If I needed my brother's authority to act on his behalf—which I don't—I'd have it. He was the one who gave me your card.'

Right. OK. So why had Finn done that? she wondered, her confidence suddenly plummeting for a moment. Was he unhappy with progress? Had he instructed Max to effectively fire her? She couldn't let that happen. She was *not* going to fail and have her dreams crumble to dust.

'You are not taking over this case,' she said, stiffening her spine and lifting her chin. Why would he even want to? She was the expert here.

'How long have you been working on it?' he asked with a deceptive yet pointed mildness that instantly put her hackles up.

'A while,' she said, wincing a little on the inside.

'Eight months, I heard.'

'It's complicated.'

'I don't doubt it.'

'Information is scarce.'

'Then you're looking in the wrong place.'

Really. She'd put in hundreds of hours of research and mined every database available. She'd built a network of operatives in Argentina and hired subcontractors of whom she asked a lot without enquiring too closely how they were going to get it. She'd looked everywhere there was to look. 'And what would you know of it?'

'Information is my business.'

'What do you do?'

'Cyber security.'

'And?'

'I have access to resources I imagine you can only dream about.'

The faint patronising tone to his words grated on her nerves even as his easy smile was setting off tiny fireworks in the pit of her stomach, and yet she couldn't help thinking, what kind of resources? Legal ones? Illegal ones? *Better* ones?

'But I have people on the ground and they're working hard.'

'They wouldn't be too difficult to find,' he countered with a casual shrug that didn't fool her for a moment because she could hear the implication and the threat behind his words. He didn't need her cooperation. There was nothing stopping him going ahead and embarking on an investigation of his own. He was just here to get a head start.

But if he *did* strike out on his own, *and* got the answers the brothers wanted, then where would she be? Bankrupt. Redundant. The failure that everyone had always expected her to be. And she wasn't having that. Max might not be the type to give up—that steely glint of his had sharpened, she saw—but then neither was she. Whether or not he had the authority to fire her or intended to do so, she was not backing down on this.

Quite apart from her professional pride and the monumental fee she was due to collect, she liked Finn and Rico. She wanted to track down every existing snippet of information about the birth and adoption of these triplets, piece together the story and give them the answers they craved. She'd started the job. She had every intention of finishing it, however hard. It was *her* responsibility, and that was all there was to it.

'I've pursued every avenue there is, Max,' she said, keeping the cool she'd developed over a decade in the police.

'I very much doubt that.'

Behind a casual smile of her own she gritted her teeth. She wasn't incompetent, despite what he clearly thought. 'I've looked into personnel records and bank accounts,' she said with what she considered to be impressive calm under very trying circumstances. 'I've examined company records and sent off freedom of information requests. Every lead has come to nothing. The orphanage

was run by nuns and closed around twenty years ago.
Everyone who worked there has either died or disappeared. There was a massive earthquake shortly after it
shut and all the archives that were held in the town hall
basement were destroyed. It was only by some fluke that
your birth certificates, which were found at the actual
orphanage, survived.

'The adoption agency, which was owned by a holding
company, was originally registered in Switzerland,' she
continued. 'It also closed down years ago. I've found no
records relating to either entity. The only possible link
I've established between the agency and the orphanage is three large payments that arrived in the orphanage's bank account around the time of your adoption,
originally made in Swiss francs before being converted
to pesos. Freedom of information requests have come
back with nothing. Swiss banking secrecy at the time
hasn't helped. The only end that isn't yet a completely
dead one is a possible future DNA match. I sent Finn's
off for analysis four months ago.'

'With no result to date.'

'No.'

'It's a long shot.'

At the dismissive tone of his voice, she bristled. 'I
am aware of that.'

He regarded her for one long moment, then arched
one dark eyebrow. 'So is that it?'

'I've done everything I can.'

'Except for one thing.'

Her brows snapped together. 'What?'

'Actually going there.'

She stared at him. 'To Argentina?'

'No. The moon. Yes, Argentina.'

OK, so, no, she hadn't done that, she had to admit

while choosing to ignore Max's derision. She'd considered it, of course, in the beginning. At great length. But she'd come to the conclusion that it could well have been an expensive wild goose chase, which, if she'd found nothing, would have eaten substantially into the budget and, worse, damaged Finn's confidence in her. So she'd stayed in London and opted for a network of local operatives instead to do the legwork on the ground, and told herself that she could always go herself as a last resort.

And that was the point she was at now, she realised with a start. She'd reached the end of the road with what she could do from London. She was all out of options, bar one.

'That was my next plan,' she said smoothly, as if it always had been, while frantically trying to remember how much she had left to spend on her credit card. 'I'll be looking at flights this afternoon.'

'No need.'

The glimmer of triumph that lit the depths of his eyes sent a double jolt of alarm and wariness shooting through her that had nothing to do with the precarious state of her finances. 'Why not?'

'I'm leaving for La Posada first thing in the morning.'

What? *What?* She guessed he'd learned about the abandoned town in which the ruins of the orphanage were located from his brothers but God, he'd worked fast. 'First thing in the morning?' she echoed, reeling.

'Rico's put his plane at my disposal. I'm making use of it. So I'd like everything you have on the case, Alex. Names. Dates. Places. Everything. And I'd like it now.'

In the face of Max's implacability and the realisation that he'd done it again, Alex's brain swirled with frustrated panic and angry confusion. How dared he go behind her back like this? These decisions weren't his to make. Why wouldn't he play by the rules? Did he think they didn't apply to him? Was he really that arrogant?

Whatever his motivation, whatever his methods, whether or not he even *knew* about the rules, he'd backed her into a corner, she realised, a cold sweat breaking out all over her skin. Her least favourite place to be. She had no room for manoeuvre. She was trapped.

But she wasn't going down without a fight. In fact, she thought grimly as a plan to get out of the tight spot he'd put her in began to form in her head, she wasn't going down at all. However high-handed, disagreeable and infuriating Max might be, she was not letting him go off on his own and potentially snatching a victory that was rightfully hers from the jaws of defeat. He was unpredictable and a threat to everything she'd worked so hard for. He needed to be reined in and controlled. How would she be able to do that if he went to Argentina all on his own? And how was she supposed to know what he found, if by some miracle he did indeed find anything, if she stayed in London?

There was only one thing for it. She was going to have to go with him. It needn't be so bad. He might even turn out to be useful. She hadn't yet established what he knew about the past. He might hold crucial information. And what were these resources of his that she could only dream about? She'd be a fool not to enquire about those.

'All right,' she said, setting her jaw and snapping her shoulders back in preparation for battle. 'On one condition.'

'Which is?'

'I go with you.'

In response to Alex's demand, every fibre of Max's being stiffened with resistance. No. Absolutely not. What she was suggesting amounted to teaming up and working together. He did neither. He operated alone. He always had. He'd grown up an only child and had learned at a very early age that he could rely on no one but himself. Now, the highly confidential nature of his work meant he trusted few. Collaboration was something he'd never sought and certainly never wanted.

That Alex's performance wasn't as flawed as he'd previously assumed didn't matter. He didn't want her involvement. Or anyone else's, for that matter. The quest for the truth was going to be intensely personal. He needed to get a grip on the resentment and anger that the call with his mother had sparked and now simmered inside him. He had to find out whether he'd ever been wanted by someone, whether he'd ever mattered. Netting all the emotions that had escaped Pandora's Box and shoving the lid back on them could get messy and no one else needed to be along for that particular ride.

'Absolutely not,' he said curtly.

Her jaw set and her shoulders snapped back. 'Absolutely yes,' she countered with steel in her voice.

'I work alone.'

'Not any more.'

'I'll match what Finn's paying you.'

'It's not just about the money.'

'I find that hard to believe. The bonus he's offered you is exorbitant.'

He could practically hear the grind of her teeth. 'My fee structure is none of your business. If you want me to share with you the information I have,' she said bluntly, 'I go with you. Otherwise you get nothing. That's my offer, Max. Take it or leave it.'

The resolve flashing in the depths of her eyes and the jut of her chin told him she was adamant. That she wasn't going to back down. Which was absolutely fine. He didn't appreciate ultimatums. He'd had enough of those growing up and just the thought of them made his chest tighten and his stomach turn. So he'd leave it. He had no doubt he could get what Alex had already found. He'd never come up against a problem he hadn't been able to solve, family conundrums aside. He didn't need her. He didn't want her—or anyone—in his space and never had. His world was his and his alone, and he'd be far more flexible and focused if he pursued the mystery surrounding his birth on his own.

And yet...

He had to admit he found Alex's fiery determination intriguing. Why was this assignment so important to her? he couldn't help wondering. Why not just take the money and move on? What was she fighting for?

And that wasn't all that was intriguing, he thought, his pulse hammering hard as he let his gaze roam over her beautiful animated face. Her prickliness was having an incredibly intense and wholly unexpected effect on him. It was electrifying his nerve-endings and firing energy along his veins. Lust was drumming through him with a power he'd never have imagined when she was the polar opposite of what he usually found attractive.

She was so defensive, so rigidly uptight. It ought to have been a turn-off, yet he badly wanted to ruffle those sleek feathers of hers, to butt up against her defences. What would it take to break them down? How far would he have to push?

She wasn't immune to him, despite her attempts to hide it. He'd caught the flash of heat in her eyes the moment they'd met. He'd noted the flush on her cheeks before she'd pulled herself together and coolly held out her hand for him to take. She was as attracted to him as he was to her. How satisfying would it be to unravel her until she was in his arms, begging him to undo her completely? How explosive would they be together?

The urge to find the answers to all the questions rocketing around his head thrummed through him. The need to hear her panting his name while writhing beneath him was like a drug thumping in his blood. So what if, instead of rejecting her proposal, he accepted it? What if he did actually allow her to accompany him to Argentina in return for everything she knew? There was little point in replicating the work she'd already done. It would only waste time. Undoubtedly, two heads would be more efficient than one.

And while they investigated he could work on unbending her. They'd have to find *something* to occupy themselves in the downtime, and seducing her would provide a welcome distraction from the more unsettling aspects of learning he was adopted.

Alex need pose no threat to his goals. He had no interest in sharing with her anything other than hours of outstanding pleasure. He wasn't cut out for anything more. He'd witnessed first-hand how thankless and manipulative relationships could be and the unhappiness they wrought. He neither believed in nor wanted commitment. He needed that kind of toxicity in his life like a hole in the head, which was why the women he dated never lasted long. The shorter the encounter, the less chance there was of disappointment and dashed expectations, of having to accommodate the feelings that someone else might develop, of becoming trapped and gradually losing the control and power to end things when he chose. Alex, despite the novel intensity of the chemistry that arced between them, would be no exception. All he had to do was persuade her to agree to a fling. It wouldn't take long. He gave it thirty-six hours tops.

'All right,' he said with a slow smile as heady anticipation at the thought of embarking on a short, sharp, scorchingly hot affair with her began to surge through him. 'London City Airport. Jet Centre. Seven a.m. Don't be late.'

Alex, with her better-to-be-twenty-minutes-early-than-twenty-seconds-late approach to timekeeping, wasn't the one who was late.

After Max had left her office she'd thrown herself into rearranging her diary, issuing instructions to Becky—who'd agreed to hold the fort—and then going home to pack. After a couple of hours of research followed by an annoyingly restless night, she'd risen at dawn and arrived at the airport with her customary two hours to spare. She'd taken immediate advantage of the private jet lounge to fortify herself with coffee while going over the notes she'd made last night and the list of questions she wanted to ask him.

Of the man himself there'd been no sign, and there still wasn't. She supposed that one of the advantages of this kind of travel was not being beholden to a schedule but she'd been told the time of their slot for take-off and in her opinion he was cutting it extremely fine.

However, that was OK with her. The more time she had to brace herself against the frustratingly edgy effect he had on her, the better. To her despair, he'd been on her mind pretty much constantly from the moment he'd walked out of her office. His scent—spicy, masculine, delicious—had lingered on the air. The intensity with which he'd looked at her was singed into her memory and she could still feel a strange low-level sort of excitement buzzing in her stomach.

Last night's dreams hadn't helped. Every time she dropped off, there he was in her office, smouldering away at her, only when he eventually rose, it wasn't to leave. It was to pull her up off her chair and spread her across her desk, and then proceed to take her to heaven and back, thoroughly and at great length. She'd lost count of the number of times she'd jerked awake, hot and breathless and aching, with the sheets twisted around her.

Why Max should evoke this strong a response in her when his brothers—so similar in looks—left her completely unmoved she had no idea. He might be mind-blowingly attractive but he still wasn't her type and she still didn't trust him one inch.

That last smile he'd given her—slow, seductive and devastating—was particularly worrying. It spoke of secrets, of being privy to information that she wasn't, and if there was one thing she detested it was secrets. Her ex-husband had had many—mainly of the female kind—and when she'd found them out they'd crucified and humiliated her.

What did Max have to be secretive about? she wondered, draining her fourth coffee of the morning and setting the delicate porcelain cup in its matching saucer. She wished she knew. She had the disturbing feeling that it somehow involved her.

Not that what lay behind the smile really mattered, of course. She wasn't interested in any of his secrets, even less in ones in which she might feature. She was here to work, nothing more. And she could easily manage the strangely wild effect he might still have on her. As a thirty-three-year-old divorcee with a career like hers, she was no naïve innocent. She'd seen things, met all manner of people and been through her fair share of struggles. She'd become adept at hiding her true feelings beneath an ultra-unflappable surface and she saw no reason why that shouldn't be the case now.

It wasn't as if Max was similarly affected by her. It had been very clear that he wasn't interested in anything other than the information in her possession, which was a huge relief. The assignment was far too important to risk screwing up by either or both of them getting distracted.

As soon as he showed up she'd make a start by finding out what he knew. Assuming he was still intending to actually catch this flight, of course. Personally, she didn't know how he could operate like this. What was the point in stipulating a time to meet if you were going to completely disregard it? His website had revealed that he consulted for clients across the globe. Apparently he was some kind of computer genius, in constant and high demand. Truly, the mind boggled.

On the other hand, she had first-hand experience of how deceiving appearances could be. Look at the nonchalant way she'd sauntered into the private jet lounge as if she travelled this way all the time when she very much did not. Take her work, which proved it on a daily basis. Or her ex-husband, who'd been impossibly charming, handsome and initially doting, yet had also been a lying, cheating rat. And then there were her parents and siblings, whose willingness to break the law was staggering, who lied, cheated and stole as naturally as breathing while managing to maintain a perpetual air of injured innocence.

Just because Max chose to live life on the edge timewise, it didn't automatically mean he was reckless and rash. And just because he'd turned up in her office dishevelled and wearing crumpled clothes, it didn't mean he couldn't don a suit if necessary.

He'd certainly look good in one, she thought absently, staring out of the window and remembering the breadth of his shoulders and the leanness of his frame. A navy one, perhaps, to match the colour of his irises. With a crisp pale blue shirt open at the collar to reveal a wedge of chest. Although, frankly, he'd probably look better in nothing at all…

No.

This wasn't on. She had to get a grip. She really did. How Max conducted his affairs was none of her business. His attitude towards timekeeping and clothing was entirely up to him.

The reason her reaction to him yesterday had been so strong was because the shock and the relief at the breakthrough he presented, followed by the fear and panic that he intended to take the case over and cut her out of it, had momentarily rocked her foundations. Now, however, those foundations were solid, unassailable. Now she was prepared. She had to be.

Breathing deeply to ease the tension in her muscles and calm the annoying anticipation nevertheless rippling through her, Alex reached into her bag for her laptop. She flipped it open and determinedly concentrated on her emails, but barely two minutes passed before she felt the air around her somehow shifting. A prickly awareness washed over her skin and a pulse kicked in the pit of her stomach. Stiffening her spine and reminding herself of just how impregnable she was, she abandoned her emails and glanced up.

Max stood at the entrance to the cabin, being accosted by one of the two cabin crew on board, who seemed overly concerned with a desire to assist him. Alex mentally rolled her eyes, because how much help could an athletically built six foot plus man of thirty-one really need? But to her relief—because, quite honestly, she could do without having to sit through thirteen hours of simpering and flirting—he responded to the inviting smile with a quick, impersonal one of his own and a minute shake of his head.

'Good morning,' he said, heading towards her and tossing his bag on one of the two soft leather sofas the colour of buttercream.

'Good morning,' she replied, reminding herself sternly that it was of no concern to her how he responded to an invitation. 'So much for not being late.'

At her arch tone, his dark eyebrows lifted. 'Am I?'

Well, no. Technically, he wasn't, but for some reason it felt as though a swarm of bees had made their home in her stomach and as a result everything had the potential to make her tetchy. 'You're cutting it extremely fine.'

'Let me guess, you've been here for hours.'

'There's no need to sound quite so dismissive,' she said, bristling at the hint of mockery she could hear in his voice. Admittedly, she might have been a tad overzealous with the two hours, but then she'd only ever flown economy. She'd never had the luxury of private jet travel, with its gorgeous gleaming walnut surfaces, cream carpet and real china. 'Punctuality isn't a bad thing.'

'Punctuality is the thief of time.'

Hmm. 'I think you'll find it's procrastination that's the thief of time. But, either way, mine is equally valuable as anyone else's.'

'I don't disagree. But, seeing as how I'm not late, the point is moot.'

Max folded his large frame into the seat opposite hers

and buckled up. His knee bumped against hers and the jolt it sent rocketing through her could have powered a city for a week.

What was wrong with her? she wondered dazedly, her heart pounding like a jack hammer. One brief contact and she'd felt it like lightning. She was normally so steady and calm. Where was her composure? What was going on? Why him? Why now? More importantly, when was the air-con going to kick in? It was so hot in here.

Thankfully, Max was looking at his phone so couldn't have noticed her absurd overreaction to his touch. A minute later the engines started up and they were taxiing away from the terminal. As the plane accelerated down the runway, Alex gave herself a severe talking to. Her response to the gorgeous man once again sitting opposite her was not only ridiculous, it was wholly unacceptable. She had to pull herself together. How was she going to make any headway on the case if she couldn't work alongside him without turning into a quivering wreck? That wasn't who she was. And how dangerous would it be if he knew how strongly he affected her? That she'd been dreaming about him? He might well consider her unprofessional as well as incompetent and neither was the case.

By the time they were in the air, the slow steady breaths she'd been taking to calm her raging pulse and the pep talk had had the desired effect and she'd got herself under enough control to at least make a start on the questions she'd compiled.

'How was lunch?' she asked, determined to focus on the job. When she'd spoken to Finn yesterday afternoon to subtly check that he wasn't intending to fire her, he'd mentioned the three brothers planned to spend the afternoon together. Max must have told him that they were teaming up and heading to Argentina together because Finn had also, bizarrely and unexpectedly, requested she take care of him. She knew that both he and Rico had had issues concerning their adoption but, quite honestly, in Max, she'd never met a man who needed taking care of less.

He glanced up and, despite all her efforts to control her response to him, her breath nevertheless caught at the bright intensity of his gaze. 'Good,' he said. 'Lengthy. It stretched into dinner and then drinks. I ended up crashing in one of Finn's hotel rooms.'

'You must have had a lot to catch up on.'

'We did,' he said with the quick flash of a genuine blinding smile.

'Do you get on well?' she asked, determined not to be dazzled.

'Exceptionally.'

He was obviously over the moon at having found his siblings, Alex thought, unable to prevent a dart of envy lancing through her. She had three siblings, with whom she had absolutely nothing in common other than a mutual lack of understanding.

How great would it be to have or find just one person who instinctively got you? Who unconditionally accepted you for who you were, warts and all. Not even her ex had truly understood her, or genuinely loved her for herself, possibly not even at all. But then, repenting at leisure was what came of marrying in haste. If she hadn't been so desperate for security and conventionality she could have saved herself years of heartache.

'Did you know you were adopted?' she asked, yanking her thoughts back on track since her relationships with her siblings and her ex weren't remotely relevant to the conversation.

'Not until the day before yesterday.'

'How did you feel when you found out?'

'Relieved.'

'Oh?'

'It's complicated.'

'In my experience, family generally is.'

His gaze sharpened and turned quizzical. 'In what way is yours complicated?'

Hers? Hmm. In what way *wasn't* it complicated? She was so different to the rest of hers that, ironically, for years she'd thought *she* had to be adopted.

She'd grown up on a rundown council estate, her parents and siblings largely relying on state support and the odd cash-in-hand job to keep them afloat. She'd been clever and wanted more, but aspiration had been thin on the ground both at school and home.

When she'd expressed an interest in university she'd been asked why she thought she was so special and told to get back in her box. In the face of such lack of encouragement she hadn't been brave enough to pursue that avenue, but had sought another way out instead. She hadn't fancied the army, with its olive drab and international danger zones, so she'd joined the police. Her family, who harboured a deep distrust of the authorities with whom they'd had more than one or two run-ins, had seen the move as a betrayal and never forgiven her.

She'd long since realised that their acceptance, their love, was conditional on conformity and it had been a price that ultimately she hadn't been willing to pay. But it still hurt, and she still wished things could have been different.

However, *her* family issues bore no relation to this case.

'I wasn't referring to mine,' she said, while thinking, well, not entirely. 'I simply meant that I've seen a lot of it through my work. Tell me about yours. It could be helpful.'

'It won't be,' he said with a frown, his jaw clenching in a faint but intriguing way.

'Let me be the judge of that,' she countered. 'Despite what you might think, Max, I am good at my job. There's a reason Finn hired me over one of the bigger, more established agencies. Not only was I highly recommended by an acquaintance of his, for whom I did some work, I leave no stone unturned. I'm tenacious like that. But I can only be the best if I have all the facts.'

He regarded her for a moment then gave a short nod. 'Fair enough. My father had a fatal heart attack seven years ago.'

'I'm sorry to hear that,' she said, feeling a faint twang in her chest, which was baffling when she hardly knew him.

'My mother lives in New York. They divorced when I was fourteen.'

'Have you spoken to her about your adoption?'

'Briefly.'

'What did she say?'

'She claims not to recall much of the detail.'

From across the table, Alex stared at him in shock. His mother didn't recall much of the detail relating to the adoption of her son? Was she ill? Had he not asked the right questions? 'How is that possible?'

'She can be difficult.'

Or could it be that his family was as dysfunctional as hers? 'I'd like to talk to her.'

'There'd be little point.'

'It's an avenue I can't leave unexplored,' she said,

noting the tension suddenly gripping him and the barriers shooting up.

'It's too early to call now.'

'The minute we land, then.'

'Have you had breakfast?'

'No,' she replied, intrigued by the abrupt change in topic but letting it go until she figured out a way of bypassing the barriers.

'Well, I don't know about you, but I'm ravenous.'

CHAPTER THREE

UNBUCKLING HIS SEATBELT, Max got up and strode to the buffet bar, upon which sat a platter of cold meats and cheeses, bowls of fruit and a basket of pastries and rolls. He didn't want to talk about his mother to anyone at the best of times. He certainly didn't want to discuss her with Alex right now, he thought darkly as he took a plate and handed it to her.

Generally, he tried to think about Carolyn Stafford née Warwick née Browning née Kentala née Green as little as possible. He'd described her as difficult but that was an understatement. She was impossible and always had been. Everything was about her, nothing was ever good enough and her ability to find fault knew no bounds.

He could still vividly recall the time he'd broken his leg at the age of eight. She'd had to cancel a lunch date to take him to hospital and on the way there had let him know in no uncertain terms exactly how inconvenient he was being. The memory of the chilly silences she'd subjected him to as a child, when he'd failed to live up to one expectation or another, had had the ability to tighten his chest and accelerate his pulse for years.

Even now, she twisted words and situations for her own benefit and tried to manipulate and control him.

The difference these days was that the armour he'd built over the years to protect himself from her—and from his father, for that matter—was inches thick and strong as steel. Everything now simply bounced off it.

So no, he thought, excising all thoughts of his mother from his head and piling breakfast onto a plate of his own, what he *wanted* to do was grab Alex by the hand, lead her into the bedroom he'd spotted at the back of the cabin and keep her there until they landed.

After departing her office yesterday morning, he'd put her from his mind and headed back to Finn and Rico, the need to reconnect with them before the flight out his number one goal. Lunch had extended into the afternoon and then to dinner and drinks late into the night, the conversation and his fascination with his brothers absorbing every drop of his attention.

Yet the minute he'd stepped onto the plane he'd felt Alex's gaze on him like a laser, and every single thing discussed and learned and every accompanying emotion that had swept through him had vaporised. It was as if he'd been plugged into the national grid. The tiny hairs at the back of his neck had shot up and electricity had charged his nerve-endings, the effects of which still lingered.

This morning she was wearing a smart grey trouser suit, her hair up in a neat bun, her glossy fringe not a strand out of place, but, once again, none of that was as off-putting as he might have assumed. On the contrary, it only intensified his intention to unwind her and find out exactly what lay beneath the icy cool surface.

Was it a concern that he was so tuned to her frequency? No. The tiny gasp she'd let out when his knee had bumped hers was merely encouraging. The hint of defensiveness and the faint stiffening of her shoulders he'd noticed when they'd been talking about complicated families was nothing more than mildly interesting, because he didn't buy for one moment that she hadn't been referring to hers.

Nor was the fact he found her obvious disapproval of him so stimulating anything to worry about. Sure, it was unusual and unexpected—especially given how much censure he'd grown up with—but it wasn't as if he was after anything other than a purely physical relationship with her. She'd already turned what he'd always considered he found attractive on its head and her opinion of him was irrelevant.

And, quite honestly, there was no need to overthink it.

'So, by my calculations,' said Alex, cutting through his thoughts and snapping him back to breakfast, 'if you factor in the change in time zones, we should be landing at La Posada some time this afternoon.'

'We're making a stopover in the Caribbean first,' Max said, breaking open a roll and drizzling olive oil onto it.

A pause. Then, 'Oh?'

'Isla Mariposa. It's an island off the north coast of Venezuela. I live there. We should land mid-morning local time. We'll leave for Argentina tomorrow.'

There was another, slightly longer pause. 'I see.'

At the chill in her voice, Max glanced up and saw that her eyes were shooting daggers at him and her colour was high, which was as fascinating as it was a surprise. 'Is that a problem?' he asked with a mildness that totally belied the arousing effect her glare was having on him.

'Yes, it's a problem.'

'We'll need to refuel and the crew will need a break,' he said, shifting on the seat to ease the sudden tightness of his jeans. 'I also need to pick up some clothes. It's cold where we're heading.'

La Posada stood three thousand four hundred metres above sea level and had a cold semi-arid climate. At this time of year, August, the temperature, which averaged seventeen degrees centigrade by day, plummeted to minus four at night.

'I know that,' said Alex somewhat witheringly. 'I checked. *That's* not the problem. Nor is refuelling and giving the crew a break, obviously.'

'Then what is?'

'You are,' she fired at him. 'You unilaterally making decisions that involve me without discussing them *with* me is the problem.'

In response to her unanticipated wrath, Max sat back, faintly stunned. 'If I'd known it was so important I'd have sent you the flight plan.'

'It's not just the flight plan,' she said heatedly. 'It's the way you set up a meeting with Rico and Finn when you were specifically requested to go through me. And then the commandeering of Rico's plane to fly to Argentina completely on your own.'

'Would you rather have flown commercial?'

'That's not the point. I'm the expert here. This is my field, Max. And it's *my* case.'

'No, it's not,' he replied, unable to resist the temptation to see how far she could be pushed.

'Yes, it is.'

'I prefer to think of it as *our* case.'

Alex threw up her hands in exasperation and he could practically see the steam pouring out of her ears, which would have put a grin on his face if he hadn't thought it would result in her throwing a croissant at him.

'But you're right,' he said a touch more soberly when it looked as if she was going to get up and storm off in vexation. 'I apologise. This is the first time I've worked with someone.'

Alex eyed him suspiciously for a moment but remained seated. 'Seriously?'

'I have a great respect for confidentiality.'

'You trust no one?'

'Not with work.' Or with anything else, but she didn't need to know that.

'Well, you're going to have to start,' she said, stabbing a chunk of kiwi with her fork. 'You'll soon get used to working with me.'

No, he wouldn't. This was a one-off and temporary. Joking aside, he didn't do 'our' anything and never would. A long-term relationship was way out of his reach, even if he had wanted one. Any hope he might have once had for love had been eroded so long ago he couldn't remember what it felt like, and thought of emotional intimacy, the kind he supposed might be required for such a thing, made him shudder. However, constant confrontation would hardly entice her into his bed.

'I'll endeavour to do better,' he said with what he hoped was the right amount of conciliation. 'And, with that in mind, my villa has a guest suite that I thought you might like to use, but feel free to book into a hotel if you'd prefer.'

The scowl on her face deepened for a moment, but then it cleared and she seemed to deflate, as if he'd whipped the wind of indignation from her sails. 'No, your guest suite would be great,' she said grudgingly. 'I wouldn't want to incur any unnecessary costs.'

'You're welcome.'

'Thank you.'

'This investigation means a lot to you, doesn't it?'

he said, deeming it safe to continue with breakfast and adding a slice of ham to the roll.

'Every investigation means a lot to me,' she said archly. 'And they all come with rules.'

Did they? 'I'll have to take your word for it.'

'So I'd appreciate it if you would respect them as much as you say you respect confidentiality.'

Respect them? She had no idea. 'No can do, I'm afraid.'

'Why on earth not?'

'Rules are made to be broken.'

'Mine aren't.'

'You seem very definite.'

'I *am* very definite.'

Max watched her neatly slice a pain au chocolate in half and thought that if that kind of a statement wasn't irresistible to someone who'd never come across a rule he hadn't instinctively wanted to trample all over, he didn't know what was.

His days of rebelling against authority and challenging the system were over long ago. A brush with the Feds at the age of twenty for hacking into the digital billboards of Times Square had made him reassess his need to foster anarchy and create chaos, but that didn't mean the urge had disappeared altogether. 'That sounds like a challenge.'

She looked up and glared at him warningly. 'Believe me, it absolutely isn't.'

'What's the attraction?' He took a bite of his roll and noted with interest that her gaze dipped to his mouth for the briefest of moments before jerking back to his.

'Well, for one thing,' she said with a quick, revealing clearing of her throat, 'society wouldn't function without them. They maintain civilisation and prevent lawlessness. Everyone knows what's what, and there's security in that.' She paused then added, 'But on a personal level I will admit to liking order and structure.'

'Why?'

'I grew up without much of either. I came to see the benefits.'

'The complicated family?' he said, catching a fleeting glimpse of disappointment and regret in her expression.

'Maybe,' she admitted with a minute tilt of her head. 'My upbringing was chaotic.'

'In what way?'

'It just was.'

Her chin was up and her eyes flashed for a second and he thought that if she didn't want to talk about it that was fine with him. Her family problems were no concern of his. He had enough of his own to deal with. 'Chaos can be good,' he said instead, reflecting on how it had got him through his teenage years before his arrest had given him the opportunity to reassess.

She sat back and stared at him, astonishment wiping out the momentary bleakness. 'Are you serious?'

'The most disruptive periods of history have produced the finest art and the best inventions. Think the Medici.'

'So have the quietest. Think the telephone. What do you have against rules anyway?'

What *didn't* he have against them? They stifled creativity. They put in place boundaries that were frequently arbitrary and often unnecessary. Mostly, though, they represented authority that he'd once seen no reason to respect.

Max had started hacking at the age of twelve as a way of escaping from the rowing at home, his mother's constant criticism and his father's lack of interest in him. Not only had he got a massive kick out of breaking the law; more importantly, he'd found a community to become part of, one that considered failure a valuable learning tool, celebrated the smallest of successes and accepted him unconditionally. It had given him the sense of belonging that he'd craved and that had been addictive.

His early talents had swiftly developed into impressive skills and by the age of seventeen he'd gained a reputation as being the best in the business. He'd had respect—of the underground type, sure, but respect nevertheless—and he'd welcomed it.

While some of his acquaintances had stolen data to sell to the highest bidder and others held companies to ransom by installing malware, the more nefarious paths he could have chosen to take had never appealed. His interest had lain wholly in breaking systems and creating chaos. He'd relished and needed the control and the power it had given him when home was a place where he had none.

Now he had control and power that he'd acquired through legitimate routes and chaos no longer appealed, but there was still part of him that missed those days and always would.

'I'm a rebel at heart,' he said, giving her a slow grin which, intriguingly, made the pulse at the base of her neck flutter.

'Well, just as long as you don't make it your mission to lure me to the dark side,' she said pointedly, 'we should get along fine.'

It was all very well for Max to dismiss her need for rules, thought Alex, smiling her thanks to the flight attendant, who was clearing away breakfast with an obligingly professional rather than flirtatious manner, to treat them as some kind of joke. He couldn't possibly understand the hunger for stability and peace that she'd developed growing up.

Home had been a noisy, disruptive place. There'd been six of them initially, living in a cramped three-bedroom flat on the eighteenth floor of a tower block decorated with graffiti, lit by dim, flickering light bulbs and littered with cigarette ends and fast-food packaging.

She'd shared a bunk room with her sister and then the baby, her niece, as well, when she'd arrived. Her older brothers, who'd shared another of the rooms, had come and gone at all hours, where and to do what she'd never dared to enquire. Her parents had considered discipline and regular meals too much of a challenge to bother with properly, and school had been optional. Somehow, though strangely, there'd always been enough money.

Since it had been impossible to study at home with the racket that went on, Alex had spent much of her time at the local library and it was there that she'd happened upon Aristotle and his thoughts on the rule of law.

What she'd read had been liberating. When she'd re-alised that there was nothing to celebrate about the reckless, irresponsible way her family lived, she'd stopped trying to mould herself into something they could accept—which was proving impossible anyway when she'd rejected the idea with every fibre of her being—and turned her sights on escape.

Rules had given her a path out of the chaos. She'd diligently followed the school curriculum despite little encouragement, taken every exam available and set her sights a career in the police, which, with its hierarchy and methodical approach to things, had appealed to her need for structure.

Sticking to them was hardly an adventurous or daring

course of action, but it was a safe one and one which she knew she could rely on. She'd experienced the fallout from zero adherence: the worry about where her father was and when he'd be back; jumping every time there was a knock on the door and knowing with a feeling of dread that the law stood on the other side; a diet so deficient it gave you anaemia that made you faint.

The knowledge that she shared her family's DNA was a constant worry. What might happen if she let go of her grip on her control? How quickly would genes win out and consign her to a future of petty crime and little hope? She couldn't let that happen. She didn't want to live the way her parents and siblings did. She wanted a steady, law-abiding, chaos-free existence, one in which she knew where she was going and how she was going to get there.

Max, on the other hand, for some reason evidently saw rules as something to bend and to break. A challenge. So what did that mean going forwards? Would he try and break hers? If he did, how many and which ones? How far would he go? And how would she respond?

Well, she'd fight back with everything she had, of course, because his love of breaking rules was not more important than her need to abide by them. That had been set in stone years ago and further cemented by embarking on a career as a woman in a man's world, which meant that she'd had to work twice as hard for her reputation.

Besides, she would not have him messing with her plans, her *life*, just because he felt like it. That tiny little thrill she could feel rippling through her at the thought of being the object of his focus could take a hike. It was wholly unacceptable and not to be indulged. She didn't want to be the object of his focus. Of *anyone's* focus, for that matter. She was very happy on her own, and had been since her divorce. She didn't need the stress and potential failure of another relationship, even if she ever could find it in her to trust again. The occasional date whenever she started to feel a bit lonely, where *she* called the shots, was more than enough.

Not that Max fell into the date category or ever would. Even if he had shown any sign of being attracted to her, he was too unpredictable, too much of a threat to her peace of mind. He was chaos with a capital C and therefore completely off-limits, despite the insane attraction she felt for him.

But he was also nothing she couldn't handle, she told herself sternly as she turned her mind to work. She'd come across far more temperamental personalities. He might have broken through her unflappable exterior with his decree about the stopover, but there'd been extenuating circumstances. She'd been provoked one time too many. It wouldn't happen again.

And, in any case, they'd be busy with the investigation. There wouldn't be time or space for Max to challenge her rules. There'd be no upheaval, no chaos. It would be fine.

While Alex set up a workspace at the table, Max grabbed his laptop from his bag, kicked off his shoes and stretched out on the sofa, still thinking of interesting and inventive ways to 'lure her to the dark side'.

It might not be as simple as he'd first imagined, he acknowledged, firing up the machine and revisiting their conversation. He hadn't counted on rules. But he didn't envisage too much of a problem. However mighty her will and however noble her intentions, the attraction they shared was a thousand times stronger. If it drummed through her the way it did through him—hot, insistent, all-consuming—it wouldn't take long for her resistance to buckle under the pressure. Maybe not quite within the thirty-six hours he'd so confidently predicted yesterday lunchtime, but well within forty-eight.

'Making yourself comfortable?'

At Alex's dry question he glanced over and saw that her gaze was fixed on his bare feet. No doubt she disapproved, which naturally made him want to do something even more unprofessional—say, strip off his shirt—just to see her reaction.

'Why don't you join me?' he said with a grin, briefly wondering what the chances were of her letting her hair down in both senses of the phrase and taking up a position on the sofa that sat at right angles to his.

'Thanks,' she muttered, returning her attention to her laptop, 'but I'm fine over here.'

As he'd thought. Minuscule. But that was all right. Now he was beginning to see how she operated, he could adapt his strategy to seduce her into his bed accordingly. 'What are you doing?'

'Emails.'

'Haven't you forgotten something?'

She frowned. 'What?'

'Your side of our deal. If I allowed you to accompany me this morning,' he said, his choice of words deliberately provocative, 'you'd give me all the information you have on the investigation so far.'

Her eyes narrowed for a moment and he felt a little kick of triumph. She was too easy to wind up. Less clear was why he found it so tempting to try.

'Sure,' she said with a disappointing return to her customary cool. 'I'll send everything over right now.'

The emails dropped into his inbox, one after the other,

and as Max clicked on the attachments, opening up reports, birth certificates, a letter from Rico's adoptive parents to their son and even the analysis of Finn's DNA, his preoccupation with undoing Alex and pulverising her rules evaporated.

Reading the names of his birth parents, Juan Rodriguez and Maria Gonzalez, made his throat tight and his pulse race. Were they still alive? Who were they, what were they like, and did he resemble them in any way? What were the chances of finding them? And which of the three certificates was his? Would he ever get to know who he truly was? Would he ever find out why he'd been given up?

Rico's letter, a translation into English from the original Italian, was deeply personal and filled with loving thoughts as well as the name of the adoption agency. Somewhere deep inside Max's chest the words and the sentiments detonated a cocktail of resentment and pain that he hadn't experienced in years, followed hot on the heels by searing envy, which he wasn't particularly proud of since Rico's parents had died in a car accident when he was ten. But at least his brother had had a decade of affection and love, which was more than Max had ever had.

The analysis of Finn's DNA was less affecting but equally gripping. Their heritage was seventy-five per cent Latin American, twenty per cent Iberian, with a smattering of Central and Eastern European representing the remaining five per cent. Revelations included the low likelihood of dimples and the high possibility of a lactose intolerance. He scoured the data for similarities and found many.

Alex might consider this to be her field and her case, Max thought, methodically going through the reports supplied by her subcontractors, the details spinning around his head. But it was his history, his *family*. She could have no idea what it was like growing up sensing that somehow you were part of the wrong one, that you were unwanted but didn't know why. Nor could she know what it was like to obsessively wonder now how different things might have been if you'd grown up loved, wanted and happy in the right one. He'd spent thirty years not knowing his real parents. Thirty years apart from his brothers, with whom he'd shared a womb. So many memories unformed and opportunities lost…

'You mentioned having resources that I could only dream about,' Alex said, jolting him out of his thoughts, which was welcome when they'd become so tumultuous and overwhelming.

'You've been pretty thorough,' he said, clearing his throat of the tight knot that had lodged there. 'However, I can call in a few favours to see if we can't get round the Swiss banking secrecy issues and access Argentina's national archives.'

'Some favours they must be.'

'They are.' He'd once resolved the hack of a major Swiss bank and fixed a number of issues in systems controlled by the Argentinian government. 'But, other than that, I'm not sure what more I could legitimately add.'

'An interesting choice of words,' she said shrewdly. 'What about illegitimately?'

'It's a quick and efficient way of getting things done.'

Her mesmerising blue eyes widened for a second. 'Would you be willing to break the law for this?'

'I could,' he said, instinctively working through how he might go about it. 'And once upon a time I would have done so without hesitation. But not now. Now I have no intention of screwing up my career for a quick thrill.'

These days he exerted his control and power in other ways, and accessing the systems to locate his brothers had been risky enough.

She looked at him steadily and he could practically see the pieces slotting into place in her brain. 'Were you a hacker?'

He nodded. 'A long time ago.'

'Is that how you got into cyber security?'

'It seemed like a good career move.'

Following his arrest, in an unlikely turn of events, Max had been offered a deal by the FBI: if he worked for them, he'd avoid jail. Initially he'd rejected the proposal. He hadn't even needed to think about it. Every millimetre of his being had recoiled at the thought of being employed by the authorities he despised. A sentence, however lengthy, would be infinitely preferable to selling out his principles.

But they'd given him forty-eight hours to reconsider, two days in a cell with nothing else to think about, and eventually he'd changed his mind. He was now on the authorities' radar. Escaping them in the future would be tough and actually he quite liked his freedom. The risks were beginning to outweigh the rewards, so maybe it was time for the poacher to turn gamekeeper.

From then on he'd been inundated with job offers, which ranged from finding weaknesses in firewalls and fixing them to providing advice on how to stay one step ahead of the hackers and disrupters in an exceptionally fast-moving field. None of his prospective employers had a problem with his brush with the law. His incomparable skills easily overrode what had gone before.

Despite being presented with some exceptionally generous packages once he'd paid his debt to society via the FBI, he'd opted to go it alone, to take his pick of the work. He'd never regretted the decision to be in sole control of his future, and not just because he had millions in the bank.

'How long have you been doing it?'

'Ten years.'

'I read you have clients all over the world.'

'I do.'

'Then I'm surprised you have time to work on the investigation.'

'I'm between contracts.'

'Handy.'

'I'd have made time regardless.'

Her gaze turned quizzical. 'It means that much to you?'

'Yes.'

'Why?'

There was no way he was going into detail about his upbringing, his efforts to overcome it and the emotional disruption the discovery of his adoption had wrought. He could barely work it out for himself. 'I'm good at solving puzzles,' he said with a casual shrug. 'I developed that particular skill while I was at MIT.' Or at least he had until his arrest, at which point he'd been stripped of his scholarship and kicked out.

'Computers are your thing.'

'They are,' he agreed, glancing at his laptop and feeling a familiar sense of calm settle over him. They were a damn sight simpler than people, that was for sure. They were devoid of emotion and didn't demand the impossible. They were predictable, easy to read if you knew what you were looking for and generally did what they were told. 'Like rules are yours.'

'Tell me more about the hacking.'

'What do you want to know?'

'Everything,' she said, getting up and moving to the sofa next to his, taking up a position that was too far away for his liking. 'Call it professional interest. There's a big gap in my knowledge of this particular area. How did you get into it?'

'I was given a computer for my tenth birthday,' he said, remembering with a sharp stab of pain how excited he'd been until his mother had told him in no uncertain terms that she expected it to improve his grades, otherwise it would be removed. 'I spent hours messing about on it, learning the language and writing programs, before discovering forums and chats. I got talking. Made friends. Things went from there.'

She leaned forward, avid curiosity written all over her face. 'How?'

'What do you mean?' he said, slightly taken aback by her interest in him and faintly distracted by the trace of her scent that drifted his way.

'Well, lots of people mess about on computers and chat online,' she said. 'Not many go down the hacking route.'

'Not many are good enough.'

She tilted her head. 'You say that with pride.'

'Do I?'

'You shouldn't.'

'Probably not.'

'What sort of things did you get up to?'

'The first thing I did was change a grade for a math test when I was twelve. I got an F. I should have got an A. I just hadn't studied. The F was a mistake.' More than that, though, he'd been terrified his mother would act on her threat and take his computer back.

She stared at him, appalled. 'How on earth could you not have studied for an exam?'

Because, since it was a subject he'd found easy, with the arrogance of youth, he'd assumed he'd wing it. 'Surely that isn't the point.'

'You're right,' she agreed. 'It isn't. What else?'

'I regularly set off the fire alarms and sprinkler systems at high school. I travelled round the city for free and was behind a handful of denial of service attacks. At one point I ran an operation cancelling parking tickets.'

'That's really bad,' she said, tutting with disapproval he'd come to expect. 'If the US authorities treat that kind of thing the same way the UK ones do, you risked years in jail.'

And that had been part of the appeal. The power, the control, the extremely high stakes and the respect he'd garnered that had made him feel so alive. It had given him a sense of identity, of purpose and he'd revelled in it. 'The commission I earned paid my rent while I was at college. I never caused anyone harm. I never even wanted to. Maximum disruption was my only goal.'

'And making money.'

'That was just a coincidence.'

'What did your parents think of what you were doing?'

'They never knew,' he said, hearing the trace of bitterness he was unable to keep from his voice and hating that old wounds he'd assumed were long gone appeared to have been ripped open. 'They were too wrapped up in themselves.'

'Ah,' she said, with a nod and smile he couldn't quite identify but which, for some reason, shot a dart of unease through him. 'Did you ever get caught?'

'Eventually. While I was at MIT, I hacked into the billboards in Times Square. I took down all the adverts and announcements and replaced them with my avatar.'

'Why?'

'Because I could. Because I was young and hubristic. Twenty-four hours later I had the FBI knocking on my door.'

'How did they find you?'

'A dark net contact of mine got sloppy and then did a deal to save his own ass.'

'Did you go to jail?'

He shook his head. 'I traded my principles for my freedom.'

'You got off lightly.'

'I was lucky.'

Very lucky, in retrospect. Forty-eight hours in the cells had been ample time to contemplate the journey that had landed him there. It hadn't taken him long to figure out that everything he'd done had been a reaction to the environment at home. His father's neglect, his mother's emotional vampirism. Operating in the shadows had given him the respect, approval and appreciation that he hadn't even known he'd been missing. His many successes had earned him recognition. His few failures had fuelled his determination to be better.

But he hadn't liked thinking about how weak and vulnerable he'd been as a kid. Nor had he enjoyed dwelling on why he'd carried on with his double life even when he'd escaped to MIT. He didn't want to admit to the fear that without it he didn't know who he was.

He'd never get the opportunity to work that out if he didn't give himself a chance, he'd eventually come to realise. And he had to stop being so angry. It didn't mean he'd forgiven his parents for the effects of their behaviour on him, but he could either allow the bitterness to take over or let it go. He'd chosen the latter, determinedly putting it all behind him, and gone on the straight and narrow, building his business and maintaining minimal contact with his parents. And everything had been going fine until he'd seen the video of his brothers and the fragile reality he'd created for himself had imploded.

'You'd get on well with my family,' said Alex with a dry smile that bizarrely seemed to shine through the cracks in his armour and light up the dark spaces within.

'In what way?' he asked, absently rubbing his chest.

'They have an unhealthy disrespect for the law too. Not quite on your level, admittedly. One of my brothers has a habit of shoplifting. My sister claims benefits but also works on the side. My father describes himself as a wheeler-dealer, but he treads a fine line.'

'Yet you went into the police.' Yesterday, he'd looked her up. The idea of a former law enforcement officer hooking up with a former criminal—albeit a non-convicted one—had held a certain ironic appeal.

'It was *my* escape.'

'How did that go down?' he asked, conveniently ignoring the comparison while thinking that she was way too perceptive.

'They've never forgiven me.'

'That I can understand. My mother's never got beyond my arrest.' Not even his subsequent success, which she tended to either diminish or ignore, could make up for that.

'I'm very much the ugly duckling of my family.'

'There is nothing ugly about you.'

'Nor you.'

A strange kind of silence fell then. Her cheeks flushed and her gaze dipped to his mouth. He became unusually aware of his heartbeat, steady but quickening. Her eyes lifted back to his, darkening to a mid-blue, and she stared at him intently, as if trying to look into his soul, which shook something deep inside him. The tension simmered between them. The air heated. He was hyperaware of her. The hitch of her breath. The flutter of her pulse at the base of her neck. He wanted to kiss her so badly it was all he could think about.

And then she blinked.

'Right,' she said briskly, snapping the connection and making him start. 'I'm going for a nap. Unlike some, I had a very early start. See you later.'

And as she leapt to her feet and fled the scene, Max had the oddly unsettling feeling that it was going to be a very long flight.

CHAPTER FOUR

NEVER HAD SHE been so glad of fresh air and space, Alex thought six hours later as she sat at the back of Max's speedboat, which was whisking them from Simón Bolívar International Airport, just north of Caracas, to Isla Mariposa, where he lived. She lifted her face to the glorious mid-morning sun while the warm Caribbean Sea breeze whipped around her, willing it to blow away the excruciating tension gripping every cell of her body.

So much for a nice refreshing nap. She felt as refreshed as a damp, dirty dishcloth, on edge and gritty-eyed, but then that was what came of not being able to catch up on a broken truncated night. She wished she could have blamed her tossing and turning on turbulence, but the flight had been smooth and uneventful. The only turbulence she'd experienced had been within.

She'd met many criminals in her time, but never a hacker and none as devastatingly attractive as the man standing at the wheel, handling the boat so competently. Beneath the blazing sun she could make out fine golden streaks in his dark hair. His eyes were even bluer in the bright mid-morning light. Once again he'd kicked off his shoes and once again she was transfixed.

Alex had never had a thing about feet before. If she'd had to provide an opinion on them she'd have said function over form was generally the case and the more hidden away they were the better. It would appear she had a thing about his, however, because they were things of beauty. She could stare at them for hours. She had, in fact, at length, on the plane, when he'd been talking about his early career and she'd been rapt. But at least it made a change from trying not to stare at his mouth, which was proving an irritatingly hard challenge.

What was the matter with her? she wondered, taking a sip of water from her bottle and surreptitiously running her gaze over him. Why were Max Kentala and his many physical attractions occupying so much of her brain? He really wasn't her type. It wasn't about his looks any longer. In that respect, it had become blindingly obvious that he was exactly her type, hair in need of a cut and jaw in need of a shave or not.

But with regard to everything else they were chalk and cheese. Their poles apart attitudes towards time-keeping notwithstanding, he'd been a law-breaker. She'd been a law-enforcer. He clearly embraced turmoil while she craved the security of stability and predictability. He considered engaging in criminal activity *a quick thrill*. They couldn't have more opposing values or be more different.

What she couldn't understand, however, was why she found this dichotomy so fascinating. The pride she'd noted when he'd been talking about the illegal ways he'd deployed his considerable IT skills, which had lightened his expression and made him look younger, more carefree and, unbelievably, even more gorgeous, wasn't something to be applauded. Hacking into the Times Square billboards wasn't cool or fun or imaginative. It was reckless, irresponsible and downright illegal.

The walk on the wild side he'd once taken was everything she abhorred, everything she avoided like the plague. That he'd so obviously enjoyed it should have dramatically diminished his appeal. But it didn't. Instead it seemed to have *augmented* it, which was baffling and more than a little concerning, as was the still unacceptable thrill that was begging to be indulged with increasing persistence.

Could it be that their many differences were somehow mitigated by their few similarities? They were both problem solvers who'd forged successful careers from nothing. They'd both had disapproving parents and had once upon a time sought an escape from their families. Both were equally invested in uncovering the truth, although she didn't quite believe that for him it was just a problem to solve.

So could their unexpected commonalities somehow explain her one-eighty swing from reproach to sympathy? *Something* had to account for that oddly heart-stopping moment they'd shared just before she'd legged it to the bedroom.

She hadn't meant to confess that she found him attractive. She was sure there was nothing to read in his comment along the same lines. Yet he'd suddenly looked so sincere it had caught her off-guard. Her gaze had collided with his and the intense heat she'd seen darkening the blue to navy had dazzled her. Her mouth had dried. Her pulse had pounded. She'd wanted to get up and move to his side. To lean down, pin him to the sofa and cover his mouth with hers. She'd very nearly done it too, to her horror, hence the sudden excuse of a nap.

She had to put the whole plane journey from her mind, she told herself firmly for what felt like the hundredth time in the past hour. She might not be able to make head or tail of her attitude towards Max but one thing was certain: his ability to derail her focus was wholly wrong. The unexpectedly sexy way he put on his sunglasses, pulling them from the V of his shirt and sliding them onto his nose, bore no relevance to anything. That the fine hair on his beautifully muscled forearms was a shade lighter than that on his head was not something she needed to concern herself with. And who cared that he'd been strangely monosyllabic and tight-jawed ever since they'd landed?

All she wanted was to crack this case and secure her future.

As they rounded a small headland Max slowed the boat and Alex turned her gaze to the shore. At the sight of the house that hove into view, her jaw dropped. Beyond the water that sparkled jade and turquoise and was so clear she could see right down to the bottom, above the curving swathe of palm-fringed white sand, the villa stood nestled among the trees that rose up behind. Four low-level triangular wooden roofs stretched out above huge glass windows and doors. In front, overlooking the sea, was a series of connected terraces. On one she thought she could make out a pool. At each end, a flight of wooden steps descended between the boulders to the beach.

Even from this distance she could see that it was a building sympathetic to its surroundings and stunningly beautiful. It was the kind of place she'd only ever seen in magazines, in which, incredibly, *she* was getting to stay. And yes, it was for work, just as the private jet had been, but that didn't stop her mentally sticking two fingers up at the teachers who'd told her repeatedly and scornfully that with her family she didn't stand a chance of ever making anything of herself. Nor did it stop her wishing her parents could see her now, not that there was any point to that at all.

Max brought the boat to a near stop and lined it up to the dock. He tossed a loop of rope over a mooring bollard with easy competence and a flex of muscles that, to her despair, made her stomach instinctively tighten, but she had the feeling that for the greater good she was just going to have to accept the way she responded to him and ignore it.

Displaying an enviable sense of balance, he unloaded their luggage and then alighted. He bent down and extended his arm. 'Give me your hand.'

For a moment Alex stared at his outstretched hand as if it were a live grenade. She couldn't risk taking it. If she did, she might not be able to let go. But she didn't have his sense of balance. One wobble and she could well end up in the sea, and quite frankly she felt jumpy enough around him without adding looking foolish into the mix.

'Thanks.'

After hauling Alex up off his boat and then dropping her hand as if it were on fire, Max grabbed their bags and strode up the steps to the house without bothering to see if she was following. He was tense. Tired. On edge.

As he'd suspected, it had been a very long flight. Once he'd rid his head first of images of Alex lying on the bed in the cabin of the plane alone and then of what would happen if he joined her, he'd found himself revisiting their conversation. Every detail, no matter how minute, appeared to be etched into his memory, and his unease had grown with every nautical mile, twisting his gut and bringing him out in a cold sweat.

Which was odd.

Generally he had no problem talking about his career

or what he'd done to get there. He didn't have anything to hide. Most of it was in the public domain for anyone interested enough to go looking for it. It wasn't as if he'd given away a piece of himself or anything. He'd long ago come to terms with his mother's ongoing ignominy of having a son with a criminal background.

So why had their conversation unsettled him so much? Alex clearly disapproved of the things he'd got up to in his youth, but so what? Her opinion of him genuinely didn't matter. They were absolute opposites in virtually every respect, and he wasn't interested in her in any way except the physical.

Perhaps it was her curiosity in him which, despite her assertion to the contrary, had seemed more personal than professional. He couldn't recall the last time anyone had genuinely wanted to know what made him tick. Neither of his parents ever had. And these days most people just wanted to hear about his exploits. But Alex had wanted to know what lay behind them. She'd looked at him as if trying to see into his soul and it had rocked him to the core.

Or perhaps it had been that 'ah' of hers, the one she'd uttered when he'd told her that his parents couldn't have cared less about what he'd got up to. It suggested she'd caught the trace of bitterness that had laced his words and it smacked of sympathy and understanding, which he really didn't need. That they had parental disapproval and lack of forgiveness in common meant nothing. What did it matter that she was as much of a disappointment to her family as he was to his?

He was beginning to regret accepting Alex's ultimatum and allowing her to come with him. He should have stuck to his guns and listened to his head instead of his body. He had more than enough going on without her adding complications. He hated the confusion and uncertainty currently battering his fractured defences. He'd thought he'd overcome that sort of thing a decade ago. To realise that he might not have dealt with the past as successfully as he'd assumed was like a blow to the chest. At the very least he should have booked her into a hotel for tonight.

But there was nothing he could do about any of that now. However tempting it might be, he could hardly leave her here while he continued to Argentina alone. They'd made a deal and, for all his many faults, for all his crimes and misdemeanours, he'd never once gone back on his word. And booking her into a hotel now, when he'd already offered her his guest suite, would indicate a change of plan he didn't want her questioning.

At least where he was putting her up was separated from the main house, he thought grimly, striding past the infinity pool and heading for the pair of open doors that led to the suite. It wouldn't be too hard to ignore her for as long as it took for him to get a grip on the tornado of turmoil that was whipping around inside him. His plans for seduction could handle a minor delay while he regrouped.

'Here you go,' he said, stalking through the doors and dumping her bag beside the huge bed that stood before him like a great flashing beacon. 'Make yourself comfortable.'

'Thank you. This is an incredible house.'

'I like it.'

What he *didn't* like, however, was the fast unravelling of his control. Him, Alex, the bed… On top of everything else, the hot, steamy images now cascading into his head were fraying his nerves. The sounds she'd make. The smoothness of her skin beneath his hands and the soft silkiness of her hair trailing over him as she slid down his body.

He shouldn't be in here. He should have simply handed her her bag and pointed her in the right direction. He had to get out before he lost it completely. He whipped round to leave her to it, but she was closer than he was expecting. He slammed to a halt and jerked back, as if struck.

'Are you all right, Max?' she said with a quick frown.

No. He wasn't all right at all. 'I'm fine.'

'You don't look fine.' She put her hand on his arm and her touch shot through him with the force of a thousand volts. 'Your jaw looks like it's about to snap. You've been tense ever since we landed. Has something happened?'

What *hadn't* happened? Forget the fact that the last forty-eight hours had been more tumultuous than the last ten years. *She'd* happened. He couldn't work out why that should be a problem, but it was. As was the compassion and concern written all over her beautiful face. He didn't need that any more than he needed her sympathy or understanding. What he *did* need was space. Air to breathe that wasn't filled with her scent. Time to get himself back under control.

And yet he could no more move than he could fly to Mars. She was close. Very close. He could see a rim of silver around the light blue of her irises and he could hear the soft raggedness of her breathing. The concern was fading from her expression and the space between them started cracking with electricity, the air heavy with a strange sort of throbbing tension. Her pupils were dilating and her gaze dipped to his mouth and still her hand lingered on his arm, burning him like a brand.

The desire that thudded through him was firing his blood and destroying his reason, but he welcomed it, because this he understood. This he could command. She leaned into him, only the fraction of an inch, so minutely she probably wasn't aware she'd done it, but in terms of encouragement it was the greenest of lights and one he couldn't ignore.

Acting on pure instinct, Max shook her hand off him and took a quick step forwards. He put his hands on either side of her head and, dazed with lust, lowered his mouth to hers. Her scent and heat stoked his desire for her to unbearable levels and his ability to think was long gone, but he nevertheless felt her jolt and then stiffen and was about to let her go when she suddenly whipped her arms around his neck, pressed herself close and started kissing him back.

With a groan of relief, he pulled her tighter against him and deepened the kiss, the flames shooting through him heating the blood in his veins to bubbling. The wildness of her response, the heat and taste of her mouth robbed him of his wits. He was nothing but sensation, could feel nothing but her, could think only of the bed not a dozen metres away and the painful ache of his granite-hard erection, against which she was grinding her pelvis and driving him mad.

He deftly unbuttoned her jacket and slid a hand to her breast, rubbed his thumb over her tight nipple, and she moaned. He moved his mouth along her jaw, the sound of her pants harsh in his ear, sending lightning bolts of ecstasy through him. She burrowed her fingers into his hair, as if desperate to keep him from going anywhere, which was never going to happen—

And then a door slammed somewhere inside the house.

In his arms, Alex instantly froze and jerked back, staring at him for what felt like the longest of moments, her cheeks flushed and her eyes glazed with desire. But all too soon the desire vanished and in its place he could see dawning dismay. She shoved at his shoulders and he let her go in a flash, even though every cell of his body protested.

'What's wrong?' he muttered dazedly, his voice rough and his breathing harsh.

'What's wrong?' she echoed in stunned disbelief. 'This is.'

'It seemed very much all right to me.'

'It was a mistake,' she panted, smoothing her clothes and doing up the button of her jacket with trembling hands while taking an unsteady step back. 'I'm here to work.'

It very much hadn't been a mistake. It had been everything he'd anticipated. More. 'Work can wait.'

'No. It can't,' she said, swallowing hard.

'We're not leaving until tomorrow. There's no rush.'

'I'd planned to call your mother as soon as we landed. Now would be that time.'

At that, Max recoiled as if she'd slapped him. What the hell? If that door hadn't slammed they'd be on the bed getting naked just as fast as was humanly possible. She'd clung to him like a limpet. Kissed him as if her life had depended on it. And now she was talking about his mother? Well, that was one way to obliterate the heat and the desire.

Had that been her intention? If it was, she'd succeeded, because now instead of fire, ice was flowing through his veins, and instead of lust and desperate clawing need, all he felt was excoriating frustration and immense annoyance.

'Sure,' he said, reaching into the back pocket of his trousers and pulling out his phone, while his stomach churned with rejection and disappointment. He scrolled through his contacts and stabbed at the buttons. 'I've sent you her number,' he added as a beep sounded in the depths of her handbag.

'Thank you.'

'Call her whenever you like.'

'Don't you want to be in on it?'

'I already know what she's going to say.' And he didn't need to hear it—or anything else she might choose to add—again. What he needed was to get rid of everything that was whirling around inside him as a result of that aborted kiss, the agonising tension and the crushing disillusionment. 'Help yourself to lunch when you're done,' he said curtly. 'I'm going for a swim.'

Alex watched Max stride off, six foot plus of wound-up male, and sank onto the bed before her legs gave way.

What on earth had just happened? she wondered dazedly, her entire body trembling with shock and heat and confusion. One minute she'd been filled with concern for his well-being since he'd looked so tormented, the next she'd been in a clinch so blistering she was surprised they hadn't gone up in flames.

Touching his arm had been her first mistake, even though she'd desperately wanted to know what had been troubling him. Her fascination with the clench of his muscles beneath her fingers and the feel of his skin, which had meant she hadn't wanted to let him go, had been her second. Then she'd become aware that he'd gone very still and was looking at her with an intensity that robbed her of reason and knocked the breath from her lungs, and the mistakes had started coming thick and fast.

She shouldn't have allowed the enormous bed and the two of them entwined on it to dominate her thoughts.

She should have spun on her heel and fled to the sanctuary of the terrace. But she hadn't. She'd been rooted to the spot, utterly transfixed by the inferno raging in his indigo gaze. Unguarded, fiery, havoc-wreaking heat, directed straight at her.

She didn't have time to wonder at the startling realisation that the attraction she'd assumed to be wholly one-sided could, in fact, be mutual. Or to even consider what was happening. A second later she'd been in his arms, her heart thundering so hard she'd feared she might be about to break a rib.

And, oh, the feel of him… The strength and power of his embrace and the intoxicating skill of his kiss. Her head was still swimming from its effect, her blood still burned. His mouth had delivered on every single promise it made. Heat had rushed through her veins, desire swirling around inside like a tropical storm. When he'd moved his hand to cup her breast the shivers that had run through her had nearly taken out her knees. If it hadn't been for that door, she'd have ended up in bed with him and she wouldn't even have cared. She'd have *relished* it, and that was so wrong she could scarcely believe it.

Where had that response come from? It had been so wild, so abandoned. Mortifyingly, she'd practically devoured him. So much for the professionalism she'd always prided herself on. She hadn't so much blurred the lines as erased them altogether.

What on earth had she been *thinking*? she asked herself, going icy cold with stupefied horror at what she'd done. Had she completely lost her tiny little mind? And where the hell had her rules been in all of this? Max had simply taken what he wanted and she'd let him. She'd had ample opportunity to push him away but she hadn't until it had been shamefully late. And before that she hadn't even thought about it. He might have taken her by surprise when he'd first kissed her but she hadn't for a moment considered not kissing him back.

God, she had to be careful. He was so much more dangerous than she'd imagined. He was such a threat to her rules, not because he saw them as a challenge necessarily, but because he made her want to break them herself. He made her forget why she had them in the first place.

But that couldn't happen. She couldn't afford to have her head turned or give in to the blazing attraction they clearly shared. Her future plans were at stake, and how good would it look if Finn ever got wind of what had just happened? He'd have every right to fire her after that lapse of professionalism. If it happened again or, heaven forbid, went any further—which it absolutely wouldn't—and got out, her reputation would never recover.

A chill ran through her at the thought of how easily she could lose everything she'd worked so hard for. How precariously she teetered at the top of a very slippery slope. She couldn't allow another blip when it came to reason. Or make any more mistakes. She would not be governed by forces which threatened her very existence and over which she had no control. She would not turn into her family. She had an entirely different future to forge.

Three hours after Max had disappeared to go for his swim, Alex sat on a sofa beneath the shades that covered the terrace, nursing a glass of mint tea while largely ignoring the laptop open in front of her. How on earth could she concentrate on emails when she had so many other things occupying her mind?

Like that kiss…

No, not the kiss, she amended firmly. Hadn't she decided she wasn't going to think about it ever again? Wasn't she supposed to be completely ignoring the irritating little voice inside her head that demanded more of the delicious heat of it? She had and she was, and besides, it wasn't as if she didn't have anything else to think about. Such as the extraordinary conversation she'd just had with Max's mother.

As he'd told her, Carolyn Stafford had nothing to add to the investigation. With regard to Max's adoption, her then husband, the first of four and Max's father, had dealt with all the practicalities. He was the one who'd found the agency, arranged the payment and booked the flights to Argentina. She couldn't even recall filling in any forms. When it came to actually picking Max up, she had the haziest of recollections involving a woman whose name she couldn't remember, which struck Alex as very peculiar when it had to have been a momentous occasion.

The minute she'd established that Mrs Stafford could be of no further help, Alex should have hung up. The rest of the conversation had borne no relevance to anything. She didn't need to know about the issues in the marriage, the troubles they'd had conceiving and the belief that adopting a baby would somehow fix everything. The impact the divorce had had on Mrs Stafford was neither here nor there, although the way she hadn't spared a thought for how Max might have taken it was telling. She evidently held her son to blame for failing to repair the marriage, which didn't seem at all fair, and obviously considered him lacking in pretty much every other area. The digs and barbs had been well wrapped up and so subtle as to be easily missed, but Alex had noted them nonetheless.

But, to her shame, she hadn't hung up. Instead she'd listened to his mother's litany of complaints with growing indignation. She hadn't recognised anything about the man being described and at one point a sudden, inexplicable urge to put things right had surged up inside her, the force of it practically winding her.

But she'd known it would achieve precisely nothing.

Firstly, given that she'd only met Max yesterday, she was hardly qualified to provide an in-depth commentary on his character, even if she did have an extremely thorough knowledge of his mouth. Secondly, early on in her career with the police, Alex had done a course on psychopathic personalities and it sounded as if Max's mother was a narcissist. She'd come across as self-absorbed, condescending and unfairly critical. Everything had been about her. Any attempt to stand up for Max would have fallen on deaf ears, and that wasn't part of the job anyway.

She couldn't exactly start questioning him on it, she reminded herself, taking a sip of tea and staring out to sea, regardless of how much she might want to deep down. Not only was it none of her business, she was here to work, nothing more. She didn't need to know and, in any case, he wasn't around to ask.

And that was something else that was beginning to bother her, even though it surely shouldn't. Max had been gone for three hours. Wasn't that quite a long time for a swim? What if something had happened? Could he have been caught in a rip tide? What if he'd got a cramp and drowned? He might be a grown man who lived by the sea and presumably swam a lot, but maybe she ought to contact the coastguard. Just in case.

Trying to keep a lid on her growing alarm, Alex picked up her phone and opened up the browser to look for the number, when her gaze snagged on something moving in the water. A figure broke through the shimmering surface of the azure water, and she froze.

First to emerge was a sleek dark head, followed by a set of broad shoulders that she hadn't had nearly enough time to explore before. A swimmer's shoulders, she thought dazedly as she put the phone down, since there was clearly no need to contact the coastguard. Max, looking like some sort of Greek god, rising from the deep, master of all he surveyed, had not perished in the waves.

As he waded through the shallows, giving his head a quick shake that sprayed water off him like droplets of sparkling sunlight, more of his body was revealed. She was too far away to make out the details, but his bronzed shape was magnificent and by the time his long powerful legs emerged, undiluted lust was drumming through her, drugging her senses and heightening her awareness of everything. Her mouth was dry. Her breasts felt heavy and tight, and she was filled with the insane urge to get up and meet him and pull him down onto the sand with her and finish what they'd started back there in the guest house.

Having reached the shore, Max bent and picked up a towel off a lounger. He rubbed it over his head, slung it around his neck and started striding up the beach towards the steps, which gave her approximately thirty seconds to compose herself. It wasn't nearly enough, she realised, taking a series of slow deep breaths to calm her racing pulse and rid her body of the dizzying heat that she'd thought she'd obliterated hours ago.

But she managed it somehow, until he came to a stop right in front of her, blocking her view of the sea with an even better one, and she realised that her efforts had been in vain.

He didn't have an ounce of fat on him. He was all lean hard muscle. The depth of his tan suggested he spent a lot of time shirtless in the sun. Judging by the definition of his six-pack, he wasn't completely desk-bound. And she didn't need to wonder what might lie at the base of the vertical line of golden-brown hair that bisected his abdomen and disappeared enticingly beneath the waistband of his shorts because she'd felt it. She'd pressed her hips against it and wanted it hard and deep inside her, and that was exactly what would have happened if only that door hadn't slammed.

But she wasn't going to think about earlier. She certainly wasn't going to bring it up. If Max did, she'd brush it off as if it had meant nothing. Which it hadn't. And she was *relieved* that door had slammed, not disappointed.

But whatever.

Denial was the way forward here, even though she generally considered it an unwise and unhelpful strategy. In her line of work, knowledge was power. If her clients could accept what was going on, they could handle it. Right now, however, confronting what had happened when she was on such unsteady ground around him seemed like the worst idea in the world, and if that made her a hypocrite then so be it.

'How was the swim?' she said, nevertheless struggling to keep her tone light and her gaze off his chest.

'Good.'

'You were gone a long time.'

A gleam lit the depths of his indigo eyes. 'Were you worried about me, Alex?'

Maybe. 'No.'

He gripped the ends of the towel, which drew her attention to his hands and reminded her of how warm and sure they'd been, first on her face and then on her body.

'There's a floating bar the next bay along. I stopped for a drink.'

'A floating bar?' she echoed, determinedly keeping the memory of his kisses at bay. Was there no end to the incredibleness of this place?

'I'll take you for dinner there this evening.'

'I didn't bring a swimsuit.'

His gaze roamed over her, so slowly and thoroughly that she felt as if her clothes were simply falling away like scorched rags, and he murmured, 'That's a shame.'

No, it wasn't. The assignment didn't include swimsuits, dinner in a floating bar or the shedding of clothing. 'This isn't a holiday for me, Max,' she said, setting her jaw and pulling herself together. 'I was expecting to be heading straight to La Posada.' Which was situated six hundred kilometres inland. 'I didn't pack for a Caribbean island stopover.'

'All right. Forget the swimsuit,' he said, which immediately made her think of skinny-dipping with him in the gorgeous water beneath the moonlight. 'We'll go by boat.'

'No.'

'I apologise,' he said with a tilt of his head and a faint smile that lit an unwelcome spark of heat in the pit of her stomach. 'How would you feel about going by boat?'

The same. It wasn't going to happen, however he phrased it. She wasn't here for fun, and dinner out felt strangely dangerous. 'I'd rather you called in the favours you mentioned.'

'I already have.'

What? 'When?' she asked with a frown. How could he have wrong-footed her yet again?

'Earlier. On the plane.'

'What happened to working together?'

'What do you mean?'

'We had a deal, Max. You asked me to hand over everything, which I did. The least you could do is include me in your decision-making.'

'You were taking a nap.'

His reasonableness riled her even more than his unpredictability. 'Still,' she said frostily, not quite ready to accept that he'd done the right thing, given what had happened when the two of them had found themselves in close proximity to a bed. 'You should have told me.'

'I just have.'

Agh. 'You're impossible.'

His grin widened. 'Did you eat lunch?'

'No.' She hadn't felt comfortable raiding his fridge.

'Neither did I, and it seems neither of us is at our best on an empty stomach. So shall we meet back here in, say, half an hour?'

To her despair, Alex was all out of excuses. Any further protest and he might start questioning what was behind it. There was no way she wanted him guessing how much their kiss had unsettled her. Or how confusing she found the switch in demeanour when the last time she'd seen him he'd been all troubled and tense. And she badly needed him and his near naked body out of her sight. His mention of stomachs was making her want to check out his and she feared she wouldn't be able to stop there.

'Sounds great.'

CHAPTER FIVE

STALKING INTO HIS en-suite bathroom, Max stripped off and grabbed a towel. He secured it round his waist, rolled his shoulders to ease the ache that had set in as a result of his lengthy swim and, with a quick rub of his jaw, turned to the sink.

As he'd hoped, vigorous exercise, a cold beer and easy conversation had assuaged his earlier excruciating tension. It had taken a while, however. He'd been ploughing through the warm tropical water for twenty minutes at full speed before he'd been able to stop thinking about what would have happened had he and Alex not been interrupted.

His imagination had been on fire, and it had occurred to him as he'd cracked open a beer at La Copa Alegre that that was unusual because, despite his mother constantly telling him that his was very vivid whenever he'd tried to correct her memory about certain things as a kid, he'd never thought he had much of one. His ability to see outside the box and apply lateral thinking to problem-solving was second to none, but it was always done in the context of data. Facts. Systems, processes and algorithms. Lurid was not a word that had ever applied to his thoughts. It was now.

On emerging from the sea he'd intended to head

straight for the house. But he'd felt Alex's eyes on him like a laser and had instead deviated towards her as if drawn by some invisible force. She'd taken off her jacket, he'd noticed once he'd been standing in front of her. The pale pink T-shirt she'd had on had been tight. The alluring curve of her breasts had not escaped his notice, and as a bolt of heat had rocketed through him at the memory of how she'd felt in his hand, tightening his muscles and giving him an erection as hard as granite, he'd been grateful for the loose fit of his shorts.

She might have chosen to opt for denial with regard to the chemistry they shared, he thought now, lathering up his jaw, reaching for a razor and setting about methodically cutting swathes through the foam, but he wasn't. That kiss had blown his mind. He wanted more. A lot more. And so did she. She'd barely been able to keep her eyes off his bare chest just now. The hunger in her gaze had been illuminating. It gave him ideas. Would it be playing dirty to capitalise on her interest in his body? Might it not simply lead her to realise that little bit faster that making out with him hadn't been a mistake?

He couldn't deny that the idea of pushing more of her buttons appealed. He liked the way her eyes narrowed and flashed when she was riled. It gave him a kick, as did the thought of demolishing her barriers and persuading her to break her own rules. The end would more than justify the means. Based on the wild heat of the kiss, he had little doubt the end would be spectacular.

There was no need to dwell on the other ways in which Alex bothered him, he told himself as he rinsed his face. He wasn't interested in any similarities in their upbringings. Or their myriad differences in outlook. He'd never meet her family. It didn't matter that she'd looked very comfortable sitting on his sofa on his terrace drinking his tea. Or somehow *right*. No one had been or ever would be right.

Love didn't exist, in his experience—certainly not the unconditional kind that people banged on about—and he was through long ago with trying to conform to someone else's expectations in the futile hope of reward. But even if he had believed in it, even if he had deserved it, he would have steered well clear.

Love, he'd decided while cooling his heels in that prison cell all those years ago, was likely to be unpredictable and tumultuous. It would follow no formula and the outcome would not be dependent on the input. If love were a flowchart, it wouldn't be nice and neat, with square boxes and straight arrows. It would be a mess of thought bubbles filled with dramatic declarations and angst amidst a tangle of wiggly lines, a constant state of confusion and turmoil, and who needed that kind of hassle?

Sure, he'd had a few wild and wacky girlfriends as a youth, but he'd subsequently come to the conclusion that it was far safer to focus on his own world and his place in it. To be in total control of his actions and opinions and emotions, and responsible for those alone. Relationships meant having to take someone else's feelings into account, and he'd never been shown how to do that. He wouldn't know how to do such a thing even if he'd wanted to.

No, when it came to women, he was supremely content with keeping things short and simple, one or two nights, a week at most, avoiding emotional involvement and unmeetable expectations, and how he felt about Alex was no different. The strength of his desire for her might be unique, but she wasn't. All he wanted, he thought as he stepped into the shower and switched on the water, was her in his bed. Anything else was totally irrelevant. So tonight he'd focus on that.

La Copa Alegre was as fabulous as Alex had imagined. The two-floor wooden platform was anchored to the seabed three hundred metres offshore and floated on the surface of a literal sea of cerulean. In the centre stood the grass-roofed bar. At one end, giant sails of fawn fabric shaded the deck, upon which sat half a dozen double sunbeds. At the other was the grill that had cooked the sublime seafood platter which had arrived at their table twenty minutes ago. Strings of softly glowing lights looped around the structure and sultry Latin American beats thumped out of the speakers situated on the top floor that was a sun deck by day and dance floor by night.

So in no way was it the venue making Alex regret not being firmer in putting her foot down about dinner. That was all down to Max, who for some reason had decided to switch on the charm.

It was hard enough to resist him when he was being irritatingly unpredictable and immensely frustrating. It was almost impossible when he kept up a flow of easy conversation while flashing her devilish smiles. And then there was the revelation that he was fluent in Spanish. She didn't speak a word, so she could only take an educated guess at what he actually said when he issued greetings and ordered drinks and food, but the sexy accent and the deep timbre of his voice when he rolled his 'r's were spine-tingling.

So much for her intention to stick to mineral water and keep a clear head, she thought exasperatedly, taking a sip of her drink and despairing of how badly wrong this whole occasion was going. She'd given in to his suggestion of a margarita with embarrassing speed. But then she'd needed something strong to dampen the insane heat and desire that had been rushing along her veins and repeatedly knocking her sideways ever since he'd reappeared on the terrace on the dot of the appointed hour.

That he'd been on time had been a surprise. The fact that he'd shaved was another. On the one hand it was rather exciting to be able to gaze at the strong line of his jaw, but on the other she missed the stubble that had, only this morning, grazed the ultra-sensitive skin of her neck and whipped up such a whirlpool of sensation inside her.

And then there were all the tiny touches that had happened along the way. The warm palm at the base of her spine as he'd led her to the boat, burning through the fabric of her top and scorching her back. The firm grip of his fingers around hers when he'd helped her first board and then alight on arrival at the bar. Why hadn't he let her go as abruptly as he had this morning? Why had his hand lingered on hers? More annoyingly, why couldn't she stop thinking about the kiss?

Under any other circumstances, with the attention Max was paying her, this evening might feel like a date. Yet it wasn't. It couldn't be. Nor was any of it remotely relaxing. The margarita was doing nothing to assuage the desire flooding every inch of her being. Her pulse thudded heavily in time to the music vibrating through her. She'd changed into a sleeveless top and a pair of loose trousers, but her clothes felt too tight. Every time she moved, the fabric brushed over her body and her hypersensitive skin tingled.

She was overdressed, that was the trouble. The rest of the select, beautiful clientele were far more scantily clad, and that included Max. He was wearing a pair of sand-coloured shorts and a white shirt that he hadn't bothered to button up, and that was yet another source of discomfort. His bare chest, just across the table, was insanely distracting. She couldn't look away. She wanted to lean over and touch. To put her mouth to his skin and see if she could taste traces of salt from his swim. At one point he'd lifted his bottle of beer to his mouth and a drop of condensation had landed on his right pec. It had sat there, not going anywhere, snagging her attention, and she'd wanted to lick it off. She'd wanted to trace her tongue over the ridges of his muscles and run her fingers over the smattering of hair that covered them.

The clamouring urge to do all this—and more—was not only crazy, it was intolerable. She would never give in to it. It would not be professional to embark on anything with someone who was part of an assignment. If she did and it got out, her reputation would be destroyed. But even if there had been no assignment and they'd met under entirely different circumstances, Max would still be off-limits. Firstly, he'd never allow her to call the shots and, secondly, he posed a huge threat to her control and could easily give her a push down the genetic slippery slope she feared so much.

No, she had to focus on work and stay strong. Her resolve must not weaken, however great the provocation. She had to call a halt to the nonsense going on inside her.

She set her glass down with rather more force than was necessary and determinedly pulled herself together. 'So I spoke to your mother,' she said, taking a prawn from the platter and peeling it. 'You were right. She doesn't have anything to add to this case.'

'I thought not.'

Max appeared to have nothing further to add to that, but she needed to pursue this line of questioning if she stood any chance of keeping her thoughts out of the gutter. 'Aren't you interested in what she did have to say?'

'I can't think of anything I'm less interested in right now.'

His languid gaze drifted over her, electrifying her nerve-endings, and the prawn she'd just put in her mouth nearly went down the wrong way, but she was not to be deterred.

'You said she was difficult,' she said, clearing her throat and ignoring the sizzling heat powering through her veins. 'I can see what you mean.'

'Have I told you how lovely you look this evening?'

At his compliment her temperature rocketed, despite her best efforts to stay cool. 'We only met yesterday,' she said, determined not to let it or the unsettlingly alluring gleam in his eyes detract her. 'I look like this all the time.'

'And still very professional.'

Now that was a compliment she could get behind. If he recognised that their relationship was to remain purely professional it would make her life a whole lot easier for the next week or two. 'Thank you.'

'Do you ever let your hair down?'

She frowned. What did that have to do with anything? 'Literally or metaphorically?'

'Either. Both.'

'Metaphorically, I run. The generally wet, perpetually grey pavements of London aren't a patch on your lovely Caribbean waters, but I like them.' And literally, her hair was tied back in a ponytail this evening, which was really rather relaxed for her. But they were getting off topic. 'So. Back to what I was saying, I—'

'Alex.'

'Yes?'

'Stop.'

'Stop what?'

'I'm not going to talk to you about my mother,' he said, the cool evenness of his tone totally belying the shutters she could see slamming down over the gleam. 'Not this evening. Not ever.'

Why not? What was the story there? She badly wanted to know, because there definitely was one, and these days she couldn't come across a mystery without needing to solve it. But his jaw was set and his shoulders were tight, and what could she do? Wrestle the information out of him?

'All right,' she said, suppressing the instant vision of exactly how that wrestling might play out and parking the topic of his mother until later.

'Good.'

'Have any of those favours you called in produced anything useful?'

'Not yet.'

'It's insanely frustrating.'

'And far too nice an evening to be talking about the investigation,' he said, his eyes glittering in the candlelight and the faint smile now curving his lips doing strange things to her stomach. 'There'll be plenty of time for that when we arrive in La Posada tomorrow. Why don't you take a break tonight?'

Take a break? He had *no* idea. 'I haven't taken a break in years,' she said, flatly ignoring his effect on her.

'All the more reason to do so now.'

What did he know about it? 'How much time do you take off?'

'Three or four months a year.'

Seriously? 'What do you do?'

'I surf. Hang out with friends. Travel.'

Alex stifled the pang of envy and then consoled herself with the realisation that he'd been his own boss twice as long as she had. 'Has your business never given you a moment's concern?'

He leaned forwards and regarded her thoughtfully for a second. 'Honestly?' he said, turning his attention to the seafood platter. 'No. Ever since I was arrested I've had so much work come my way that I've been able to pick and choose.'

'An unusual outcome to an arrest, I imagine, but lucky you.'

'It's not luck. I'm exceptionally good at what I do.'

And what else might that be? she couldn't help wondering as her gaze snagged on his hands, which were deftly dealing with a lobster claw. How skilled would they be on her? Not that they'd ever *be* on her again, obviously. The kiss had been a never-to-be-repeated aberration, and he was still talking.

'Your website says that you were in the police for ten years before you started up your own agency five years ago.'

'That's right,' she said, ruthlessly removing the scorching images of his hands on her body from her head and biting into the slice of lime that garnished her margarita in the hope that the sharp acid hit might jolt some sense into her.

'What made you swap?'

This was better. A conversation about work she could handle. 'Years ago, when I suspected my then husband was cheating on me, I hired a private investigator to find out what was going on and report back to me. Which he did. But not with a whole lot of sympathy or tact. I saw a gap in the market for a more sensitive approach and decided to fill it. We started off investigating cases of suspected infidelity, then expanded to work on missing persons and fraud. There's very little we don't now cover.'

'Impressive.'

She put down the slice of lime and sat back. 'I have big plans, which I will allow nothing and no one to ruin,' she said pointedly.

'I'm surprised that you'd take the risk.'

Oh? 'Why?'

'You said you liked order and structure. A career in the police reflects that. Setting up your own business doesn't.'

Hmm. So that was true. She'd never really thought about it like that. She'd only ever focused on her need for security. But maybe she was more of a risk-taker than she'd thought. Professionally, at any rate. Only time would tell whether hers would pay off, but if it didn't it wouldn't be because she hadn't tried her hardest.

'Yes, well, there was also the complication that my ex worked for the police too,' she said, hauling her focus back to the conversation. 'We met on the training course and were posted to the same area. The divorce made things difficult. I was under no obligation to leave but it was hard. Especially when he started dating another colleague.'

'He should have been the one to go,' Max said bluntly.

'I agree,' Alex replied. 'But once I got my head around it and started making plans it was exciting. I wanted to move on anyway. From everything.'

'What went wrong?'

So that was none of his business. That strayed from the professional into the personal, and it was a step she wasn't sure she wanted to take. She didn't like to talk about the mistakes she'd made or even think about how naïve and foolish and desperate she'd once been.

And yet, if she shared more of herself with Max, maybe he'd feel obliged to do the same with her. Her curiosity about his relationship with his mother was killing her. She wanted to know everything about it, for the case, naturally, but she suspected it would not be forthcoming without serious leverage. Perhaps not even then, but she had to give it a try, and since she'd got over the disaster of her marriage long ago, it wouldn't exactly be traumatic.

'I got married far too young and far too quickly,' she said, twirling her glass between her fingers and resisting the urge to down the remainder of her drink. 'I'd already left the chaos of my family behind. A solid relationship seemed to me to be the next step and I guess I thought that in one I'd find the emotional connection I'd been missing at home. I was embarrassingly desperate to go down the conventional route. I thought I'd found a partner for life and we were engaged within three months.'

'So it was a whirlwind romance.'

'Hardly,' she said dryly. 'He broke our vows within months of the ink drying on the certificate. Yet it took me five more years of trying to fix things before realising that I had to end it for good.'

'That's a long time.'

'Far too long, in hindsight. God knows where my self-respect was. But I hated the thought of failing. I gave him endless chances and believed too many of his promises. I tried to change, more fool me. I even turned down a promotion because it meant more time away from home and he wasn't happy about that.'

'You left no stone unturned.'

'Exactly. But none of it worked.' She shook her head

and gazed at the shadowy horizon for a moment before giving herself a quick shake. Regrets were futile. All she could do was ensure that if she ever did get over her trust issues enough to embark on another relationship, she wouldn't make the same mistake again. 'Looking back, I don't know what I was thinking. I guess I was going through some kind of identity crisis. Police officers are supposed to have sound judgement. Mine was a disaster.'

'The man was an idiot.'

'Well, he was young too,' she said, a little confused by the ribbon of warmth that was winding through her at Max's terse pronouncement. 'And my career was moving faster than his, which I think he found intimidating. He used to make these sly little comments to undermine my confidence and belittle me.'

'Like I said, an idiot.'

'The only good thing to come out of the whole sorry mess was that I made a promise to myself that never again would I try and be what someone else expected me to be. I've learned to be exceptionally resilient on that front. Very little shocks me these days. Except people's propensity for self-centredness. That still floors me every time. I don't know why.'

'What did your parents want you to be?'

'Definitely not a police officer,' she said, unable to prevent a quick stab of hurt and regret from piercing her heart. 'I grew up in a very working class area of east London, except "working" class is a bit of a misnomer. It was a sink estate with lots of crime and many social problems. My school had a forty per cent truancy rate. No one cared. I once told my teacher that I wanted to go to university and she first just stared at me and then burst out laughing. At that point I realised that if I wanted to achieve anything I'd have to do it on my own. Joining the police was a way out.'

'Do your parents still live there?'

'Yes.'

'Your job must have made visiting tricky.'

'It made it impossible. But then I wasn't welcome anyway. I'm still not.'

'Do you want to be?' he asked, something about the intensity of his expression suggesting that he was really interested in her answer.

'I'm not sure,' she said with a sigh. 'Sometimes I think I do, which is nuts, right?'

'Not at all. As we've already established, families are complicated. Yours is probably jealous.'

She stared at him for a moment as that sank in. 'Do you think so?'

He shrugged. 'It's a possibility, I guess, although I'm no expert. But, ultimately, whatever lies at the heart of it, it's not your problem. You can't change anything. You'd be better off letting it go.'

Easy for him to say. 'And how do I go about that?'

'I wish I knew.'

A shadow flitted across his expression and she wondered suddenly if perhaps it wasn't easy for him to say. Could it be that he wasn't as laid-back as he liked to portray, and was, in fact, far more complex a character than she'd thought? It was a more appealing idea than it should have been. 'Let me know when you figure it out.'

'Likewise. But, for what it's worth,' he said, 'I think that what you've achieved under the circumstances is remarkable.'

Did he? She scoured his face for signs of insincerity but found none. Well, well, well. A little boost to her self-esteem from a man who was her opposite in almost every way. Who'd have thought? 'Thank you.'

'You're welcome. Would you like some dessert?'

Yes, was the answer on the tip of her tongue. For dessert she wanted him. A little salt, a little sweetness, a whole lot of spice. However, since that wasn't going to happen and she was full of shellfish and margarita, she ought to decline. But, for some bizarre reason, she couldn't get the 'no' out. Despite how very on-edge she was feeling, she didn't want the evening to end. And, besides, he owed her now, and this time she wouldn't be letting the debt go unpaid. 'Dessert would be lovely.'

CHAPTER SIX

MAX DUG HIS spoon into a bowl of coconut sorbet and thought that he could easily understand Alex's determination not to conform to someone else's expectations. How many times as a kid had he tried to do the exact same thing, with equally disappointing results? How long had he spent pointlessly trying to figure out what it was his mom wanted from him and then attempting to provide it, to no avail? It had never ended well. The inevitable failure ate away at a person's confidence and crushed their spirit until either they were ground to dust or got out. Like him, Alex had chosen the latter. He wondered if, also like him, she inwardly recoiled at the word 'compromise'.

Her ex-husband was the biggest fool on the planet. She was beautiful, intelligent and capable. To be cherished, not cheated on, if a long-term relationship was your thing. Any idiot could see that. How pathetically insecure must he have been, to handle her successes with such disparagement. How difficult that must have been to live with. Max had experienced both, having been on the receiving end of endlessly crippling insincerity and belittling while growing up, and his admiration for her grew.

Not that Alex's marriage was any of his concern, beyond the fact that it had ended and she was now single. How much he admired her was irrelevant. The stab of sympathy he'd felt when she'd been talking about disappointing her family had been wholly unnecessary.

What was important here was that his plan to get her into bed worked and, infuriatingly, with the way things were going, it didn't look as if it was going to. All evening he'd been as charming as he knew how—which had had great results in the past—and he'd deliberately left his shirt undone, but she'd seemed remarkably unmoved by his efforts. She'd generally responded to his flirting with an arch of an eyebrow and a glare of disapproval and hadn't ogled his chest once.

He, on the other hand, was anything but unmoved by her. She'd changed out of the trouser suit of earlier into a pair of loose-fitting trousers and a sleeveless top and looked effortlessly chic, which was a result he was sure she hadn't intended. The breeze had loosened her ponytail so that tendrils of hair fluttered around her face. He wanted to peel the clothes from her body and pull the band from her hair with a need that bordered on desperate.

While eating, she kept making all these appreciative noises, even groaning at times, and he'd instinctively contemplated all the ways *he* might be able to make her groan, should the opportunity arise. Desire was drumming through him and he was so hard it hurt and all he could think about was what it would take to erode her resolve. What more could he do? The not knowing, the possibility of failure, was driving him nuts.

'What you've achieved is remarkable too,' she said, cutting through his frustration and making him glance up at her.

'What do you mean?'

'It doesn't sound like you had the easiest of child-hoods either.'

He didn't want to talk about that. He wanted to talk about the chemistry they shared that she seemed determined to ignore, or, better still, act on it. And what did she know of his childhood anyway? How long had her conversation with his mother lasted?

'As I told you before,' he said so smoothly she'd never guess how churned-up inside he was feeling, 'that subject is off-limits.'

'Was it that bad?'

It had been traumatic and difficult and he had no wish to take a trip down that particular memory lane. 'It bears no relevance to anything.'

The look she levelled at him was pointed. 'Neither did mine.'

Now what was that supposed to mean? That because she'd talked to him he was under some sort of obligation to reciprocate? To hell with that. He'd hardly forced her to spill out the details of her marriage. He hadn't even been that interested. He owed her nothing.

And yet...

Maybe it wasn't such a bad idea. What if opening up to her succeeded where the flirting and his bare chest hadn't? What if she was the sort of woman to be lured into bed with sincerity and connection rather than flattery and visuals?

He wanted her more than he'd wanted anyone and failure hadn't been an option since the moment he'd left the police station a reformed character. So perhaps he should take a leaf out of her book and leave no stone unturned in his quest to seduce her.

Any connection created would hardly be deep and it sure as hell wouldn't be binding. It wasn't as if his experiences were any great secret. It was just that he'd never felt the need to share before. He'd never had a conversation where this aspect of his past came up. But it had now, and if he continued to deflect she might suspect there was more to it than there really was, and for some reason that didn't appeal. Besides, with her background, she'd hardly be likely to judge.

'All right, fine,' he said, nevertheless bracing himself as he set his spoon into his empty bowl and met her gaze. 'The environment I grew up in was a toxic one.'

She sat back and regarded him steadily, and he was strangely relieved to see in her expression no sign of victory that she'd succeeded where no one else ever had. 'You said your parents argued.'

'It was more than just that,' he said darkly. 'It was frequently a full-on war. My mother is obnoxious.'

'Your mother is a narcissist.'

At her blunt observation, Max frowned. 'What makes you say that?'

'Well, I'm no expert, obviously, but I once did a course on psychopathic personalities and, from what I recall, she fits the profile.'

'Which is?'

'A constant demand for praise and attention, ignoring the needs of others and a belief of being special, for a start.'

That sounded very familiar. 'How about an inability to tolerate criticism, never-ending attention-seeking and an obsessive need to control the lives of others?'

She nodded and took a sip of her drink. 'All that too.'

'Then you could be right.' He'd always known his mother was utterly self-absorbed, but he had to admit now that was probably the least of it.

'The conversation I had with her earlier today was extraordinary.'

'What did she say?'

Alex tilted her head and regarded him for one long heart-stopping moment. 'I thought you didn't want to know.'

Well, no, he hadn't then. But he did now. Because, to be quite honest, he was sick to the back teeth of being in the dark. The dark was where a man could get hurled off course, where doubts set in and chaos reigned, and three days of it was more than enough. 'Humour me.'

'It's not pretty.'

'I can take it,' he said, thinking that that was hardly news. Nothing about his family background was pretty. How bad could it be?

'You won't shoot the messenger?'

He had entirely different plans for the messenger if this strategy of his played out. 'No.'

'OK, then,' she said, taking a deep breath, her gaze unwavering. 'She told me that the marriage was in trouble and that she'd decided a baby—you—would fix things. Your father initially refused but she told him that if he loved her he'd do this for her, and fast.'

Even though he'd been expecting the worst, the information still struck him like a blow to the gut. Yet another ultimatum, he thought, acid and bitterness swilling around inside him. How he hated them. So he really *hadn't* been wanted by his parents. He didn't know why it was such a shock when the evidence had always been there, but it was nonetheless.

'She said she doesn't remember anything about picking you up,' Alex continued, oblivious to the turmoil he was experiencing, 'and I don't know if that's genuinely the case or if, once it had been done, it had served its purpose and didn't require any more thought. Given her narcissism, I suspect the latter. She laid a lot of the blame for things at your feet, wholly unfairly. That kind of behaviour can be very destructive. I'm so sorry.'

He loathed the pity in her eyes and wished he could shrug casually, but he couldn't. 'It's not your fault,' he said, thinking that the old adage 'be careful what you wish for' had never been more appropriate.

'My father should have stood up to her. He should have been stronger. He should have said no.'

'Narcissists can be very persuasive and manipulative.'

She was right about that. To the outside world, his mother was beautiful and charming. It was only with her family that she showed her true monstrous self. Appearances were everything, which was presumably why their disaster of a marriage had limped on for so long. But still.

'He was weak. He was worse than I was in his efforts to please an unappeasable woman.'

'A toxic environment indeed.'

'And yet he left me there.' For which Max had never forgiven him. But perhaps the adoption explained that. Perhaps he'd never considered Max his true son.

'Didn't they share custody of you?'

'My mother was keen to keep control over me and my father couldn't have cared less.'

'How devastating.'

'It wasn't great.'

'Did you see much of him before he died?' she asked, her voice cracking a little and her eyes shimmering.

'Twice.' That was it. Neither visit had been a success. He'd harboured a lot of anger and his father had clearly just wanted to put everything behind him. 'He moved to Los Angeles after the divorce,' he said flatly, ruthlessly clamping the lid down on all the old memories and feelings that were bubbling up.

'The other side of the country.'

'It wasn't a coincidence.'

'And you choosing the Caribbean as your home, which is what, two thousand miles from New York?'

She was too clever by half. 'That's not a coincidence either.'

'I didn't think so. What about your stepfathers?'

'They were never around for long.'

'Used and then discarded?'

'Either that or they swiftly saw through the deceptively beautiful facade and got the hell out.'

She shook her head. 'I can't imagine what it must have been like.'

He was glad she couldn't. He wouldn't wish it on anyone. 'It wasn't much fun,' he said with staggering understatement. 'My dad couldn't have cared less about me while my mom was obsessed. She had to control everything. My friends, my clothes, even the music I listened to. Weakness and failure weren't allowed. They reflected badly on her. Expectations were impossibly high and I rarely met them, and the criticism was relentless. Nothing I did was ever good enough and she had no problem with letting me know that. If I put a foot out of line, she'd go very still and very quiet and then simply walk out of the room. In the end I figured it was less hassle to keep my opinions and feelings to myself. She wouldn't let me stay out of her way, so I just bided my time and bit my tongue until I got accepted at MIT.'

'How on earth did you get through it?'

'I had the hacking and its community.'

'Like I had studying,' she said with a slow nod of what looked like understanding. 'I spent most of my time at the library. That was where I realised my family chose to live the way they did and that I could choose not to.'

'Hence the rules?'

'Via the classics.'

'Everyone needs some form of escape.'

'And everyone has expectations to face,' she countered, 'although in my case, they were low rather than high. I still don't meet them and I've come to terms with that, so I have no idea why I still feel guilty about it.'

Her too? 'I was angry for a very long time.'

'I think I still am.'

'You should try a couple of days in jail. There's nothing like it for reflecting on what's going wrong and why. Break a law or two. It's a lot cheaper than therapy.'

'I'll bear that in mind,' she said with a faint smile. 'But you do realise your parents' behaviour is none of your fault, don't you?'

'In theory, yes. In practice, it's complicated.'

'As I know only too well. So is all that why you're so keen to track your biological parents?'

'I need to know who I am and where I come from,' he said, once again struck by her perception as much as the effect of her smile on his lungs. 'How I ended up with parents who didn't give a crap about me. With a mother who can't even remember travelling halfway across the world to pick me up and a father who barely spared me a thought. I've spent the last decade believing I'd dealt with it and living in relative peace. But one twenty-minute interview three days ago blew that peace to smithereens and I need it back. I hate not knowing what's going on. With so much information about my history missing, I suddenly feel like half a person. I need that information. I need answers.' Deep down, he also desperately hoped he'd find out that, whatever the circumstances that had led to his adoption, he'd once been wanted, but there was no way in hell he was going to share that with her. Exposing that level of vulnerability to another human being was never going to happen. Instead, he said, 'You have no idea what it's like to have your life so suddenly torn apart.'

'Well, I do have some idea,' she said with a tilt of her head. 'When I first found out my husband was cheating on me, my world collapsed. Not just my marriage, but everything I'd been working towards. Structure. Normality. A life of conventionality. It took me a while, too, to get back on track, and God knows it wasn't easy, but I did, and nothing will push me off it again.'

'Which is why the success of this assignment is so important to you, why you wouldn't just take my money and move on.' She was fighting for her future like he was fighting for his identity.

She nodded. 'When I was young I was repeatedly told I'd never amount to anything. I've worked hard to overcome that. You were right about the importance of the fee Finn's paying me. It does matter. But his good opinion is invaluable. Much of my work comes via word-of-mouth and his recommendation would open all kinds of doors. I have big expansion plans and I won't have them derailed.'

Yeah, well, he had big plans too and didn't want them derailed either. He was done with talking about the past. It was all water under the bridge anyway. He was infinitely more interested in the present and the imminent future. The conversation had taken an unexpectedly heavy turn but that didn't mean it couldn't now be steered in a different direction. It was still early and he wanted her as much as ever. It was time to wrap things up here and move on.

'Are you done?' he asked, wiping his head of the conversation and everything it had stirred up and contemplating his next step instead.

'Yes. Thank you.'

'Then we should head back.'

The boat journey back to Max's house was conducted in silence, the warm dark night acting like a sort of blanket that prevented further conversation, which was more than all right with Alex, who was feeling all churned up inside by what she'd learned about his upbringing, such as it had been.

She couldn't get the look of torment that had appeared on his face when she'd revealed what his mother had said to her on the phone out of her head. Or the shock and the hurt that had flashed in the depths of his eyes, even if he had got it all under control with remarkable speed.

Should she have told him? was the question that kept rolling around her thoughts. If she'd known the effect it was going to have on him, she might have thought twice. But, on the other hand, if they asked, didn't everyone deserve to know the truth, however messy, whether it was to do with a faithless spouse, an embezzling employee or a narcissistic mother? Hadn't she always believed that ignorance wasn't necessarily bliss?

One of the things she recalled from her course on psychopathic personalities was that the effects of narcissistic behaviour on those around the narcissist could include feelings of not being good enough, a deep-rooted need for approval and the suppression of emotion. Before this evening, if she'd put much thought to it, she'd have remembered Max's pride in his former life as a hacker and his general air of supreme confidence and assumed that he'd overcome any suffering he might have experienced or even escaped totally unscathed.

But she'd have been wrong.

How could he not have been affected? she reflected, her heart wrenching at the thought of it, while the Caribbean breeze whipped at the scarf she'd tied around her head to protect her hair. He'd essentially been bought by a pair of people who didn't deserve to be parents, and then shamelessly used by one while being wholly neglected by the other. It was hard to know which one of them had been worse. An insecure, manipulative mother or a father who'd bailed on him and left him to the cruel whims of a woman who only thought of herself?

What a horrible, wretched environment he'd been brought up in. He'd had no siblings, no one who was going through the same thing to talk to. What must it have been like to grow up knowing that his father didn't want him? That while his mother had been physically present, every interaction she'd had with him had had an ulterior motive? Where had the love been? The affection? Not that she knew much about it, having had little of either herself.

No wonder he'd sought out an online community among which to find what he'd been missing at home. She couldn't imagine it would have been the place for a discussion of the kind of angst his upbringing must have generated, but the comradeship he had clearly found there had to have been the only way to survive, just as studying and a plan to escape had for her. If there'd been anything remotely amusing about any of it she'd have thought it was funny how they'd both drawn the short straw on the family front, but really there wasn't.

Once they were on dry land and heading up the steps to the house, Alex wondered how he felt about it all now and what effects still lingered in a way that had nothing to do with the filling of a gap in her professional knowledge. She was intrigued by the many complicated layers to him and the insanely tough journey he'd had. She couldn't imagine what he was going through now, having had his world turned so upside down by the discovery of his adoption. Her identity crisis wasn't a patch on the one he had to be undergoing.

'Nightcap?' he offered as he headed for the outdoor bar, his deep voice making her shiver despite the balminess of the evening.

'No, thank you,' she said, managing to muster up a smile to mask the thoughts rocketing around her head. 'I think I'll head to bed.' Where she would no doubt revisit their conversation at the bar and wonder if there was some way she could help him deal with everything. Where she would ponder his insight into her family's possible jealousy and her blamelessness for it instead of the way he made her feel. Where her resolve to stay strong and resist him wouldn't be challenged by the burning desire to know more about him and the dark, sensual intimacy of the terrace that was softly lit by hundreds of tiny discreet solar-powered lights.

'The night is young.'

'But today's been a big day,' she pointed out, slightly dazed by how eventful it had been, 'and tomorrow's an even bigger one.'

He turned to face her and leaned against the worktop of the bar. 'Just one drink.'

'Jet lag is catching up with me.' It was a lie. She'd never felt so energised. But she didn't trust herself. The intensity of his gaze was a threat to her reason. Where was the flirting? Where was the charm? That she could bat away. This sudden serious intent of his, on top of the intimate conversation they'd had earlier, felt so much more dangerous.

'Coward.'

She went very still. His eyes were dark, his expression unsmiling and her pulse skipped a beat. 'What makes you say that?'

'Your determination to ignore what's between us.'

Her heart thumped and her mouth went dry. So they were doing this, then. 'There's nothing between us.'

The fire burning in his gaze nearly wiped out her knees. 'Our kiss this morning would suggest otherwise.'

'Like I said, that was a mistake.' And the less said about it the better.

'I disagree,' he said, his voice low and rough. 'It nearly blew the top of my head off. If that door hadn't slammed when it did, you know we'd have ended up in bed together. And you know we'd probably still be there.'

She envied how easily he could accept what he wanted from her. He was so sure, so confident. In this, she was quite the opposite and, despite the envy, she couldn't help wishing that he'd opted for denial like she had.

She swallowed hard and fought for control. 'I know nothing of the sort.'

'I'm very attracted to you, Alex,' he said, running his gaze over her so slowly and thoroughly that a wave of heat rushed over her, tightening her nipples in a way she desperately hoped he wouldn't notice. 'As you are to me. You can carry on burying your head in the sand if you want, but that won't make it go away.'

Wouldn't it? He was probably right. The pressure crushing her was immense. How much longer could she stand it? Perhaps if she confronted the attraction, the intoxicating mystery of it would disappear and along with it the heat and the desire. Denial wasn't working and facing up to things was something she encouraged in her clients, so maybe she ought to put her money where her mouth was.

'All right,' she said, mentally crossing her fingers and wishing her heart would stop hammering quite so hard. 'It's true. I want you. A lot. And I'm not in the slightest bit happy about it.'

'I know you aren't,' he said, the tension in his shoulders easing a fraction and the ghost of a smile curving his mouth. 'But do you have any idea how rare the chemistry between us is?'

'Not really,' she admitted, thinking that if she was in for a penny she might as well be in for a pound. 'I imagine I'm considerably less experienced than you.'

'We'd be explosive together.'

Like phosphorus and air. There she was, happily sitting surrounded by water, all nicely inert and safe, and then along he came, luring her to the surface and encouraging her to break through it, at which point things would go bang.

'It's not going to happen,' she said, having to believe that for the sake of her future.

'Why not?'

'There's a huge conflict of interest.'

'As we've established, I'm not your client.'

'That's not the point,' she said, struggling for a moment to remember quite what the point was when her head was filling with images of the two of them being explosive together. 'Finding the truth about your adoption is too important to me to screw up by fooling around and getting distracted.'

'Who says we can't do both?'

'I do.'

'You want me.'

'That doesn't matter.'

He regarded her for one achingly long moment. 'You know I could prove you wrong, don't you?'

In a heartbeat. Desire was flooding through her, weakening her knees and her resistance. All he'd have to do was touch her and she'd go up in flames. 'I'd hope you have more integrity than to try,' she said, inching back out of his mind-scrambling orbit and wondering if she was expecting too much from a criminally minded former hacker.

'On any other occasion, I'd say I absolutely do,' he said with an assessing tilt of his head. 'Right here, right now, however, I'd put it at fifty-fifty.'

Her heart gave a lurch and for one appalling moment she couldn't work out which fifty she wanted. But then she pulled herself together. 'I have rules about this sort of thing.'

'Of course you do.'

'Don't mock me.'

'I'm not. But would it really be so bad if they got broken?'

'Yes,' she said firmly, squashing the little voice in her head yelling, *Would it? Really?* The risks vastly outweighed any potential reward. She couldn't allow herself to think about possible explosions.

'Why?'

'I've worked insanely hard to get where I've got and my reputation is everything to me. I would stand to lose a lot if it got out that I fraternise with people involved in a case.'

'Who would ever know?'

'I would.'

'But think of the fireworks.'

'There'd be fireworks?' What was she saying? Of

course there'd be fireworks. Mini Catherine wheels were spinning in her stomach and they weren't even touching.

He ran his gaze over her yet again, as if he *knew* the effect it would have on her, and those Catherine wheels nearly took off. 'I know what I'm doing.'

That didn't help one little bit, because now all she could think about was how spectacularly good in bed he would be. 'I wish I did.'

'You do,' he said. 'You're successful and well-respected. Finn sang your praises. He described you as tenacious and determined. He wouldn't have hired you if you hadn't come highly recommended. Your reputation would be in no danger from sleeping with me.'

Maybe it would. Maybe it wouldn't. But, actually, that wasn't the real issue.

'You're wasting your time, Max,' she said with a shake of her head, although who she was trying to warn she wasn't sure. 'We are totally different. Sleeping with you would bring chaos to my life. You're unpredictable, a loose cannon. And I don't want that, however briefly. I need to stay in control of everything. My rules aren't just about order and structure. They keep me focused. On the right track. Every morning I wake up with the feeling that if I'm not careful I could well end up like the rest of my family. That all it will take is one slip, one "it'll be fine just this once", and genes will take over and I'll lose everything I've worked so hard for. You can't have any idea what that's like.'

'I know exactly what that's like,' he said, his eyes dark and glittering. 'I've done everything in my power not to turn out like either of my parents. Doesn't matter that we share no genes. Nurture trumps nature in my case.'

'I won't risk it.'

'Some risks are worth taking.'

'Not this one.'

He took a step towards her, and her breath caught while her heart hammered. 'I don't want anything long-term, Alex,' he said, his gaze so mesmerising she couldn't look away. 'I'm not cut out for that. I simply want you, for as long as we're working together.'

'And then what?'

'We go our separate ways with no regrets.'

But she would have regrets. She knew she would. She wouldn't be able to help throwing herself into it one hundred per cent, the way she did with everything, and while it would undoubtedly be fabulous while it lasted, the fallout would be huge. He was too overwhelming, too potent—too everything. The impact of a fling with him would be immense and she didn't want to have to mop up the mess afterwards. She wasn't willing to make that mistake again and that was all there was to it.

'This might be some kind of game to you, Max,' she said, the thought of history repeating itself injecting steel into her voice, 'but it isn't to me.'

'It's no game.'

'Then have some respect for my rules. Have some respect for me. And back off. Please.'

CHAPTER SEVEN

WATCHING ALEX SPIN on her heel and head off in the direction of the guest wing, Max grabbed a beer and cracked it open, disappointment and frustration coursing through him like boiling oil. Her resolve was stronger than he could have possibly imagined. Under any other circumstances he'd applaud it. Under these circumstances, tonight, he hated and resented it.

Not that that was her fault, of course. She had every right to turn him down and she'd given a perfectly reasonable, understandable explanation for why she was so reluctant to yield to the attraction that arced between them. He knew what it was like to fear turning into your family. He'd spent half his life concerned that both his father's general weakness of character and his mother's manipulation could be hereditary and had done everything in his power to avoid both.

But right now all he could think was that he'd given it his best shot with Alex and he'd failed. The physical attraction, although mutual and scorching, wasn't enough. Opening up and allowing her a glimpse into parts of him that hadn't seen the light of day for years wasn't enough. *He* wasn't enough.

Rejection spun through him at the idea of that, leaving the sting of a thousand darts in its wake and stirring up memories of his childhood that he'd buried deep long ago. Such as seeking out his father's attention for help with a school project, only to be dismissed with a glance of irritation and a mutter of 'later'. Such as once making a birthday cake for his mother, who'd showered him with thanks before telling him that she was watching her weight and tossing it in the trash. But he shoved aside the memories and ignored the tiny stabs of pain, loathing the weakness they represented.

The impact on him of Alex's rejection was ridiculous, he told himself grimly as he lifted the bottle to his mouth and necked half its contents. It wasn't as if she were the only woman on the planet he'd ever wanted, and it wasn't as if he'd never want anyone else. There were plenty of other women in this world who would be only too pleased to spend a night or two in his bed.

Why had he tried so hard with her? What made her worth an effort he'd never had to make before? Had he really been so keen for a distraction from the disruption caused by the discovery that he was adopted? Didn't that somehow make him a bit of a coward rather than her?

Well, whatever his motivations, whatever they made him, the result was the same. Despite the sizzling chemistry that she'd even acknowledged, she didn't want him. So he'd back off. He had no interest in pursuing someone who didn't want to be pursued and she'd made it very clear that she was that someone.

Starting now he'd withdraw the smiles and the charm she disdained and channel the pure professionalism that she valued so highly. He'd prioritise the investigation, the way she had. He'd get the answers he so badly needed and haul his life back on track. It was faintly pathetic that it mattered so much. He was a grown man of thirty-one, for God's sake. Professionally, he was at the top of his game. He was envied by the best of the best. Personally, however, the events of the last few days had revealed that he languished somewhere at the bottom, unable to claw his way up, and it was frustrating as hell. He needed to get to the truth, whatever it might be, so he could move on.

None of this was a game to him, despite Alex's accusation. It mattered. A lot. And that was all there was to it.

Max and Alex had arrived in La Posada late the following evening, having landed at the airport in La Quiaca in the afternoon and picked up a top-of-the-range four-by-four to cover the hundred-and-fifty-kilometre distance by road.

The Quechuan town, home to six thousand inhabitants and situated on the eastern edge of the Andes, stood on the top of a dramatic ridge. It had been rebuilt after a devastating earthquake twenty years before, some thirty kilometres from the original site. The air was dry and dusty. The surrounding landscape was rocky, the vegetation was sparse and the sun was harsh. The contrast to the sparkle and lushness of the Caribbean could not have been sharper.

But it wasn't the lack of humidity, the aridity or even the altitude that accounted for her irritability, Alex had to admit as she breakfasted alone on coffee and bread in the restaurant of the only hotel in town. It was her apparent and alarming contrariness.

Despite knowing she'd done absolutely the right thing by laying her cards on the table, bidding Max goodnight and marching off into the house, she'd still spent a large part of the night fretting about how things between them would turn out come morning.

What would she do if he completely ignored her plea

and launched a concerted effort to change her mind? she'd agonised as she'd stared at the ceiling and listened to the chirrup of the crickets that inhabited the thickets beyond the terraces. Realistically, how long would she be able to resist his considerable charms? She'd like to think for ever, but she was only human, the attraction was impossibly strong and it had been so long since she'd had any attention.

And why had he set his sights on her in the first place? She was nothing special. Surely he had to know far more appealing women than her, gorgeous, interesting ones who were totally on his wavelength and shared his approach to rules. No doubt she was merely convenient, popping into his life at a moment when he was in between contracts and looking for a challenge to fill the time. It could hardly be anything else. Despite the intimacy of the conversation they'd had at La Copa Alegre, he was so out of her league he might as well be on another planet.

In fact, her concerns had become so troubling that at one point she'd actually considered telling him to go to Argentina on his own and simply report back, which was so baffling and downright wrong that she'd had to give herself a mental slap to get a grip while reminding herself at length that never again was she going to allow how she felt about a man get in the way of work. Nor was she going to keep on wondering how explosive was explosive.

However, she needn't have worried. Max had clearly taken on board what she'd said. The smiles had gone and had been replaced with polite distance. He hadn't touched her once since they'd met on the deck to catch his boat to the airport. He'd barely even looked at her. On the plane he'd been professionalism personified. He'd opened his laptop the minute they'd taken off, and had only stepped away to make some calls.

Alex, on the other hand, had hardly been able to concentrate on anything. She'd been restless, as if sitting on knives, and the plane had felt oddly claustrophobic. Even Becky, with whom she'd checked in somewhere over north Brazil, had queried her distraction, for which she hadn't had much of an answer.

Bizarrely, with every nautical mile, she'd found herself growing increasingly irritated by Max's aloofness. Surely it was over-the-top. Surely they could have settled on somewhere in between flirty and frosty. To her confusion and consternation, that irritation still lingered.

None of it made sense, she thought frustratedly, taking a sip of freshly squeezed orange juice to wash down the last few flakes of delicious buttery *medialuna*. She should be glad he'd backed off. She shouldn't be feeling piqued that he'd done what she'd asked. And as for the disappointment that had lanced through her yesterday evening when the hotel he'd booked had had another room available, which he'd accepted without a moment's hesitation, what on earth had that been about? She didn't want to be put in a situation where they had to share a room. Or at least she shouldn't. And she ought to have been delighted not disappointed when, after checking in, he'd ordered room service before heading off, not to be seen again for the rest of the evening.

She couldn't work out what was wrong with her. Max was showing respect for her rules, for *her*, so where was the satisfaction? Where was the relief? Why was she missing the smiles, the conversation and even the dangerous edge of the night before last? Why did she keep willing him to actually meet her gaze for longer than a fleeting second or two? When exactly had she become so obsessed with his hands that she could practically feel them on her body?

She'd had nearly twenty-four hours to ruminate these baffling questions but, to her exasperation, she was no closer to an answer. But at least his imminent arrival at her table would give her a welcome break from that particular madness.

God, he was gorgeous, she thought, watching as he made his way across the room, weaving through the tables, all lithe grace and powerful intent. This morning he'd foregone the shave and her fingers itched to find out whether the light stubble adorning his jaw was as electrifying as she remembered. His hair was damp and, as a vision of him in the shower, standing beneath the jets while hot, steaming water poured over him and ran in rivulets down the contours of his body, flew unbidden into her head, she felt a throb between her legs.

'Good morning,' he said with a quick impersonal smile that she'd inexplicably grown to loathe.

Was it? It seemed very hot for this time of day. And she clearly hadn't got used to the altitude because she was suddenly finding it hard to breathe. 'Good morning.'

'Did you sleep well?'

To her surprise she had, but maybe it shouldn't have been unexpected, given the restlessness of the nights that had gone before. 'Like a log. You?'

'Same.'

Hmm. He didn't look as if he had, she thought, assessing him carefully as he took the seat opposite her and poured himself some coffee. Despite the tan, his face was slightly paler than usual, and drawn. Faint lines bracketed his mouth and the frown creasing his forehead looked as if it had been there a while. But his expression was unreadable and his eyes revealed nothing.

She wished she knew what he was thinking. It took no great leap of imagination to suppose this had to be hard on him. By his own admission, the discovery that he was adopted had turned his life on its head. She couldn't even begin to envisage what kind of upheaval it must have generated.

And now here they were in the country of his birth, the land of his heritage. Not only that, they were half an hour from the orphanage where he'd spent time before being taken to the US. It had all happened a long time ago, certainly, but surely it had to be having some kind of effect on him. He'd acted so swiftly on hearing the news and then moved so decisively. Those weren't the actions of a man who was largely indifferent. So could it be that deep down he was all over the place emotionally, and stoic detachment was his way of handling it?

'How are you feeling?' she asked, wondering if there was any way she could help, if there was indeed something troubling him.

'About what?'

'Well, everything, really,' she said, watching him closely for a reaction or a sign, however minuscule. 'But principally, being here in Argentina.'

'I'm feeling fine. Why?'

'I was thinking that today's visit to the orphanage might be difficult for you.'

'Not in the slightest,' he said as he reached for a roll.

'Are you sure?'

'Yes. It'll be fine.'

Right. So that was two 'fine's in a row. In her experience, nothing suggested a problem more. 'What time shall we leave?'

'There's no need for you to come.'

So that wasn't happening. For one thing, she wasn't

being cut out of the loop. For another, his shoulders were tight. His jaw now looked as if it was about to shatter. He was very much not 'fine'. There was no way she was letting him go through whatever he was going through alone. Her chest tightened and her throat ached at the mere thought of it and he'd had to deal with enough on his own.

'I disagree,' she said with a tiny jut of her chin as resolve surged inside her.

'Too bad.'

'This is my case too, Max. I've been working on it exclusively for eight months. I'm as invested as you are.'

His eyes met hers finally, incredulity shimmering in their indigo depths, along with a good deal of scepticism. 'You couldn't possibly be as invested as I am.'

Debatable, but also possibly an argument for another time. 'Consider me moral support then.'

'I don't need support,' he said flatly. 'Moral or otherwise.'

Yes, he did, despite the waves of rejection and denial radiating off him. She could understand why he might want to push her away. For him this had to be intensely personal. They weren't friends. They certainly weren't lovers. They were colleagues at most and she'd told him to back off. Why on earth *would* he want to share the experience with her?

But he could protest all he liked. Just because she'd put an end to the chemistry and the flirting, it didn't mean she didn't care. What if he *did* turn out to need the support? She was the only person to provide it right now and, in her admittedly biased opinion, she was also the best. A large part of her job was handling the fallout of her investigations with perceptiveness and sensitivity, and she excelled at reading emotionally fragile situations, instinctively knowing when to step in and when to stay back. She'd also learned to look beneath the surface, and beneath Max's, beneath the outward stoicism and steely control, she sensed great, seething turmoil.

'You have it, whether you want it or not.'

'You once asked me to back off, Alex,' he said warningly. 'Now I'm asking you to do the same.'

'This is different,' she said, having no intention of getting into a tit-for-tat. 'I'm worried about you, Max, and I have lots of experience in picking up pieces, should there be any. So I'm coming with you.' If he continued to reject her offer, then so be it, but if he said 'fine' again she'd know it was the right thing to do.

He let out a deep sigh of defeat and gave a shrug as if he couldn't care less. 'Fine.'

The drive to the Santa Catalina orphanage took longer than expected. Not only was the road riddled with potholes and strewn with rocks, they had to keep stopping for meandering alpaca. It was taking every drop of Max's concentration to avoid the hazards, yet with every passing kilometre his pulse thudded that little bit faster and his stomach churned that little bit harder.

Despite what he'd told Alex, in the hope she'd stop her damn prodding and leave him alone, he'd been feeling off-kilter ever since they'd landed. At first the unease had been vague, a mild cocktail of anticipation and uncertainty. But overnight the pounding of his head had intensified and a tight knot had lodged in his chest.

He didn't appreciate that he hadn't been as successful at hiding the mess of his emotions from Alex as he'd hoped, but he couldn't deny she'd been spot-on about the reasons for it. The minute he'd set foot on the land of his birth, he'd been rocked in a way he could never have anticipated. Arriving in La Posada, knowing that the orphanage he'd spent time in was so close, had compounded the unsettling sensation that his foundations were cracking.

But why any of that should be the case, he couldn't work out. Argentina was a country like any other. Largely destroyed in the earthquake, the orphanage was just a pile of stones. He'd read a report and seen a photo of the place in one of the attachments Alex had forwarded him. How traumatic could the reality actually be?

Nevertheless, he recognised that he was standing on shaky ground, metaphorically if not literally. He had been for days now. He'd held the chaos at bay by focusing on getting Alex into his bed, but, thanks to her determination to resist the attraction, that shield had shattered and, without it, havoc prevailed. The emotions he thought he'd got a handle on over a decade ago now crashed around inside him, fierce and volatile. If he didn't keep a tight grip on them, they could all too easily result in the hot mess of an eruption he'd once predicted, and he wanted no witnesses.

So why had he caved and allowed her to accompany him today? He could have simply taken off without her. He hadn't had to wait for her to meet him at the car. Yet his resolve, already weakened by the tempest whipping up a storm inside him, had crumbled to dust with petrifying speed.

Why did the idea of her support appeal so much? He'd survived perfectly well without it—or any support, for that matter—previously. The last thing he wanted was her picking up his pieces in the event there were any to pick up. And what did it matter if he couldn't recall the last time anyone had worried about him? He was totally used to being on his own and worrying about himself, well, *himself.*

For all he knew, Alex's concern and the support were just an excuse, and for her it was all about the job anyway. She'd made it blindingly clear how important the assignment was to her, so of course she wasn't going to give up the chance to find any more evidence for herself, or, if there wasn't any, closing down that line of enquiry once and for all. If he had any sense at all he'd be focusing on that instead of allowing himself to get side-tracked by contemplating other, more unsettlingly appealing motivations she might have, such as simply wanting to be there for him, which he knew, after their post-dinner conversation, couldn't be the case.

However, regardless of everything going on inside him, he was oddly relieved that she hadn't been deterred by his attempts to push her away. He was glad she was here, whatever her reasons. And because that was confusing as hell when she'd so flatly rejected him, and because he didn't have the wherewithal to analyse it right now, he thrust it from his mind and focused instead on navigating a patch of vegetation that had encroached onto a section of the road.

After consulting the map that the hotel receptionist had sketched out, Alex directed him off the main road and along a track lined with the remains of what looked like houses.

'It must have been quite an earthquake,' she said, gazing at the devastation all around.

'Seems risky, building a new town quite so close.'

'Better materials and modern methods, I suppose. There it is,' she said, pointing at a dilapidated building a couple of hundred metres ahead on the left and effectively cutting off his attempt at a distraction.

Max parked up, the hammering of his pulse and the thumping of his head more intense than ever, and got out. A dry, dusty wind was whistling down the abandoned streets and around the ruins. The only signs of life were a couple of goats, wandering about and nibbling on the odd wrecked tree. It was bleak and desolate and eerie, and there was a chill in the air despite the warmth of the midday sun.

Barely aware of Alex now, he walked on, as if being pulled in by some invisible force. The front door had long gone, as had the windows. Most of the walls had fallen in and there was no roof.

How on earth had he and his brothers wound up here? was the thought pummelling away at him as he moved from one destroyed space to another, numbly picking his way through the rubble. Who had left them here? Why? Had they been happy? Well-fed and cared for? How could they have been separated? What kind of adoption agency would have allowed such a thing?

In the absence of memories, speculation flooded through him, blurring his vision and quickening his breath. Babies. Kids. The noise, the bustle, the nuns. He could be standing on the very spot where he and his brothers had once slept...

But there were no clues here. This place had been stripped of anything useful or valuable long ago. The rusty filing cabinet that was bolted to what was left of a wall had already been emptied of documents by Alex's on-the-ground contact, who'd found his birth certificate and those of his brothers within. Nothing else remained.

He didn't know what he'd expected to find, he realised, his throat aching and his chest tight. Or why he'd come, when the place had been thoroughly searched already. The rashness of the decision, the uncertainty and the confusion indicated a weakness that he hated. If he'd somehow hoped to find a connection with his past, it had been a hugely self-indulgent move.

In fact, this whole experience was making him feel sick. His hands were clammy and his head was swimming, the nausea rolling through him threatening to overwhelm him. The world seemed to be spinning around him and he could hardly breathe. The blood was draining from his head and the strength was leaching from his limbs.

What if he never got the answers he sought? What if neither he nor Alex ever uncovered the truth? How would he be able to get a grip on everything that was going on inside him and figure out what his life really meant? What if he never recovered a sense of peace? What if this chaos was for ever?

He needed to get out, away from the thoughts and the emotions ricocheting around him. His control was unravelling faster and more wildly than ever before, and it was terrifying. He couldn't handle any of this any longer. It brought back unwanted memories of vulnerability and desperation, and it was making him unhinged.

Forget wanting to find out who he might have once been. He didn't need to know that to work out who he was now. The future was his to decide. This trip had been a mistake. For a decade he'd been all about looking forwards with a single-minded focus that had not wavered once. So what the hell had he been *doing* this last week?

'Alex?' he yelled, summoning up some strength from

who knew where and striding off in the direction of the exit, the car, sanity.

'Over here,' came the response from somewhere to his left.

'We're leaving.'

CHAPTER EIGHT

'ARE YOU ALL RIGHT?' said Alex, a little breathless as she half walked, half jogged to keep up with Max's long quick strides and a lot concerned with the way he appeared to have the hounds of hell at his feet.

'No, I'm not all right,' he muttered, a deep scowl darkening his face, his jaw clenched and his hands curled into fists.

'What's wrong?'

'I'm through with this.'

Her chest squeezed in a way that had nothing to do with the burn in her lungs. She shouldn't have left him alone, she thought, her throat tight and her pulse galloping. She'd wanted to give him space and privacy and so had taken herself off, which had clearly been an error of judgement, but at least she was here now, to help him navigate this stage of his journey.

'This has to have been a lot to deal with.'

'I don't just mean today,' he said curtly, unlocking the door of the car and yanking it open. 'I mean the entire bloody investigation.'

Alex opened her own door and clambered in, her mind reeling with shock. 'What?'

'I'm done.'

Having buckled up, he fired the engine, released the

handbrake and hit the accelerator with such force that the wheels spun and kicked up a cloud of dust so large it completely obscured the ruined town that he seemed intent on putting as far behind him as possible.

'What are you talking about?'

'I'm leaving,' he said tightly, his gaze on the road, his fingers gripping the steering wheel as if his life depended on it. 'Going home.'

She clung to the door handle, for a moment too stunned for words. 'No, you can't do that,' she said once she'd regained the power of speech.

'Keep the plane. I'll make my own way back.'

What had happened? What was going on? 'But why?'

'Work.'

That made no sense. Hadn't he told her he was between contracts?

'You said all you needed to work was your laptop,' she said, thinking of the device he'd been so occupied with on yesterday's flight.

'You don't need me here.'

'I do.'

'In what possible way?'

Well, quite. She'd managed on her own for eight months. It was an entirely fair question. She didn't need him here, in truth. But her mind had gone blank. She couldn't think. All she knew was that she didn't want him to leave. She'd got used to having him around. They were supposed to be working *together*. Besides, he clearly wasn't in a good place at the moment and how was she supposed to keep an eye on him for Finn if Max went home on his own?

'I don't speak Spanish,' she said, her head spinning as she grappled for an excuse.

'You're competent and driven. You're more than capable of finishing up here. You'll manage.'

'I know, but this isn't right, Max.'

'It's my call.'

'I have a plan.'

A muscle hammered in his jaw. 'I'm sure it's great.'

It wasn't particularly, but at least it was something.
'Step one is checking out all the hospitals within a hun-
dred-kilometre radius of here. Step two is taking a gam-
ble on your biological parents living close by. It's you
parading around town on the off-chance that someone might recognise you. That can't happen if you're
not here.'

The brief glance he threw her way was incredulous.
'That won't happen even if I am.'

'It's worth a try.'

'It's even more of a long shot than a DNA match.'

'I am aware of that,' she said, determined to keep her
cool so she could work out what to do. 'But I am also
aware that the three of you reuniting after thirty years
apart has little to do with me. Rico found out about
Finn because of a photo he'd seen in the financial press,
and you showed up because of the interview, which was
originally suggested by Carla.' Rico's fiancée. 'Even
the feelers we have out with the Swiss bank and the Argentinian government are yours. Nothing *I've* tried has
worked and I'm not ready to give up.'

'Has it occurred to you that we might never discover
the truth?'

'Yes, it has,' she said, her heart giving a quick lurch
at the thought of defeat, of failure. 'But I can't dwell on
that. I have to see it through.'

'I'm not stopping you.'

'You need to see it through too.'

'No, I really don't,' he said, his jaw tight. 'I'm done with digging around in the past. It can't be changed. I'm going to focus on the future. That's how my brothers have handled things. They're all about looking forwards, not back.'

Yes, well, they had partners to help them and children in various stages of development to focus on. Max had no one. And while he might not think it at the moment, he needed to deal with this. The truth was what he sought. She wouldn't let him throw away the chance to find the answers because of what could quite possibly be a knee-jerk reaction to what had to be a very stressful set of circumstances. Not without further consideration anyway.

'They've had far longer to process things,' she said, her heart in her throat as the car swerved violently. 'And it wasn't easy for either of them at first.'

'Then all I need is time.'

He needed more than that. 'Pull over.'

'What?'

'Stop. Please. You're in no fit state to drive.'

'I'm fine.'

'You nearly hit an alpaca just now.'

'What alpaca?'

'Exactly.'

She could practically hear the grind of his teeth, but a moment later he'd pulled over, killed the engine and tossed her the key. They got out and swapped seats and Max did up his seatbelt, but Alex had other plans. She twisted to face him and it tore at her heart to see the torment he was trying so hard to contain.

'The key goes in the ignition, Alex.'

'Let's look at this calmly,' she replied, ignoring his

sarcasm as much as the sizzling effect of his proximity on her.

'I am calm.'

No, he wasn't. He was anything but calm. The tension gripping his whole frame buffeted hers. There was a wildness to his movements and his words that suggested he was a man fast reaching the end of his tether.

'What's going on?'

'Stop trying to psychoanalyse me, and drive.'

'In a moment.'

'Am I going to have to get out and walk?'

'If that's what you need.'

'What I need is to get back to the hotel so I can start packing.'

That was the last thing he needed, in her opinion. But how was she going to keep him here? If he was determined to go, there was nothing she'd be able to do to stop him. Could she appeal to his better nature? Did he even have one? What incentive would work? He was so wound up. How could she get him to relax enough to be able to realise she was right?

But hang on…

'Why don't we take some time out?' she said as the idea of relaxing triggered a memory from dinner at La Copa Alegre and inspiration struck.

He whipped round and stared at her as if she'd sprouted a second head. 'Some time out?'

'The last few days have been incredibly intense for me,' she told him, steeling herself against the blaze of astonishment and turmoil she could see in his eyes. 'I can't imagine what they've been like for you. I read that there are some salt flats not far from here, just across the border. They could be worth a look.'

'Are you mad?'

She'd never felt saner in her life. 'We'll go out there,' she said, more convinced it was the right thing to do with every passing second. 'After lunch. Check out the nature. Take advantage of the new moon and gaze at a few stars once the sun has set. There's even a luxury lodge. We could stay the night there and come back refreshed tomorrow.'

'*Refreshed?*'

His disbelief was fierce but she refused to quail. 'You did say I should take a break.'

'You don't need me for that.'

'And you don't need me for anything,' she said, reminding herself that this wasn't about her. This was about him. And even if it hadn't been, she ought to be glad he thought he didn't need her for anything because that was exactly what she wanted. 'I get it. But I won't let you mess this up, Max. You need to give it a chance. For the sake of your brothers but, more importantly, for yourself. I know what it's like to not know who you truly are, and I know how petrifying it can be to have to work that out. But I also know the relief that comes when you're through it. You'll regret it if you leave. Running away doesn't solve anything.' She let that sink in for a moment then leaned forward a fraction, keeping her gaze firmly fixed on his. Injecting as much persuasion into her tone as she could, she said, 'So let's be tourists for a while. We won't talk about the case. We'll just take the opportunity to relax and forget ourselves for once. We can start again tomorrow. It would be less than twenty-four hours. What do you think?'

Max didn't want to hang out in any salt flats and relax. He couldn't think of anything less appealing than doing the tourist thing and stargazing with a woman who'd so ruthlessly rejected him yet to whom he was still wildly attracted. He'd have to be some kind of masochist to agree to it when all he wanted to do, but couldn't, was reach out, pull her tight against him and run his hands all over her, before kissing her until neither of them could think straight.

He didn't want conversation of any kind with her. They'd talked plenty—too much, in fact—and they were already staying in a perfectly good, if basic, hotel in La Posada. And what did she know about relaxing anyway? Could she even do it? Not once in the brief but impactful time he'd known her had she shown any evidence of it. The kiss they'd shared, the one that she'd been able to dismiss so easily but still tormented him night and day, hadn't been in the slightest bit chilled. Even during dinner at La Copa Alegre her conversation had been laced with wariness, her body gripped with tension.

And what the hell gave her the right to tell him that he'd regret it if he left? he wondered, his stomach churning and his head pounding. She knew nothing about anything. He wasn't petrified. He wasn't running away. He'd just had enough. He was completely overwhelmed by everything that had happened recently, that was all, and God, he was tired. He'd barely slept recently. He'd hardly been able to breathe. He wanted to go home, crash out for a month and wake up to the realisation that the last week had been nothing but a bad dream.

But it wasn't. It was reality. His new reality, in fact, and much of it—namely the discovery of his brothers— he was delighted about. The rest of it, not so much, but, if he was being brutally honest, he probably wasn't going to be able to escape that by simply going home. No matter how much he tried to convince himself that the past was of no interest or importance to him, it was, and it would follow him wherever he went, evermore festering away inside him and corroding his identity and his self-worth the longer it went unaddressed.

He needed to track down his biological family in order to find out whether he'd been wanted. If he'd once mattered to someone, to anyone. It was only on meeting his brothers and feeling somehow anchored by them that he'd realised how adrift he'd always been, how unsure of his place in the world at large, knowing somewhere deep down inside that he was entirely on his own.

But now he had the chance to make sense of it all, so what choice did he have but to stay and see it through to the bitter end? Whatever the outcome, and he was aware that he might not get the results he so badly hoped for, at least then he'd know he'd given it everything. At least then he could process it and, somehow, move on.

Whether she knew it or not, Alex's point about not letting Finn and Rico down had struck him deep in the gut. He shouldn't need their approval, or anyone's, but he craved it nonetheless. He liked them, he valued the relationship they were developing, and he'd do nothing to jeopardise it. He'd told them he'd do what he could to get to the truth and, while he was all for breaking rules, he didn't break promises. How could he have forgotten that?

He hadn't been thinking straight for days now. Could it be that he wasn't thinking straight now? Could Alex be right and he *did* need a breather? The thought of handing over even the minutest modicum of control made him want to recoil in sheer horror, but perhaps he'd be wise to concede to her on this. The tumultuous news of his adoption and all it entailed sat like a rock on his chest, crushing him with its ever-increasing weight, and his judgement wasn't exactly firing on all cylinders at the moment.

And, in any case, this wasn't just about him. It was about Alex too. Her career and her future. He'd agreed that they'd work together and so far she'd kept her end of the bargain. In fact she'd gone beyond it. She hadn't let him push her away, no matter how hard he'd made it for her. She'd been resolute and unshakeable. He'd never had that kind of steadfast unconditional support. He didn't know quite what to do with it, but at the very least he owed it to her to stick around a little while longer.

Besides, maybe she *did* know how to relax. Despite the stress and turmoil storming his defences, he couldn't deny that he found the idea of it intriguing and alluring, a tiny beacon of light piercing the dark maelstrom of chaos. He'd failed to entice her into his bed, but if he could get her to lower her guard and ease up, he would at least be able to claw back some kind of pride.

'The salt flats it is.'

They set off after lunch and spent two hours driving along huge, wide, empty roads that bisected great swathes of desolate rocky landscape before reaching their destination. En route they passed cactus fields, a stretch of bubbling geysers and abandoned towns made entirely of salt. The jagged mountains that rose majestically in the distance were awe-inspiring. In every direction, as far as the eye could see, bright white salt sparkled in the sun, the light reflecting off it dazzling. They came across flocks of flamingos, wild vicuña and ruby-red lagoons. The sky was cloudless and the air clean and raw. It had to be one of the most isolated, most beautiful places on earth.

Heading out here had been the best idea she had had in ages, Alex reflected as she and Max sat on the viewing platform attached to the one dome-shaped pod-like cabin that had been available, watching the sun dip beneath the horizon, having dined on a feast of yucca soup followed by grilled *paiche* served with a delicate risotto and then, to finish, an exquisite mousse of dark chocolate and eucalyptus. She had to admit that she needed the break. It felt so wonderful to throw off the shackles of work for a while. To put aside her worries, even temporarily, and lose herself in the wonders of the world.

As agreed, she and Max hadn't talked about the case or family or anything, really, of a personal nature. Instead, the conversation had meandered through a wide variety of largely neutral subjects—travel, food, books. It had hardly been scintillating but, even so, she hadn't been able to get enough of it. She wanted to know everything about him, and she didn't even bother to try and convince herself that her interest was professional. It wasn't. It was entirely personal. Those complex layers of his that she'd identified during the floating dinner, that she'd caught a glimpse of at the orphanage, drew her attention like the brightest of beacons and were impossible to ignore.

But now, with the fire crackling in the pit that stood in front of them, the conversation had petered out. Max seemed to be as lost in thought as she was and she wondered whether he too had been struck dumb by the mesmerising reflection of the sun on the mirror-like surface of the ground and the staggeringly beautiful streaks of reds and gold slashing across the vast blue sky or if he could possibly be thinking the same thing she was, namely the fireworks he'd mentioned.

Despite her best efforts, she hadn't been able to scrub them from her mind, but that was what came of spending so much time cooped up with him in a car, however large and luxurious. The distance between places here was immense. Five minutes was all it took for her to become achingly aware of him sitting beside her, his shoulder mere centimetres from hers, and then she found she spent the rest of whatever journey they were on trying not to lean into him and keeping her eyes on the scenery and not on his profile, which inevitably was agony.

And then there was the lodge. If she'd known it was billed as a honeymooners' paradise and that the half a dozen domes came with a king-size bed only she'd never have suggested staying the night. The air of romance was everywhere, from the double shower in the en-suite bathroom to the intimacy of the tables set for two in the dining room to the cosy sofa they were sitting on out here. Not only did she feel like a fraud, she couldn't stop thinking about how exciting their kiss had been, how desperately she wanted more and how nearby and enticing the bed was.

Max, on the other hand, clearly wasn't suffering from the same kind of struggles. He hadn't batted an eyelid about there only being one dome available. He'd dismissed her suggestion they drive back, saying it was too far, and told her he'd take the floor, as if it didn't bother him in the slightest that they'd have to share a room. He still hadn't touched her. His distance was polite. His smiles were entirely impersonal. She both envied and resented his ability to simply switch off the attraction. How did he do it? she wondered for what had to be the hundredth time in the last hour.

And what would it take to switch it back on again?

It was a question that shouldn't have been of the remotest interest but, despite everything, she badly wanted to know the answer. The longer he obeyed her request to back off, the more she wanted him to dishonour it. She desperately yearned for him to deploy that rebellious streak of his and break every single one of her rules, which made no sense at all.

Or did it?

As she gazed up at the vast canopy of stars that now spread out above them like a giant glittering blanket, her heart began to thump that little bit harder while her head began to spin that little bit faster. The sky was so big out here, the universe so huge. She could make out the Southern Cross and the Milky Way and suddenly she felt very small and very alone. At least Max had his brothers now. She had no one. No one on her side, no one to turn to for support.

She'd been so lonely for so long and just for one night, maybe a few more, she didn't want to be. She was so tired of keeping how she felt about Max at bay. Constantly fighting it when she was achingly aware of every movement he made, every breath he took, his scent, his warmth, the impact of his gaze on her, took more effort than she could possibly have imagined and she was running on fumes.

Why shouldn't she sleep with him? she thought, her mouth going dry and her entire body heating as the last of her defences bit the dust. Why shouldn't they have the fling he'd proposed the night she'd told him she would never act on the attraction they shared? It needn't be complicated. Sex with him wouldn't mean anything beyond a release of tension and, she hoped, outstanding, mind-blowing pleasure.

He'd certainly be a boost for her self-esteem, if the kiss was anything to go by, and God, she could do with one of those. How she hated the angst and insecurity she'd developed about her body, thanks to her ex. She wanted to feel good about herself, physically as well as professionally, and if Max was as skilled as he said he was she knew she'd feel amazing.

But what about her rules?

Well, those no longer seemed quite as important as they once had. As he kept reminding her, he wasn't a client. Neither of them was looking for anything long-term and, as he'd pointed out, no one else need ever know.

So what if she let a little bit of chaos into her life? She could handle it. She'd spent years building up her armour against precisely this sort of thing. She didn't need to worry about possible heartbreak and misery. There'd be no regrets. Things would never get that far. It wasn't as if she wanted a relationship with him. Or anyone, for that matter. Even if she could overcome the major trust issues her husband's many infidelities had engendered, the possibility of failure, the potential upheaval when it all went wrong was too distressing to contemplate and deeply unappealing. But a fling? With Max? That she would welcome. That she wanted with an all-consuming hunger that was fast becoming unbearable.

So what was she going to do? Was she brave enough to find out whether, despite the discouraging signs, he still wanted her too? Was she prepared for the very real yet faintly sickening prospect that she'd killed the attraction he'd once had for her? If she had, could she somehow manage to rekindle it?

Whatever the outcome, she had to try, she thought, her heart hammering as desire and longing rushed through her blood. She had to know. Because she couldn't go on like this. She didn't want to for ever wonder, what if. She'd had enough of the loneliness and the constant battle to ignore how he made her feel. And, above all, despite what he might think of her, she wasn't a coward.

* * *

'Look,' said Alex, wonder tingeing her voice as she pointed up at the sky. 'A shooting star.'

In response, Max just grunted. He didn't trust himself to speak right now. If he opened his mouth, there was every possibility it would be to beg her to change her mind about sleeping with him, because he was finding it increasingly hard to remember her rules and respect her wishes.

With hindsight, he should never have agreed to this whole ridiculous taking a break thing. What had he been thinking? Had he gone completely mad?

The afternoon had started off great. He'd never been to Bolivia. The landscape was stunning and fascinating. Alex was an amusing and interesting travelling companion, and with the investigation and the drama of the last few days firmly, if temporarily, put to one side he'd felt the chaos recede and a modicum of calm descend. It might have taken every ounce of strength he possessed but he'd ignored her proximity, and dismissed the fanciful idea that he could listen to her talk about nothing for ever, and had instead forced himself to concentrate on nature in all its vast and varied glory.

Things had started to fall apart for him when they'd arrived at the lodge and there'd only been one dome available to book. It had been too late to head back, he'd realised, deep unease setting in as the consequences dawned. The roads were unlit and wildlife with a death wish had a tendency to appear out of nowhere.

He'd briefly toyed with the idea of leaving Alex to occupy the dome while he slept in the car, despite the temperature dropping to sub-zero overnight. But he'd pulled himself together and reminded himself that his control wasn't that unreliable. He didn't have to face hypothermia. Alex could have the bed. He'd take the floor. She'd viewed that as an acceptable compromise and, quite honestly, how hard could it be?

Then he'd walked into the sumptuously furnished, seductively lit room, which was mostly bed and very little floor, and realised he was in for a night of pure, agonising hell.

'And there goes another one,' she said, yanking him back to the deck and the dazzling display of stars. 'You're meant to make a wish.'

That was a joke. The only thing he wanted right now wasn't going to happen, and the frustration was excruciating.

'Yeah, well, you were meant to be relaxing.'

'I am.'

No, she wasn't. She was huddled up at her end of the sofa, as far from him as she could get, practically clinging to the arm of it as if it were a lifebelt.

'I don't bite,' he muttered, loathing the fact that she didn't trust him.

'That's a shame.'

What the hell did she mean by that? he wondered, whipping his head round to find her watching him in a way that had his pulse suddenly racing. She'd loosened her death grip on the sofa and turned to face him, but why was she looking at him like that, sort of nervous yet hopeful? What was going on?

He was about to ask precisely that when she suddenly reached up and back, pulled off the band holding her hair back and, to his utter shock, shook out her hair. It fell in great, soft, dark brown waves around her shoulders, the tendrils framing her face shining in the light that came from the firepit, and it was every bit as exciting as he'd imagined.

'What are you doing?' he said, shock and desire turning his voice into almost a growl.

'I thought I would let my hair down.'

'It's beautiful,' he said before he could stop himself.

'Thank you.'

'All of you is beautiful.'

'Do you really think so?'

How could she possibly doubt it? Her smile, her eyes, everything about her, was lovely and he liked it all. He also liked their conversation, their differences and their similarities, not to mention her interest in him and the support she offered, but he couldn't go there, not even in his head. All that mattered, all that ever mattered when it came to women, this woman in particular, was the physical. 'Yes.'

She took a deep breath and leaned forward an inch, dizzying him with her scent and confusing him beyond belief, because what was she doing? 'You're the most attractive man I've ever met,' she said, the words coming out of her mouth in a rush. 'And the most dangerous.'

His heart gave a great lurch. 'In what way?'

'You make me want to break my own rules.'

Yeah, well, he knew that. But he'd failed. And he'd had enough of this. He was tired and turned on and in for eight hours of agony.

'We should call it a night,' he said gruffly. 'You in the bed. Me on the floor.'

Her gaze dropped to his mouth and the chilly air between them thickened with heat and tension. 'Is that really what you want?'

'Not by a long shot,' he said, the truth drug he appeared to have taken continuing its effect.

'Neither do I.'

He went very still, his gaze locking onto hers, his

heart hammering as her intentions became clear, but he wasn't taking anything for granted. Not this time. 'What are you saying?'

'I want us in the bed together.'

God. 'You know where that will end up.'

'I know where I'd like it to end up,' she said, the desire and heat shimmering in her eyes stealing the breath from his lungs. 'I want you, Max. So much I'm going out of my mind. And I'm sick of trying to convince myself otherwise.'

Not giving in to the need drumming through him and reaching for her was taking every drop of control he possessed. His head was spinning. He was so hard he hurt. But he couldn't get this wrong. He didn't think he could take yet another rejection.

'You have rules.'

'They don't seem very important at the moment.'

'Prove it.'

CHAPTER NINE

ALEX DIDN'T EVEN HESITATE. Max had flung open the door she'd feared might be permanently shut and she was going to head on through it before she thought better of it. Excitement and anticipation rushed through her, obliterating the nerves and the doubt. In a flash she tossed aside the blanket, and with one quick move she was astride him, sitting in his lap, wrapping her arms around his neck and crushing her mouth to his.

And oh, the *relief* when he instantly started kissing her back, clamping his hands to her hips to hold her in place while the kiss burned hotter than the fire in the pit. Tongues tangled and teeth clashed and when he ground her pelvis against his, the rock-hard length of his erection rubbing her where she ached for him so desperately, she actually whimpered.

That seemed to trigger his inner caveman because suddenly he tried to take control of the kiss, but she used the advantage of her weight on and above him to push him back and increased the pressure because *she* was in charge right now. She had something to prove and she wasn't going to stop until she absolutely had to, so it went on and on, battering every one of her senses with the most delicious of assaults.

He filled her vision. He tasted of chocolate and

whisky, dark and wicked. His touch set her alight and his scent dizzied her head. The desire that was sweeping through her was intense and undeniable, which was absolutely fine because she didn't want to deny any of this any more.

'Is that enough proof for you?' she said huskily when they finally broke for breath, noting with satisfaction that his eyes were glazed and a flush had hit his cheekbones.

'Are you sure about this?' he muttered, his voice spine-tinglingly low and gravelly.

'I've never been surer about anything.'

'You're not going to tell me it's a mistake or a conflict of interest?'

'No,' she said with a tiny shake of her head and a faint smile. 'Well, it's probably both, but I don't care.'

'Good.'

Without breaking contact, Max surged to his feet, his arms like steel bands around her back. She wrapped her legs around his waist and tightened her arms around his neck, and felt as light as a feather as he strode into the dome. He kicked the door shut and then fell with her onto the bed in a tangle of limbs before rolling her onto her back and pinning her to the mattress with *his* weight.

He didn't seem to have a problem with her attributes, judging by the hardness of his erection and the fierce intensity of his gaze that was locked to hers. He wouldn't care that her boobs were on the small side and she didn't have much in the way of hips. This was going to be everything she'd hoped for, she could tell.

And then she stopped thinking altogether because his head came down and his mouth landed on hers and once again she was nothing but a molten mass of need.

'I've wanted you since the moment we met,' he muttered against her jaw while he slid his hand beneath her clothes and up her side, making her shiver and shake.

'Really?' she breathed raggedly, clutching at his shoulders and wishing he wasn't wearing so many layers.

'I took one look at you in your tight skirt and neat top and I wanted to strip them off you then and there.'

'Likewise. Only in your case it was your worn jeans and crumpled shirt.'

'It made no sense.'

'I know. We're so unalike.'

'You can't imagine the agony I've endured.'

'I do have some idea,' she panted as he reared up to whip the clothes off his upper body. 'That kiss... I haven't been able to stop thinking about it, and that's been driving me nuts.'

Having hurled his clothes onto the floor, he set about hers. 'Your willpower is both awe-inspiring and frustrating as hell,' he muttered, removing her layers with flattering speed and throwing them in the general direction of his.

He undid her bra with impressive dexterity and tossed that to one side too. Her spine seemed to have dissolved because all she could do beneath the heat of his gaze was lie back, as if granting him permission to look, which he did for one heart-stopping moment, and then touch, which, to her relief, he decided to do too.

When he bent his head to her breast and swept his tongue over her nipple she nearly jack-knifed off the bed. He held her down and did it again and she moaned. After what felt like far too short a time, he transferred his attention to her other breast, whipping up such staggering sensations inside her that she could scarcely breathe, and she jammed her fingers in his hair to keep him there for ever.

But Max obviously had other ideas and, true to form, he simply did what he wanted. Just when she thought she couldn't stand the electric shocks stabbing through her any longer, he moved lower, sliding his mouth down her stomach, the hint of stubble setting her achingly sensitive skin aflame.

When he reached the waistband of her trousers and pants, she instinctively lifted her hips and he eased them down and off. Then he settled back between her legs, holding her thighs apart, and put his mouth to where she was so hot and needy.

Her entire world centred on what he was doing to her and, at the sparks zinging through her, her head fell back while her fingers tightened in his hair. The tension was unbearable, the pleasure so intense she felt as though she were on a roller coaster, going faster and faster and higher and higher. He slid two long, strong fingers inside her and she moaned and gasped. And then he did something clever with them and quite suddenly that roller coaster left the rails and soared into the ether and she broke apart into a million tiny glittering pieces, wave after wave of ecstasy washing over her.

'I knew you'd be good at this,' she managed once the world had stopped spinning and she'd got her breath back.

'Alex, sweetheart, we've barely begun.'

He levered himself off her, his face dark and intense and his jaw so tight it could have been hewn from granite, and he jerked away to locate his wallet. Having found what he was looking for, he stripped off his jeans and shorts and ripped open the foil packet. Her breath caught as she watched him roll the condom onto his impressively long and thick erection with hands that seemed to be shaking, and her entire body trembled.

And then he was back with her, parting her knees

and positioning himself before thrusting inside her, filling and stretching her so sensationally that she thought she might pass out with the indescribable pleasure of it.

When he began to move, she lost the ability to think altogether. She moaned and he kissed her hard. She clutched at his shoulders, feeling the flex of his muscles beneath her fingers and revelling in the masculine strength and power of his body. Her hips rose and fell instinctively to meet his movements and the pressure inside her swelled unbearably.

'Don't hold back,' she breathed on a sob, and it was like putting a match to a touch paper.

He moved harder and faster, his increasingly wild, fierce thrusts driving her higher and higher, their kisses becoming frantic and desperate until, without warning, she shattered again, the waves of pleasure hitting with such intensity that she cried out. Max followed her over the edge moments later, lodging hard and deep and groaning as he pulsated inside her before collapsing on top of her, his chest heaving and his entire body shaking.

For several long moments they lay there recovering, and then Max eased out of her and shifted onto his side.

'So,' she said with a giddy grin once she'd got her breath back. 'Fireworks.'

His gaze, as he looked down at her, was glittering and wild. 'Told you.'

'I saw stars.'

'That'll be the glass roof.'

'Not just the glass roof. You certainly know how to give an ego a boost.'

'Was yours in need of one?'

God, yes. 'When someone cheats on you repeatedly you find yourself…doubting your attractions.'

He frowned at that. 'You have many, as I think I just

made pretty obvious,' he said, reaching out and running a hand slowly over her, making her sensitive skin shiver and her breasts tighten. 'But if you're still not convinced, I'd be more than happy to prove it again.'

'You know what?' she said huskily as fresh desire began to thud through her. 'I'm not sure I am.'

Yesterday, the overnight timeout suggested by Alex had felt to Max like aeons. At two in the morning, however, after the events of the last six or so hours, it didn't seem like nearly enough.

He'd never had sex like it, he thought, wide awake and staring up at the billions of stars through the roof made up of glass equilateral triangles while beside him Alex slept. She'd been insatiable and he'd been beyond desperate and they'd already got through half the box of condoms located in the drawer of the night stand, thoughtfully supplied by the lodge that clearly catered to honeymooners.

The edge of sexual tension and frustration he'd been living with since he'd met her had gone and, whatever the reason for her volte face, he couldn't be more satisfied with the way things had turned out. He'd known she'd be unable to resist in the end. It had taken longer than he'd anticipated but if there was one thing he *could* be sure of at the moment it was the power of chemistry.

He had to hand it to her, though. There was definitely something to be said for taking a break from reality, especially when that reality sucked. He felt he could breathe out here. Some of the chaos had calmed. Getting the answers he needed was still a top priority, despite the blip at the orphanage, but this little bubble that he and Alex were in at the moment didn't suck at all and, if he was being brutally honest, he wasn't quite ready for it to burst.

She'd suggested they head back to La Posada today to continue with her plan, which, frankly, didn't seem a particularly solid one, but what was the rush? There was plenty more to see and do here, and not just inside their dome. What would be the harm in staying another day or two?

It wasn't as if the investigation was moving apace and required their immediate attention, and it wasn't as if he hadn't chilled out with women before in a heavy-on-the-sex, light-on-the-conversation kind of way. None of them had been anything like Alex, it was true, but that didn't mean anything. All this was, was sex. Spectacular, head-wrecking sex, but just sex, nonetheless.

And sticking around a bit longer would do her good too, he thought as she turned in her sleep and sort of snuggled against him, which he found he didn't mind at all. Everyone needed a holiday, however brief, and by her own admission she hadn't taken one in years. He understood why she had an issue with letting her hair down, but she ought to do it more. Because he had to admit he liked the relaxed version of Alex, with her guard lowered and her inhibitions history. He liked her a lot.

Well, wasn't she full of good ideas at the moment, Alex thought with a wide satisfied grin as she sprawled across the bed and ogled Max, who was standing at the coffee machine wearing nothing but an open shirt and underwear, his hair damp from the shower.

Last night, and this morning, had been unbelievable, better than her wildest dreams, and God knew she'd had a few of those. The things he'd done to her... The things she'd done to him... Her confidence, so badly knocked by her lousy ex, was back with a vengeance and her self-esteem was higher than it had been for years. Max didn't seem to have an issue with any part of her body. In fact, he couldn't seem to get enough of it, and he'd made her feel like a goddess.

Taking up the challenge of proving that her rules no longer mattered had been a risk, but it had paid off in spades, and as she watched him stick a pod in the coffee machine, close the lid and stand back to let the machine do its thing, she wondered if maybe she ought to be a bit braver in other areas too. Maybe she ought to have it out with her family once and for all, and tell them exactly how she felt about the way she'd been brought up, how damaging it had been. It wouldn't change anything when the chasm between them now was wider and deeper than the Grand Canyon and equally unbridgeable, but at least then she'd have closure and the grip the past had on her would ease.

She knew now that she had what it took to be a success. As Max had pointed out yesterday when they'd been talking about work in a very vague sort of way, given the confidentiality that governed both their fields, she was still in business after five years, which was no mean feat when most start-ups failed within the first twelve months, and word-of-mouth recommendations were still coming in.

If this trip was the end of the road with regard to the investigation—and she had to face the fact that it could well be, because not only had Max heard back from his contacts, who'd come up with nothing, she didn't want him breaking the law and hacking into whatever systems he'd have to when he'd put such things behind him—would that really be the disaster she feared so much?

OK, so perhaps her track record would be broken and her expansion plans might have to be put on hold, but what was the hurry? Wasn't it a bit pathetic to still be trying to prove something to people who couldn't care less? After all these years? During dinner at the floating bar, Max had suggested she just let it go and perhaps it really was as simple as that.

It would be no reflection on her if this investigation ended now. She'd done everything she could. She badly wanted Max to have the answers he sought for his own peace of mind, but in reality there were no avenues left to pursue. The three brothers had found each other after thirty years apart and were intent on forging a relationship going forward, and that was huge.

So wouldn't everyone be better off by simply moving on? In her considerable experience, not to mention her own *personal* experience, answers didn't always fix things. Look at all the investigations she'd run. Look at the mess of her marriage. Sometimes, success resulted in more unhappiness, more uncertainty and often innumerable other problems. Even if they did by some miracle get a breakthrough, it could well be the case that the truth was harrowing, more so than anyone could have imagined, and hadn't Finn, Rico and Max suffered enough? Didn't they need some sort of closure too?

Max handing her a cup of coffee snapped her out of her thoughts, and as her gaze fixed on his bare chest, which she'd explored at great length and now knew in exquisite detail, she flushed with heat.

'What is it with you and buttons?' she said huskily, taking a sip and feeling the welcome hit of caffeine suffuse her blood.

'What do you mean?'

'You have a habit of forgetting to do them up.'

'No, I don't.'

Her eyebrows lifted. 'You mean it's deliberate?'

'It might be,' he said with the hint of a grin as he grabbed a coffee of his own and stretched out on the bed beside her.

'At dinner the other night too?'

'I don't know what you mean.'

He knew exactly what she meant. 'It wasn't that warm and there were mosquitoes. You had an ulterior motive.'

'I didn't think you'd noticed,' he said, shooting her a look of pure wickedness.

'I noticed.' Oh, how she'd noticed.

'And it bothered you.'

'I didn't think it was very professional.'

'Perhaps this is simply how I roll on holiday.'

'You were showing off.'

'I was getting desperate.'

At the thought of how much he'd wanted her, desire flooded every inch of her body. 'It worked.'

'Ever play poker?'

'No. Why?'

'You'd be very good at it. No one would ever be able to tell what you were thinking.'

'Can you tell what I'm thinking now?'

'You're thinking what I'm thinking,' he said, his gaze dropping to her mouth, and it was so tempting to lean in for a kiss that would blow her mind and lead to another hour of outstanding pleasure, but it was getting late and check out was looming.

'Sadly, I don't believe I am. I was thinking we should be getting going and heading back,' she said with real regret because, even if they carried on sleeping together back in La Posada, there was something magical and special about this place.

'I disagree.'

'Oh?'

'I think we could do with more refreshing.'

Her heart began to hammer. 'What do you suggest?'

'Another couple of nights here.'

Her willpower was no match for the excitement beginning to ripple through her. If she were stronger she'd insist on leaving now, as had been the plan. But being out here, just the two of them with no cares, no work between them, was intoxicating. There was something about the freshness of the air and the vastness of the scenery that made everything else seem very insignificant. Max had eased up yesterday afternoon while they'd been exploring the landscape and she longed to see more of the man behind the assignment, to burrow further beneath those layers of his. Besides, after eight months, what was another couple of days?

'I could get behind that.'

'And then we head back to La Posada. Where the investigation will resume and this,' he said, indicating the both of them, 'will continue.'

'Until either we find the answers we seek or we decide to call it quits,' she said, for some reason feeling it needed confirmation.

'Exactly.' His expression sobered then and his smile faded. 'You should know, Alex, I don't do long-term. I don't do relationships.'

She understood where he was coming from but she needed no warning. She was entirely on the same page. She wasn't in danger of being swept up in the romance of the place and mistaking this for something it wasn't, no matter how many of his layers she managed to peel back. People didn't change, even if they promised over and over again to try, and in any case she didn't want him to.

'Neither do I.'

'Because?'

'Oh, you know,' she said lightly. 'A number of trust issues, thanks to a cheating ex. Not wanting to experience the monumental chaos of a breakup ever again. That kind of thing. You?'

'I witnessed the fallout of a disintegrating marriage,' he said, a shadow flitting across his face. 'Nothing would ever persuade me to go there. And, as I may have mentioned once or twice, these days I prefer my life free from chaos too.'

'Have you ever had a relationship?'

'Not since I went on the straight and narrow.'

'Why not?'

'I don't need the hassle. One night, one week, maybe two, suits me fine.'

'Me too.' Although she could count on one hand the number of dates that had ended up in the bedroom since her divorce and have fingers left over.

'A woman after my own heart.'

'Your heart is of no interest to me,' she said, even as hers gave a quick lurch. 'Nobody's is.'

'You don't believe in love?'

'It's not that I don't believe in it,' she said, thinking with a shudder of the potential pain and devastation a badly broken heart could cause. Hers had merely been dented by her ex, but even that had been difficult enough to recover from. 'On a theoretical level I can understand that true love exists, but the only kind I've ever experienced is conditional.'

'I haven't experienced any kind. What my parents felt for me was not love.'

No, it most certainly wasn't.

'Girlfriends?'

'They're never around long enough.'

'Deliberately?'

'It's just the way things pan out.'

Hmm. That didn't exactly answer the question.

'My family has always made it perfectly clear that unless I conform to their standards they want nothing to do with me,' she said. 'I know now that that's not a price I'm willing to pay.'

'Nor me.'

'Just as well that we're in this just for the sex then, isn't it?'

His eyes glittered, the look in them turning predatory, and as he took her cup off her and set it and his own on the night stand, his intention clear, desire began to sweep through her. 'I couldn't agree more.'

By the following morning, Max and Alex had taken a trip in a hot-air balloon, had a picnic lunch on a shimmering sea of white and bathed naked in hot springs. Once again, the day had been warm and sunny, the night cold, clear and starry. And, once again, the minute the door of the dome closed behind them after dinner, clothes were shed and hands met skin and the temperature hit boiling point.

Unlike the day before, however, the talk had been anything but small. A thousand feet above the ground, catching Max at a moment his defences had been blown away by the sheer magnitude of the view, she'd drilled down into the nitty-gritty of his upbringing and rewarded him with details of her own. Over lunch he'd found himself telling her about why the need to find his biological family burned so much more intensely in him than in his brothers, how badly his self-worth needed him to have been wanted by somebody, and she'd reciprocated by confessing how she'd hated the insecure, needy woman she'd become after she'd found out about her husband's cheating, which had made him want to hunt the man down and throttle him.

The glimpses Max had caught of the woman behind the rules were fascinating. Who'd have thought Alex had such a dirty laugh? If someone had told him the day they'd met that she couldn't pass a bottle of glittery nail varnish in a shop without buying it and that her collection was now in the hundreds he'd have scoffed in disbelief.

But then who'd have thought he'd find her beams of appreciation so addictive? Who'd have thought he'd do pretty much anything to elicit one of her blinding smiles of approval, whether it was simply building and lighting a fire in the pit, helping her climb into the hot-air balloon or closing down the hot springs site so they could have privacy?

She was like a drug running through his veins and making him feel invincible, and while part of him was all for the high, another part of him was troubled by the growing sense that things were heading in a dangerous direction. The connection between them didn't feel purely physical any longer. Feelings were developing, he could tell, and his subconscious shared that unease because in the middle of the night he'd woken abruptly from the most erotic yet unsettling dream of his life.

He'd been sitting in his study back home, staring at his screens and trying to figure out how to fix a piece of code that wasn't quite right. Alex had sidled in wearing nothing but a half open shirt and a smouldering smile and had then planted herself between him and his desk. From there she'd proceeded to blow his mind several times over and he hadn't even had to leave his chair.

But when, still trembling in his arms, dream Alex had held him tight while murmuring that she was there and everything was going to be all right, an odd chill had swept through the room, freezing the blood in his veins and sending icy shivers down his spine. The more she'd continued to whisper reassurances and soft words of support in his ear, the more he'd wanted to get up and run. But he couldn't because firstly she was sitting in his lap, pinning him to the chair, and secondly his arms were wrapped around her and wouldn't loosen, no matter how much he ordered them to.

Now, he was sitting on the terrace in front of their dome, watching the most stunning sunrise he'd ever seen while tapping his phone against his thigh and remembering how, at dinner last night, a warm light seemed to have taken up residence in her eyes and her smiles had been somehow different, although he couldn't put his finger on quite why, and that added to the apprehension because he didn't know what to make of them.

His foundations, already on shifting sands, seemed to be cracking. His stomach churned with a low-level sort of anxiety and his mind wouldn't rest. He felt as if he could skid off the rails at any moment and he didn't know how to stop it.

'What are you doing out here?'

At the sound of Alex's voice behind him, husky with sleep, the anxiety ratcheted up a notch.

'Watching the dawn.'

'Are you all right?'

Why did she keep asking him this, as if she cared? Why did he hope she did?

'Fine.'

'You look a little tense.'

'I've had a text from Rico.'

'Is everything OK?'

'It's our birthday next month,' he said, telling himself that this was what was bothering him, with its stirring-up of unwelcome memories of birthdays gone by. 'He wants to know whether I'd be up for a celebratory dinner.'

'And are you?'

He wouldn't miss it for the world. 'I guess. I haven't celebrated my birthday for years.'

She pulled the blanket around her tighter and came to sit beside him, which simultaneously made him want to shift closer and leap to his feet. 'Why not?'

'When I was a kid, my mother chose my friends, what I wore, what I ate. That didn't let up on my birthday.'

'My birthdays weren't much fun either,' she said dryly. 'No one ever even remembered. At least you got presents.'

'Only because they could be repurposed as weapons. She used to use the threat of taking them away as a punishment for whatever I did wrong.'

Her eyes shimmered. 'What a bitch.'

'Yup.'

'You're so lucky to have found your brothers,' she added with a wistfulness that, for some bizarre reason, made his throat tighten.

'I know.' He'd filled her in on the conversations they'd had and how much meeting them had meant to him. Now he came to think of it, there'd been a wistful look on her face then too.

'You now have family that cares about you. That gets

you. You have an instant connection with people you met a week ago. I've known my family for thirty-three years and have no emotional connection with them at all. I have no such connection with anyone.'

She had an emotional connection with him. The thought spun into his head before he made it spin right out again. That couldn't be the case. The only connection they shared was a physical one. All that was between them was sex. He wasn't the one for her, even if she had wanted something more. He wasn't the one for anyone. Ever.

But he didn't like the clench in his chest at the thought of her all alone in this world, and he liked even less the jealousy that speared through him at the thought of her with someone else.

The dream, still fresh in his mind, was unsettling. He couldn't work out what was going on and he didn't want to, so it was a good thing that just then her phone, which she'd brought out with her to take pictures of the dawn as she'd done the morning before, beeped to alert her of an incoming message.

She focused on the device for a second or two, hitting a button there, scrolling up and down there, and then she gasped, 'Oh, my God.'

'What?'

When she lifted her gaze from the screen and looked at him, her eyes were wide and stunned. 'Remember I told you Finn had sent his DNA off for analysis?'

As if he'd ever forget anything he'd learned about his new-found family. 'Yes.'

'So it turns out it wasn't such a long shot after all.'

He went very still at that and his heart gave a great crash against his ribs. 'What are you saying?'

'There's a match.'

CHAPTER TEN

As Alex's pronouncement hit his brain, each word detonating on impact, time seemed to stop. Max's head emptied of everything but this one massive revelation and then began to spin as questions started hurtling around it. His pulse thundered, his stomach churned and he couldn't seem to make any of it stop.

The facts. That was what he had to focus on. The facts.

'Who is it?' he said, his voice sounding as though it came from far, far away, even to his own ears.

'I don't know,' she said, sounding as dazed as he felt. 'A woman. A Valentina Lopez. The message is in Spanish.'

She held out the phone and for one moment he just stared at it as if it were about to bite. Valentina Lopez? That name hadn't come up in any of Alex's research. So who could she be? He ought to be snatching the phone out of her hand to find out, and yet he hesitated. There was an odd unexpected security in uncertainty. Once he read the message there'd be no going back. He could be on the brink of finding out everything he needed to make sense of his life, his value and who he was, or he could be opening a whole new can of worms.

But then he pulled himself together. This was precisely why he'd made the snap decision to fly from the Caribbean to London in the first place. Why he'd taken up Rico's offer of his plane and agreed to work with Alex, who'd been right that morning she'd stopped him leaving. He had to investigate this. For his brothers and, more importantly, for himself.

Bracing himself, he took her phone and glanced down at the screen. The details were blurry so he blinked, gave his head a quick shake and forced himself to focus.

'It would appear we have a first cousin,' he said a moment later, his limbs suddenly so weak he was glad he was sitting down. 'She's twenty-five. She's a marketing assistant and lives in Salta.'

'Oh, my God,' Alex breathed. 'That's five hundred kilometres south of La Posada. Does she say anything else?'

'That she'd like to meet.'

'Do you think she might know something?'

'I have no idea.'

'What are we going to do?'

As with so much that had happened over the last week, Max didn't have a clue. That he had more blood relatives was blowing his mind. His parents had both been only children, his grandparents long dead, so it had always been just them. But if he had a cousin here then he had an aunt and uncle and who knew how many more. He might have biological parents and grandparents. More siblings. An instant family, with the relationships and history and everything that entailed, things he'd never had. Or he might not. The chaos that had receded over the last couple of days was back with a roar, expanding and intensifying with every passing second, and it was making it impossible to think.

Or maybe that was Alex, who was sitting looking at him with a combination of wariness, hope and excitement, who still managed to stir up desire in him, even now, with this, and who, he realised with a jolt, confused the hell out of him.

What on earth had he been *doing* lately? he wondered wildly as he tapped out a reply, which took an age since his fingers were shaking so much he kept hitting the wrong letters. What had he been thinking?

All the things he'd told her… His angst over his parents, the doubts he had about who he was and the reasons behind his drive to get to the truth… None of that was in the public domain. None of that she'd needed to know for the case. And what about the compromises he'd made, the lengths he'd gone to to please her, all so she would think more of him, better of him? He'd vowed never to change, to never again mould himself into being something someone else wanted, but that was exactly what he'd been doing.

For some reason his guard hadn't just lowered, it had disappeared altogether, and he felt as though he were on the edge of a precipice and about to hurl himself off it. She hadn't robbed him of the control and power he valued so highly and needed so much. He'd handed both over to her on a platter, without blinking an eye. He'd allowed her to break all the rules he hadn't even known he had. She'd pierced his armour. He was beginning to feel things he didn't want to feel, couldn't allow himself to feel, didn't deserve to feel.

He should never have allowed it to happen, he thought as panic began to set in. Hubris had been his enemy once again; in his arrogance he'd assumed he'd have this fling with Alex firmly under his control. But he'd been weak and foolish in his need for her and she'd sneaked beneath his defences. He'd become too involved. Their affair was supposed to have been a purely physical thing.

It was never meant to have involved the discussion of innermost thoughts and emotions.

He shouldn't have indulged himself by analysing how alike they were, or wondered how the hell she couldn't see it, he realised, his throat tight and his head pounding as he hit the send button on his reply to Valentina Lopez. He shouldn't have granted her access to so many fragments of himself that she'd seen the whole.

But it wasn't too late to put a stop to it. To get some breathing space and perspective and regroup. He was going to Salta on his own. He was more than capable of handling whatever he found there alone. He'd spent thirty-odd years doing precisely that. He didn't want Alex there for any fallout. She'd already seen far too much of him and the thought of exposing any more of his vulnerabilities to her made him feel physically sick. It was now a question of survival.

'Well, I don't know about you,' he said bluntly, throwing up a shield of steel behind which he could restore his strength and fortify his defences, just the way he had as a kid whenever his mom had been particularly vicious or his father particularly uninterested, 'but *I'll* be leaving for Salta just as soon as possible.'

What the hell?

Stunned and confused, for one heart-thumping moment Alex just sat there watching as Max leapt to his feet and strode back into the dome. One minute she'd been desperately hoping that he would invite her to his birthday dinner—which was insane when what they were doing together firstly stayed in Argentina and secondly definitely did *not* involve birthday dinners—the next she'd been receiving a text from Becky with the instruction Check your emails!!!!!!, which she'd done and received a shock that had knocked her for six. As if all that wasn't enough to make her reel, Max's blunt declaration that he was flying solo on this whipped the air from her lungs and the strength from her limbs.

But, whatever was behind it, it wasn't happening. They were beyond unilateral decision-making. He had to be in shock. She'd noticed that his fingers had trembled as he tapped out a reply and the tension in his jaw. That was what this was about, she was sure, and as a result he needed her more than ever.

Filling fast with energy and determination, Alex sprang into action and ran after him. 'Wait,' she said, faintly alarmed by the frenzy with which he was gathering up his things and tossing them into his bag.

'What?' he snapped distractedly.

'Don't you mean *we* will leave as soon as possible?'

He didn't even look at her. He looked as if he was somewhere else entirely and her chest tightened with sympathy and alarm.

'No,' he said flatly. 'I mean "I".'

He sounded resolute and tension radiated off him like some kind of force field designed to keep her out. And as it dawned on her that he was not going to yield on this, was not going to talk to her about what he was feeling, hurt sliced through her.

'You want to cut me out of the loop now?' After everything they'd talked about? Everything they'd done?'

'It's nothing personal.'

The sting of that lodged deep in her chest and twisted. 'It is to me, Max,' she said, her throat tight, her voice cracking. It was deeply personal for a whole host of reasons she couldn't begin to unravel right now. 'This is *my* success,' she said, going for the simplest. 'I've waited eight months for a breakthrough like this. I need to be part of it.'

'It's *my* family. There's no point in you coming. You don't speak Spanish. You literally wouldn't understand.'

Another arrow pierced her heart, dipped in envy for the family, the connections, the love and acceptance he might find, and yet more pain. No, she didn't speak Spanish, but she could be there, in the background if necessary. She *would* understand. She could see what he was going through. She wanted to help him. But he wasn't letting her and that was more agonising than she could ever have imagined.

'I'd like to be there for you.'

'I don't need you to be there for me, Alex,' he said, his horribly and bewilderingly blank gaze finally meeting hers. 'I don't *want* you to be there for me. That isn't what this is. You knew the score. You *agreed* with the score.'

Yes, she had, but still. Wow. Just wow. It was as if he'd punched her in the stomach and sliced her heart in two. Her head was spinning and she couldn't breathe.

'We'll head back to La Posada now,' he said, tossing her bag on the bed and then striding into the bathroom. 'I'll drop you off at the hotel and then go on to the airport. I'll be back this evening and fill you in on the details then. Get packing.'

Max wouldn't be filling her in on the details this evening, or at any other time, Alex thought dully as the powerful four-by-four ate up first the Bolivian and then the Argentinian kilometres. She wasn't sticking around when she clearly wasn't wanted. What did he take her for? Some kind of sap he could use when it suited him and discard when it didn't? Well, that wasn't her.

She understood that the news that he had a cousin—

and therefore quite possibly more relatives—must have come as an almighty shock, but how could he dismiss her so brutally? Didn't she deserve more than that?

If she was being completely honest, the thing between them had never been purely physical. She'd been fascinated by him from the moment they'd met and not just because of his devastating good looks. Somewhere along the line she'd started thinking that maybe it was the same for him. The things he'd told her had been freely shared. She hadn't had to prise anything out of him. She'd sensed his trust in her in his touch, in the strength of his need for her.

Yet the security she'd been starting to feel with him had been entirely false. One huge toss of the sea and Max had retreated behind his feet-thick walls, keeping her well and truly out, more determinedly, more successfully than before, and now everything was falling down around her like a house of cards.

How could she have been such a fool? What on earth had made her think her support, her help, would count for anything? He'd never asked for it. He clearly didn't want it. And why would he when he'd never had either before, and had presumably adapted to that? Where had that arrogance of hers come from?

This was precisely why she didn't get involved, she reminded herself, the blood in her veins chilling at the thought of how close a shave she'd had. This was why she had rules. To protect herself from hurt. To ward off weakness. To prevent the kind of emotional turmoil that could destroy her focus and threaten her future. She ought to be grateful that Max had revealed his true self before she'd tossed aside what remained of her rules and found herself in too deep. Before she wound up trying to find ways to prolong the investigation and therefore their affair too, believing that it could turn into something it wasn't.

As soon as he dropped her at La Posada and left, she'd make her way home. Her work here was done. Once she was back in London, free of Max's impact and the cruelty of his whims, she'd focus on the fact that, after all these months of nothing, her long shot had paid off. She'd had the breakthrough she'd so badly needed. In terms of progress, she'd gone from zero to a hundred. Because of a recommendation *she'd* made. Once the implications had fully registered she'd be on cloud nine. She was sure she would.

To hell with what Max discovered in Salta. If she wanted to know she'd find out from Finn. She would not wonder how he got on or how he dealt with whatever it was that Valentina Lopez had to say. She would not regret that she couldn't be there to share the joy or the sorrow he might feel. She would not allow the pain of his rejection to linger or indulge the many what-ifs she could feel crowding at the edges of her mind.

In fact, she wouldn't think of him at all.

Max arrived back in La Posada at midnight, wrecked and battered by the events of the day, to discover that Alex had checked out. She'd left a brief note at Reception, informing him that she was closing down the investigation and going home and wishing him luck for the future, before signing off with her full name and professional title.

And that was absolutely fine, he told himself, his chest aching and his stomach churning as he strode into his room, kicked the door shut and cracked open the bottle of bourbon he'd procured from the bar on his way up, the words of her bald little note ricocheting around his head. Better that she wasn't around to see him like this, actually, and what had he expected anyway?

He'd had plenty of time to reflect on this morning's conversation. He hadn't handled the news of the match well, he knew now. In his mind's eye he could still see the hurt on Alex's face when he'd told her he was going to Salta alone, could still hear her gasp of shock when he'd told her why. That he'd been both knocked for six by the news that he had a cousin and thrown into a spin by various realisations about the nature of their affair was no excuse.

He'd planned on apologising and explaining, as well as confessing that he deeply regretted rejecting her support because all too soon he'd realised he could have done with her there, even though he wasn't entirely sure why. He'd have got on his knees to beg her forgiveness, if it had come to that. He'd have done whatever it took to calm the storm that was raging through him.

But none of that was necessary now, he reflected numbly, splashing bourbon into a glass and swallowing it in one. There'd be no grovelling, no recounting of the meeting he'd had with his cousin and no forgiveness and acceptance. No arms around him when he broke down over the fact that his biological mother had died six years ago and, his father had been a one-night stand she'd had when she was sixteen, and no soothing insight into how he might go about dealing with the heart-breaking fact that he would never know if he was like either of them or who he truly was.

But at least there was also no risk of him crashing through his shield of steel and begging Alex to agree to continue their fling even after the case closed, which was not only impractical when they lived half a world apart and unprecedented when he rarely reversed a decision once made, but also so very, very dangerous.

He wasn't good enough for her, he told himself, pouring himself another glass of liquor and again downing the contents. He wasn't good enough for anyone. How could he have forgotten that? Wanting to be wanted by her would lead to nothing but misery and disillusionment. Even if this morning had gone differently and by some miracle she'd agreed, how long would it be before he screwed up so badly that her approval and appreciation turned to disappointment and regret?

No. As he'd always known, he was far better off free from the emotional havoc of a relationship that he'd inevitably mess up through ignorance and inexperience. He neither wanted nor deserved the responsibility of Alex's happiness and well-being. He wouldn't know how to take care of them. He could scarcely believe he'd even contemplated it. Hell, he didn't even know who he was. The confused, unwanted, unloved kid? The cocky, rebellious hacker? The cool-headed cyber security expert? Or a man being torn apart by pointless feelings for a woman he could never have?

He'd survive. He always did. And he had his brothers now. He'd take the bundle of unopened letters Valentina had given him to England. He'd read them with Finn and Rico instead of with Alex. It was much more appropriate that way anyway.

He had no doubt that tomorrow he'd realise that things had turned out for the best today. He'd treated Alex appallingly and the regret and shame scything through him were nothing more than he deserved. He'd been wise to put a stop to their affair before it had got out of hand and he'd done even more damage. He didn't think he could bear it if he made her unhappy, which he inevitably would.

He picked up the bottle for the third time and figured that since the bourbon was doing such a good job of dulling the pain he might as well finish it off. In the morning, with hindsight, he'd see that he'd had the luckiest of escapes and, more importantly, so had she.

But if he'd had such a lucky escape, thought Max three tumultuous days later as he sat with his brothers in Finn's drawing room in Oxfordshire, the letters strewn across the vast coffee table that sat between two enormous sofas, why was Alex all he could think about? Why did the fact that she'd sent her invoice to Finn the day she'd got home, as if she hadn't been able to wait another minute to sever the connection they'd once had, cut him up so painfully?

He'd assumed, an inch from the bottom of the bottle, he'd have no trouble wiping her from his head. He'd told himself that he had more than enough to worry about and did not need either the confusion she wreaked or the hassle she caused. He'd deal with what was going on inside him somehow. He'd done it before. He could do it again. She was out of his life and it was a relief.

But, if that was the case, why was he still feeling so out of sorts?

Outwardly, he was just about holding it together, but inside he was falling apart. Every time a memory from the time he and Alex had spent together slammed unbidden into his head, the impact of it nearly wiped out his knees. When he recalled the way she'd smiled at him, warmth spread through him like a blanket seeping into every corner of him, even those parts that had always been so cold and empty, before it was whipped away by regret.

He was untethered, adrift, and he itched to return to his old ways. He wanted to break laws and hack into a system or two, just to claw back some kind of control and power over what was happening to him. He wanted to immerse himself in the dark web and find out what his former colleagues were up to and maybe lend a hand. It was only the thought of Alex's disapproval that stopped him and that was baffling, since her opinion of him was neither here nor there any more.

It wasn't as if he didn't have anything else to occupy his mind. Once he'd sobered up he'd gone home, where he'd spent two days translating the letters their mother had written, and what a weekend that had been.

The letters, which ran to dozens of pages each, detailed a history of her life and as much of theirs as she'd known. They were filled with explanations and reasons and the hopes she'd had at first of finding her sons and then, when that had looked less and less likely, the dreams she'd had for them. Her anger, her sadness, her love poured from the lines, and reading them, analysing them as he'd translated them, had completely wrecked him.

It seemed to be wrecking his brothers too. For two hours they'd been studying the letters, largely in silence, and jaws were tight and brows were furrowed. The struggle for self-control seemed to be as tough for them as it had been for him.

'Bit dusty in here,' said Finn gruffly, clearing his throat as he put down the final page, the one in which their mother's heartbreak at knowing she was going to her grave without ever finding them had ripped Max to shreds.

'I appear to have something in my eye,' said Rico, looking as if swallowing was hard.

Finn rubbed his face and got to his feet. 'I think I'll go and find Georgie.'

Rico shoved his hands through his hair and did the same. 'I'm just going to call Carla.'

They exited the room, leaving Max alone with nothing more than a pounding head and a racing pulse. His chest ached. His vision blurred. He could hardly breathe with emotions that were crushing him on all sides, one in particular scorching through him like lightning.

It was envy, he realised with a jolt as the room began to spin. He envied his brothers. For the relationships they had and the women they loved. How did they do it? He wished he knew. Because, deep down, he didn't want to be alone. He wanted Alex, in the way Finn had Georgie and Rico had Carla. Not only to help him navigate the choppy waters he was in, but to sail along with him even when they weren't choppy. In other words, all the time.

Which meant what? That he'd been the biggest fool on the planet to turn her away? Well, that seemed pretty much spot-on. Despite his attempts to convince himself otherwise, Alex *was* different to the other women he'd hooked up with over the years. Quite apart from the fact that what they'd been doing was far more than 'hooking up', they'd travelled similar paths. They understood each other. Until he'd been spooked into falling back into bad habits and internalising his fears, everything had been going great.

So could he have pushed her away deliberately, sabotaging something good before it blew up in his face? Had it been his way of maintaining control over a situation that was fast slipping out of his grip? It wasn't beyond the realms of possibility. But what if it didn't blow up in his face? What if he'd thrown away the best thing that had ever happened to him because of some ridiculous concern that he might not survive it?

He had to take responsibility for his behaviour, he realised suddenly as he sprang to his feet and began to pace the length of the drawing room. His hang-ups about the past might be valid, but his response to what happened now was his own. He had a choice, and he could either continue to allow it to eat him up with bitterness and resentment or he could let it go.

He was fed up with dwelling on the past. Shouldn't he take a leaf out of his brothers' book and start looking forwards rather than back? It would be charting new territory and that was scary as hell, but that was no excuse not to do it. That smacked of cowardice.

Could the future hold Alex? He desperately wanted it to, because he could see her in it. He wanted her in it. Was he in love with her? How would he know? Where was a flowchart when he needed one? But *something* had to account for the gaping hole in his chest and the tightness in his throat. The ache in his heart and the spinning of his head whenever he thought of her, which was pretty much all the damn time.

He had to be in love with her, he thought, going dizzy at the idea of it. He probably had been from the moment they'd met. That was why he'd found it so much fun to provoke her. That was why he'd been so determined to make her his. Why he craved her smiles and wanted to make her happy.

Their mother's letters proved that he and his brothers had once upon a time been loved. Very much. He'd mattered and been wanted. And now he realised that he wanted to matter to Alex, as much as she mattered to him.

And all those worries of his? Pathetic. He hadn't changed. He hadn't moulded himself into anyone. He'd made no sacrifices. She'd demanded nothing of him. The compromises he'd made had made him happy too. He had nothing to fear from love or a relationship. It didn't have to be toxic or manipulative.

Who he'd been was of no importance. What was important was the sort of man he wanted to be, and that was a man who deserved her, and if she had expectations of him, well, he wanted to spend the rest of his life attempting to meet them.

This morning Finn had asked him if there was anyone he wanted to invite to their birthday dinner on Saturday. He'd flatly said no, but here, now, he'd changed his mind. He wanted to invite Alex. He wanted a second chance. He could only hope it wasn't too late.

CHAPTER ELEVEN

WHEN ALEX HAD arrived back on UK soil, she'd hit the ground running. Finn had settled her invoice with much appreciated efficiency and she'd wasted no time in paying off her debts before hiring a recruitment consultant and calling up a commercial estate agency.

In the midst of the flurry of activity she'd paid her family a visit, which had been a tense and unpleasant hour, not least because her elder brother had put in a request for ten grand and then spat at her feet when she'd refused. In that moment, any qualms she might have had about cutting them out of her life for good had evaporated, and once she'd got everything she wanted to say to them off her chest she'd left with no looking back and no regrets. She was wholly on her own now, but she was independent and strong, utterly content with who she was and her place in the world.

True to his word, Finn was already recommending her agency, and Becky, who'd done a great job of holding the fort while she'd been away and whom she was on the point of promoting, was taking more calls than she could handle. The plans for expansion were once again within touching distance and the new kit Alex had ordered was scheduled to arrive imminently. The future looked bright and brilliant and she was marching straight into it.

She didn't have time to think about Max, nor did she care to. She'd been so upset, so angry at the abrupt, careless way he'd dismissed her and, for some unfathomable reason, so damn sad, but by the time she'd landed in London after a lengthy journey that involved a number of changes and a lot of analysis, she'd been totally over it. And him. She couldn't believe that at one point she'd actually been hoping their affair might turn into something more. Anyone who could be that cruel didn't deserve her and wasn't worth her head space, no matter how many times he'd rocked her world.

And that was why, when the invitation to the triplets' black-tie thirty-second birthday celebrations at Rico's house in Venice had dropped into her inbox, Alex had seen no reason not to accept. She hadn't dressed up in months. She'd never been to Venice. She might even make a long weekend of it. Besides, she'd like to see Finn and Rico again and meet Georgie and Carla and it wasn't as if she was going to go all dewy-eyed over Max. That was the very *last* thing that was going to happen. Thank God she hadn't done anything stupid like gone and fallen in love with him. That really would have been recklessly insane.

If she'd made the guest list, she was, no doubt, one of a hundred guests, so she'd probably hardly even see him. And in the unlikely event she did, well, her unflappable facade was in place and these days it was impregnable. There'd be no shock, no thundering rush of lust, just polite professionalism and cool distance.

So what if she'd bought a new dress? She could hardly wear a trouser suit to a black-tie dinner. Her hair was loose tonight but that was because the style suited her outfit, not because Max liked it like that. The fact that she'd brought him a present had nothing to do with wanting to show him they could be given freely, without any strings attached. It was merely polite. She'd brought gifts for Finn and Rico too, although the books she'd selected for them were far less personal than the tiny bag of Bolivian salt she'd had sent over at vast expense for him. And if her heart was pounding so hard she feared it was in danger of escaping her chest…well, that was entirely down to the exhilaration of the boat ride across the lagoon.

But when Alex's water taxi approached the jetty and she saw Max standing there, tall, solid and so handsome he took her breath away, frowning out across the water as if looking for her, she realised, with a nosedive of her heart, she'd been kidding herself.

Everything she thought she'd successfully buried shot to the surface, all the hurt and misery she'd felt on the plane home, and she knew, with a sinking of her spirits, that she was no more over him than she could fly to the moon.

How on earth had she managed to ignore the X-rated dreams she'd had, which woke her up on a regular basis in a tangle of sheets and a puddle of lust, her heart aching with regret and sorrow?

How many times had she had to stop herself calling him up to tell him how well her business was going and to find out what he was up to?

How much had she wished he'd been there to hold her after she'd cut her family out of her life, which had been hard, even if completely the right thing to do?

Taking a couple of deep shaky breaths, Alex ordered her galloping pulse to slow and pushed the memories and the flush of heat that came with them aside. It was only natural that her subconscious would remember the best sex she'd ever had and miss it. It meant nothing. She could handle it. And how could she have missed *him* when he'd been so horrible? Her plans for the future were of no interest to him and he wouldn't have been there to hold her anyway. That wasn't what their affair had been about and she mustn't forget that.

'Hi,' he said with the ghost of a smile that annoyingly melted her stupid soppy heart.

'You look awful.' His face was gaunt, she noted as she alighted. There were bags under his eyes, his cheekbones were sharp and the black suit he was wearing fitted a little more loosely than she suspected it should or indeed than she'd once imagined.

'You look beautiful.'

Well. She wasn't going to be distracted by that, no matter how much of a flutter it sparked in her stomach. She was still so angry. 'Thank you.'

He thrust his hands in the pockets of his trousers and she refused to notice how lovingly the fine fabric pulled across the powerful muscles of his thighs. Nor would she think about how much she'd missed wrapping her arms around his broad, strong shoulders, or how heavenly he smelled.

'How have you been?'

'Good.' He didn't look it. He looked as if he'd been to hell and back, and yet there was something remarkably calm in his indigo gaze, something sort of settled, which she just couldn't put her finger on. 'You?'

'Very well,' she replied, intent on keeping her tone impersonal. 'Busy.'

'Work going well?'

'Work is going very well, thank you,' she said coolly.

'I'm glad you're here.'

'I can't imagine why.'

'You left without saying goodbye.'

He'd given her no option and what did he care anyway?

'The case was closed, Max. My work was done. Once you'd gone to Salta there was no need for me to stay.'

He tilted his head, his gaze turning quizzical. 'Don't you want to know what happened?'

She did. She badly did. She deliberately hadn't asked Finn. She'd worried she wouldn't be able to stop herself from asking about Max too, which was pathetic when this case had taken up nearly nine months of her life.

'All right, fine,' she said with a casual shrug, as if it were neither here nor there. 'What happened?'

'I met with Valentina,' he said as they started walking up the jetty to the magnificent villa she could see peeking through the towering cypress trees.

The early autumn sun was low in the sky and the heat of the day still lingered. That was why she was so warm. It had nothing to do with the man walking with her, so close that he was taking up all her air, so close that she'd barely have to move her hand to be able to hold his. She had to focus and stay strong if she stood any chance of getting through this evening which she was beginning to regret with every passing second.

'Did she know anything?'

'Not a lot. She never met our mother, whose name, by the way, was Silvia Solana, contrary to what appears on our original birth certificates.'

'Was?'

'She died in Buenos Aires six years ago. Pancreatic cancer.'

She tried not to care but it was impossible when her chest ached for him. He had to have been *so* disappointed. 'I'm so sorry.'

'It's fine.'

'How can it be?'

'She left us letters.'

'Letters?'

'Twenty-six of them. She wrote to us once a year on our birthday and then one last one a few weeks before she died. In them she explains everything.'

'What happened?'

'She had a one-night stand with a guy she met in a bar when she was sixteen. She didn't know who he was and she never saw him again.'

'What was she doing in a bar at the age of sixteen?'

'Rebelling.'

'Like mother, like son.'

He cast her a quick startled glance and then grinned, and he looked so carefree that she found she could hardly breathe. 'I guess so,' he said. 'Perceptive as always.'

He made it sound as if he knew her, which he didn't or he'd never have treated her so badly, but, before she could tell him that, he continued, 'Her parents were deeply religious and when they discovered she was pregnant they sent her to a convent. We were removed from her by the nuns when we were two months old. She was never told where we were taken or what ultimately happened to us. She escaped the convent, went to Buenos Aires to find work and never spoke to her parents again. When they died, she established contact with her sister, but by then she was ill and didn't have much time left.'

'That's so sad.'

'She never stopped looking for us.'

'She must have loved you all very much.'

'She did.'

Alex cleared her throat to dislodge the knot that had

formed there against her will. 'Do you have other relatives?'

'We have aunts and uncles and cousins galore. Some in Salta, some in Buenos Aires. One cousin lives in New York, oddly enough.'

'Will you visit them?'

'Some time.'

'That would be good.'

'Would you like to read the letters?'

God, yes. But the case was closed. They were done. 'I've moved on to other things.'

'Have you?'

'Very much so.'

'I'm sorry I didn't take you to Salta with me, Alex. I needed you there.'

She steeled her heart not to melt. His apology came far too late. 'Don't worry about it,' she said with an airiness that she didn't feel at all. 'It's all water under the bridge. No hard feelings. We agreed to a short-term thing that was going to last just as long as the investigation and it ended. It's completely fine.'

'Is it?'

Something in his voice made her meet his gaze and her pulse skipped a beat at the dark intensity that shimmered within. It wasn't fine, she thought with a sudden surge of alarm. It wasn't fine at all. 'Absolutely.'

'What if I told you I loved you?'

The world stopped for a second and then began to spin, but she couldn't let herself go there. She was in such a good place at the moment and she'd worked hard for it. The risk of upending everything for a man who played fast and loose with her emotions was too great. 'I'd say we've known each other for less than two weeks and ask what you were on.'

'I know it's been quick but I *am* in love with you, Alex. I think I have been since the moment we met.'

'You could have fooled me.'

'The only person I've been fooling is myself.'

She badly needed a drink and to mingle, to be able to remove herself from his presence in order to be able to think straight, and they'd reached the pretty terrace now, which overlooked the lagoon and was decorated with strings of light. But where was the party? Why was the table set for six?

'Where's everyone else?' she asked, confused and alarmed by the absence of other people.

'Finn and Georgie are putting their son to bed. Rico and Carla are in the kitchen doing something clever with pasta.'

And that was it? This wasn't a party. This was an intimate dinner. A family dinner. What did that mean? She couldn't work it out. All she knew was that Max had whipped the rug from under her feet yet again and coming here had been a mistake.

'I'm sorry,' she said as panic swept through her like the wildest of fires. 'I can't do this. I should go.'

Of all the responses Max had expected to his apologies and his declaration of love, Alex spinning on her very sexy heel was not one of them. Yet she was charging back down the steps towards the jetty and he was so stunned it was a full ten seconds before he sprang into action.

'Stop,' he said, even though, this being an island and her water taxi having left some time ago, she couldn't actually go anywhere.

'No.'

He caught up with her and put a hand on her arm which she threw off, but at least she stopped and turned to face him, even if the torment on her face sliced straight through his heart. 'What's wrong?'

'This is.'

'In what way?'

'We had an agreement,' she said wretchedly.

'I know.'

'You don't do love.'

'It turns out I do, with you.'

'Then how could you have pushed me away like that?' Her eyes filled with sadness and he felt physically sick at the knowledge that he'd put it there.

'I'm so sorry I did that,' he said, his chest aching with regret. 'You'll never know how sorry. I guess I was trying to protect myself. I learned early on in life to suppress my emotions. The only way to survive was not to care and so I didn't. I grew up believing I was worthless and unwanted, which was compounded by the discovery that I was adopted, and that's a hard habit to break.'

'You hurt me badly.'

The ache turned into pain of the sort he'd never felt before. 'I know and that guts me. Not that it's any excuse, but I was struggling to work out who I am.'

'You should have just asked. I know who you are.'

'You're the only person in the world who does,' he said, not taking his eyes off her for even a second, willing her to believe him because his entire future depended on it. 'You came along and crashed through my defences, Alex, and it was terrifying at first and now it isn't at all. You knowing me and me knowing you makes me incredibly happy. I love you and I'd like to spend the rest of my life proving it to you.' He took a deep breath, his entire world now reduced to this woman and what she said next. 'The only question I have is, how do you feel about me?'

* * *

Alex didn't know. Max had stirred up so many emotions inside her and she couldn't unravel any of them. But he was waiting for an answer and, with the way his gaze bored into hers, it mattered. A lot.

'Volatile,' she said, wishing she was better at explaining it.

He jerked back as if she'd struck him and she wanted to hug the shock out of him, but if she did that she might not be able to stop and they'd have resolved nothing. 'Volatile?'

'Like I'm on the top of the world one minute and at the bottom of a pit the next. It's not the way I want to be. It's not the life I want to live. I need stability and security. I always have.'

'I'll give it to you.'

No doubt he thought he could, but it was impossible. That wasn't who he was. 'How?' she said desperately, all pretence of control gone. 'You are chaos and unpredictability. You don't want to change who you are any more than I want to change who I am, and that's fine because I wouldn't want you to.'

'It's far too late for that,' he said, his gaze on hers steady and sure. 'I already have changed and I'm OK with it. I'm done with the chaos. I figure it's a choice and I choose, well, not that. I choose you. I've always feared the idea of being responsible for someone else's feelings. But I want to be responsible for yours. Trust me with them, Alex. Take a risk with me. You won't regret it.'

Wouldn't she? How could he be so sure? How could anyone? He was so calm, while she was the one who felt wild and out of control, and yet the longer she stared into his eyes, the more she could feel the wildness ease. It was as if they'd swapped roles, as if she'd rubbed off on him and he'd rubbed off on her.

Could she do it? That was the thought ricocheting around her head, making her breath catch and her heart race. Could she take the risk? Did she even want to?

Yes, yes and, God, yes.

Because she was in love with him too, she realised as the walls she'd built around her heart on the plane home crumbled to dust. Madly and irreversibly. She'd been so miserable these past couple of days, so sad. Just being here with him, colours were brighter, sounds were sharper. When he pushed her buttons she loved it. She never felt more alive than when he was challenging and provoking her. He was the polar opposite of everything she'd ever thought she wanted but she'd been wrong. They were like two sides of the same coin.

'I've missed you,' she said, her voice shaking from the force of the emotions rushing through her.

'I've missed you too.'

'I cut all ties with my family.'

'That was brave.'

'It had to be done, even if I am now all alone. I could give you tips, if you want.'

'You aren't alone, Alex. You have me. If you want me. You need never be alone again.'

She did want him, desperately, but… 'What if it all goes wrong?'

'It won't.'

'You don't know that. It did for me before.'

'I do know that,' he said with quiet certainty that filled her with confidence and brushed away the doubts. 'I won't allow it. I don't want you to be anyone other than who you are, Alex. Why would I when you are absolutely brilliant?'

'You are *not* worthless,' she said, her throat thick.

'I know. Silvia's letters prove it. I love you and I will always be there for you, the way you've been there for me.'

She had to trust him. She wanted to trust him. All she had to do was take a risk, and it wasn't even that much of a risk. This might have been quick, but she'd never been surer of anything in her life, and they could work out the logistics later.

Her heart was pounding and her eyes were swimming as she took a step forwards, but nothing was going to stop her telling him how she felt now.

'I love you too,' she said, winding her arms around his neck, her heart so filled with happiness it felt too big for her chest.

He pulled her close and she lifted her head as he lowered his, and their mouths met in a kiss that was hot and tender and went on and on until the sun dipped beneath the horizon.

'Happy birthday,' she murmured raggedly when he finally lifted his mouth from hers.

The smile he gave her was blinding. 'It's a *very* happy birthday.'

EPILOGUE

Christmas Day, three months later

THE NORDIC FIR standing in Finn and Georgie's drawing room in their sprawling mansion situated in the Oxfordshire countryside was so tall it nearly touched the ceiling. Strings of fairy lights were draped over thick wide-spreading branches from which gold and silver baubles hung, and tinsel sparkled in the bright winter sunlight.

Outside in the snow, under a cloudless blue sky, two-and-a-half-year-old Josh was building a snowman with his mother, Georgie, and his aunt, Carla. Alex was searching for sticks, presumably to be turned into its arms. Inside, the rich aroma of roasting turkey and stuffing filled the house and carols rang out from speakers hidden in the ceiling.

This year the dining room table was set for seven. Next year, wherever they chose to spend it—London or Oxfordshire, Venice or the Caribbean—there'd be more. Georgie and Finn were expecting a daughter via surrogate in May. Carla was due in August, and only this morning Alex had told Max that come September they too would be welcoming the patter of tiny feet.

Before the roaring fire, the brothers stood side by

side, each nursing a glass of Scotch as they gazed out of the window at the activity outside.

'I'd like to make a toast,' said Max, raising his glass and thinking how unbelievably lucky he was, how unbelievably lucky all three of them were, to have found each other and have the love of incredible women.

'To the best Christmas in thirty-two years?' said Rico.

'To many more in the future?' said Finn.

'To family.'

* * * * *

A CONTRACT FOR HIS RUNAWAY BRIDE

MELANIE MILBURNE

MILLS & BOON

To Denise Florence Monks. You were not just
our help in the house—and in the garden and with
house-sitting—but our help and support during some
very difficult times. I will always treasure my memories
of you. Your love and compassion for our family, our
pets and even our friends was amazing. Even right
to the end you were thinking of others. Rest in peace.

CHAPTER ONE

ELODIE CAMPBELL GLANCED at her designer watch and muttered a colourful curse. The one time in her life when she was bang on time for an appointment and she was kept waiting. Who was this guy who thought it was okay to leave her out here with her nerves ripping her stomach to shreds?

This meeting was her last chance for financial backing. It had to go ahead.

To fill the time—and to settle her anxiety—she'd glanced through the artfully splayed glossy magazines five times. One of which featured a spread of her on a photo shoot in Dubai. Then she'd consumed two expertly brewed black coffees. Maybe the second coffee hadn't been such a good idea. Restless at the best of times, now she was so fidgety she wanted to pace the floor…or punch something.

She crossed one leg over the other and kicked her top foot up and down in time with the tick-tock of the second hand on the clock above the receptionist's desk.

The clock went around another eight and a half minutes and Elodie was close to screaming. Not just a scream of frustration but one that was so loud it would shatter the windows of the swish-looking office tower. Normally people had to wait for her. Her identical twin, Elspeth, had inherited the punctuality gene. Elodie had got the chronically late one.

The longer she waited, the worse her anxiety spiked. What if this meeting turned out like the last? Her options were running out—especially since the recent scandal attached to her name. Her previous financial backer had pulled out once he'd heard about her role in sabotaging a society wedding. Urgh. What was it with her and scandals? If she couldn't secure financial backing, how could she leave her lingerie modelling career behind? She was tired of playing on her looks. She wanted to prove she had more than a good body. She wanted to design her own label of evening wear, but she needed an investor in her business to get it off the ground.

Another five minutes crawled past like a snail on crutches.

Elodie blew out a breath and sprang up from the sofa in the plush reception area on the top level of the London office tower. She strode over to the smartly dressed receptionist with a smile so forced it made her face ache. 'Could you give me an update on when Mr Smith will be available?'

The receptionist's answering smile was polite but formal. 'I apologise for the delay. He'll be with you shortly.'

'Look, my appointment was—'

'I understand, Ms Campbell. But he's a very busy man. He's made a special gap in his diary for you. He's not usually so accommodating. You must've made a big impression on him.'

'I haven't even met him. All I know is, I was instructed to be here close to thirty minutes ago for a meeting with a Mr Smith to discuss finance. I've been given no other details.'

The receptionist glanced at the intercom console where

a small green light was flashing. She looked up again at Elodie with the same polite smile. 'Thank you for being so patient. Mr...erm... Smith will see you now. Please go through. It's the third door on the right. The corner office.'

The corner office boded well—that meant he was the head honcho. The big bucks began and stopped with him. Elodie went to the door and took a deep calming breath, but it did nothing to settle the frenzy of flick knives in her stomach. She gave the door a quick rap with her knuckles.

Please, please, please let me be successful this time.

'Come.'

Her hand paused on the doorknob, her mind whirling in ice-cold panic. Something about the deep timbre of that voice sent a shiver scuttling over her scalp like a small claw-footed creature. Elodie ran the tip of her tongue over her suddenly carpet-dry lips, her throat so tight she couldn't swallow. Surely her nerves were getting the better of her? The man she was meeting was a Mr Smith. But how could this Mr Smith sound so like her ex-fiancé? Scarily like him.

She turned the doorknob and pushed the door open, her gaze immediately fixing on the tall dark-haired man behind the large desk.

'*You?*' Elodie gasped, heat flooding into her cheeks and other places in her body she didn't want to think about right now.

Lincoln Lancaster rose from his chair with leonine grace, his expression set in its customary cynical lines— the arch of one ink-black brow over his intelligent bluey-green gaze, the tilt of his sensual mouth that was not quite a smile. His black hair was brushed back from his high forehead in loose waves that looked as if they had last been combed by his fingers. He was dressed in a three-piece suit that hugged his athletic frame, emphasising the broadness of his shoulders, the taut trimness of his chest, flat abdomen and lean hips. He was the epitome of a successful a man in his prime. Potent, powerful, persuasive. He got what he wanted, when he wanted, how he wanted.

'You're looking good, Elodie.'

His voice rolled over her as smoothly and lazily as his gaze, the deep, sexy rumble so familiar it triggered a host of memories she had fought for seven years to erase. Memories in her flesh that were triggered by being in his presence. Erotic memories that made her hyper-aware of his every breath, his every glance, his every movement.

Elodie shut the door behind her with a definitive click. She clenched her right hand around her slimline purse and her other hand into a tight fist and stalked towards his desk. 'How dare you lie to me to get me here? You know I'd never willingly be in the same room as you.'

His eyes shone with amusement, which only fuelled her anger like a naked flame on tinder. 'You answered your own question. I wanted to meet with you and this seemed the only way to do it.'

'Mr Smith?' She made a scoffing noise. 'Couldn't you be a little more original than that? And why not meet me at your Kensington office?'

'In another life, Smith could well have been my name.'

There was a cryptic quality to his tone and a flicker of something in his expression that piqued her interest.

'I'm using this office for a few weeks while my other premises are being renovated.' He waved a hand at the plush chair in front of his desk. 'Take a seat. We have things to discuss.'

Elodie remained standing, her fists so tightly balled she could feel her fingernails cutting half-moons into the skin of her palm and the soft leather of her purse. 'I have nothing to discuss with you. You've no right to waste my valuable time by luring me here under false pretences.'

'Sit.' His one-word command was as sharp and implacable as the steely *don't-mess-with-me* glint in his eyes.

Elodie raised her chin, a frisson skittering over her flesh at the combative energy firing between them like high-voltage electricity. Fighting with Lincoln had formed a large part of their previous relationship. Their strong wills had often clashed and their passionate fights had nearly always been resolved in bed. The thought of *this* fight ending that way made her heart race and her pulse skyrocket.

'Just try and make me.'

She injected her tone with ice-cold disdain to counter the fiery heat pooling between her legs. Only Lincoln Lancaster could have this effect on her, and it made her furious to think he still had the power to make her feel things she didn't want to feel. Dangerous feelings. Overwhelming feelings. Feelings she couldn't control.

One side of his mouth came up in a half-smile, and the slow burn of his gaze sent tingles cascading down the length of her spine to pool in a ball of molten heat in her core.

'Tempting as that is, right now, I want to discuss a proposal with you.'

'A proposal?' She unclenched her fists and gave a bark of scathing laughter. 'There's nothing you could ever propose to me that I would find irresistible.'

There was a long beat of silence. A silence so weighted, so intense, it sent goosebumps popping up along the skin of her arms.

His unreadable eyes held hers in a lock that made her blood tick with excitement. It was an excitement she wished she could quell, but it seemed her body had a mind of its own when it came to Lincoln.

And somehow, she suspected he knew it.

Lincoln came around to perch on the corner of his desk, close enough to her for her to catch a tantalising whiff of his aftershave. The citrus notes were fresh and clean, the base notes a little more complex, reminding her of the rich, earthy scent of a densely wooded forest after rain. His eyes were an unusual mix of green and blue—a bottomless ocean with flashes of kelp and green sea glass swirling in their unreachable depths. She couldn't drag her eyes away from the dark shadow of regrowth peppering his jaw. How many times had she run her fingers over that prickly stubble? How many times had she felt its sexy rasp on the sensitive skin of her inner thighs?

Her gaze drifted to his mouth and her stomach bottomed out. Suddenly she found it hard to breathe. Those sensually curved lips had explored every inch of her body, stirred her into cataclysmic pleasure time and time again. She had never had a more exciting lover than Lincoln Lancaster. His touch had set fire to her body, making it erupt into roaring flames of need only he could assuage. Every lover since—not that there had been many—had been a bitter disappointment. It was as if Lincoln had ruined her for anyone else. No one could ignite her flesh like he had. No one could make her feel the things he made her feel. It seemed her body was programmed to respond to him and him alone.

'How about we start again?' His voice had a disarmingly gentle note, but his gaze was still unwavering on hers. 'You're looking good, Elodie.'

The pitch of his voice went down half a semitone to a deep burr that put her resolve to resist him in Critical Care. He was impossible to resist when he laid on the charm.

Elodie swallowed the choking lump of her pride, intrigued by his change of tactic. Intrigued by why he had set up this meeting under a false name and in a high-rise office tower that was on the other side of town from his London base. Intrigued to find out exactly what he was proposing. Office renovations aside, surely he could have contacted her without the need for pretence?

'Thank you.' She glanced behind her to locate the chair and sat—not because she wanted to do as he had commanded earlier, but because right then her legs were feeling decidedly unsteady. She positioned her leather purse on her lap, her fingers absently fidgeting with the silver clasp. 'You said you had something to discuss with me? A proposal?'

Lincoln rose from his perch on the edge of the desk and went back to sit in his office chair. He rolled the chair forward and then rested one of his forearms on the desk. His other hand reached for a sheaf of papers.

'A business proposal.' His gleaming eyes met hers and he added, 'You weren't expecting any other type of proposal, were you?'

Elodie schooled her features into cool impassivity. 'I can't imagine you'd be interested in repeating past mistakes.'

An inscrutable smile tilted one side of his mouth. 'I hear you're interested in some financial backing for your own evening wear label.' He drummed his fingers on the paperwork beneath his hand. 'Are you interested in hearing my terms?'

Elodie ran the tip of her tongue over her lips, aware of another moth-like flicker of excitement in her blood. Could this be her chance to fulfil her dream at last? She had never aspired to be a lingerie model, but she had played the role with aplomb. *Smart, successful, sassy, sophisticated* and *sexy* were the five words to describe her brand. A brand she had never intended adopting in the first place but had somehow drifted into. Lincoln was offering her an escape route—but he'd mentioned terms. What would they be? Dared she even ask? He was one of the most successful self-made businessmen in the country. He turned around ailing businesses within a year or two for a sizeable profit. Did he see her venture as a sure bet?

'You want to finance me? But…but why?'

He shrugged one broad shoulder, his expression as unreadable as a mask. 'I never allow emotions to get in the way of a good business deal.'

Did that mean he was confident she could succeed? How strange that he of all people believed in her potential. 'You think I can be successful?'

His gaze was suddenly laser-pointer-direct. 'Do you?'

'I…' Elodie chewed at the inside of her mouth and lowered her gaze from the penetrating heat of his. 'I think so.'

'Not good enough. You have to believe in yourself or no one else will.'

The chiding edge to his tone made her straighten her back in her chair. She brought her gaze back to his. 'I do believe in myself. I've wanted to get out of modelling for a while now. I want to prove I have more to offer the world than my looks.'

'A wishbone and a backbone are two different things. How much do you want it?'

She disguised a tiny swallow. 'More than anything.'

One dark eyebrow lifted over his mercurial gaze. 'Are you sure about that?'

Elodie lifted her chin, locking her gaze on his. 'Positive.'

Lincoln pushed the paperwork across the desk to her. 'Good. Because in here are my terms. You can read them at your leisure, but I can summarise them for you here and now if you like.'

Elodie laid her purse on the floor and took the sheaf of documents, but she knew it would take her ages to read through it carefully due to her dyslexia. And so did he. Not that he had ever made an issue of her learning problems in the past—if anything he had been surprisingly accommodating and understanding. It was another way he had charmed her into thinking he cared about her for more than her looks—more fool her.

'Please do.'

He leaned back in his chair, one forearm still resting on his desk. His posture was casual—almost too casual, given the searing intensity of his gaze. 'I'll put forward the necessary finance for you to launch your label.'

He named a sum that made her perfectly groomed eyebrows almost fly off her face. She knew he was wealthy, but surely that was a ridiculous amount of money to be offering her—especially given the way their relationship had ended.

Elodie rapid-blinked, her heart thumping like a hard fist against her ribcage. *Ba-boom. Ba-boom. Ba-boom.* 'But why would you want to do that?'

He held up a hand like a stop sign, his expression difficult to read. 'Allow me to state my terms without interruption.' He lowered his hand to the desk and continued. 'The money is yours if you'll agree to be my wife for six months.'

Elodie stared at him with her mind reeling, her pulse racing, her stomach freefalling. *His wife?* Was he joking? Was this some sort of candid camera prank? And why only six months? Wasn't a marriage meant to be for ever?

The money was more than enough to launch her label. Along with her own savings, the money would mean she would be able employ the necessary staff to help her achieve her dream. But to become his wife? To live with him, sleep with him, spend every day with him…? *Risk the chance of falling in love with him?*

She had come perilously close to losing herself in their relationship in the past.

Could she risk the same happening again?

Elodie narrowed her eyes and leaned forward to place the papers back on his desk. 'Is this some kind of joke?'

Lincoln picked up a gold cartridge pen and rocked it back and forth between two of his long, tanned fingers. 'It's no joke.'

His gaze remained marksman-steady and it sent a shiver of reaction through her body. Could he see how much his presence unsettled her? Could he sense the magnetic power he still had over her? A power she fought to resist with every cell of her body…

She swallowed and tried not to stare at his fingers—tried not to recall how those fingers felt when they touched her, excited her, pleasured her. She forced her gaze back to his, her heart thumping so loudly she was surprised he couldn't hear it. 'You know I can't do that.'

He tossed the pen to one side and it rolled up against a glass paperweight with a soft tinkle that seemed overly loud in the silence. 'Your call. But I should warn you this offer is only open for twenty-four hours. After that, it's off the table and won't be repeated.'

Elodie rose from her chair in one agitated movement, her arms going around her middle. She wanted to slap him for being so arrogant as to think she would accept. She wanted to grab him by the front of his shirt and…and… press her mouth to… *No.* She slammed the brakes on her wayward thoughts. She did *not* want to go anywhere near his sensual mouth.

'I can't believe you're doing this. What can you possibly hope to achieve?'

'I need a wife for the period of six months. It's as simple as that.'

She curled her top lip. 'I'm sure you have plenty of willing candidates to choose from.'

'Ah, but I want you.'

The silky smoothness of his tone threatened to put her willpower on life support, but Elodie raised her chin at a defiant angle, determined to hold her ground for as long as she could.

'What about the woman I saw you with last time we ran in to each other? She looked like she was madly in love with you. I was surprised you could still breathe with her arms clasped around your neck like that.'

His smile was indolent, his eyes glinting. 'She was in love with me. And that's why she's not suitable for this position.'

Elodie frowned so hard even a hefty shot of Botox wouldn't have prevented her wrinkling her brow. 'I don't understand… Are you saying you don't want—?'

'I can hardly want someone to be in love with me if I only want them to be my wife for six months.'

Elodie stood behind the chair and grasped the back with both hands. Something low and deep in her belly was doing somersaults. Rapid somersaults that made her intimate muscles twitch in memory of his rock-hard presence.

'Why only six months?'

He rose from the desk and slipped off his jacket, hanging it on the back of his chair. His movements were methodical, precise, as if he were mentally preparing a speech. His expression was cast in lines of gravitas she was not used to seeing on his face.

'My mother is terminally ill. She wants to see me settled before she dies.'

Elodie's frown deepened to one of confusion. 'Your mother? But you told me your mother died a couple of months before we met.'

His lips moved in a grim smile—a stiff movement of his lips that had nothing to do with what a smile was meant to be. 'That was my adoptive mother. I only met my biological mother a couple of years ago.'

Her eyes widened and she became aware of a sharp pain underneath her heart. A burrowing pain that almost took her breath away. He was adopted? Why had he never mentioned it? She knew every inch of his body, knew how he took his coffee, what brand of suit he preferred, knew his taste in literature and film, knew how he looked when he came… But he had never told her one of the most important things about himself.

'You never told me you were adopted. Did you know when we were—?'

'I always knew I was adopted.'

'But you chose not to tell me, the woman you asked to be your wife?'

Anger laced her tone and the pain in her chest burrowed a little deeper, a little harder, as if working its way towards her backbone like a silent drill. Why hadn't he told her something as important as that? It only confirmed the suspicions she'd had all along—he hadn't been in love with her. He'd been attracted to her, but love hadn't come into it at all. He had chosen her for her looks, not for *her*.

And wasn't that the miserable story of her life?

CHAPTER TWO

'But you chose *not* to be my wife, remember?' Lincoln said, with an edge of bitterness that even after all these years he couldn't quite quell. Nor did he want to. His bitterness had fuelled the phenomenal success he'd achieved in the seven years since Elodie Campbell had left him standing at the altar.

He would never admit it to her, but she had actually done him a favour by jilting him. It had galvanised him, motivated him to build an empire that rivalled some of the largest in England, if not the world. He had quadrupled his income, built his assets into an enviable portfolio that gave him the sort of security most people only dreamed about. Aiming for success had always been his passion, a driving force in his personality, but her rejection had amped up his drive to a whole new level. Everything he touched turned to gleaming gold. He *made* it do so. Nothing stood in his way when he was on a mission to achieve a goal.

Nothing and no one.

But seeing her again stirred other feelings in him that were equally difficult to ignore. Feelings he had squashed, buried, disposed of with ruthless determination.

Her beauty had always been captivating. Her long wavy red-gold hair hung halfway down her back like a mermaid's. Her heart-shaped face with its aristocratic cheek-bones, retroussé nose and uptilted bee-stung mouth gave her a haughty, untouchable air that had drawn him from the first moment he'd met her. Her body was slender, and yet her feminine curves made him ache to skim his hands over them as he'd used to do.

She was strong-willed and feisty, passionate and impulsive, and no one had ever excited him or stood up to him as much as her. He had never forgotten the thrill of arguing with her. A fight with her had not been just a fight—it had been a full-on war that always ended explosively in bed. He got hard just thinking about it.

No one had ever pushed back against him the way Elodie did.

And no one had ever humiliated him the way she had.

The business proposal he was offering now was his way of ruling a line underneath their relationship. If she accepted his terms he would be the one to end their relationship this time. He had loved her and lost her, and he would never give her, or indeed anyone, the power to make a fool of him again.

Elodie moved away from the chair she was holding on to and wrapped her arms around her middle. 'It seems my decision to jilt you was the right one.' She threw him a glance so frosty he wished he hadn't taken off his jacket. 'How could you have withheld something so important from me?'

Lincoln shrugged one shoulder. 'It wasn't something I talked about to anyone.'

'But why? Were you ashamed of it? Were you upset at being relinquished as a baby?'

'I was neither ashamed nor upset.'

Lincoln had known since he was old enough to understand the concept that he had been adopted. His adoptive parents had been loving and supportive parents and his childhood mostly happy. He had also known his younger brother and sister were his parents' biological children. But instead of feeling pushed aside and less important, he had been reassured by his parents that he was the reason they had been able to have their own biological children. That their love and nurturing of him had unlocked their unexplained infertility.

'But while we're on the subject of withholding information—why did you choose to run away on our wedding day instead of talking to me about your concerns? You've never adequately explained your actions, and nor have you apologised to me face to face.'

Twin circles of colour bloomed in her cheeks and her gaze slipped out of reach of his. 'I'm sorry if you were embarrassed. I—I just couldn't go through with it.'

Lincoln let out a stiff curse. 'The least you could have done is told me to my face. It would have saved a lot of unnecessary expense.'

'Oh, so it was the money angle that upset you the most?' Her voice had a cutting edge, her blue gaze flashing fire. 'You were the one who wanted a big wedding and insisted on paying for everything.'

'Only because I didn't want to put that sort of load on your mother. I knew your father wouldn't help out.'

Elodie bent down to pick up her purse off the floor near her chair, her long glossy hair momentarily hiding her expression. She straightened and shook her hair back over her shoulders. 'I have to go.'

He ached to run those silken strands through his fingers, to lift handfuls of her fragrant hair to his nose and breathe in her exotic scent. It had taken him months to get rid of the smell of her perfume in his house, even though he had instructed his housekeeper to remove every trace of Elodie. Every room had seemed to hold a hint of her distinctive scent, lingering there to silently mock him.

Look what happens when you fall in love. You are left with nothing but memories to taunt you.

'I want your answer by five p.m. tomorrow.'

Her defiant gaze met his and a lightning bolt of lust slammed into his groin. 'I gave you my answer. It's an emphatic, don't-embarrass-yourself-by-asking-me-again *no*.'

Lincoln leaned his hip against the corner of his desk and folded his arms across his chest. He hadn't expected her to say yes at the first meeting. It wasn't in her nature to do anything without a fight and, frankly, he admired that about her. But seeing her again had proved to him she wasn't immune to him, and that gave him the assurance that she would eventually agree to his terms.

That he wasn't immune to her was an issue he would have to address at some point. He would not allow her the same sensual power she'd had over him in the past. The sensual power that had made him propose marriage within a couple of months of meeting her. The stunning physicality of their relationship had blindsided him to the reality of her using him, rather than loving him. She had said the words but she had still bolted. That was not love—that was betrayal of the highest order. And he would not allow it to happen again.

'Don't let your emotions get in the way. I can help you achieve your dream. It can be a win-win for both of us.'

'Why are you doing this?'

'I told you—I need a temporary wife.'

'But marrying someone you don't love and who doesn't love you is hardly honouring your biological mother in the final weeks or months of her life. Won't she be able to tell it's not a love match?'

'Nina Smith knows you jilted me seven years ago. She's

a hopeless romantic who believes I'll never be happy until we get back together. She disapproves of my playboy life-style and wants to see me settled before she passes on.' His mouth stretched into a cynical smile and he added, 'You were good at pretending to love me in the past. I'm sure you'll do an excellent job this time around—especially given the amount of money I'd be paying you.'

Her lips were tightly compressed. 'If—and it's a big if—if I accept your offer, I won't sleep with you.'

Lincoln pushed himself away from his desk and picked up the sheaf of papers, held them out to her. 'You won't be required to. It's written in the contract. You'll find it on page three.'

She took the papers from him as if he was handing her a dangerous animal. She laid them on the desk and began to read painstakingly through the pages. Then her eyes rounded and she lifted her gaze back to his. 'A paper marriage?'

Lincoln smiled a victor's smile. 'Won't that be fun?'

Later, Elodie would barely recall leaving Lincoln's office. She'd only vaguely remember stalking past the smartly dressed receptionist and getting into the lift. Her mind was numb all the way down to the ground floor. It was still barely functioning by the time she met her twin, El-speth, for coffee in Notting Hill half an hour later.

'I was about to give up on you,' Elspeth said as soon as Elodie dropped into the chair opposite with a thump. 'Hey, are you okay? You look a little flustered. What's wrong?'

'Sorry I'm so late.' Elodie placed her purse on the table. 'My meeting ran over time.'

'How did it go?'

Elodie was reluctant to share every detail of the meeting with her twin, even though they were close. It was still too raw.

Lincoln didn't want to sleep with her. It was to be a paper marriage.

The one thing they had got right about their relationship was sex. They'd been dynamite together. No one could ever say there had been something wrong with their sex life. They'd been more than compatible. Why, then, did he want a hands-off arrangement? Did it mean he would have someone else on the side? That she would be humiliated by him conducting numerous affairs under her nose?

'It was…interesting.'

Elspeth leaned forward, her eyes bright. 'So, what was this Mr Smith like? Was he keen to back your label?'

'He was very keen.'

'So why are you frowning?'

Elodie let out a sigh and poured herself a glass of water from the bottle on the table. 'Mr Smith is an alias.' She glanced at her twin's intrigued expression and added, 'It was Lincoln.'

Elspeth's eyebrows shot up. 'Lincoln?'

'Yup. He wants to back my label.'

'Wow.' Elspeth sat back in her chair, her expression puzzled. 'Why would he want to do that?'

Elodie gave her a look. 'Because he wants something in exchange.'

She couldn't keep this to herself any longer. Raw as it still was, she had to talk it through with someone, and who better than her twin?

'Me.'

Elspeth's eyes rounded to the size of the saucer under her coffee cup. 'He wants you back? Oh, how romantic. I always thought he still had feelings for you, and—'

Elodie pursed her lips and shifted them from side to side. 'Not exactly. He wants me to marry him for six months. A paper marriage.'

Elspeth's mouth dropped open. 'A paper marriage? You mean no sleeping together? Seriously? What did you say?'

'I said no.'

'No?'

Elodie frowned. 'Why are you looking at me like that? Do you think I should agree to such a preposterous proposal?'

'I guess if you said yes it would give you both time to sort out your differences. There's clearly unfinished business between you. And if he's going to finance your label—well, surely that's a bonus?'

Elodie leaned her elbows on the table and, bending forward, rested her forehead on her splayed fingertips. 'Argh! I hate that man *so* much. I thought I knew him so well, and yet he kept one of the most important things about himself from me.'

She lifted her head out of her hands and filled her twin in on the circumstances behind Lincoln's proposal.

'I knew I was right to jilt him. This proves it. He didn't allow me to know him. The *real* him.'

Elspeth stroked a gentle hand over Elodie's wrist. 'If you can't bear the thought of accepting the money from him, then let Mack help you. He's happy to finance your label and—'

Elodie raised her face from her hands and sat up straighter in her chair. The thought had crossed her mind before, but she knew she could never ask her twin's fiancé for financial help. She wanted to keep her financial affairs separate and under her control.

'No. I can't accept money from Mack. I have twenty-four hours before I have to give my final answer to Lincoln.' She drummed her fingers on the table for a moment, her thoughts going around on a hamster's wheel. 'You know, there could be a positive spin on this… Imagine the press exposure I'd get if I went back to Lincoln. Who doesn't love a romantic reunion story? The news of us getting back together would go viral. It would boost my profile enormously. Lincoln said it could be a win-win, but I didn't see how until just now.' She beamed at her twin. 'He thinks he has me under his control, but he's in for a big surprise.'

Elspeth chewed at her lower lip, her face etched in lines of concern. 'I hope you know what you're doing.'

Elodie tossed her hair back over her shoulders. 'I know exactly what I'm doing. And, what's more, I can't wait to do it.'

Elodie dressed carefully for her follow-up meeting with Lincoln. She wasn't vain, but she knew the good-looks fairy had been especially generous to her and her twin. And years of being in hair and make-up sessions had given her skills that rivalled some of the top professionals.

Her make-up highlighted the blue of her eyes and the updo of her hair showcased the slim length of her neck. She put on diamond droplet earrings—a gift from one of the lingerie designers. She slipped on an emerald-green designer dress gifted to her after a photo shoot. It came to just above her knee and had a deep cleavage.

She smoothed the close-fitting dress over her slim hips and turned from side to side in front of her full-length mirror. Lincoln might think he could keep her at arm's length, but she had a point to prove. A point to win. A score to settle. He might not have ever loved her, but he'd desired her with a ferocity she knew she could trigger in him again. She'd seen the way he'd looked at her, his scorching gaze running over her body, the way he'd kept glancing at her mouth.

She smiled at her reflection. 'Let's see how long you can keep your hands off me now, Lincoln Lancaster.'

Lincoln was reading through some paperwork in his home office when he caught sight of Elodie on the security camera screen on his desk. He dropped the pen he was holding and stared at her for a long moment, drinking in her feminine form like a badly dehydrated man might stare at a long, cool glass of water, hardly daring to believe it was real.

She was dressed in a stunning green dress that left little to the imagination—and he didn't need much imagination, because he remembered every sexy curve of her body. He had explored and tasted every inch of it, and spent many a night since their breakup aching to do so again. No one had ever worked him up as much as Elodie Campbell. And that irritated the hell out of him.

The desire to settle down had come upon him the moment he'd met her. At twenty-one, she'd been bright and funny and wildly entertaining. He'd been twenty-eight years old, and still reeling from the sudden death of his adoptive mother. Falling fast and hard for Elodie had made him long to recreate the secure family unit he had grown up with. And watching his father slide into a deep depression had only reinforced Lincoln's desire to settle down. He'd figured it would offer his dad some hope for the future—a beautiful daughter-in-law, grandkids at some point…

Elodie's energy and vitality had lifted him out of his own funk of grief and within a couple of months he'd found himself on bended knee with an expensive diamond ring in his hand. He had never been the impulsive, spurof-the-moment type, but something about her bewitching personality had unlocked the armour around his heart.

It was a decision he had come to regret, and bitterly, but now he had the power to end their relationship—this time around on his terms.

The only thing he was grateful for was he had never actually told her he loved her out loud. He had shown it in a thousand ways, but saying the words had been difficult for him. Elodie, on the other hand, had professed to love him many times—which just showed how empty those three little words could be. They were cheap, and overused, and he had been fooled by them, but he would not allow himself to be taken in by them again.

Elodie used people to get where she wanted to go, and she had used him callously and deceptively. She had been a virtual unknown before her fling with him, but her career had taken off after she'd jilted him. She had ruthlessly used him to get the social exposure she'd craved. That was the thing that niggled at him the most—she had used *his* public humiliation to launch her career.

Now she needed him in her quest for a career-change and he was happy to help. More than happy to help. Because this time around he would call the shots. Each and every one of them. Or die trying.

Elodie shifted her weight from foot to foot, annoyed that Lincoln was keeping her waiting again. She knew he was home, for his top-model sports car was parked in the driveway and there were lights on in his Victorian mansion.

She pressed her finger on the bell once more and looked directly into the security camera positioned above the entrance. She considered waving, but then the stained-glass and glossy black arched double front doors suddenly opened automatically, and she stepped inside.

The doors whispered shut behind her with a barely audible click, somehow giving her a vague sense of being imprisoned. She shook off the sensation and straightened her shoulders. She wasn't one to be intimidated by anyone or anything—even if this house did hold some memories she wished she could forget. Disturbingly sexy memories that made her body feel hot all over.

'Hello?' Elodie's voice echoed eerily in the spacious foyer.

The floor was light-coloured Italian marble with grey flecks and the walls a chalk-white. From the high ceiling hung a large crystal chandelier, and a grand sweeping staircase with black balustrading wound its way to the upper floors. A walnut and brass inlaid drum table with curved pedestal legs was positioned in front of the staircase, and a cymbidium orchid in luscious full bloom was situated on top, with a selection of hardback wildlife and wilderness books.

On the other side of the foyer there was a large brass inlaid dresser with twin crystal lamps either side of a gold-framed mirror that made the area seem even more spacious. Another orchid was positioned between the lamps, and either side of the dresser were two dark grey velvet wing chairs, which gave a welcoming and balanced feel to the formal entrance.

The sound of a footfall on the staircase brought her gaze up and she watched as Lincoln came towards her. She was glad it was him and not his crotchety old housekeeper, who had never made her feel welcome in the past. Hopefully Mean Morag had long gone.

Lincoln was wearing casual latte-coloured chinos with a light blue open-necked casual shirt that made the blue in his eyes dominate the green. The shirt was rolled halfway up his strong tanned forearms, the rich dusting of masculine hair spreading from his arms to the backs of his hands and along each of his fingers reminding her of the potent male hormones surging through his body.

'I've been expecting you.'

His voice held a trace of amusement, and she wondered how long he had been watching her via the security camera.

'It took you long enough to open the door.' Elodie threw him a churlish look. 'I was freezing my butt off out there.'

His eyes ran over her outfit from head to toe, lingering a moment on the deep valley of her cleavage. 'Then maybe you should have worn a coat.'

And spoil the knock-his-socks-off effect? No way.

Elodie sent her gaze around the foyer once more. 'You've redecorated since I was here last.'

No doubt he'd gone to great expense to rid his house of every trace of her. She seemed to recall he'd had a fling with an interior designer a few years ago. One of many glamourous women he'd been seen out and about with in the seven years since their cancelled wedding. Lincoln could barely change his brand of toothpaste without the press commenting on it, which was why her decision to accept his proposal would be so lucrative and important for launching her label.

'What do you think?' he asked.

She gave an indifferent shrug. 'It's nice enough.'

Lincoln's smile was sardonic, making her wonder if he could read her mind. 'Would you like a drink?'

'Sure.'

He led the way to a grand sitting room off the foyer, which had three large windows on one side overlooking the formal garden. A large sofa and matching armchairs were positioned in the middle of the room on a luxurious rug that left a wide boundary of the parquet floor on show. The grand fireplace had a large mirror above the mantelpiece and another crystal chandelier hung from the ceiling. Lamps were tastefully situated between each of the three large windows, on antique tables, and there were fresh flowers on the round coffee table in front of the sofa and chairs.

Elodie plonked herself down on one of the chairs and crossed her legs, watching as Lincoln went to a cleverly hidden drinks cabinet complete with fridge on the wall further along from the fireplace. 'Have you still got the same housekeeper?'

'I have, actually.' Lincoln took out a bottle of champagne and set it on the top of the cabinet with two tall crystal flutes. 'Will that be a problem for you?'

Elodie inspected her nails rather than meet his gaze. 'Why should it be?'

He popped the cork on the champagne. 'I seem to recall you and Morag never quite hit it off.' He proceeded to pour dancing bubbles into the two glasses.

'That's because she didn't respect me. I was your partner…your fiancée. But behind your back she treated me like I was gold-digging trailer trash. It was one of the first things she said to me when I met her. "You're only after his money and fame".'

That she had benefited from that fame after their breakup was neither here nor there, in her mind. Elodie had not agreed to marry him for any other reason than she wanted to be with him. Because… Because she'd been a silly little fool back then, who'd thought lust equalled love.

A taut line formed around Lincoln's mouth, as if he recalled every heated argument they'd used to have over his housekeeper. 'Perhaps you didn't treat her with the respect she deserved.'

He came over with the two glasses of champagne, handing one to her. Elodie did everything she could to avoid touching his fingers as she took the glass, but in spite of her efforts a tingle shot up her arm when his fingers brushed hers.

'Or perhaps she always knew you weren't going to stick around.'

Elodie made a snorting noise and took a generous sip of her champagne. 'She was just plain rude to me. She should have retired years ago.'

'Elodie.' The was a heavy note of censure in his tone and a frown was carved deep into his forehead.

She gave a nonchalant shrug and took another sip of champagne. 'So, aren't you going to ask me what I've decided about your proposal?'

Lincoln sat opposite her on the large sofa and stretched one of his strongly muscled arms along the back. 'I already know what you've decided. You wouldn't be here if your answer was still a flat-out no.'

Elodie circled one of her ankles round and round, not sure she was comfortable with him being able to read her so well. 'I've thought it through and I agree with you. It can be win-win for both of us—especially with the on-paper-only clause.' She raised her glass in a mock toast, painting a sugar-sweet smile on her lips. 'I would never have accepted without that.'

Lincoln rose from the sofa and placed his champagne glass on the coffee table between them with a thud. He straightened and nailed her with his gaze. 'There are some ground rules we need to establish from the get-go. Just because we don't sleep with each other doesn't mean we sleep with anyone else during the duration of our marriage. Is that clear?'

Elodie raised her eyebrows and whistled through her teeth. 'My, oh, my... That's going to be harder for you than me, isn't it? Celibacy isn't quite your thing, as I recall. You had someone else in your bed within a week of our cancelled wedding.'

His jaw became granite-hard. 'And that rankled, did it?'

'Nope.' She injected her tone with insouciance. 'I didn't want you, so why would I be upset someone else did?'

His eyes bored into hers with the intensity of an industrial strength drill, but Elodie was determined not to look away first. The tension in the air was palpable. A vibrating, pulsating tension that travelled along the invisible waves of silence like an electric current.

'But you want me now.' A cynical smile slanted his mouth and his eyes glinted challengingly.

Elodie laughed and tipped back her head. She drained her champagne glass, then leaned forward to set it on the coffee table next to his. 'Actually, I think you've got that the wrong way around. It's you who wants me.'

'And you know this because...?'

Elodie rose from the sofa and sashayed over to where he was standing, driven by an irresistible and recklessly rebellious urge to make him eat his words. She stood right in front of him and, locking her gaze on his, slid her hands up his muscular chest to rest on the tops of his impossibly broad shoulders. She breathed in the intoxicating scent of him—the wood and citrus and salty male scent that sent her senses into a tailspin. His eyes were hooded, his expression inscrutable, but she could sense a palpable tension in him.

'I know this because of the way you look at me.' She ran her index finger down the straight blade of his nose.

'It's the way you've always looked at me. Like you want to lick every inch of my body.' She kept her voice husky and whisper-soft, her gaze sultry.

He drew in a breath and let it out in a jagged stream. 'I told you the rules.'

Elodie moved a little closer, so her breasts brushed against his chest. A wave of incendiary heat swept through her at the contact, making her inner core contract with longing. She lifted her finger to his lips, tracing the sensual shape with deliberate slowness. 'You know all about me and rules.'

Lincoln grasped her by the upper arms in a hold that hinted at the coiled tension in his body. His eyes were diamond-hard, his expression grimly determined. 'We're not doing this.' The words were bitten out through tight lips.

Elodie stood on tiptoe, which pressed her breasts even more firmly against his chest. Her mouth was so close to his she could feel the warm waft of his breath mingling intimately with hers. 'But we both want to, don't we?'

She brushed her lips against his firm ones but he didn't respond. Goaded by his intractability, she pressed her lips on his and then slowly stroked her tongue along the seam of his mouth. He smothered a groan-cum-curse deep in his throat and crushed his mouth to hers.

It was a kiss that contained so many things—unruly and fiery passion, frustration, and even a little anger. Elodie didn't care. All she wanted was his mouth on hers, working its old magic on her senses. His tongue entered her mouth with a commanding thrust so like the way he'd used to enter her body she almost came on the spot. The taste of him was so familiar it triggered a firestorm of lust in her flesh. She groaned against his lips, winding her arms around his neck, needing, wanting, aching to be closer to the hard ridge of his erection.

No one could turn her on like Lincoln. No one. His touch was so electric, his kiss so explosively passionate, she had no hope of resisting even if she'd wanted to.

But just as quickly as the kiss started it ended, as if a cord had suddenly been tugged out of an electric appliance.

Lincoln pulled away from her with a cynical smile. 'Not going to happen this time, baby.'

Elodie disguised her disappointment behind a cool smile. 'Let me guess—there's someone else? I hope you're not going to humiliate me by seeing her while you're married to me.'

'You're a fine one to accuse *me* of humiliation.' There was no mistaking the bitterness in his tone, or the rigid set of his jaw. 'I think you deserve the prize for that.'

Elodie wasn't proud of the way she had ended their relationship, but at the time it had seemed her only escape route. She had let things go too far without talking to Lincoln about her career plans and her worries over how their relationship would cope. How she would juggle being a wife with being a lingerie model.

He had said he wanted children at some point. Even his father had mentioned how much he was looking forward to grandchildren. But what would have happened to her career if she'd got pregnant sooner rather than later? At the age of twenty-one, having children wasn't even on her radar. And even now, at twenty-eight, she still hadn't heard a single peep from her biological clock. Her career was her focus. Her drive and ambition left no room for anything else.

'I understand how embarrassing it must have been for—'

'But it achieved what you wanted it to achieve, didn't it? You were a nobody until you got involved with me.

Jilting me got you the press attention you always wanted, and you built your career off the back of it.'

Elodie stared at him speechlessly for a long moment, her mind whirling like clothes in a tumble dryer. He thought she had *used* him? That nothing about her involvement with him had been more than a tactical move to gain fame? That might be her plan now, but back then she *had* loved him. Truly loved him. Had told him so many times. Her feelings for him had been overwhelming—so much so they had contributed to her rash decision to jilt him.

She had sensed that if she married him, her career would never be a priority. Her priority would be him. His priority would never be her. To Lincoln, all she would have been was a trophy wife. He had never told her he loved her, and until the last moment she had been too star-struck by him to see that was a problem—an alarm bell she should have paid far more attention to. She had fooled herself into believing he was one of those men who wasn't comfortable with expressing his emotions. She had fooled herself into thinking he actually *felt* the emotions just because their lovemaking was so incredible.

But complete strangers could have incredible sex—love had nothing to do with it.

Elodie walked over to the drinks cabinet, where Lincoln had left the champagne bottle, and brought it over to refill her glass. She placed the bottle down on the coffee table and sent him a sideways glance. 'I find it highly amusing that you're accusing me of using you when all you wanted was for me to be a trophy wife, a bit of arm candy to show off to all your friends and business associates. You didn't love me.'

Lincoln compressed his mouth into a flat line. 'At least

we're equal on that score. Love was never a part of our relationship.'

There—he had admitted it. He had never loved her. Elodie did everything in her power to disguise the pain his words evoked. But then she had always been good at masking her emotions, and if she couldn't mask them she ran away from them.

Growing up with a twin with a life-threatening nut allergy had taught her how to play down her panic, to keep cool under pressure, never to show the turmoil she was actually feeling at the thought of losing her sister. In a perverse kind of way, she had adopted a devil-may-care approach to life. And her rebellious streak had strengthened as her mother's overzealous attention had focussed more and more on her twin. Negative attention was better than no attention, and it was a pattern that had followed her through life.

'I'd like to know more about what you expect of me during our six months marriage,' she said, with no trace of the turmoil she was feeling. 'What are our living arrangements, for instance?'

Lincoln picked up his glass of barely touched champagne but didn't drink from it. 'We'll live together but have separate rooms.'

Elodie raised her brows. 'And what's your housekeeper going to think about that?'

Would she have to endure more rejection? More stinging little asides from the housekeeper about how she wasn't good enough for Lincoln and never would be? Words that had been reinforced by the rejection of her father and everyone else who had never believed in her and only seen value in her looks, not in her as a person.

'She'll think what I pay her to think.'

'You're not worried she might leak the truth about our relationship to the press?'

'No.'

Elodie twirled the contents of her champagne glass, her eyes still trained on his masklike expression. 'What about when either of us needs to travel for work? Are you going to come with me and expect me to come with you?'

'We'll be together as much as possible, when work and other commitments allow.'

Elodie wondered what his 'other commitments' might be. For a man with such a healthy and robust sexual appetite, she couldn't imagine him taking on celibacy for six days, let alone six months. And how would she cope with living with him in close proximity? Especially given their passionate history? The sexual chemistry between them was ever-present. It was like a current in the air...a humming, buzzing frequency that sent tingles all over her flesh.

She took a sip of her champagne and then asked, 'Are we having a big wedding? I mean, it would look more romantic and convincing if we—'

'No.' The word was delivered bluntly. 'We'll be married in a register office with only two witnesses.'

'No press?'

His gaze was steely. Impenetrable. 'I'll make an announcement once we are officially married.'

'And when will that be?'

'Tomorrow.'

Elodie widened her eyes, felt her heart slipping sideways in her chest. 'That soon? Don't you have to get a license and stuff?'

'Already done.'

How had he been so confident of her agreeing to his proposal? Did he think she still had feelings for him? Feelings he could take advantage of to suit his own ends? But her feelings for him were in deep freeze. She had locked her heart in a block of ice that was resistant to his charm. She could not afford to fall for him again.

'You were so sure I'd say yes?'

'I've learned that nothing is ever a certainty with you, but let's say I was quietly confident.'

'You do know I'm only doing it for the money, don't you?'

His half-smile was cynical. 'But of course.'

Elodie put her glass down and tucked a loose strand of hair behind her ear. 'And when do I get to meet your mother?'

'The following day. We'll fly to Spain and spend a couple of days there.'

'She lives in Spain? Is she Spanish, or—?'

'English. But she enjoys the warmer climate there. It's where she wants to spend the rest of her days.'

'What if it doesn't suit me to fly to Spain?' Elodie asked, not sure she wanted to agree to his plans without some token resistance, even though Spain was one of her favourite destinations and she was increasingly intrigued to meet the woman who had given Lincoln up as a baby.

What had been her reasons? Her circumstances? What had made her feel she had no choice but to hand her baby over to others to rear?

'People will expect us to have a short honeymoon. And I'd prefer you to meet Nina as soon as possible. Her health is unreliable. Her doctors can't seem to agree on how long she's got.'

Elodie could only imagine how sad it must have been for him to have finally found his birth mother, only to face the prospect of losing her all over again. He obviously cared about her, otherwise why go to the trouble and inconvenience of marrying his ex-fiancée, the woman who had publicly humiliated him seven years ago?

Elodie wanted to make a good impression on Nina—not for Lincoln's sake but for the woman herself. But how could she, given the train wreck of their history? How much had he told his birth mother about her? And what if Nina had already done her own research? The internet was full of the scandals that clung to her name, with the latest one naming her as the 'other woman' in a misnamed 'love triangle' that had seen a society wedding cancelled—eerily, like hers had been—at the altar.

Her twin, Elspeth, had been there, in a twin-switch, because Elodie had had a financial meeting that meant she hadn't been able to get there for the rehearsal in time. Then the meeting had been extended, which had given her the perfect excuse not to go to the wedding at all. She had dreaded the fallout if the bride had ever found out she'd had a one-night stand with the groom…

The only good to come out of it had been Elspeth meeting the groom's older brother, Mack MacDiarmid, and now they were happily in love and getting married in a month's time.

'But what if Nina doesn't like me?'

'She'll love you, because she believes you to be the love of my life.'

Elodie couldn't hold back another frown. 'Is that what you told her?'

His expression was unreadable. 'It's what she wants to believe.' He lifted his glass to his lips and drained the contents. He lowered the glass to the coffee table with a definitive thud and added, 'And you will do everything in your power to make sure she continues to believe it. Understood?'

Elodie gave him a mocking salute. 'Loud and clear.'

Lincoln held her defiant gaze for a beat or two. 'I'll pick you up at ten in the morning. Pack what you need for the time being, and anything else can be picked up later. I'll cover the rent on your flat for six months. The ceremony isn't until twelve, but we have some legal paperwork to see to first. And I'd appreciate it if you'd keep up appearances with all your friends and family and associates. We'll have a dinner celebration here with my family—and yours, if they can make it. I know it's short notice, but I don't want anyone to suspect our relationship isn't the real deal in case it gets back to Nina.'

'You mean lie to them?'

'I'm sure it won't impinge on your conscience too badly.' He flicked an invisible piece of lint off his rolled-up sleeve and continued, 'I heard about your deception at Fraser MacDiarmid's wedding. It created quite a scandal. How did Elspeth cope with pretending to be you for the weekend?'

'She got herself engaged to Mack MacDiarmid, so I'd say very well indeed. But that raises another issue. Their wedding's in a month's time, and since you and I'll be married you'll be expected to be there with me. It's likely to be a big affair. Will you be able to act like a devoted husband who's madly in love with his wife?'

'I'll do my best.'

'And we'll have to share a room if everyone thinks we're in love and sleeping together.'

The thought of it sent a tremor of unease through her body. Not because she was worried he would take advantage of such a situation, but because she wasn't sure she could resist him if he did. There was a particular intimacy about sharing a room, even if not sharing a bed. Taking turns to use the bathroom, dressing and undressing and moving about the space they shared… It would stir a host of memories she had spent the last seven years doing her level best to forget.

Lincoln's smile didn't reach his eyes. 'We will have to give the appearance of being in an intimate relationship at all times and in all places. And, judging from your kiss a few minutes ago, that's not going to be too hard for you to achieve.'

'That kiss was hardly one-sided. I thought you were going to make—'

'I wasn't.' His tone was adamant and it cut her like a knife. 'I meant what I said about the rules. A paper marriage is a lot easier to dissolve than a consummated one. Once the six months is up we'll get a simple annulment and move on with our lives.'

He made it sound so simple, so clinical, when her feelings about him and their arrangement were anything but. Six months as his wife on paper. Six months acting the role of devoted intimate partner. But another way of looking at it was to think of it as six months building her career, making the most of the time to launch her own label. Being Lincoln's wife would lift her profile like nothing else could.

His wife… How those words made her insides tighten with unruly desire.

Elodie leaned down to pick up her purse. 'I'd better get going. I'll need my beauty sleep for the big day tomorrow.'

Lincoln placed a hand on her wrist as she straightened. 'I won't be made a fool of twice.'

She held his determined gaze, her skin tingling where his fingers curled around the slender bones of her wrist. 'Nor will I.' She brushed off his hand with a stiff smile.

'Let's leave the intimate touching for when there's an audience, shall we? Or have you already changed your mind?'

A devilish glint appeared in his eyes. 'If I do, you'll be the first to know.'

CHAPTER THREE

ELODIE TOOK OVER an hour to decide what to wear for her wedding day. *Her wedding day.* What a mockery those words were in the context in which she was becoming Lincoln Lancaster's wife.

Her wedding day seven years ago had involved a team of hair and make-up experts, a designer gown and a hand-embroidered veil that had had a train two metres long. Her bridesmaids, including her twin, Elspeth, had attended her, along with a cute flower girl and a cheeky little boy who had been ring bearer. The church, complete with an angelic-sounding choir, had been packed with guests and flowers.

A fairy tale setting without the happy ending.

She didn't like to think too deeply about her regrets over how she'd ended her relationship with Lincoln. She knew she had hurt her mother and her twin—especially Elspeth, who'd had received a lot of undeserved criticism when everyone had assumed she must have known something.

But even Elodie hadn't truly known what she was going to do until she'd done it. It had been an impulsive decision that, at the time, had felt like her only option. She suspected the only hurt she had inflicted on Lincoln was to his pride. He hadn't been in love with her, so it wasn't as if his heart had been shattered by her jilting him. But even so, she did feel a twinge of guilt that she had bolted without talking to him face to face.

And now she was facing another wedding day with Lincoln. But what had changed in seven years? He still didn't love her, and he was only marrying her to give his birth mother her dying wish to see him settled. Elodie couldn't help feeling compromised about lying to someone who had so little time left. What if his mother saw through their act? What if his mother was like his housekeeper and disliked her on sight?

The streak of rebelliousness in Elodie's nature had her reaching for a black dress for their wedding. But then she thought of Lincoln's mother and changed her mind, and chose a cream one instead. There would be photos of the event, and no doubt they would go online. She couldn't afford for anything to look amiss—especially when she hoped to use her marriage to Lincoln as a platform to build her own success.

She made sure her hair and make-up were perfect, and she put on pearl earrings and a pearl necklace that teamed nicely with the classic cut of her calf-length dress.

The doorbell sounded and Elodie took a deep calming breath and addressed herself in the mirror. 'You can do this.'

The door opened and Lincoln's breath stalled in his throat. Elodie didn't have to try too hard to look stunning at the best of times, but right now she could have stopped traffic. Air traffic. Her cream dress had a swirly skirt with a chiffon overlay that fell to her shapely calves, and the upper part of the outfit clung to her curves in all the right places. Places he had touched, kissed and caressed in the past and wanted desperately to do so again.

His continued desire for her was a problem, given the terms of their marriage. He wanted no complications, and sleeping with Elodie Campbell would be one hell of a complication. Not because it wouldn't be exciting, thrilling and deeply satisfying—because it would be all that and more. But sleeping with her in the past had made him fall in love with her, and he couldn't allow his feelings to be triggered again. Besides, he was only allowing six months for their marriage. His mother's doctors hadn't been precise on her expected lifespan, but they had all agreed it would be a matter of three or four months, tops.

'You look stunning,' he managed to say once he could get his voice to work.

'I dragged this old thing out of the back of the wardrobe,' Elodie said. 'I figured you wouldn't want me to wear my old wedding dress.'

Lincoln frowned. 'Do you still have it?'

A fleeting sheepish look came over her face. 'It was custom-made and cost a fortune.'

'You could have sold it.'

'Nah, too much trouble.' She turned to collect her purse and keys and her phone off the small hall table. 'I keep it as a reminder not to do stupid things.'

'Do you still have your engagement ring?'

She turned to look at him with a frown pulling at her brow. 'I took it back to your house. Didn't you find it?'

'When did you bring it?'

'I dropped it off after I left the church when I…left. No one was home, so I used my key and left that as well, with a note.'

Lincoln wasn't sure he should believe her. The ring had been ridiculously expensive, and would have fetched a decent sum if she had sold it. He hadn't specifically asked for it back. He hadn't been interested in any contact with her after that humiliating day. But it had niggled at him all these years that she hadn't done the decent thing and at least offered to return it. And if she had returned it, why hadn't his housekeeper mentioned it? Surely Morag would have found it in her spring-cleaning efforts the following day? Trusting Elodie was not something he was prepared to do.

He slipped his hand inside his jacket pocket and took out a ring box and handed it to her. 'Just as well I have a backup.'

Elodie took the ring box from him, her forehead still cast in a small frown. She prised open the lid and stared at the classic halo diamond ring he had chosen. It was far simpler than the one he had purchased for her seven years ago, but no less expensive. Money wasn't an issue for him when he had a goal to achieve. And making Elodie his wife for six months was his primary goal.

'Aren't you going to try it on?'

'Sure.' Elodie took the ring out and handed him back the box. She slipped the ring over her finger and held her hand up to the light to inspect the quality of the diamond. 'It's lovely. But I'll definitely give it back to you in person once we end our marriage.'

Lincoln held her gaze for a beat. 'No. You can keep it as a souvenir—like the wedding dress.'

She gave him a defiant look. 'I'm not the sentimental type.'

He gave a crooked smile and leaned down to pick up the two large suitcases near the door. She had never been one to travel light. 'Come on. We have some paperwork to sign before we get married.'

'You mean a pre-nuptial agreement? That sort of thing?' Elodie said on her way with him to his car.

'We both have assets to protect. As I said before—it will make an annulment a lot less complicated.'

'You didn't get me to sign one seven years ago.' There was an accusatory note in her voice.

'I didn't have as many assets back then, and nor did we actually get married, so it's a moot point.'

'But what if we had got married and subsequently divorced? Weren't you taking a risk by not insisting on a pre-nup?'

Lincoln shrugged one shoulder and opened the passenger door for her. 'Maybe I trusted you back then.'

'But you don't now?'

A wounded look came into her blue eyes. He held her gaze for a pulsing moment. 'Trust has to be earned once it's been broken.'

'I was never unfaithful to you. And I did bring back your damn engagement ring.'

She got into the passenger seat and swished the skirt of her dress out of the way, her expression stormy.

Lincoln closed the door of the car and walked around to the driver's side. He slipped in beside her and pulled down his seatbelt, clipped it into place. He turned to look at her, but she had turned her head to look the other way.

'Elodie, look at me.'

'No.'

He reached out his hand and captured her small, neat chin, gently turned her to face him. He frowned at the shimmer of tears in her eyes. He blotted an escaping one with the pad of his thumb.

'Tears?'

He couldn't keep the surprise out of his voice. He had never seen her cry—not even when they'd had furious arguments with each other in the past. She'd always given as good as she got and never resorted to floods of tears.

Elodie batted his hand away, her expression churlish. 'I'm not crying. It's just a reaction to my new eyeshadow. I—I think I must be allergic to it or something.'

Lincoln brushed his bent knuckles across the creamy curve of her cheek. He couldn't stop his gaze from drifting to the plump contours of her mouth.

'Hey…'

His voice came out low and deep and husky, and her shimmering eyes crept up to meet his. Something in his chest came loose, like a tight knot unravelling. He brushed the pad of his thumb over the cushion of her lower lip, back and forth, watching as her pupils dilated and her lips softly parted. He leaned closer and lowered his mouth to hers in a feather-light kiss. It was a mere brush of his lips across her soft ones, but it sent a shockwave of ferocious lust through his body.

He eased back to gaze into her eyes before he was tempted to take the kiss deeper. 'Let's see if we can get through the rest of today without fighting, hmm?'

She brushed at her eyes with an impatient flick of her hand. 'Good luck with that.'

Their meeting with his lawyer was held in a smart office a few blocks from where they were to be married. There were documents to read and papers to sign, but Elodie found it almost impossible to concentrate. Her lips were still tingling from Lincoln's brief kiss in the car, and her emotions were see-sawing.

She couldn't remember the last time she had shed tears. She didn't do emotional displays—she had taught herself not to—but for some reason Lincoln's lack of trust in her had stung far more bitterly than it should. So what if he didn't believe her about the stupid engagement ring? She knew the truth, even if he didn't believe it.

How could two people be so unsuited to marry? They were enemies, not lovers. There was so much residual angst between them and yet they were about to become man and wife. Lincoln had called a truce, but how long would that last?

A short time later they arrived at the register office. Lincoln had organised two employees from his office to act as witnesses.

The ceremony was conducted with brisk efficiency and zero sentimentality. Had that been Lincoln's plan? To make this ceremony as different as it could possibly be from their wedding day seven years ago? There were no flowers, no angelic-sounding choir, no bridesmaids, no flower girl and impish little ring bearer. Just two people she had never met before, witnessing what was supposed to be the happiest day of one's life.

'You may now kiss the bride.'

Elodie was jolted out of her reverie when Lincoln drew her closer. His hands framed her face and his mouth came down to hers in a kiss that totally ambushed her senses.

His kiss was gentle, and yet passionate, tender and yet determined, and she was swept away on a rushing tide of longing. She forgot where they were…was not conscious of anything but the exquisite sensation of his lips moving sensually on hers. Her lips remembered every contour of his mouth, every movement of his lips as they stirred her senses into rapture.

She opened her mouth under the delicious pressure of his, and while he didn't deepen the kiss, it was no less thrilling. In fact, it intensified the experience, heightening all her senses to every subtle movement and sensation. The soft press of his lips on hers, the intake of his breath, the audible gasp of hers, the tilt of his head as he changed position, the slight rasp of his masculine skin against her soft feminine skin, the splay of his fingers as he cradled her face in his hands.

It was a kiss that stirred sleeping feelings into wakefulness—feelings Elodie had thought would never come back to life. Feelings she didn't want to come back to life because they threatened to take over her life and her dreams and aspirations.

That could *not* happen.

It *would* not happen.

She would not *let* it happen.

The repeated clicking of a camera shutter was the cue Elodie needed to pull away. She kept her features in a mask of pretend happiness for the photographer, knowing that every photo would be crucially important to achieving her goal.

Lincoln put his arm around her waist and led her outside, where some paparazzi were waiting. 'This shouldn't take too long,' he said in an undertone. 'Leave the talking to me.'

Elodie glanced up at him with a frown. 'Why? I can speak for myself. I handle the media all the time. Besides, I want to make the most of the attention on us. It will put a spotlight on my new label like nothing else could.'

His lips tightened momentarily, as if he was going to argue the point with her, but then he gave a sigh. 'Fine, but don't overplay it.'

One of the journalists pressed forward with a recording device. 'Congratulations to you both. Can you tell us how you got back together?'

Elodie beamed at the journalist and leaned her head lovingly on Lincoln's broad shoulder. 'We realised we'd never fallen out of love and decided to get married as soon as we could.'

'We're happy to be together again,' Lincoln said, his

arm around her waist tightening. He led her down a series of steps to the footpath, with the group of journalists moving backwards in order to keep snapping pictures.

'Lincoln, congratulations on winning back your runaway bride. Does this mean we'll be hearing the patter of tiny feet any time soon?'

'We haven't made any plans in that regard,' Lincoln said with a cool smile. 'Now, if you'll excuse us, we're looking forward to some time alone to celebrate our marriage.'

Lincoln led Elodie to his car, half a block away, with the paparazzi following all the way, taking numerous shots of them together. Elodie kept her blissful bride face on, but inside she was ruminating on his comment about children.

Did he still want children some time in the future? Obviously not with her, as their marriage was not going to be long-term. But did he one day want to settle down and raise a family, similar to the one he was raised in?

Even though she didn't feel any particularly strong maternal urges, she couldn't help feeling a twinge of jealousy that another woman, one day in the future, would be the mother of Lincoln's children. But what place did her jealousy have in a six-month marriage agreement? None. She had signed the paperwork and she had accepted the terms. Their marriage was not the happy-ever-after type. It was an agreement so that she could receive the necessary finance for her label and Lincoln could assure his mother, before she died, that he was finally settled with the 'love of his life'.

Lincoln helped Elodie into his car and was soon behind the driver's seat and pulling away from the kerb. 'Nice work back there. You almost had me convinced you'd fallen madly in love with me.'

'Ha-ha.' Elodie gave him the side-eye and then turned to smile sweetly for the lingering journalists. Once they had driven clear of the paparazzi, she twisted in her seat to look at him. 'That comment you made about kids back there to the paps… *Are* you planning on having a family one day? I mean, after we end this arrangement?'

There was no change in his expression, but his fingers tightened ever so slightly on the steering wheel. 'No.'

Elodie frowned. 'But when we were together seven years ago you talked about having a family.'

'That was then—this is now.'

'I understand that you don't want any kids with me, especially since we'll only be married a matter of months, but I thought you'd still want to—'

'I don't.' His tone was curt.

'But why?'

His gaze was fixed on the road ahead, his jaw set as hard as granite. 'Meeting my biological mother changed my mind.'

'But I thought you liked her? She's obviously someone you care about, otherwise why would you be marrying me to make her happy in her final months of life?'

He sent her a grim look. 'I care deeply about her.'

'Have you met your biological father?'

'He died before I was born.' There was no trace of emotion in his voice, and yet she sensed a deep sadness behind his dispassionate answer.

'How?'

'Car crash.'

'How sad for your mother. Did that have something to do with why she gave you up?'

'We haven't discussed it much. She seems reluctant to talk about it, so I don't push it.'

Elodie studied his inscrutable features. What was the story behind his conception?

Thankfully, the forced adoptions of several generations ago were no longer common. Most women who relinquished a baby these days did so because they wanted their child to have better opportunities than they could provide. It was still a difficult decision, and no doubt there were still elements of pressure on some women from their family of origin. But these days there were safety measures in place to give the relinquishing mother a chance to change her mind during the process of adoption. There was even open adoption now, where children maintained their contact with the birth mother while being raised by adoptive parents.

'How are your brother and sister?' she asked.

'Aiden and Sylvia are both doing well.'

Elodie nibbled at her lower lip for a moment. 'Are they adopted as well?'

'No, my parents naturally conceived Aiden a year after adopting me, then Sylvia came eighteen months after him.'

'Wow, that's amazing. But did it make you feel on the outside at all?'

'Not really. My parents were devoted to us all, and my mother in particular insisted that she wouldn't have been able to have her own children if I hadn't come along. She said it so often I eventually believed it.'

'She sounds like she was an amazing person.'

'She was.'

Elodie had seen photos in the past of his family, and never once questioned Lincoln's place in it. She had even met them in person at their engagement party, and they had seemed like a normal family. He even looked a little like his adoptive father, Clive. It still hurt that he hadn't told her he was adopted. It made her feel shut out and in-significant—feelings which had added to the reasons she had run away from their wedding day.

'How did Aiden and Sylvia take the news of our re-union? Are they coming tonight to celebrate?'

'They're looking forward to seeing you again.'

She glanced at him in surprise. 'So they've forgiven me for jilting you?'

'You'll have to ask them yourself.'

She rolled her eyes and gushed out a theatrical sigh. '*Really* looking forward to that.'

He gave a wry sound of amusement. 'Did you manage to convince any of your family to come tonight?'

'Actually, Elspeth and Mack happen to be in London at the moment, so they'll come. Which reminds me—El-speth has a serious nut allergy, remember? I'll have to talk to Morag about making sure her food is not contaminated.'

'I've already spoken to her.'

'Thanks, but I'm not afraid of her, you know.'

Elodie was touched he'd remembered her twin's al-lergy, but wouldn't have minded a showdown with Morag to establish some boundaries. *Start as you mean to go on*, was her credo now. She was not going to allow the house-keeper to walk all over her feelings this time around.

'I know, but I want things to go as smoothly as possible.'

Elodie shrugged and continued. 'Mum can't come, but not because she didn't want to—she's in Ireland with her new partner, visiting his family.'

She decided against telling him she had told her twin the truth about their marriage. She could trust Elspeth to keep quiet and play along with the charade.

'Were your mother and Elspeth surprised by your an-nouncement?'

'Mum is impossible to surprise these days. I think it's because of all the impulsive things I've done in the past.'

He gave a wry *been-there-experienced-that-first-hand* grunt. 'What about Elspeth? Was she surprised when you told her?'

She swivelled in her seat to look at him. 'No, because she thinks you've always been in love with me.'

Lincoln's mouth tightened just a fraction. 'Then let's hope she keeps that fantasy going for the next six months.' He changed gear and added, 'Is your father coming tonight?'

Elodie gave a mirthless laugh. 'No way. I know better than to ask him. He's always got something more important to do.'

She felt rather than saw the weight of Lincoln's glance on her, and mentally kicked herself for revealing her father issues. Showing vulnerability was a no-no in a relationship such as theirs. A transactional relationship that had no place for sharing emotional baggage. Not that she had ever shared much of her baggage in the past… She hated showing any sign of emotional neediness, especially to someone like Lincoln, who was so in control of his emotions—if he had any, that was.

'What about your father? Has he forgiven me too?'

'You won't have any problems on that score. He forgave you long ago.'

But have you? Elodie wanted to ask, but she stayed silent.

If the roles had been reversed, she would have found it near impossible to forgive him if he had jilted her. Rejection was her worst nightmare.

Her fear of being abandoned came from her childhood. Her father had proudly paraded his cute twin girls around until they'd stopped being cute. As a young child Elodie had gravitated towards her father, because her mother had been so obsessed with keeping Elspeth safe from her nut allergy.

Elodie had thought she was her father's favourite, like Elspeth was her mother's. But how wrong she had been. She'd lost her first tooth and her father in the same week. He'd moved on to build a new life and a family with another woman. He hadn't even made the time to come to her ill-fated wedding.

But then, why would he have needed to? He had given her away years ago.

CHAPTER FOUR

THE CELEBRATORY DINNER was not something Lincoln was particularly looking forward to, but he was immensely glad of the distraction. Acting the devoted husband was going to be a stretch, but he preferred it to the alternative. Going home to be alone with Elodie until they flew to Spain the following day was too tempting to think about.

Their kiss at the wedding ceremony had stirred up a host of erotic memories he had tried for years to suppress. The hands-off paper marriage he was insisting on was not going to last long if he didn't pull himself into line. He needed to prove to himself that he could resist her this time around. But resisting her would be so much easier if he could ignore the way she lit up a room as soon as she entered it.

It wasn't just her natural beauty—it was her vibrant energy that spoke to him on a cellular level. He had never met a more exciting lover, and the thought of revisiting their passion was a persistent background hum in his body. A hum he was finding it increasingly difficult to ignore.

Lincoln led the way inside his house and then shrugged off his jacket and hung it over one of the velvet wing chairs in the foyer. 'We have a couple of hours before our guests arrive. I have some emails to deal with in my office. I'll leave you to re-familiarise yourself with the house. Morag has put you in the guest room next to mine.'

Elodie raised her neat eyebrows, her eyes alight with mischief. 'The one with the connecting door?'

Lincoln flattened his mouth into a firm line. 'The door will remain locked.'

She raised her chin, her eyes still glinting. 'Which side is the key on?'

He had to force himself not to stare at the perfect curve of her mouth. That pillow-soft mouth he could still taste on his lips. 'My side.'

She made a moue with her lips. 'Shouldn't there be one on my side too? I mean, fair's fair and all that.'

'I can't imagine any circumstances in which you would need to enter my room.'

Elodie's eyes danced as they held his in a challenging look. 'Oh, can't you?'

A hot shiver ran down his spine and set spot fires in his groin. He reached up to his neck to loosen his tie, which right then was all but strangling him. 'I'll see you later.'

He began to walk away, but one of her slim hands landed on his forearm in a light but electrifying hold. Another shiver shimmied down his spine and hot, hard heat filled his pelvis.

'Don't you think we should rehearse how we're going to behave in front of our guests tonight?'

'Rehearse?'

She moved closer, sliding her hand down his arm, her fingers ever so lightly brushing over the back of his hand. His skin tingled and his pulse quickened. He could smell the exotic notes of her signature scent—a mix of musk, tuberose and something that was unique to her.

'We'll need to look comfortable touching each other like lovers do.'

Her smile had a sultry tilt that made the heat in his groin smoulder to boiling point.

'Right now, you look tense and uncomfortable.'

Tense was right. He had never felt so hard in his life. He placed his hands on her wrists, intending to put her away from him, but somehow, he found himself doing the opposite. The magnetic pull of her body called out to the humming need in his. He brought her flush against him, not caring that she could feel every throbbing beat of his blood against her lower body.

'Is this the sort of thing you mean? Getting up close and personal?' He kept his tone cynical, but his mind was whirling with the possibility of tweaking the rules.

Elodie moved against him, her yielding softness against his hardness sending a torrent of lust through him. She eased her wrists out of his hold and wound her arms around his neck, her cinnamon-scented breath teasing his senses into overdrive.

'You want me so bad…'

Her voice had a throaty quality to it that only did more lethal damage to his self-control. Lincoln put his hands on her slim hips, holding her to the jutting ridge of his arousal. The feel of her against him sent his senses spinning. She was impossible to resist in this playfully seductive mood. But resist he must.

'We'll embarrass our guests if we don't show some restraint.' His gaze lowered to her mouth and his heart rate spiked. 'Kissing is fine, holding hands, hugging… but that's all.'

Elodie stepped on tiptoe and planted a soft-as-air kiss to his lips. She pulled away so slowly her lips clung to his like silk catching on something rough.

She sent the tip of her tongue over her lips and smiled

at him, her eyes still twinkling. 'Is that chaste enough for you, baby?'

Her purring tone was almost his undoing. *Almost*. He knew she was toying with him and he wasn't going to be so easily manipulated—even though every male hormone in his body was begging him to give in to the temptation she was dangling before him. No one could turn him on like Elodie Campbell. Smart, sassy, sophisticated, sexy—all the things her brand defined her as were catnip to him. But he had to resist her for as long as he could. To prove to himself she no longer had the power over him she'd once had.

Lincoln took her by the upper arms and put her from him, keeping his expression impassive. 'You're playing a dangerous game, sweetheart. And you won't win it.'

Elodie gave a carefree laugh and reached up and pulled her long hair out of its updo, letting the silken tresses fall about her shoulders in fragrant bouncing waves. 'Don't bet on it.'

She blew him a kiss and turned on her sky-high heels and walked away, leaving him burning, burning, burning with rabid lust.

Elodie entered the bedroom next to Lincoln's and closed the door and leaned back against it with a whooshing sigh. She knew it was dangerous, tempting Lincoln into changing his mind about the terms of their marriage. But knowing he wanted her gave her a sense of power—an addictive sense of power she couldn't resist exercising.

Lincoln was a man who held strong opinions. Once he made up his mind he found it difficult to change it. It was one of the reasons they'd locked horns so much in the past. They were both strong-willed and opinionated and neither of them wanted to back down.

If by some miracle she managed to change his mind, she would be flirting with even more danger. The danger of allowing her feelings into the passion they shared. That had been her mistake in the past—falling for him because he was such a fabulous lover. She had confused physical chemistry with emotional attachment. How had she been so foolish to not recognise it? Just because a man knew how to make your blood sing, it didn't mean he was in love with you.

Seven years ago, Lincoln might have been in lust with her—just as he was now—but love had never been part of his commitment to her. He had been willing to marry her, to live with her and have a family with her, but he hadn't been willing to offer her his heart. What sort of star-struck, lovesick idiot had she been to accept him on those terms back then?

Since their breakup Elodie had never felt anything for any of her lovers—not that there had been many. She had actively encouraged a party girl image to go with her smart, successful, sassy, sophisticated and sexy brand. Those five S-words sold the lingerie and swimwear she modelled. But no one had come close to exciting her the way Lincoln had.

Sex for her had been a purely mechanical thing before she'd met him. She had never orgasmed with a lover before him and she hadn't since. It was as if he had cursed her to be unable to fully function sexually without him. Which was part of her reason for wanting to revisit their passion. She needed to know if he still had the same sensual power over her. Judging from the kisses they had shared, it was looking highly likely.

Why was he so insistent on keeping their marriage on paper? It didn't make sense. They both stood to gain from their arrangement—why not exploit it to the fullest extent?

Elodie came downstairs a few minutes before their guests were due to arrive. She wandered into the kitchen to get a glass of water and came face to face with Morag, the housekeeper. A shiver of apprehension scuttled over her flesh, her heart-rate increased and a sense of dread as heavy as stone filled her stomach. She mentally prepared herself for attack, knowing it would be a miracle for the housekeeper to welcome her with open arms, especially after the way she had left Lincoln standing at the altar seven years ago.

She hid her unease behind a breezy smile. 'Hi, Morag. Nice to see you again.'

The older woman's lips pursed. 'So, you're back.'

Elodie waved a hand in front of her body. 'As you see. And blissfully happy. Aren't you going to congratulate me?'

'Congratulations.'

Never had someone sounded less sincere.

'Thanks. It's nice to be back.'

Morag wiped her hands on a tea towel and tossed it to one side, her expression set in disapproving lines. 'How long are you staying this time?'

Elodie gave a tinkling laugh. 'For ever, of course.'

The lie slipped off her tongue with such ease it was almost scary.

Morag harrumphed and picked up a paring knife. She began slicing into an avocado, her brow heavily furrowed. 'If I thought you truly loved him I'd be happy for you.'

Her voice had the stern quality of a buttoned-up schoolmistress dealing with a rebellious child.

Elodie shrugged off the housekeeper's comment with a nonchalant up-and-down movement of one shoulder. 'You're entitled to your opinion, I guess.'

Morag glanced at her with a narrow-eyed look. 'He deserves better than the likes of you.'

Elodie tried to suppress the bubble of anger that rose in her chest, but it was like trying to hold back a flood. And along with the toxic tide of anger there was a deep twinge of hurt because the housekeeper saw her as a taker, not a giver.

She wasn't by nature a people-pleaser. She went her own way and didn't give a damn what people thought about her—or at least she pretended she didn't give a damn. What was it about her that Lincoln's housekeeper disliked so much? It had irritated her in the past, but now, for some strange reason, it hurt as well. Was there something about her that both Morag and her father saw? A flaw that made her unacceptable? Unlikeable? Unlovable?

She moved to the other side of the kitchen to find a glass, but because the kitchen had been remodelled she couldn't find one. 'Where do you keep the glasses?'

'Third cupboard on the right.'

'Thank you.' Elodie found a glass and took it over to the sink and filled it with water. She drank the water and then placed the glass upside down on the draining board. Then she turned and leaned back against the sink to look at the housekeeper. 'Did you know Lincoln was adopted when we were together seven years ago?'

Morag continued artfully arranging the sliced avocado on the seafood starters she was making for dinner. 'I knew.'

Elodie couldn't hold back a frown. He'd told his housekeeper and not her? How was that supposed to make her feel? How could she not feel upset and unimportant? Someone under his employ knew the intimate details of his life, and yet the woman he had asked to marry him did not. He had chosen *not* to tell her.

'Did he ask you not to mention it to me?'

Morag lifted her gaze from her food preparation to meet hers. 'I only knew because his mother Rosemary mentioned it to me in passing one day. Lincoln never told me himself and I didn't see it as my business to tell anyone else.'

'Not even his fiancée? The woman he'd chosen to be his wife?'

The housekeeper gave her an unwavering look. 'I think you already know the answer to that question. It's why you didn't go ahead with the wedding. You didn't love him the way he deserves to be loved.'

Elodie pushed herself away from the sink in agitation. Her feelings about Lincoln had always been the issue. The depth, the intensity, the overwhelming need of him she knew could put her in a vulnerable situation from which she might never escape.

'I wasn't ready for marriage back then. I was young—only twenty-one.'

'And you're ready now?' Scepticism was ripe in the housekeeper's tone.

Elodie straightened her shoulders, her chin at a defiant height. 'You bet I am.'

The first guests to arrive were Elspeth and Mack. Seeing her twin hand in hand with her gorgeous Scottish fiancé made Elodie feel faintly jealous. Not that she wasn't happy for her twin—she was. It was so nice to see her shy and reserved sister enjoying all the things she had missed out on before. But it was obvious Mack adored Elspeth—he could barely take his eyes off her and Elspeth glowed like never before. She was practically incandescent with love.

Elodie had once fooled herself that Lincoln looked at her the same way Mack did her twin. But she had mistaken lust for love and she wasn't going to be so stupid as to do so again. But the lust was real. It still throbbed between them and she was determined to bring him to his knees with it.

She smiled a secret smile. She knew how to seduce Lincoln. She had done it so many times before. He was holding out on her to prove a point. He wanted control this time around. But so did she. And she would damn well get it.

While Lincoln was chatting to Mack, Elodie quickly lured her twin aside to speak to her in private. She led Elspeth to a small room a few doors down from the formal dining room and closed the door once they were inside. 'Els, you're not supposed to know my marriage to Lincoln isn't the real deal, so please keep it under wraps. And, whatever you do, don't tell Mum.'

Elspeth frowned. 'But what about Mack? I've already told him and—'

Elodie let out a stiff curse. 'Will he say something to Lincoln, do you think?'

'I don't think so. He's the soul of discretion at the best of times.'

'Better have a word to him, just to make sure.'

Elspeth took one of Elodie's hands in hers. 'You probably should tell Lincoln that I know. It's not good to keep secrets in a marriage.'

Elodie gave a cynical cough of a laugh. 'Try telling Lincoln that. He's the one who didn't tell me anything about himself when we were together before.'

'Maybe you didn't spend enough time getting to know him. You did have rather a whirlwind relationship.'

'Look who's talking!'

Elspeth blushed a delightful shade of pink, her blue eyes shining with happiness. 'I know, right? It was crazily fast, and I still can't believe Mack and I are getting married next month. He's everything I ever dreamed of in a partner. I only wish you and Lincoln could sort things out and be—'

'Not much chance of that,' Elodie said, and opened the door to return to the dining room. 'Come on. Mean Morag, the crotchety old dragon of a housekeeper, will blame me if dinner is spoilt.'

Lincoln watched Elodie and her twin walk together into the dining room, where the other guests were assembled. The twins were eerily alike, but while he had only seen them together a handful of times, he could always tell them apart. Elspeth was a more introverted and reserved version of Elodie. But that was what had drawn him to Elodie in the first place—her vibrant zest for life and her devil-may-care attitude. She didn't just dare to step where angels feared to tread—she stomped in with her sky-high heels and laughed while she did it.

She was smiling now, her beautiful white teeth framed by a vivid red lipstick, her make-up perfect, her hair a voluminous cloud around her slim shoulders. She had changed into a tight-fighting black dress that clung to her feminine curves in a way that made him fantasise about peeling it off her later.

But the rules were the rules and he needed them in place. He had rushed into a fling with her in the past and it had blown up in his face. This time he wanted control. And falling madly in love and lust all over again was not going to help him maintain it.

Elodie came over to him and nestled against his side, gazing up at him adoringly. He had never said she wasn't a good actor. No one would ever think she wasn't thrilled about being married to him. But then, she was getting a heap of publicity out of their reunion. The photos of their wedding had already gone viral, and he was fielding dozens of requests for an exclusive interview. No doubt so was she.

Lincoln slipped his arm around her waist, the feel of her against his side sending shivers down his spine. 'Come and say hello to Dad, and to Aiden and Sylvia and their partners.'

He led her to where his family were gathered, enjoying the drinks and nibbles provided by Morag.

'Welcome home, Elodie, my dear,' Clive Lancaster said with a warm smile. 'This is my partner, Jan.'

Elodie smiled and greeted everyone in turn. 'It's so nice to see you all again. And so good of you to be here to celebrate with us tonight at such short notice.'

Clive clapped a hand on Lincoln's shoulder, his eyes shining with warmth and fatherly affection. 'I wouldn't have missed it for anything. I've waited a long time for Lincoln to settle down with the only woman he has ever loved. And maybe I'll get those grandbabies now, eh?'

'Ri-i-i-ght...' Lincoln smiled and ignored the twinge of guilt in his gut about the truth of his marriage to Elodie.

He didn't like lying to his family, but needs must in this case. He had to provide his biological mother with the peace she longed for before she passed away. Nina still agonised over her decision to relinquish him as a baby. She longed to see him happily settled, to have the assurance that her decision hadn't permanently damaged his ability to love and be loved.

But love wasn't part of his arrangement with Elodie and nor had it ever been, in spite of her regular and gushing declarations of it in the past. If she'd loved him she wouldn't have jilted him. In his mind it was a simple as that. If she had truly had deep feelings for him she would

have expressed her concerns about their relationship—
not left him standing in front of a congregation of guests
looking like a fool.

There was a part of him that would never forgive her
for that. The humiliation had stung then and it still stung
now—which was why he was keeping firm control of the
way things would play out between them going forward.

Elodie sipped glass after glass of champagne and nibbled
at the delicious food the housekeeper had placed in front
of her and the other guests. Lincoln was seated at the head
of the long dining table, his father at the other end. Elodie
was on his left and felt acutely conscious of everyone—
particularly the members of his family, who were watching her every movement, gesture or expression.

Her face was aching from smiling, and her brain was
fried from trying to make convivial conversation with everyone. Normally she loved a good party. She could work
any room like a pro without a moment's worry about putting a foot wrong or, indeed, about what anyone thought
of her.

But for some reason it felt wrong to be pretending
to Lincoln's family that their relationship was genuine.
The only thing that was genuine was the lust simmer-
ing between them. She was aware of the pulse of it every
time Lincoln took her hand, his fingers warm and strong
around hers. Every time he locked gazes with her, every
time he brought her hand up to his mouth and kissed her
bent knuckles, or the ends of her fingers, a lightning-fast
current of erotic energy passed from his body to hers,
leaving her wanting, wanting, wanting…

Clive rose towards the end of the meal, glass in hand.
'Let's toast the happy couple. To Lincoln and Elodie. May

your future be bright and happy and fulfilling and blessed with children.'

Elodie reached for her glass but, anxious, somehow managed to knock it over instead. 'Oops.'

Lincoln righted the glass and refilled it within seconds. He held his glass against hers. 'To us.'

She clinked her glass against his, her expression as radiant as her twin's. 'To us.'

But then, she was good at masking her true feelings. No one would ever guess at the turmoil inside her at the thought of having Lincoln's baby. He didn't love her. How could she raise a family with someone who didn't love her? It was asking for heartbreak. The sort of heartbreak she had run away from seven years ago. The sort of heartbreak her mother had suffered.

Where was the 'for ever love' Elodie's father had once claimed to feel for his wife and his cute twin daughters? It had gone away like a wisp of smoke as soon as someone more interesting came along.

'Now for the first dance,' said Sylvia, Lincoln's young sister. 'Go on, you two. Show us your moves.'

Elodie wasn't the type of person to blush, but as soon as Lincoln gathered her in his arms a rush of heat flowed from her cheeks to her core. He held her close, hip to hip, thigh to thigh, cheek to cheek, as they danced to the music Aiden had jumped up to put on the sophisticated sound system.

It was a romantic ballad that was poignant and bittersweet—which perfectly described her situation. It wouldn't matter if she were married to Lincoln for six months or six decades. She would never be able to guarantee he would love her the way she longed to be loved. He could *act* as if he did. No one looking at him now would think he wasn't madly in love with her. But she was too much of cynic to think he would ever open his heart to her. She was still a trophy wife—a beautiful bit of arm candy to show off to his dying mother and convince her she hadn't done the wrong thing in relinquishing him as a baby.

Lincoln tipped up her chin and looked into her eyes. 'Did I tell you how beautiful you look tonight?'

Elodie smiled, even though his words kind of proved her point. He loved the way she *looked*. He didn't love *her*.

'You look pretty damn awesome yourself.' She linked her arms around his neck and swayed against him with the music. 'You feel pretty damn awesome too.'

His hands grasped her hips but he didn't separate their bodies. He brought her harder against him, in spite of their watchful audience. His blue-green gaze blazed with lust… the same lust she could feel pounding in her own body.

He lowered his mouth to just below her ear, his lips sending shivers coursing down her spine as he spoke in an undertone. 'You're enjoying yourself a little too much, aren't you?'

Elodie gave a breathy laugh and rolled her head further to one side, to give him better access to the sensitive skin of her neck. 'You're making it hard not to enjoy myself. No one would ever think you weren't desperate to get me alone right now.'

His hands tightened on her hips and his lips moved across her skin as lightly as a feather, stirring her nerves into a frenzy.

'I am desperate to get you alone…but not for the reason you think.'

His voice was a low, rough burr of sound that made her spine tingle from top to bottom. She framed his face in her hands, staring into his eyes with brazen defiance.

'You mean you're *not* going to make mad, passionate love to me on our wedding night?'

'You know the rules.'

His eyes glinted with determination and she could feel the war going on in his body. He was fighting their mutual attraction, but she was confident she would bring him down.

She smiled a sultry smile. 'I just love it when you draw a line in the sand.'

'Why?'

'Because I get such a kick out of stepping over it.'

And then she planted her lips on his.

CHAPTER FIVE

FOR A MOMENT Lincoln forgot they weren't alone. As soon as her lips met his a fire erupted in his body. An inferno of lust that left no part of him unaffected. His groin tightened, the backs of his legs tingled and his self-control scrambled to get back on duty.

But it was always this way with Elodie. Her passionate and rebellious nature spoke to him in a raw, primal way that was nothing short of overwhelming. Need pummelled through his flesh, making him hot and tight within seconds.

He had existed for seven years without this heady rush of excitement. How had he done it? It seemed impossible that he had lived in a wasteland of substandard sensuality when he could have had this fiery intensity of lust. Her mouth was soft and yet insistent, and he answered it with the thrust of his tongue, mating with hers in a playful duel that sent another rush of blood to his groin.

'Get a honeymoon suite, you guys!' called out his brother Aiden with a laugh.

Lincoln lifted his mouth off Elodie's with a cynical smile only she could see. 'We'll finish this later.'

One way or the other, he *had* to get control of his desire for her. She was exploiting it and he was in danger of caving in like a horny teenager lusting over his first crush.

'Ooh, I can hardly wait.' Her eyes danced with mischief and she eased out of his arms to go and sit next to her twin.

Lincoln went back to the table and pretended to listen to a conversation between Mack and his father. He picked up his wine glass and took a token sip, but no amount of alcohol could make him as drunk as Elodie's sexy mouth. That soft and supple mouth had in the past been all over his body, sending him to the stratosphere multiple times.

He suppressed a shudder and picked up his water glass instead and took a long draught. He put the glass back on the table and caught Elodie's eye. She smiled and gave him a fingertip wave, and another rush of heat flowed through his flesh.

It was probably only a few minutes later that everyone began to leave, but to Lincoln it was like hours. Finally, the door closed on the last of their guests and Lincoln and Elodie returned to the dining room, where Morag was busy clearing everything away.

'Let me help you with that,' Elodie said, stepping forward to help stack some plates.

'Leave it,' Morag said, without even turning from the table to look at Elodie. 'You'll only end up breaking something.'

Lincoln frowned at his housekeeper's clipped tone. He had never heard her be so brusque with Elodie—or indeed with anyone before. But then, Morag hadn't seen him enter the room with Elodie, as her back was to the door. He'd always thought Elodie had exaggerated the housekeeper's behaviour towards her in the past. Elodie was a bit of a drama queen and liked being the centre of attention. Morag's no-nonsense, stay-in-the-background personality was the total opposite. But now he wondered if he would have done better to keep an open mind. He had known his housekeeper a lot longer than Elodie and sided with her. Had that been a mistake?

Elodie continued stacking the plates, her lips in a tight line, her handling of the top-shelf crockery not exactly gentle. The clatter and clang of cutlery and china was obviously her way of showing how upset she was.

'It may surprise you, Morag, but I'm quite domesticated these days. I can stack a dishwasher, do my own laundry and cook a decent meal.'

'You'll need more skills than that to keep your husband happy,' Morag shot back.

Elodie placed the plates on the trolley that would ferry them back to the kitchen. 'I have plenty of *those* skills too.'

Her tone was pure sass, and her *don't-mess-with-me* expression a warning even he took note of. He knew all about those skills of hers. The sensual skills that gave him thrills like no other person ever had before or since. The sensual skills he was trying not to be tempted by. But he realised he had vastly underestimated the explosive chemistry that still existed between them. Would it lessen if he indulged it or would it get out of control?

'Morag, why don't you leave this for us to clear away?' Lincoln said. 'You've worked long enough today. Go home and we'll see you when we get back from Spain.'

Morag turned from the table and wiped her hands on her apron, her expression unrepentant. 'She'll only bring you trouble. She doesn't love you.'

'It's none of your damn business *what* I feel about him,' Elodie flashed back, blue eyes blazing.

'Elodie—' Lincoln began in a calming tone, but she was having none of it.

'You always side with her,' Elodie said, turning to him. 'I'm your *wife*, for God's sake. You're supposed to... Oh, never mind.' She tossed the cutlery she was holding with a loud clatter on top of the plates on the trolley. 'I'm going to bed.'

She stalked out, slamming the door behind her.

Lincoln sighed and raked a hand through his hair. Drama and Elodie were never far away from each other, but he would have to get used to it—and so would his housekeeper. Otherwise the following six months would be unbearable.

Sacking Morag wasn't an option. She had been a stalwart support for more years than he could count—first to his mother, as a long-term friend, and since his mother's death Morag had been his link to her—one he wasn't ready to sever. She often gave him little vignettes of the two of them growing up as close friends, stories of their escapades and adventures and childhood games that kept his mother alive for him in his mind.

'Morag, go easy on her, yeah? I want things to work this time.'

The housekeeper's mouth tightened. 'She'll break your heart again. You mark my words.'

He wanted to tell his housekeeper that he hadn't had his heart broken, just his pride, but Morag had witnessed first-hand the fallout from Elodie jilting him.

'I'm not going to allow anything like that to happen,' he said, with the utmost confidence.

He was in control now. Emotions were not part of their relationship this time around and he was going to keep it that way.

Elodie was in her en suite bathroom, taking off her make-up, when there was a knock at the door. 'Go away.'

'Come on, sweetheart, open up,' Lincoln said, rapping his knuckles on the door again.

She slammed the toner bottle down on the counter and

tossed the cotton pad in the bin. She opened the door and glared at him. 'If you've come to give me a lecture about being nicer to your housekeeper, then you're wasting my time and yours.'

'I've come to apologise.'

Elodie knew she shouldn't be mollified so easily, but something about his tone made her anger melt away. Her shoulders went down on a sigh and she came out of the bathroom, tightening the ties of her wrap around her waist a little more firmly.

'You're seven years too late with your apology.' She threw him a petulant look from beneath her lowered lashes. 'She's always been unnecessarily rude to me.'

Lincoln came over to her and raised her chin with his index finger, locking his gaze on hers. 'I'm sorry I didn't listen to you about that in the past. I can see there's tension between you.'

Elodie made a scoffing noise. 'Tension? You don't know the half of it.'

He placed his hands on her shoulders and gave them a gentle squeeze. 'I thought you didn't care what people thought of you?'

She lowered her gaze from his to stare at the collar of his shirt. 'I don't. But I don't think someone you employ to take care of your house should treat your…your… wife like she's gold-digging trailer trash. I earn my own money—heaps of it, actually. Not enough to launch my own label, but still…'

Lincoln raised her chin again, to mesh his gaze with hers. 'I've spoken to Morag and you shouldn't have any trouble in future.'

'And if I do?'

He drew in a breath and released it in a long exhalation. 'Then I'll deal with it.'

'How? By firing her?'

He released her, stepped back and rubbed a hand over his face. 'I don't know. She's worked for me a long time. She was a friend of my mother's—they went to primary school together. She had a rough time growing up, then she married a brute of a man who physically abused her every chance he got. They had a couple of kids who both ran off the rails and barely speak to her now. She finally got the courage to leave him and has worked for me ever since. Plus, she developed Type Two diabetes recently. She would probably find it hard to get another job that pays as well and with such flexible hours.'

Elodie sat on the edge of the bed with her hands resting either side of her thighs. She was secretly impressed by his commitment to his housekeeper. Morag was clearly a vulnerable person who had been taken advantage of in the past. Her heart ached for her and what she had been through. It was no wonder she didn't find it easy to let people into her life. It reminded her a little bit of herself.

'My God. I'm sorry to hear Morag has been through all that. She doesn't deserve to be treated that way. No one does. But hurt people don't heal themselves by hurting others. You have to work through your own pain rather than project it on to someone else.'

Lincoln twisted his mouth into a grimace. 'I guess that's how it plays out sometimes. She's a little set in her ways.'

Elodie flopped backwards on the bed, flinging her arms above her head. 'Oh, God, I'm so tired of how the world can hurt people. It's one of the reasons I want to work for myself. You would not believe the rubbish I've had to put up with for years.'

Lincoln came and sat beside her on the bed, but he didn't touch her. Even knowing he was within touching distance made every cell in her body throb with awareness.

'What sort of stuff? Sexual harassment?' His frown was heavy, his expression gravely serious.

She rolled her eyes like marbles in a jar. 'Nothing I couldn't handle on my own.'

He reached out and brushed a strand of hair back from her forehead. 'You shouldn't have to handle that stuff on your own. That stuff shouldn't happen in the first place.'

'Yeah, well, it still does.' She rolled over so she was facing him on her side, even more conscious of how close his body was to hers. 'Thanks for listening. I don't talk to anyone about this stuff except Elspeth, and half the time I don't tell her the full extent of it. It would shock her too much.'

'You try to be strong for her, don't you?'

Elodie let out a puff of air. 'Yes, well... I'm not the one with the life-threatening allergy, am I? When our father left...' She frowned and then continued, 'I didn't see it coming, you know? I thought he would always be there for us, and for me in particular, because he always called me his favourite girl. It was all lies. He didn't love anyone but himself.'

'I'm sorry you had such a jerk of a father. I can only imagine how that has impacted on you.'

Elodie met Lincoln's gaze, finding in it a warmth and an emotional connection that was completely disarming. 'I think I've spent a lot of my life pretending to be someone I'm not. The cutesy outgoing twin, the cheeky extroverted kid who caused drama wherever she went. The blissfully happy bride-to-be...until I got cold feet, when the reality of being your wife—anyone's wife, for that matter—hit me.' She twisted her mouth and continued, 'I've had to be tough all my life. And I can see now why

Morag is the way she is. It's emotional armour to keep from getting hurt.'

His eyes held hers, his pupils dark as black holes in outer space. 'It was never my intention to hurt you or block you from your dreams.' He took one of her hands in his and gave it a gentle squeeze. 'I wish you'd talked to me about this stuff way back then.'

'Yes, well… We didn't do a lot of talking, as I remember. Apart from arguing. And then having make-up sex.' She gave a rueful smile and continued, 'It was nice being with your family tonight, although I couldn't help feeling guilty about all the pretence.' She frowned and added, 'I can't help worrying that they'll be terribly hurt when we end this. I mean, your father seemed so convinced I'm the love of your life.' She gave an incredulous laugh and added, 'I can't imagine being the love of *anyone*'s life. I'm too much hard work.'

Lincoln stroked his fingers through her hair in a slow, mesmerising fashion, sending shivers over her scalp and down her spine.

'Sometimes hard work brings its own rewards.'

His eyes became hooded and drifted to her mouth, and a wave of longing coursed through her. He leaned on one elbow, his other hand stroking up and down the length of her satin-covered thigh.

'I like your sister's fiancé, Mack. They seem a good match.'

'Yes, she's very happy and I'm happy for her.' Elodie toyed with one of the buttons on his shirt and added, 'I consider myself a bit of a matchmaker, actually. If I hadn't got her to go in my place to the wedding she might never have met Mack.'

There was a beat or two of silence.

'Why did you have a one-night stand with Mack's

brother Fraser that night?' Lincoln asked. 'The night we ran into each other at that bar in Soho?'

Elodie shuffled away and sat upright and hugged her knees. 'I hope you're not going to go all double standards on me about having a one-night stand. You've had plenty.'

'I'm not denying it, but it seemed out of character for you.'

She gave him the side-eye. 'Were you jealous?'

'No.' His expression was masklike, except for a knot of tension in the lower quadrant of his jaw.

Elodie got off the bed and smoothed her hands over her satin wrap. 'It was awful, if you want to know…'

She wasn't sure why she was telling him about a night she would rather wipe from her memory for good. Running into Lincoln with his latest squeeze had rocked her far more than it should. The stunning young woman had been draped all over him, her adoration for him obvious for all to see. It shouldn't have upset Elodie one iota, but for some reason it had thrown her into a tailspin. His partner had looked *so* in love with him. The same way Elodie had once looked up at him—as if he was the only man in the world who could make her happy.

Her mind back then had run through a reel of thoughts—would he announce their engagement soon? Would they settle down and have the family he had once wanted with her?

To distract herself, she'd flirted outrageously with Fraser MacDiarmid, determined to show Lincoln she was completely and utterly over him, but it had backfired spectacularly a few months later.

Lincoln rose from the bed in a single movement and came over to her. 'Did he…hurt you?' A thread of anger underpinned his voice and his expression was a landscape of concern.

Elodie hugged her arms around her middle and gave him a stiff, no-teeth-showing smile. 'It was consensual but crappy sex.'

His eyes held hers. 'You didn't enjoy it?'

'If you're asking did I come, then, no, I didn't.'

Why are you telling him that?

But it seemed now she'd opened her mouth, she couldn't stop confessing the rest. She gave him a pointed look. 'It's your fault, you know. You've spoilt me for anyone else.'

A frown formed on his forehead. 'What do you mean?'

She blew out a long breath. 'I haven't enjoyed sex since we broke up.'

There was a weighted pause.

'Have there been many lovers?' Lincoln's tone was mild—casual, almost—and yet she sensed an undercurrent of avid interest he was trying his best to hide.

Elodie unwound her arms from around her middle. 'Not as many as I've led people to believe.' She speared a hand through the loose tresses of her hair and continued, 'I suppose that gives your male ego a massive boost? That I can't come with anyone else?'

His expression didn't register surprise, for hardly a muscle moved on his face, and yet she still suspected he was shocked. Deeply shocked. And why wouldn't he be? The press had documented her every move over the last seven years, linking her with various high-profile men. She had played to the cameras, using every opportunity to lift her profile. Some of the men she had had flings with—many she had not.

'Casual sex isn't for everybody.' His tone was as hard to read as his expression.

Elodie gave a mirthless laugh. 'You seem to do all right. As I recall, you didn't even wait a week before finding someone else after our breakup.'

Seeing him in a gossip magazine with an attractive partner within a week of their aborted wedding had struck at her heart like a closed-fist punch. If he had cared for her even a little, wouldn't he have waited just a while in case she changed her mind? But, no. He'd moved on so rapidly it had confirmed she had done the right thing in calling off their wedding. For if he had loved her wouldn't he have at least tried to change her mind rather than replace her?

Lincoln rolled his bottom lip over his top one in a contemplative gesture, his eyes still holding hers. After a long moment, he released a long-winded sigh. 'I didn't sleep with anyone for months after we split up.' His voice was low and rough around the edges.

Elodie stared at him, her heart skipping out of its normal rhythm. 'But…but I thought… *Really?*' She leaned on the word, suddenly desperate to know the truth. 'Why not? And why did you give everyone the impression you'd moved on so quickly?'

Lincoln looked down at the floor, where he was idly using the toe of his shoe to straighten the fringe of the Persian rug. When he raised his gaze back to hers his expression was still unreadable.

'I'd better let you get some sleep. We fly first thing in the morning.' He moved across to the door with long, purposeful strides.

'But wait,' Elodie said, following him, placing a hand on his arm before he could open the door to leave. She looked up into his enigmatic features, her mind whirling from what he'd told her. 'Was it because you were hoping I'd come back to you? You thought I might change my mind?'

He held her gaze in an unwavering lock for endless seconds, but there was no clue to what he was thinking. It was like trying to read the expression on a marble statue.

'Do you really think I would've taken you back?' he said at last, in a cynical tone that stung far more than it should.

Elodie kept her expression as masklike as his. She removed her hand from his arm and stepped back. 'No.'

The door closed behind him and she let out a rattling sigh.

Why would he if he hadn't loved her in the first place?

The journey to Valencia in Spain the following day took just over six hours door-to-door. Elodie spent most of it with her head buried in a collection of fashion magazines, determined to keep her distance, knowing that as soon as they were in Nina Smith's presence the charade of being a happily reunited loved-up couple would begin.

Lincoln seemed just as disinclined to talk—he had business papers in his briefcase and wore a preoccupied frown for most of the journey.

A car was waiting for them at the airport, with a young uniformed driver called Elonzo. *'Buenas tardes, Señor Lancaster.'* He smiled shyly at Elodie and added, *'Señora, mucho gusto.'*

'It's nice to meet you too,' Elodie said, with an answering smile that made the young man blush in spite of his olive complexion.

Lincoln helped Elodie into the car and they were soon on their way to the villa at Sagunto, about twenty minutes' drive from the airport. The sunshine was blindingly bright, the air warm in comparison to the chilly autumn weather back home.

'Have you been to Sagunto before?' Lincoln asked.

'No, but I've been to a few other places in Spain. It's one of my favourite destinations. The people are so friendly, the food is great—and don't even get me started about the weather.'

Lincoln gave a lazy smile and laid his arm along the back of her seat. 'You've already won over one heart.' He nodded towards the young driver, who was shut off from them by a panel of glass for privacy. 'Let's hope Nina is as easy to win over.'

Elodie angled her head to look at him. 'You don't call her "Mum" now that your adoptive mother has passed away?'

He absently toyed with the loose strands of her hair, sending electrifying tingles down her back.

'I don't think it's appropriate. My adoptive mother will always be my mother, so too my father. They earned the titles by the love and care they gave me all those years.'

'Given you had such a nice childhood, I find it intriguing as to why you no longer want children yourself.'

His hand stopped playing with her hair and went back to resting along the back of her seat. A line of tension formed around his mouth. 'When my mother died I was thrown off course, as were my father and siblings. Pancreatic cancer took her so quickly. One minute she was well, the next she was critically ill, and she died within a few weeks. Dad went into a slump. I'd never seen him so low…' He released a long sigh and continued, 'Then I met you and I suddenly saw a future. A bright and happy future that would include kids and family life—the sort of family life my parents had given me.'

Elodie frowned, not sure she liked his reasons for wanting to marry her back then. They didn't seem to have anything to do with *her*. She could have been any suitable woman to fill the role as his wife and future mother of his children. He had liked what she represented—a beautiful wife to grace his home—but he hadn't loved *her*.

'But you don't hanker after that family life now?'

'Aiden and Sylvia are planning on having kids with their partners,' Lincoln said. 'My father will be thrilled to have a bunch of grandkids to dote on. I can concentrate on my work and on living life the way I prefer.'

'Footloose and fancy-free.' She didn't state it as a question but as a statement of fact. 'Once a playboy, always a playboy.'

Lincoln gave a mercurial smile. 'My inner playboy is on pause for the next six months.'

Elodie gave him a pointed look. 'Can I trust you on that?'

His eyes drifted to her mouth and then back to her gaze. 'The discipline will be good for me.'

CHAPTER SIX

NINA WAS WAITING for them in the salon, where bright
shafts of sunlight were coming in from the large windows,
casting her in a golden, almost ethereal glow. She rose
from the sofa and came towards them with both hands
outstretched, her expression warm and welcoming.

'It is so lovely to meet you at last, my dear. Lincoln has
told me so much about you.'

Elodie took the older woman's soft hands in hers and
gave them a gentle squeeze. 'It's wonderful to meet you
too. And lovely of you to have us stay with you for a couple of days.'

Nina kissed Elodie on both cheeks and then, releasing
her hands, turned to Lincoln. Her eyes watered, as if she
could barely believe he was really standing there in front
of her. It touched Elodie to see the love in Nina's eyes.

'Lincoln, darling, thank you for bringing your beautiful wife to meet me. I know you're terribly busy, and I
really do appreciate it.'

Lincoln enveloped his biological mother in a gentle
hug. It was as if he was worried he might break her. She
was indeed a little thin, and had a frail air about her, but
her eyes were sparking and clear.

'It's always good to see you. How have you been?'

Nina eased out of his hold with a crooked smile. 'So-

so. Some days are better than others. But today is a good day.' She beamed at Elodie. 'Shall we have a drink to celebrate your marriage? Alita has made some sangria. We can go out to the terrace and enjoy the view.'

A short time later they were sitting under a large umbrella on the terrace with tall glasses of delicious and refreshing sangria in front of them. Elodie couldn't take her eyes off the stunning vista in front of her: ancient Roman ruins, including an outdoor theatre, interspersed with lush green hills and the port of Sagunto in the distance.

'Wow, it's so lovely…' She put her glass down before she was tempted to drain it. The last thing she wanted to do was get tipsy in front of Nina. But then, being here with Lincoln, especially with him sitting so close and holding one of her hands, was enough to make her feel drunk.

'It's my happy place,' Nina said, with a smile that encompassed Lincoln as well.

'Have you lived here long?' Elodie asked, reaching for one of the marinated olives on the tapas plate on the table.

'Two years,' Nina said and, glancing lovingly at Lincoln, added, 'Lincoln bought the villa for me as a birthday gift soon after we met. So very generous of him.'

Elodie put the pit of her olive on the little dish set on the table for such a purpose. She knew all about his generosity. He had bought her expensive gifts in the past—the missing engagement ring being a case in point. It still irked her that he didn't believe she had taken it back to his house. But if he hadn't found it, surely his housekeeper had? It couldn't have disappeared unless someone had stolen it—someone else who'd come into the house that day. Her new engagement ring was even more expensive, but she realised with a jolt that it was his trust she valued the most. That, to her, was priceless. Would he ever give it to her?

'I guess he missed a lot of your birthdays, so it was his way of making up for it.'

Nina's smile faded and she sighed and looked away into the distance. 'Yes, a lot of birthdays…'

Lincoln released Elodie's hand and stood, bending down to drop a light kiss to the top of her head. 'If you will excuse me? I'm going to have a chat to Elonzo about some maintenance that needs doing. I'll see you at dinner.'

Elodie waited until he had walked down the stairs from the terrace that led into the expansive gardens below before she turned back to look at Nina. 'It must have been very difficult to give him up all those years ago.'

Nina's eyes shimmered and her chin gave a distinct wobble. She reached for her glass of sangria but didn't drink from it. Her fingers moved up and down the frosted glass in a reflective manner.

'I wanted to keep him so much. It tore my heart out to give him up. But I was young and left reeling after the death of Lincoln's father. He was killed in a motorcycle accident on his way to see me when I was four months pregnant. I didn't have my family's support. They were deeply religious, and I knew bringing a born-out-of-wedlock child into the family would have a negative impact on the child in the long run.'

She glanced at Elodie, her expression pained.

'I decided to give Lincoln away to give him the best chance in life. I always thought I did the right thing, but when I met him a couple of years ago…' She gave a long sigh and continued, 'I could see he wasn't happy. Oh, he was successful, and wealthy beyond belief, and he'd had a good childhood thanks to his wonderful adoptive parents… But in himself… No. Not happy.'

She looked into Elodie's eyes.

'I blamed myself for that. I tortured myself with it. But

now he is back with you he will be content at last. I know it in my heart of hearts.'

Elodie painted a smile on her face, feeling her own heart cramping in her chest at the deception she was complicit in. She was surprised Nina couldn't see through it—but then, didn't people who wanted something so badly see it even when it wasn't there? Nina wanted Lincoln's happiness more than anything else in the world. She believed that happiness and fulfilment could be achieved through being reunited with his runaway bride—*her*.

'I'm surprised you're not angry with me for walking out on our wedding day seven years ago.'

Nina put her glass down and took one of Elodie's hands, holding her gaze once more. 'I didn't know you or Lincoln back then. But I can see you love him now. That's all that matters, yes?'

Elodie looked down at their joined hands, her emotions in turmoil. How could she blatantly lie to a dying woman? It seemed morally wrong to continue the pretence. She sensed a bond with Nina…a connection that was beyond explanation. Or was it because they both loved Lincoln?

'The thing is… I'm not sure he loves me the way I love him.'

There was a silence broken only by the rustling of leaves as a breeze passed by and the tweeting of birds in the shrubbery. In the distance, a motor scooter revved and whined as it went up one of the winding hills leading to the ruins of a castle.

Nina gently stroked the back of Elodie's hand. 'You've always loved him, yes? Even when you called off the wedding seven years ago?'

Elodie met the older woman's gaze, deciding to be honest not just to Lincoln's mother but also to herself. 'I was frightened I was going to lose myself in our relationship back then. Lincoln is so driven and focussed—success is everything to him. And I knew it would be hard to make my own mark on the world while living in his shadow.'

She pulled her hand away and laid it on her lap, curling up her fingers so her engagement and wedding rings caught the light.

'I saw it happen to my mother when my sister developed a nut allergy. She gave up everything to be at home with Elspeth. My dad walked out when we were six, leaving her with the burden of taking care of two little kids, one of whom could die at any moment from anaphylactic shock.' She let out a sigh and continued, 'Mum didn't just lose her career, she lost her potential to be the person she wanted to be. The person she thought she *would* be. I didn't want that to happen to me.'

'We all make choices we have to live with.' Nina gave a wistful smile. 'I've revisited my choice about giving up Lincoln so many times. I wasn't lucky enough to have any other children. I thought I was being punished for not keeping him. Not a day went past that I didn't think of him, wondering what he looked like, what he sounded like, what he was good at and so on. I'd walk past young men in the street and wonder if one of them could be him. I positively ached to find him, but I couldn't summon up the courage until two years ago—I was too terrified that he wouldn't want anything to do with me. I was blessed that he did. And then I realised he wasn't truly happy. I wondered if it was my fault he found it hard to express love because of being relinquished as a baby. You know…what if the bonding issue was ruined for him way back then?'

'But you did what you thought was the best for him at the time. And he had a happy childhood. His parents loved him as their own.'

'I know, and I'll be forever grateful for that. But, like me, you now have to get to a point where you forgive and accept yourself and your choices. You did what you thought was right at the time by calling off the wedding. And now, like me, you've been lucky enough to get a second chance. Not everyone gets that.'

Elodie gave an answering smile touched by melancholy. 'I guess you're right.'

She might be able to forgive herself, but would Lincoln ever do so? That was the question she had no idea how to answer.

Elodie left Nina soon after, so the older woman could have a rest before dinner. The youngish housekeeper-cum-cook, Alita, escorted Elodie to the suite she had prepared with obvious pride. She opened the door of the bedroom on the first floor with a wide smile, her eyes sparkling as if she had binge-watched romantic movies and television shows for most of her life.

'Welcome to the honeymoon suite, Señora Lancaster. Elonzo brought up your luggage earlier. I hope you will be comfortable.'

'Thank you.'

Elodie stepped into the graciously decorated suite, trying not to notice the king-sized bed made up with snowy-white linen and the array of blood-red rose petals artfully scattered on top. The bed might be big enough to accommodate two people, but when those two people were her and Lincoln what would happen? His hands-off rule was going to be tested to the limit, that was what. And her self-control—never good around him at the best of times—was going to be challenged like never before.

Elodie heard the door close behind her as Alita left and let out a long, ragged breath. She moved across the wide expanse of floor to the bed, picturing Lincoln's dark head on the pillow next to hers.

Something in her belly turned over and her heart skipped a beat. She had fought for years to rid her mind of the erotic memories of being in his arms. The pleasure he'd evoked, the intense feelings he'd stirred in her like no one else. But she only had to close her eyes to recall the sensual glide of his hands along her naked flesh. His touch had sent fireworks through her blood each and every time. How could she share a bed with him and not want him?

The door opened again and she turned to see Lincoln standing there with an inscrutable expression. He shut the door with a definitive click that seemed overly loud in the silence. 'Everything all right?'

Elodie folded her arms and pursed her lips. 'The honeymoon suite has been lovingly prepared for us by Nina's delightful young housekeeper.'

He came further into the room and tossed his phone on the end of the bed. 'I'm sure we'll manage to keep our hands off each other.'

She angled her head at him. 'You think?'

He gave an indolent smile and walked over to where she was standing, stopping just in front of her. Close enough for her to see the green and blue flecks in his eyes and the dark bottomless circles of his pupils.

'What? Are you worried you won't be able to keep your hands off me?'

Elodie unfolded her arms and placed them on his chest. 'I have a feeling you *want* me to put my hands on you. You want it very much.'

Her voice came out as a throaty whisper and she felt her pulse kicking up its pace at his nearness. The salt and citrus smell of him teased her senses, and the hard muscles of his chest beneath her hands reminded her of the potent power of his male body. She could almost feel it rising in the small space between their bodies—the arousal he couldn't hide or deny.

She pressed herself against the swollen heat of his body, relishing the potent length of him responding to her in spite of his rules. There were no rules strong enough to contain the lust they felt for each other. She could feel it in the air like a third presence in the room. A throbbing invisible energy that drew them together as powerfully as a magnet to metal.

Lincoln's eyes darkened and he drew in a sharp-sounding breath, his hands going to her upper arms in a hold that was on the wrong side of gentle. But she didn't care if he left fingerprints on her flesh. She wanted him. All of him.

'You're playing a dangerous game.'

His tone was rough and deep, his fingers momentarily tightening on her arms.

'What's so dangerous about doing what we do so well, hmm? Or have you forgotten how good we were together?'

His hooded gaze went to her mouth, lingered there for a pulsing moment. 'No, damn you, I haven't forgotten.'

He brought his mouth down on hers in an explosive kiss that sent a rush of heat through her body. His hands left her upper arms to move around her, crushing her closer to him, so close she could feel the hardened ridge of his erection. A frisson passed through her—a delicious frisson that made the hairs on her head stand on end and a pool of molten heat form in her core.

He backed her up against the nearest wall, his mouth still clamped to hers. She arched her spine in a desperate quest for more intimate friction, and gasped when one of his hands lifted her dress to her hips. His hand gliding along her bare thigh sent another wave of intense heat through her core. Damp heat that smouldered and steamed and simmered in secret.

Lincoln's mouth moved from hers to kiss the ultra-sensitive skin below her ear, the movement of his lips sending shivers cascading down her spine. He moved lower to the skin of her neck, and then her décolletage, the caresses light but no less tantalising. His hand slid further up her thigh to the edge of her knickers. Fervid excitement sent her pulse-rate soaring and her stomach swooped.

'Oh, God, *yes*...' she gasped against his mouth.

He traced the seam of her body through the lace of her knickers, his intimate touch making her grind against his hand, desperate to assuage the burning ache of her flesh. He pushed her knickers to one side and his mouth came back down hard on hers, his tongue mimicking the flickering action of his fingers. The tension built in her to snapping point, a rush of sensation barrelling through her until she was swept off into the abyss on a tumultuous tide of pleasure.

Elodie clung to his tall frame, not sure her trembling legs would hold her upright as the aftershocks rumbled through her body. But, as intensely pleasurable as her orgasm had been, she knew she couldn't afford to let him think there was anything more than animal lust between them.

There wasn't and never could be.

She had loved him once, with a consuming, overwhelming love that had almost caused her to give up everything she had planned for her life. But she had come to her senses just in time.

If she had married him when she was twenty-one she would have been little more than a trophy wife. A beautiful woman who would grace his home and bear his children and then be pushed aside when she lost her looks or he got bored with her. She wouldn't have built her career to what it was today. She wouldn't have built her profile to the point where she could use it to fulfil her dream of producing her own designs.

Lincoln had never told her he loved her. She had pressed him a few times, but he had never said those three little magical words. And what was the point of hoping he might say them in the future? He had been blatantly honest about his reasons for marrying her. She was only back in his life because he wanted to give his dying mother end-of-life peace.

There was no other reason.

Elodie straightened her clothes with a sultry smile. 'You certainly haven't lost your touch.' She tiptoed her fingers down to the waistband of his chinos. 'Let's see if I've lost mine, shall we?'

Lincoln's hand captured hers in a firm hold, his expression unreadable. 'No.'

She arched her brows in a cynical manner, determined not so show how much his rejection hurt her. She pulled her hand out of his and opened and closed her fingers, her skin tingling from the heat of his touch. 'You really are serious about those rules of yours, aren't you?'

'I am.'

Elodie shifted her mouth from side to side in a musing way. 'May I ask why?'

'I told you—it will make it a lot easier to dissolve our marriage when the six months is up.'

He moved to the other side of the room, taking his jacket from where it was lying over the back of a chair and moving towards the built-in wardrobe. He slid one of the mirrored doors back and took a coat hanger from the rack. He hung his jacket on it, then placed it in the wardrobe and closed the door again. His actions were precise, methodical, as though the task helped him process his thoughts.

He turned and faced her again, with a light of determination in his gaze that struck a chord of unease in her. 'I don't want any lasting mistakes from our temporary union.'

Elodie frowned, in spite of her determination to act cool and unmoved by his stern composure and stance. 'What do you mean by "lasting mistakes"?'

His eyes bored into hers. 'Are you currently using contraception?'

'Of course.'

A low-dose pill was her only option at the moment, because she had struggled to find one that didn't affect her mood. Not that she was good at remembering to take it regularly. But she'd figured that since she hadn't exactly been putting herself 'out there' since her ill-fated hookup with Fraser MacDiarmid, it was the best alternative. And since Lincoln was so adamant their marriage was to be on paper only—well, what did it matter if it didn't have the same reliability as other methods?

Lincoln held her gaze for a pulsing moment, then his eyes drifted to her mouth and he sucked in an audible breath. 'We'll have to share the bed or Alita and Nina will suspect something is up.'

Elodie gave him a playful smile, sensing he was struggling to keep to his own rules. It gave her a sense of feminine power that sent a thrill through her flesh. He wanted her, but his fight was not with her but with himself.

'Do you want to toss for which side to sleep on? I seem to remember you like being on the right—or have you changed since we last—?'

'The right is still my preference.'

She made a little snorting noise. 'That figures.'

'Why?'

'Because you always like to be right.'

A crooked smile formed on his lips. 'So do you.'

Elodie shrugged in a nonchalant manner, and went to the dressing table where she had left her cosmetics. She picked up her cleanser and then sat on the velvet-covered chair. She caught his eye in the mirror. 'What?'

Lincoln came over and laid his hands on the tops of her shoulders, still holding her gaze in the mirror. 'I haven't really thanked you properly for agreeing to all this.'

There was a different quality to his tone—a softer, warmer note that made her heart suddenly contract.

'All this?'

'Pretending to be in love and happily married. It means the world to Nina to see us reunited.'

Elodie placed one of her hands over his, where it was resting on her shoulder. 'I really like her. It's so sad that she has so little time left with you…especially as you only found each other a couple of years ago.'

One of his hands began playing with the long tresses of her hair in an absent fashion. His touch sent shivers dancing over her scalp and down her spine.

'Life isn't always fair, but we have to deal with it.' His hand fell away from her hair, the other from her shoulder.

Elodie spun around on the chair and craned her neck to look up at him. 'How will you deal with it? Her death, I mean?'

Lincoln let out a long breath and rubbed a hand over his face. 'The same way I coped with losing my adoptive mother.'

She raised her eyebrows. 'By trying to rush into marrying a woman you barely knew and didn't even love?'

There was a beat or two of silence.

Lincoln continued to hold her gaze, but his was

screened—like a blacked-out window in an abandoned building. There was a muscle near the corner of his mouth that twitched once or twice, as if he couldn't decide whether to give a rueful smile or grind his teeth, and then he released a long sigh.

'I wish I'd searched for her earlier. I lost her as a baby and now I'm going to lose her again. When we're only just getting to know one another. She's filled the hole my adoptive mother left behind, but I'm conscious of the time ticking away. Every day that goes by is a day closer to losing her. It's…torturous, to be honest.'

'Oh, Lincoln, I'm so sorry. It must be hard for both of you.'

He gave a stiff movement of his lips that passed for a dismissive smile. 'We'd better dress for dinner. Nina likes to dine early as she gets tired. I'll leave you to get ready in private.'

Elodie watched him stride away to the door of their suite. 'Lincoln?'

His hand had almost reached the doorknob, but he lowered it to his side and turned to face her, his expression guarded. 'Yes?'

His tone was clipped, with an edge of impatience, which only made her all the more determined to get close to him. He had lowered his guard enough to tell her about his sadness over the prospect of losing Nina. What else might he reveal if she encouraged him to be vulnerable with her? Would getting close to him physically unlock more of his emotional armour? What if the Lincoln she'd been engaged to in the past was not the *real* Lincoln? What if, like her, he had kept back a part of himself he allowed few people, if any, to see?

'You don't have to leave while I get ready. We've dressed and undressed in front of each other before—

heaps of times. And we can take turns using the bathroom.' A smile played at the corners of her mouth and she added, 'I promise I won't peek.'

The line of his mouth remained tight, but his eyes darkened. 'I'm going for a walk. I'll be back in half an hour.'

He walked out and closed the door with a firm click that sounded as definitive as a punctuation mark.

Lincoln went for a brisk walk through the gardens to get himself back in line. The more time he spent with Elodie alone, the harder it was to resist her. She was flirting outrageously with him, and he would be lying if he said he didn't enjoy every moment of her playful behaviour.

He did. Too much. Way too much.

But it wasn't just the playful flirting that got to him. She had revealed more about herself than she ever had in the past, and so had he. This new emotional connection between them was strange...foreign to him...because he always kept people at a distance. And keeping Elodie at a distance was supposed to be his top priority.

But she was making it near impossible to keep his hands off her—especially as he remembered all too well how clever those little hands of hers could be. How hot and tempting her soft mouth. Kissing her had almost blown the top of his head off. And the passion that flared between them was getting harder and harder to control.

Her cheeky bend-the-rules personality had always appealed to him—mostly because his nature tended to lean towards the colour-between-the-lines conservative. She evoked in his staider personality a recklessness that was exciting to indulge. She made his flesh sing when she touched him. Her lips had set his alight and he could still taste the fresh sweetness of her. It was like a drug he had forgotten how much he craved. One taste and he was addicted all over again.

But their marriage had a short timeline, and he was adamant there would be no casualties in the aftermath. As far as he was concerned this was a business deal like any other. Emotions were not required, and in fact only blurred the boundaries. And he needed boundaries when it came to Elodie.

Firm, impenetrable boundaries.

Lincoln stood for a moment, looking at the view of the ruins of Sagunto Castle. The fortress-style castle had a history going back two thousand years. His history with Elodie was much shorter. And while the fortress he had built around himself was not quite in crumbling ruins, he would still have to be careful to keep it secure.

But... But...

A persistent voice kept niggling at him. What if he indulged himself with a little tweak of the rules? After all, he had always kept his emotions out of his sex life. Sex was a physical experience he enjoyed on a regular basis, with like-minded women who played by the same rules. No strings, no promises, no commitment other than for a brief interlude of mutual pleasure.

The pleasure he and Elodie had experienced together in the past was something he couldn't eradicate from his mind or indeed from his body. The memory of possessing her, the slick, wet tightness of her body and her passionate response to him, was something he had never been able to recreate to quite the same degree with anyone else. In fact, for years he'd had trouble having sex without his mind drifting to her.

Maybe these six months would be the antidote to his obsession with her. He could finally move on with his life once he had ruled a thick black line under them as a couple.

End of story.

No sequel.

No reruns.

Finished.

Elodie was doing the final touches to her make-up when Lincoln came back to their suite. She squinted one eye to apply her volume-enhancing mascara. 'The bathroom's free.' She blinked a couple of times and then dabbed the wand back into the container. 'I hope what I'm wearing is okay. Not too OTT?'

Lincoln would have preferred to see her naked, but decided to keep that to himself. The hot pink dress she was wearing should have clashed with her red-gold hair and creamy complexion, but somehow she made everything look stunning on her.

'You look great.'

He moved further into the room, resisting the temptation to touch her. He could smell her perfume—a rich, exotic blend of flowers and spice that teased his nostrils and tantalised his senses. Her hair was piled up in a makeshift bun that somehow managed to looked casual and elegant at the same time. But then, that was Elodie to a tee. She would look glamorous without a scrap of make-up on and dressed in a rubbish bin liner.

She reached for her lip-gloss and leaned closer to the mirror to apply it. He couldn't tear his eyes off her plump lips as she painted the glistening colour on her mouth. She pressed her lips softly together and then glanced at him in the mirror, a mercurial smile forming, her blue eyes sparkling like the diamond droplet earrings dangling from her ears.

'Nice walk?'

'Nice enough.'

She picked up a soft brush and dusted some highlighter down the slope of her nose. 'Still hot outside?'

'Yes.'

But not as hot as in here, Lincoln wanted to say, but didn't.

Heat was pooling in his groin—a fiery heat that bloomed and flared like wildfire. If ever there was a time for a cold shower, this was it. He went into the en suite bathroom and closed the door, but even in there he was surrounded by the alluring, bewitching scent of her.

There were wet towels hanging haphazardly over the rail and he suppressed a wry smile. It was certainly an improvement from her leaving them on the floor, as she had so often in the past. He had argued about it with her numerous times, but he had never managed to housetrain her. He wondered now why he'd bothered. Of course, these days Elodie had a team of people picking up after her. She had personal assistants and make-up artists and hair stylists who were at her beck and call, catering to her every whim.

Lincoln had to make sure he didn't become one of them.

CHAPTER SEVEN

ELODIE WALKED DOWN to the dining room with Lincoln a short time later. He was dressed in a casual suit with an open-necked white shirt that brought out the olive tan of his skin. She had briefly left their suite while he showered and changed, not sure she could trust herself not to melt at his feet if he came out dressed in only a towel slung around his lean hips.

Lincoln's arm slipped around her waist as they entered the dining room.

Nina looked up from her seat with a warm smile. 'You both look so good together—like movie stars or something. I love those earrings, Elodie. Did Lincoln give them to you?'

Elodie flicked one of her earrings with her finger. 'No, I was given them by a lingerie designer a couple of years ago.'

'It must be an exciting life…travelling the world and modelling lovely things,' Nina said.

'Yes, well…it's kind of lost its appeal, to be honest,' Elodie said, as Lincoln pulled out her chair for her. She flashed a smile of thanks to him and returned her gaze to Nina. 'I'm pursuing a new career now.'

'Lincoln told me you're an aspiring dress designer. How wonderfully creative. Maybe you could design something for me...' A flicker of something passed over her face and she continued in a subdued tone, 'Not that I could give you much time to do so, given my diagnosis.'

Elodie reached for the older woman's hand and gave it a gentle squeeze, her own eyes watering. So much for never showing her emotions, but something about Lincoln's biological mum's situation tore at her heartstrings.

'I'm sorry to hear you're so ill. Life can be unfair. Is there nothing that can be done? Nothing at all?'

Nina patted Elodie's hand in a resigned manner. 'There have been so many treatments and experiments and drugs, but I'm something of a mystery to my doctors. I get the feeling they don't know what to do with me now. They've run out of options. I've come to terms with it, more or less. But it will be sad not living long enough to meet my grandchildren... I would have loved that more than anything...' She gave a deep sigh and stretched her lips into a smile. 'But let's not be maudlin. I have much to be grateful for and I count each day as a bonus—especially now you two are back together.'

Elodie wasn't game to look in Lincoln's direction and kept her gaze focussed on Nina's. 'I'd love to design you a dress—in fact, a complete wardrobe of outfits. You might as well make the most of the time you have left. And there are such things as miracles. It's good to have some hope, I guess. That's better than giving up, right?'

Nina's smile was so motherly and affectionate it made Elodie's heart all but explode with emotion.

'Sweet child. I can see why my son fell so hard for you. Design away, my dear. I will be proud to wear every item.'

Elodie was so inspired to get to work on some outfits for Nina that she barely touched the delicious food placed before her during the meal. Her mind was buzzing, and colours and fabric designs were swirling about in her head as she planned a bright and colourful collection.

Finally, the meal came to an end and Nina bade them goodnight and retired to her quarters.

Lincoln picked up his still half-full wine glass and gestured to Elodie to do the same. 'Come out to the terrace for a while. It's a little early to go to bed.'

Elodie raised her eyebrows. Was he prolonging the time before the moment they'd have to go upstairs to share the suite? Surely he wasn't...*nervous*?

She curved her lips into a teasing smile. 'Since when is it too early for us to go to bed? I seem to remember us having quite a number of early nights in the past.'

A glinting light appeared in his gaze. 'That was never the problem between us, was it? The sex?'

She glanced over her shoulder to see Alita, the young housekeeper, hovering in the doorway, waiting to clear the room. 'Thanks for a lovely meal, Alita.'

'You're most welcome, *señora*.'

Elodie turned back to Lincoln. 'The terrace sounds like a good idea.'

And, picking up her own glass, she followed him out through the French doors to where a full moon was shining.

The shift of location gave her a moment to reflect on their past relationship. Making love with Lincoln had always been phenomenal. From their very first time it had showed her a world of sensuality and pleasure she hadn't experienced with anyone else before. But while it had been wonderful in every way, it had also covered up the tiny cracks in their relationship that had been there right from the start. Fine cracks that had developed into the deep fissures she had ignored until the day of their wedding, when she hadn't been able to ignore them any longer.

They hadn't communicated other than through sex. And making love was not a good substitute for effective communication. Perfect strangers could have good sex. She had never been able to share her doubts and fears and insecurities with him and he had never shared his—if he'd had any, that was.

'Actually, I think it was a big part of the problem.'

Lincoln leaned against the stone balustrade with his glass in one hand. 'What do you mean?' There was an edge of guardedness in his tone.

Elodie moved across the terrace to stand within half a metre of him and placed her glass of wine on the balustrade. The last thing she needed was more alcohol to loosen her tongue. 'I think we used the chemistry we had together as a distraction from…other things.'

'What other things?'

She half turned to look up at him, but the moonlight coming from behind him had cast his features into an unreadable shadow. 'When we argued over something, we used sex to clear the air rather than sitting down and talking through stuff. Talking about why we had argued in the first place.' She licked her lips and continued, 'It was a pattern we drifted into from the start. Fight and have make-up sex. We never resolved the underlying issue.'

'Which was?'

'We knew each other physically, but not emotionally.'

Lincoln moved so that he was looking out at the moonlit view, his forehead creased in a frown. 'I'm not saying you were totally to blame for our breakup,' he said. 'I didn't like how you went about it, that's all.'

His grip on his wine glass was so tight, she was worried it might break.

'You should've told me you weren't happy,' he added.

'But that's my point. We never *talked* about things. We

never got that far. You were always busy chasing your next big deal, becoming more and more successful, as if that was the only thing that really mattered to you. I was nothing more than an ornament to you. A plaything you enjoyed having at your disposal. I was never your equal.'

He put his glass on the balustrade too, as if he too was worried it might shatter under his grip. He turned to look at her, his expression still in shadow. 'Why did you feel you couldn't talk to me?'

The quality of his tone had changed—become softer, less defensive, more concerned.

Elodie blew out a soft breath. 'I don't know...' She gave a little shrug and continued, 'Maybe because I didn't think you would understand how important having a career was to me. I got the impression you wanted me to be a home-maker, like your adoptive mother, not a career woman. It scared me because that's what happened to my mum. She gave up everything to take care of Elspeth when she got sick. Then my dad left when we were six and poor Mum was left with nothing. No career, no money and no support other than the pittance he sent only because he was legally required to, not because he wanted to. No wonder she turned into a nervous wreck who never seemed to notice she had two children, not just one. I didn't just lose my dad when he left—I lost my mother too.'

There was a silence.

Lincoln reached out with one of his hands to brush a loose tendril of hair away from her face. 'I'm sorry. I didn't realise how hard that must've been for you. I knew your father was a bit of a lost cause, but I didn't know you felt pushed aside by your mother as well.'

Elodie grimaced. 'It's not really her fault. She did her best, and Elspeth was so sick a couple of times that losing her was a very real possibility. I learned to get attention in other ways—not always sensible ways, mind you…but, hey, it worked until it didn't.'

Lincoln's hand moved to capture one of hers, his fingers warm and gentle as he cradled it as if it was a baby bird. 'I guess none of us get out of childhood without a few issues, but it must have been terrifying to think you might lose your twin. You're still close, yes?'

Elodie smiled a little wistfully. 'Yes, she's amazing—especially now she's in love. She's really blossomed. Mack's been wonderful for her and she for him.' Her smile faded and she added, 'But I guess now Mack will be her go-to person, not me.'

Lincoln began an idle stroking over the back of her hand with his thumb, his gaze still trained on hers. 'I'm sure she'll always have a special place in her life for you.'

'Are you close to your siblings? And your father?'

He looked down at their joined hands for a moment, a slight frown pulling at his brow. 'I'm probably not as attentive a son and big brother as I should be. I'm always busy with work and travelling and so on.' He looked back at her and gave a rueful smile. 'Sylvia is always nagging me to make more time for family gatherings, but it's not the same without Mum.'

There was a thread of sadness in his tone that made her realise how deeply he still missed his adoptive mother. And now he had to face the prospect of losing his biological mother. Was it any wonder he would do anything—including marrying *her*—to make Nina's last days as peaceful and happy as possible?

Elodie found herself moving closer to him, one of her hands going to rest against his chest, the other reaching up to stroke the side of his lean jaw. 'Oh, Lincoln, I'm so sorry you lost her. And now you have to face losing Nina too.'

Lincoln settled his hands on her hips, his expression cast in grave lines. 'The thing that gets me is not knowing for sure when it will be. She looks fine at the moment—you'd hardly think anything was wrong. And yet on another day she can go down quickly and need to be in bed all day.'

'But you said the doctors told you no more than three or four months?'

He let out a serrated sigh. 'That was what they said the last time I spoke to them. It's not a long time, is it?'

'No, but I read this saying once: even the dying are still living. It's important that Nina gets to do all the things she wants to do. I meant what I said about designing a new wardrobe of clothes for her. I was mentally preparing sketches during dinner. I can't wait to get started.'

Lincoln smiled and lifted one of his hands to brush her cheek with his fingers. 'She's quite taken with you. I knew she would be.'

Elodie chewed at her lip for a moment. 'I can't help feeling a bit compromised, though. I mean, pretending we're madly in love when we can barely stand the sight of each other...'

He eased up her chin and locked gazes with her, his expression serious. 'Do you hate me that much?'

The problem was that she didn't hate him at all. She had the opposite problem—she was madly, deeply, crazily in love with him. Had she ever *not* been in love with him? She had tried to deny it, hide it, disguise it, but while it was possible to hide it from him, she couldn't hide it from herself. And hadn't Nina noticed it too? The older woman had intuitively sensed the feelings Elodie was keeping under lock and key for fear of being rejected.

Elodie gazed into the darkness of his eyes and tried to ignore the fluttering of her pulse. Tried to ignore the sen-

sual pull of his body, the magnetic energy that drew her
even closer until her hips were flush against his. 'No...
I don't hate you...' Her voice came as a whisper, as soft
as the night breeze currently playing with the tendrils of
her hair.

He framed her face in his hands, his gaze still trained
on hers. 'It would be easier if you did, you know...' His
voice was as rough as the stone balustrade that held their
wine glasses.

'Why?'

'Because then I wouldn't be tempted to do this.'

He lowered his mouth to hers in a long, drugging kiss
that sent shivers racing up and down her spine like elec-
trodes. His tongue entered her mouth with erotic intent,
the glide and stroke of it against hers sending her senses
haywire.

He made a groaning sound and drew her even closer,
wrapping his arms around her. He angled his head to
deepen the kiss, and a warm rush of longing almost overwhelmed her in its intensity. Kissing him wasn't enough.
She wanted to feel his thick, hard presence where she
needed it the most.

She moved against him, signalling her need, and he
sucked in a harsh breath and kissed her more firmly, as
if only just managing to stay in control.

After a few breathless moments, he lifted his mouth
off hers, his eyes glazed with lust. 'About those rules...'

Elodie stepped up on tiptoe and planted another playful kiss to his lips. 'Don't tell me you've changed your
mind about your silly old rules?'

He gave a lopsided smile and cupped the curves of
her bottom in his hands, holding her against the pounding heat of his aroused body. 'Then I won't tell you. I'll
show you instead.'

He scooped her up in his arms, and even though she gave a token squeak of protest continued carrying her through the French doors and all the way up the stairs to their suite.

Once they were inside their bedroom, he let her slide down the length of his body to the floor. Every deliciously sexy ridge of his toned body teased hers into a frenzy of want. Need clawed through her tingling flesh, making her wonder how she had gone seven years without feeling anywhere near this height of sensual awareness.

Lincoln crushed her mouth beneath his, the passionate pressure of his lips and the gliding thrust of his tongue into her mouth only ramping up her desire.

He raised his mouth barely a millimetre above hers, his breath mingling intimately with hers. 'No one turns me on quite like you do.'

Elodie combed her fingers through his hair, barely able to take her eyes off his mouth. How could a man's mouth—this man's mouth—create such a firestorm of need in her body?

'I hate to boost your ego too much, but it's the same for me. I want you even though my head tells me it's a mistake to get involved again.'

He stroked his thumb over her bottom lip, his touch sending tingles straight from her mouth to her core. 'It's only for six months. It's not like we're making any promises beyond that.'

And there was the kicker for her. The time frame. The temporary nature of their marriage. So different from what he had proposed seven years ago. He had once offered her for ever. This time he had only offered for now.

And yet… And yet how could she not accept the new terms? She had not truly moved on from him, in spite of all her efforts. Maybe six months of living and sleeping together as man and wife would help her reframe their relationship. Help her to see it for what it was and always had been—nothing more than a stunning physical chemistry that would eventually burn itself out.

Elodie painted a smile on her lips—a fake smile that pulled at her mouth like too-tight stitches. 'You mean we're not going to fall in love with each other? That's still against the rules, right?'

A flicker of something passed through his hooded gaze, like a blink-and-you'd-miss-it movement in a deeply shadowed forest. 'Do you think it's likely?' he asked.

'You mean for me or for you?'

'For you.'

Elodie kept her eyes focussed on the sculptured perfection of his mouth rather than meet the probing intensity of his gaze. Of course he wouldn't consider himself in any danger of falling in love with her. He hadn't before, so why would he now? He loved how she looked. He was in lust with her. Was he even capable of romantic love?

'Anything's a possibility, I guess.' She brought her gaze back to his with a carefree smile. 'But what has love got to do with red-hot lust, hey? Not much.'

Lincoln brought his mouth down to within a millimetre or two of hers. 'Speaking of lust…' He brushed her lips with a kiss that made her hungry for more. 'Do you have any idea of how much I want you right now?'

She nestled closer, delighting in the proud bulge of his erection. Her inner core tightened in anticipation. The walls of her womanhood were already slick with moisture. 'I think I've got a fair idea.'

She nibbled at the edge of his mouth with teasing little nibbles that she followed up with a sweep of her tongue.

He groaned deep in his throat and grasped her by the hips, bringing her even closer.

'I want to go slowly,' he said in a husky tone.

'Don't you freaking dare…' Elodie pulled his head down so his mouth came back to set fire to hers.

CHAPTER EIGHT

ELODIE WOKE FROM a deep, blissful sleep to find Lincoln had left the bed. She glanced at the bedside clock and frowned. It was three in the morning. She pushed back the covers and slipped on her wrap, tying the ties around her waist. There was no light on in the bathroom, but the doors leading out to the balcony were open, for she could see the billowing of the silk curtains as the night breeze stirred them. She pushed the curtains aside to find Lincoln standing against the balustrade with his back to her. He was wearing his underwear but the rest of him was naked.

'Lincoln?'

He turned and smiled at her. 'Sorry. Did I wake you?'

'Not really.' She went over to where he was standing and touched him on the arm. 'Can't you sleep?'

He picked up her hand from where it was resting on his arm and brought it up to his mouth, his eyes still holding hers. He kissed the ends of her fingers, one by one, his touch sending tremors of pleasure through her body.

'I guess I've got used to spending the night alone.'

Elodie frowned. 'Alone? I don't understand… You mean you don't spend the night with any of your…your lovers?'

Lincoln released her hand and turned back to look at the moonlit view. His hands gripped the balustrade and even in the low light she could see the straining of the tendons in the backs of his hands. 'I prefer not to.'

Elodie stared at him for a long moment, trying to get her head around this latest revelation. *He no longer spent the whole night with a lover.* Then she recalled that he had said he hadn't been with anyone for months after their breakup, in spite of the photo she had seen in the press the week after she'd jilted him. The photo that had cut at her like a flick knife, making her hate him for moving on so quickly.

She hadn't realised until she saw the photo how much she had wanted him to come after her, to fight for her, to beg her to come back to him. To reassure her that he cared about her, that he wanted to be with her, that even, by some miracle, he loved her.

But he had done none of that.

And because of that damn photo she hadn't made any effort to contact him other than the brief note of apology she had left on the hall table with the engagement ring—which, of course, he claimed he hadn't got.

'Lincoln…you said the other day you didn't sleep with anyone for months after we broke up. Why was that?'

His expression was as screened as the moon was just then by a passing cloud. 'Don't go reading too much into it.'

'But why did you actively encourage me—and the rest of the world when it comes to that—to believe you'd moved on to someone else the very next week?'

'Why would that upset you? You were the one who jilted me. You made it clear we were over. More than clear.'

Elodie shifted her gaze from his and rolled her top lip over her bottom one, a frown still pulling at her forehead.

'I know I had no right to be upset. I guess I thought you might…try and talk me round.'

He gave a short bark of incredulous laughter. 'Really? You mean come crawling on my hands and knees, begging you to come back to me? Shows how little you knew me back then.'

Her shoulders went down on a heavy sigh. 'Yes, well… that works both ways, doesn't it?'

Lincoln glanced at her, his expression still inscrutable. But then he sighed and raked a hand through his hair, before dropping it back by his side. 'Was there anything I could've said to get you to change your mind back then?'

His tone had lost its sharp, mocking edge and become deeper, almost gentle. Elodie forced a smile, not sure she wanted to reveal any more than she already had. It was funny, but she could parade in the skimpiest lingerie and swimwear on catwalks and billboards all over the world, and yet revealing her vulnerability to Lincoln was the scariest, most terrifying thing of all.

'Probably not.' She wrapped her arms around her body against the chill of the night air.

There was a lengthy silence.

Lincoln stepped closer and lifted her chin with two of his fingers, meshing his gaze with hers. 'It wasn't my best moment, having that photo circulated of me with that young woman.' He gave a rueful twist of his mouth, then lowered his hand from her face and continued, 'You should have heard the dressing-down Sylvia gave me. She thought it was unspeakably crass. But I was angry and bitter. It's not often I get blindsided by someone—especially someone who'd claimed they loved me.'

But I did love you.

The words were stuck behind the wall of her pride. The pride she needed to keep from getting hurt all over again.

Elodie moved further away from him, wrapping her arms around her middle to ward off the sudden chill of the night air. 'Look—I was young, and I had stars in my eyes. You showed me a world I'd never had access to before. A world of wealth and privilege and private jets and God knows what else. I fooled myself into thinking you cared about me, but what you cared about was having a beautiful wife. I'd have completed your successful lifestyle. A good-looking wife who you saw as an asset rather than a person in her own right. But you didn't offer me your heart in return.'

'I seem to remember you made the most of our breakup.'

The mocking tone was back, even more biting than before. And the steely look in his eyes was harder than the diamonds on her finger.

Elodie went back into the trench of her pride. 'And why shouldn't I have made the most of it? The sponsors approached me—not me them. I did realise it gave me the perfect opportunity to lift my profile, and I didn't see any reason I shouldn't use it. I was only doing itty-bitty modelling jobs before that, most of which only paid a pittance, and I found them demeaning. I wanted to get more control over the photos and the labels I wore, so shoot me for using our breakup to do it. Besides, you're the one who always says you shouldn't let emotions get in the way of a good business decision. I was simply taking your advice.'

There was a ringing silence.

Then Lincoln's mouth began to twitch with a smile. 'Methinks I've been hoist by my own petard.'

Elodie mock-pouted at him. 'That'll teach you for having one rule for you and another one for everyone else.'

He stepped towards her again and took her by the upper arms. His eyes meshed with hers, and there was a lopsided smile on his lips. He lifted his hand to her face and stroked his finger down the slope of her nose. 'That's another thing I missed about you. You always stood up to me.'

'What? No one else has since?'

He gave a rueful movement of his lips. 'Not quite like you do.' He stroked her bottom lip with his thumb. 'I'm surrounded by sycophants most of the time—people intent on pleasing me. It gets boring after a while.'

Elodie placed her hands against his chest, felt his warmth seeping into her like the rays of the sun. Her lower body brushed against his and a wave of longing swept through her. 'I'm glad you didn't find me boring. But if you were missing a good old ding-dong fight, why didn't you just call me? I'm sure we could have found something to argue about.'

She was only half joking. She had missed their fights too. In fact, she had missed way more than that. She had missed everything about him.

His eyes drifted to her mouth. 'That night we ran in to each other in Soho...' He grimaced, as if the memory pained him. 'When I saw you go off with Fraser MacDiarmid I was shocked at how much I wanted to stop you.'

Elodie arched her eyebrows. 'You said you weren't jealous that night.'

His expression had a hint of sheepishness about it. 'Seeing you again was...difficult. I'd seen you heaps of time on billboards or in magazine spreads and on television, but not in the flesh.' His eyes came back to hers, dark and glittering. 'I was jealous, angry...disappointed that it wasn't me you were going off with instead of him. The thing is, I'd never felt jealous before. It annoyed me that I felt it then.'

Elodie wasn't fool enough to think his jealousy signalled love. He was a proud man who had been publicly humiliated by her jilting him. Seeing her with another man would have triggered him in the same way she had been triggered by seeing him with his beautiful and clearly devoted new partner that night.

She lifted her hands to the tops of his broad shoulders, then slid them down his muscled arms to his strong wrists. His fingers entwined with hers and heat coursed through her body. 'We're going to have to deal with the chance of running into each other in the future—I mean, once we divorce.'

It seemed a good a time as any to remind him of the time frame on their marriage. To remind herself.

Lincoln placed one of his hands in the small of her back, bringing her up against him. 'Let's not mention the *D* word until after Nina passes.'

'But what if she doesn't die within our time frame? I mean, it can happen, you know... People go into remission, or a new drug is released, or—'

'Our agreement is six months and six months only.'

The edge of intractability in his tone was just the reminder she needed to keep her emotions in check.

'Fine.' She pulled out of his hold and sent a careless hand through her hair. 'I'm going back to bed.'

She turned and walked through the French doors, back into the bedroom, aware of Lincoln's footsteps following her. He came up behind her and placed his hands on her hips, pulling her against him. His hands cupped her breasts and a shiver of anticipation coursed over her flesh.

'Want me to join you?'

He spoke against the sensitive skin of her neck, sending another hot shiver racing down her spine like a cartwheeling fiery coal.

'I thought you didn't like spending the whole night with your casual lovers any more?'

Lincoln turned her so she was facing him. His smile was sardonic, his eyes glittering. 'You're not a casual lover—you're my wife.'

'For six months and six months only.' Elodie followed up her statement with a sugar-sweet smile. 'That's still a lot of nights sharing a bed.'

His hands skimmed down the sides of her body, from her shoulders, past her ribcage and waist, to settle on her hips, his gaze smouldering. 'Then let's not waste a single one of them.'

And his mouth came down and sealed hers hotly, explosively, possessively.

It was an urgent kiss that sent a river of fire through her blood and her body. Her inner core turned to molten lava within seconds, her need of him so intense it surged in pulsing and pounding waves through her most intimate flesh.

Lincoln tumbled with her to the bed, only stopping long enough to apply a condom. He rolled her over so she straddled him, his hands caressing her breasts with thrilling expertise. He guided himself into her, his expression a grimace of pleasure at the contact of aroused male flesh against aroused female flesh.

'You feel so damn good...' he groaned.

'You took the words right out of my mouth.'

Not to mention taking her breath away.

Elodie moved with him, the rocking motion of their bodies sending her over the edge within moments. She gasped out loud, riding out the powerful orgasm, her hair swishing wildly about her shoulders, her body so rattled and shaken by ripples of pleasure it was like being transported to another world. A world of intense sensuality where no thoughts were necessary.

This was not the time to think of the temporary nature

of their relationship. This was not the time to think about the love she had for him that put her at so much risk of heartbreak. This was the time to enjoy a moment of pure ecstatic bliss, of two perfectly in tune bodies.

Elodie came floating back down from the stratosphere to watch Lincoln shuddering through his own release. It looked and sounded as mind-blowing as her own. She scooped her hair back over one of her shoulders and smiled down at him. 'You look like you had a good time.'

He gave a deep sigh. 'The best.'

Elodie lay over him with her head on his chest, their bodies still intimately joined. His hands stroked the curves of her bottom in lazy strokes that sent goosebumps popping up all over her skin.

'If you don't stop doing that, you're going to have to make love to me all over again.'

'Maybe that's exactly what I want to do.'

'So soon?'

'You bet.'

He flipped her so she was lying on her back, then swiftly disposed of the used condom before replacing it with a fresh one. He came back to her, leaning his weight on one elbow, one of his strongly muscled legs flung over one of hers. His other hand caressed her thigh in long slow movements that sent tingles down to her curling toes.

'I could make love to you all night.'

CHAPTER NINE

THE NEXT COUPLE of days passed in a blur of activity. Spending time with Nina was clearly a priority for Lincoln, which only made Elodie love and respect him more, but he also managed to show Elodie some of the tourist spots in the town—including the Roman theatre and the fortress castle.

They walked hand in hand as they explored the sights, and she tried to pretend they were just like any loved-up couple on their honeymoon. There were even times when she caught Lincoln looking at her with an indulgent look on his face, making her wonder if some of his bitterness about their breakup was finally melting away.

Certainly, there was no trace of it in his lovemaking. The passion they shared never ceased to amaze her. It seemed to be getting more intense, and there were moments of tenderness too, that were particularly poignant given their marriage was only temporary.

It was poignant too, to see Lincoln's relationship with his biological mother growing each day. It touched Elodie to see the care he had for her, the way he made sure she had everything she needed. The villa and its grounds were immaculate, and managed with expertise, and the staff were friendly and supportive.

Elodie couldn't help comparing the lovely Alita with

Morag. How could there be two such different housekeepers? One was so helpful, the other so spiteful. One made her feel welcome, the other made her feel like trailer trash, triggering the emotions of the past, when others had done the same. It made the thought of going back to London daunting—not to mention the prospect of leaving Nina, and wondering if it would be the last time they'd see her.

The morning of their departure, Nina wrapped her arms around Elodie in a warm, motherly hug. 'Take care of yourself, my dear. Don't work too hard, will you? And promise to come and see me again soon, yes?'

Elodie blinked back tears, her heart suddenly feeling cramped inside her chest cavity. 'I promise. Thank you for making me feel so welcome.' She eased back to look at the older woman, who was also tearing up. 'I'm so glad you and Lincoln found each other at last.'

Nina's smile was happy-sad. 'I waited a long time to make contact. Too long. But I wasn't sure if he would want to meet me. After all, I gave him up as a week-old baby. Some adoptees find that very hard to understand—why their birth mother gave them away. But I always loved him. I only ever wanted the best for him.'

Elodie stood back as Lincoln hugged Nina and said his own goodbyes. He had better control over his emotions, but she sensed he was also well aware that this could be the last time he saw Nina. She saw it in the set of his jaw, the fixed smile, the shadowed eyes, the aura of sadness that enveloped him.

Once they were in the car, with Elonzo driving, on their way to the airport, Elodie placed her hand on Lincoln's thigh. 'I really like Nina. She's so warm and friendly.'

He took her hand and gave it a gentle squeeze. 'Yeah, she's great.' His voice was sandpaper-rough. 'I'm glad she liked you.'

Elodie glanced at her wedding and engagement rings, glittering on her hand. 'Yes, well…it would've been a disaster if she hadn't, given you've gone to the trouble of marrying me and all.'

His gaze met hers, his expression inscrutable. 'Has it been such a trial so far?'

She leaned closer to plant a kiss on his lips. 'No…' Her voice came out a little husky. 'But I can't say I'm looking forward to living in the same house as Mean Morag. Alita is so lovely and sweet. She falls over herself to help.'

'I hope you don't call Morag that to her face?'

'No, of course not.'

He sighed and ruffled the loose strands of her hair. 'I'll have a word with her about reducing her hours. That way you won't have to run into her so often.'

'I probably won't be home during the day much anyway. I have work to do. I've got to find a studio—preferably close to the centre of London, which will cost a bomb, but—'

'I know of a place you could use,' Lincoln said. 'It's around the corner from my office—the one that's currently being renovated. It has space for a showroom as well.'

A flicker of excitement coursed through her blood. 'Really? How much will the rent be, do you think?'

'I'll have a word with the landlord. He might do mates' rates or something.'

'Wow, that would be awesome.'

He brought her hand up to his chest, his eyes meshing with hers. 'You might not believe this, but I really want you to succeed.'

Elodie didn't ask for clarification, because she already knew what was behind his motivation for her success. Her career would be all she was left with after their marriage came to an end. It would be her consolation prize.

'I'll do my best,' she said.

* * *

Within a few of days of coming back to London, Elodie was setting up her studio with Elspeth's help. Some of the furniture had yet to arrive, and there was a lot more to do in terms of preparing her creative space, but it was like a dream come true to have her own place at last.

'I've got a good feeling about this venture of yours,' Elspeth said, unloading some fabric swatches from a box. 'I can't wait to come in and have some fancy evening wear designed for me by you.'

'Hey, I thought you didn't like dressing up?' Elodie teased. 'What happened to the shy librarian archivist who only wore brown and beige and flat shoes?'

Elspeth pulled the plastic wrapping off one of the velvet showroom chairs and gave a dreamy smile. 'I've decided it's much more fun being a butterfly than a moth.' She bundled the wrapping into a ball and added, 'You haven't told me much about your trip to Spain apart from how nice Nina was. How was it?'

'It was good.'

'Only "good"?'

Elodie took the ball of plastic from her twin and stuffed it in the box she had set aside for recycling. 'We're not having a paper marriage any more.'

Elspeth's eyes twinkled. 'Wow!'

'Wow, indeed.' Elodie picked up one of the sketching sets she'd ordered and placed it on the table. 'This is probably way too much information to share, even for a twin sister, but I've never really enjoyed making love with anyone other than Lincoln.' She glanced at her twin. 'Is that weird, or what?'

'It's not weird at all,' Elspeth said. 'It shows you care about him. You do, don't you?'

Elodie sighed. 'Way more than I should, given we're only staying married for a matter of months.'

'That might change. I mean, Lincoln might change his mind and offer you more.'

'He was pretty blunt about it. Six months and six months only.'

'But he changed his mind about the paper marriage, right?'

Elodie picked up another parcel from the box she was unloading, a small frown tugging at her brow. 'I haven't decided yet if he always intended to tweak the rules or if I managed to convince him. He's so hard to read sometimes.'

Elspeth started to unwrap another velvet chair, a small smile playing about her mouth. 'I can only imagine the lengths you went to in order to change his mind.'

Elodie laughed. 'Now, that *would* be sharing way too much information.'

Elodie got back to Lincoln's London home to find Morag preparing dinner in the kitchen. She hadn't seen much of the housekeeper since she and Lincoln had returned from Spain. She had deliberately stayed away during Morag's working hours. But now that she had no choice but to interact with her, Elodie decided to try a new tactic—to act her way into feeling more positive about the grumpy housekeeper.

It was worth a try. Anything was worth a try.

'Can I do anything to help?'

Morag wiped the back of her hand across her forehead. 'No. I can manage.'

Elodie narrowed her gaze on the older woman's strange-looking pallor. She had a greyish tinge to her skin and beads of perspiration peppered her forehead. 'Are you okay?'

Morag gripped the edge of the kitchen bench with her hands. 'I… I think I might need some insulin… I might have missed a dose…or eaten the wrong thing…'

Elodie rushed over and took her by the shoulders. 'Let me help you. Come and sit down and I'll get your insulin for you. Where is it?'

Morag sank into the chair with a sigh of relief. 'In my bedroom…' She took a gasping breath and slumped forward with her head bent over her knees. 'In the chest of drawers…top drawer, I think.'

'I'm going to call an ambulance.'

'Don't you dare. I'll be fine once I've had a dose.'

'Maybe you should lie down while I get it?' Elodie suggested. 'I don't want you to fall off that chair.'

Morag lifted her head to glare at her. 'Just bring me the insulin, will you?'

Elodie ground her teeth and ran upstairs to the top floor, where Morag had a small suite of rooms for when she stayed over. She rushed over to the chest of drawers, but the insulin wasn't in the top drawer as Morag had thought. She opened the second and third drawers, rustling through the housekeeper's belongings, but failed to find any medication.

The fourth and bottom drawer was stiff to open, and while she doubted the medication would be stored there, she thought it best to check anyway. She finally managed to get the drawer open and rummaged around the contents. Her eyes suddenly homed in on a velvet ring box, and her heart came to a complete standstill. She stared at the box for countless seconds, her heartbeat restarting with a loud *ba-boom, ba-boom, ba-boom* that made her suspect she was having her own medical crisis.

She reached for the box with a hand that wasn't quite steady, opening it to find her old engagement ring glittering there in all its brilliance. Something dropped like a tombstone in her stomach. Morag had the ring. All this time, the housekeeper had had the ring. But why?

Elodie heard the sound of Lincoln's firm footsteps coming along the corridor and quickly stashed the ring back in the drawer. She tried to shove it closed. The drawer wouldn't close all the way, but there wasn't time to worry about that. She straightened and glanced around the room, and saw an insulin kit sitting on a chair next to the bed. She snatched it up just as Lincoln came through the door.

'You found it? Great.' He took it off her and raced back downstairs, with Elodie in hot pursuit. 'I called an ambulance. It should be here any second now.'

'I offered to, but Morag insisted I didn't.'

'She can be difficult about her illness. She hasn't really accepted it.'

They got back to the kitchen and Lincoln helped administer a dose of insulin as if he had been moonlighting as a physician for years. Morag recovered within a few minutes, but by then the ambulance had arrived and Lincoln insisted she go to hospital to be checked out.

'But what about dinner?' Morag said.

'I'll sort it out,' Elodie said. 'You just concentrate on getting well again.'

Within a short time the paramedics had taken Morag away and Elodie and Lincoln were left alone.

Lincoln took Elodie by the hands, his expression rich with concern. 'Are you okay? You look like you're in shock.'

Elodie *was* in shock. Deep shock. Her heart was still pounding, sweat was trickling down between her shoulder blades, and her stomach was churning along with her brain. Here was her chance to tell him about the ring she had found, but for some reason she couldn't bring herself to do it. What if he thought she herself had planted it there? What if he didn't believe she had found it while looking for the insulin kit?

But if he did believe her, she realised it would poison his relationship with his housekeeper. The breach of trust would be hard to forgive—especially when Morag had worked for him for so long. Besides, she wanted to hear Morag's explanation first.

'I—I'm fine…' She forced a smile that didn't quite work. 'I'm not good in a crisis. Just ask Elspeth. Sick people terrify me.'

Lincoln stroked her hair away from her face, his gaze steady on hers. 'You did a great job of taking care of Morag.'

She gave a dismissive snort, her eyes drifting away from his. 'So, how was your day?'

He reached up to loosen his tie. 'Not bad. How did you go at the studio?'

'It was great. Elspeth came to help me unpack the stuff that's arrived so far. There's still heaps to do, but it feels so good to have my own space. I can't thank you enough for organising it for me.'

He gave her chin a playful brush with his fingers. 'It's my pleasure.'

Elodie plastered another smile on her lips and turned for the kitchen, saying over her shoulder, 'Give me half an hour or so and I'll have dinner ready for you.'

'You're starting to sound very wifey.'

There was a note of amusement in his tone.

She turned around to smile back at him. 'Make the most of it, baby. It's only for six months, remember?'

And then she disappeared into the kitchen.

* * *

Lincoln tugged his silk tie the rest of the way out of his collar, threading it through his fingers, a frown pulling at his forehead. Elodie was always reminding him of the temporary nature of their relationship. Was that for her benefit or his? He knew the time frame well enough—he was the one who'd put it in place. And it needed to stay in place, in spite of how well they were getting on.

Settling down to domesticity with Elodie was out of the question. Firstly, because he didn't want to lay himself open to the sort of heartache his father had gone through after losing his mother—loving for a lifetime contained certain devastation, for one partner always outlived the other. It was a fact of life and one he wanted to avoid experiencing first-hand. And secondly, because Elodie was like him—career-focussed. She had left him before because she had wanted a career more than she wanted to be with him.

Now he was doing all he could to facilitate her career—it was the least he could do to repay her for how warmly she had bonded with Nina. He had hoped they would connect, but he hadn't dared hope they would get on as well as they had. It made him feel a little less compromised about the game of charades he and Elodie were playing.

But there were times when it didn't feel like a charade.

It felt real…scarily real.

Elodie was still mulling over the engagement ring hidden in the drawer upstairs when Lincoln came into the kitchen.

She quickly hung a tea towel over the oven door. 'No peeking. I want to surprise you with dinner.'

'It smells delicious.'

'It needs a few more minutes. Do you want a glass of wine?'

'Sure. You want one?'

'Not tonight.'

The last thing she wanted was to loosen her tongue with wine. The engagement ring incident was still playing on her mind. She couldn't work out why Morag would have done such a thing. Why hadn't she sold the ring? Why had she kept it after all this time? What could the housekeeper hope to achieve by keeping it stashed away? It didn't make any sense.

'I'm having an AFD.'

'Pardon?'

'An alcohol-free day.'

'Right...'

'But you go ahead.'

Lincoln took a bottle of orange juice out of the integrated fridge. 'I'm fine with juice. Would you prefer mineral water?'

'That would be perfect.'

A short time later they were seated in the dining room. Elodie served the chicken chasseur she'd made, along with steamed beans and a potato dish with onions and a dash of cream and fresh herbs.

She picked up her glass of mineral water. *'Bon appetit.'*

Lincoln smiled and picked up his glass, clinked it against hers. 'So, when did you develop an interest in cooking? I seem to recall you could barely scramble an egg when we were together.'

She put her glass down and picked up her cutlery, sending him a glance across the candlelit table. 'Life living out of hotels can be pretty boring. The food starts to taste all the same. I made a point of using my time at home between photo shoots as a chance to experiment. I did a cooking class in Italy, and then another one in France. They were heaps of fun.'

'I'm impressed.'

Elodie shrugged off his compliment. 'It's not that hard. But I freak out a bit when I cook for Elspeth.'

'Because of her allergy?'

'Yeah.' She shuddered and continued, 'Seeing Morag collapse like that was a bit triggering, to be honest. What if neither of us had been home? What if she'd lost consciousness and we'd found her on the floor, and it was too late, and—'

'Elodie, sweetheart.' His voice cut across her panicked speech with calm authority. 'It didn't happen, okay? She's safe and sound in hospital and she will be back to work tomorrow, if I'm any judge.'

Elodie put her cutlery down, her appetite completely deserting her. 'Sorry.' She flashed him an effigy of a smile. 'It's been a long day. I think I'll just clear away and go to bed.'

She put her napkin to one side and began to push her chair back. Lincoln rose from his own chair and came around to help her. He took her in his arms and gathered her close, resting his chin on the top of her head.

'Seven years ago you never really told me much about what it was like for you, growing up with Elspeth and her allergy. You've told me more in the last few days than you did the whole time we were together.'

Elodie laid her cheek against his chest, enjoying the warmth and protectiveness of his embrace and the deep reverberation of his voice beneath her ear. 'I guess we talked about other stuff or didn't talk at all. Or at least not about stuff that was deep and serious.'

He lifted her chin from his chest and meshed his gaze with hers. 'I should have told you about my adoption. I have a habit of compartmentalising my life. I'm not sure it's a healthy or wise thing to do.'

She slipped her arms around his waist. 'At least you're aware of doing it. That's half the battle, surely? Awareness.'

'It sure is.' He placed his hands on her hips, his expression warm and tender. 'I'll clear this away while you go upstairs and get ready for bed. I'll be up soon.'

'But I'm such a messy cook. There's stuff everywhere in the kitchen.'

'You're not the only one who's become a little more domesticated in the last few years. Now, off you go. I won't take no for an answer.'

Elodie would have put up more of a fight, but she suddenly realised how completely exhausted she was. Her emotions were in a whirlpool and she didn't know how to process them. She was used to blocking out things she didn't want to think about. Used to pushing thoughts to the back of her mind and leaving them there, like stuffing old clothes she didn't want to wear again to the back of the wardrobe.

But the engagement ring sitting in that drawer in Morag's room was playing on her mind so much it made it hard to think about anything else.

Should she tell Lincoln, or leave things until she could talk to Morag? How could she tell Lincoln and be sure he would believe her?

Sure, they were talking and communicating in a way they hadn't done in the past, but it didn't guarantee he would trust her version of events. She had been the one to publicly humiliate him by jilting him. It would be reasonable for him to assume she had sold the ring to finance her career. If she produced it now, it would be her word against his long-term housekeeper's. And he had never trusted her word against Morag's in the past.

It had always been difficult for her to put her trust in

someone, to believe they'd have her back no matter what. That they'd *believe* her. She had been portrayed in the press as scatty and fickle—a wild party girl who couldn't care less what people thought of her.

But she did care.

Was it foolish to hope Lincoln might finally trust her now?

Lincoln worked at restoring order to the kitchen for the next forty minutes. Elodie hadn't been wrong when she'd called herself a messy cook—it looked as if she had used every pot and utensil. He was used to good food—his housekeeper was an excellent cook, who always prepared nutritious and interesting meals. But seeing the effort Elodie had gone to over dinner—especially after experiencing the shock of Morag's medical episode—deeply impressed him.

He was learning more and more about her upbringing, and he realised now how little he had understood her in the past. No wonder she had looked done in and gone to bed early. She had been triggered by his housekeeper's sudden collapse—no doubt because of all the times she had witnessed her twin suffering an attack of anaphylaxis.

What could be more terrifying to a small child than to see her twin sister desperately ill? He hadn't realised how pushed aside she had felt by her mother's overprotectiveness of Elspeth. Of course any parent would struggle to balance the needs of their children under such difficult circumstances. But Elodie had hinted at the way she had fought to be noticed—by seeking attention by negative means. Hadn't she done that during their previous relationship? Hadn't her constant bickering over inconsequential things been a continuation of that pattern of behaviour?

Lincoln finally made it upstairs, only to find Elodie soundly asleep. She was curled up in a ball like a sleeping kitten, her hair a red-gold cloud splayed across the pillow. He pulled the covers up a little more and then leaned down to press a light-as-air kiss to the top of her head. She made a soft murmur and burrowed deeper into the mattress, her eyes remaining closed, her dark lashes like miniature fans resting softly against her cheeks.

He stood looking at her for a long moment, and felt something in his chest tightening, straining, like a silk thread pulling against his heart. This subtle shift in their relationship was bringing up other issues he wasn't sure he wanted to face.

But the timeline was set.

He had insisted it was non-negotiable.

Damn it, it *was* non-negotiable.

And yet something about being with Elodie now made it harder for him to imagine going back to his playboy lifestyle. Or was it because he didn't like thinking about her with someone else? He hadn't considered himself the green-eyed monster type, but thinking about her with someone else tied his gut into knots. Strangely, he had found himself confessing to her how eaten with jealousy he had been that night they'd run into each other in Soho—even though he had rigorously denied it before.

Showing any hint of vulnerability was normally anathema to him. He didn't do it in his professional life. He didn't do it in his personal life.

He didn't do it, period.

So why was he even tempted to do it now?

CHAPTER TEN

ELODIE SIGHED AND rolled over in bed, opening her eyes to find Lincoln lying on his side, watching her in the moonlight. She ran a lazy hand over the dark stubble on his jaw. 'You really are a dreadful insomniac these days, aren't you?'

He gave a crooked smile that made something slip sideways in her stomach.

'I like watching you sleep.'

She wriggled closer, her legs tangling with his beneath the bedcovers. 'I'm not asleep now.'

'So I see.'

Her hand drifted down to the proud rise of his erection. 'What are you thinking about?' she asked.

'Right now?' His tone was so dry it almost crackled, his eyes glittering darkly.

'Right now.'

'I'm a little cognitively impaired right at this very moment, with you touching me like that.'

'Like this?' Elodie ran her hand up and down the length of his shaft, her own arousal intensified by feeling the insistent throb of his.

He groaned and pulled her hand away, moving over her so she was beneath the weight of his body. He caged her in with his arms, his gaze holding hers in an erotic lock that sent tingles to her core. 'I want you.'

The raw urgency in his voice matched the desire pounding through her body. 'I want you too—just in case you hadn't picked up on that vibe.'

'You're not exactly subtle.'

She gave him a twinkling smile. 'Do you want me to be?'

'God, no. I love it when you're so forthright. It turns me on.'

He lowered his mouth to hers in a spine-tingling kiss that lifted each and every hair on her head. His tongue tangled with hers, darting and diving and duelling in a cat-and-mouse caper that thrilled her senses.

He lifted his mouth off hers to work his way down her body, leaving a hot pathway of kisses along her naked skin. He caressed her breasts with his lips and his tongue, sending waves of pleasure through her as strong as electrical pulses. He worked his way down her stomach, circling her belly button with the teasing touch of his tongue. She sucked in a breath as he went lower, his lips exploring her most intimate flesh of all.

She arched her back like a sinuous cat, giving herself up to the sensual attention of his mouth. He knew her body so well, so intimately, there was no question of her not responding. She did—powerfully, passionately, volubly. Her panting cries were almost primal, the thrashing of her body equally so. Her orgasm went on and on, carrying her along on a rushing tide that was almost frightening in its intensity.

She finally collapsed back against the pillows. 'Oh, God, I can't believe you did that. I thought it was never going to end.'

Lincoln gave her a smouldering look and leaned across her to access a condom. He slipped it on and came back to her, one of his hands brushing her wildly disordered hair off her face. 'I love watching you come.'

Elodie scrunched up her face self-consciously. 'Eek! I can only imagine how ugly I look.'

'You couldn't look ugly if you tried.'

She traced the strong line of his collarbone with her finger, her gaze lowered from his. 'Beauty isn't everything…and it fades eventually.' She raised her eyes back to his. 'Millions of people have seen me in sexy lingerie and swimwear, but I don't think they actually see *me*… the real me…mostly because I haven't wanted them to.'

'But now?'

She chewed one side of her mouth. 'I've played on my looks for as long as I can remember. I've used them to get where I wanted to go. Unlike Elspeth, who tried not to be noticed at all. But I want more now. I want to be noticed for my skills as a designer—not because I rock a skimpy bikini.'

'I'm going to miss seeing you in those skimpy bikinis.'

She angled her head at him. 'So you've been checking out some billboards and magazine spreads, have you? I noticed one in your office. Did you know I was in it or was that just a lucky purchase?'

'Lucky purchase.' His eyes shone like wet paint. 'Although coming across you on a billboard almost caused me to run off the road a couple of times.'

'No doubt because you were furious with me for having the audacity to use our breakup as a platform for my success.'

There was a small silence.

'I was angry…livid, actually…' His voice trailed away as if something had changed in his attitude towards her since then.

'But not now?'

He brushed another strand of hair off her face, tucking it gently behind her ear. 'It's hard to be angry with you when you're lying naked in my bed.'

Elodie stroked her hand down his flat abdomen, her smile teasing. 'Do you want me to get dressed?'

His gaze glinted and he lowered his mouth to just above hers. 'Not yet.'

Elodie linked her arms around his neck, the thrill of his lips and tongue against hers sending her pulse racing off the charts all over again. He entered her body with a deep thrust that sent shockwave after shockwave of pleasure through her. His movements were slow at first, but he gradually increased his pace, driving her closer and closer to the point of no return.

The tension built in her body—the delicious tension that incorporated each and every piece of intricate tissue and muscle in her feminine flesh. She arched her pelvis to seek more friction, wanting more, needing more, aching for more. He slipped his hand between their bodies and caressed her swollen flesh, sending her over the edge within seconds. The orgasm rippled through her in smashing, crashing, tumbling waves, sending her senses into a whirlpool of earth-shattering ecstasy.

Lincoln followed her with his own release, the vigorous pumping action of his body sending another wave of tumultuous pleasure through her slick and swollen flesh. He gave a guttural groan and pitched forward over her, giving a whole-body shudder as he spilled his essence.

It was not often Elodie was rendered speechless, but her body was so acutely aware of every part of his where it touched her. The aftershocks were still rumbling through every inch of her flesh, and her heart was hammering against his chest where it was pressed against hers. The physical bliss was unlike any she had experienced with anyone else. And she knew without a doubt that even if she went on to have dozens of subsequent partners no one would ever be able to draw from her such a mind-blowing response.

The realisation of what lay ahead of her once their six months were up—the aching loneliness, the emptiness of shallow going-nowhere relationships—almost made her cry. Almost.

She bit down on her lower lip and squeezed her eyes closed over the sting of tears. She had no right to be upset. She had agreed to the terms and was already enjoying the benefit of them. Her bank account was full of money. More money than she had ever dreamed to see there. Luxury fabrics were on order, due to arrive this week. The studio was just about up and running. She had dozens of sketches in her workbooks and on her laptop. She had staff interviews set up in the coming days. Promotional work to see to…interviews and planning meetings. She even had clients waiting for her to design for them—not just Elspeth and Nina, but other friends and acquaintances.

Her dream was finally coming to fruition and she wanted to cry? She had to get a grip on herself. Emotions and business didn't mix, right? That was Lincoln's mantra and it had to be hers.

It *had* to be. Otherwise she would get her heart smashed to pieces.

Lincoln rolled her over so she was lying face to face with him on her side. He propped himself up on one elbow and stroked his other hand down the slope of her cheek, his frowning eyes searching hers. 'What's wrong?'

She forced her lips into a tight smile and rolled away, sitting upright and tossing her hair back over one shoulder. 'Don't mind me. I'm just trying to recover from having multiple orgasms for the first time in seven years.'

He sat up and shuffled over so he was sitting beside her on the bed. One of his hands stroked down the length of her spine—a warm, soothing stroke that loosened each and every vertebra.

'If it's any comfort, I'm a little shell-shocked too.'

He bent his head and planted a soft kiss to the top of her shoulder, the touch of his lips making her skin tingle.

'More than a little, actually.'

Elodie turned her head to meet his blue-green gaze. She lifted her hand to his face and traced the prominent line of each of his eyebrows. 'That's good. I'd hate to be the only one feeling dazzled.'

He slid his hand under the curtain of her hair and brought his mouth down to just above hers. 'That's what you do best, sweetheart. Dazzle.'

And he closed the distance between their mouths with a blistering kiss.

It was almost two weeks later when Morag returned to work. Elodie was due home first, as Lincoln was flying back from a meeting in Dublin later that night. He'd asked her to go with him and stay a couple of extra days, but she'd declined, citing another staff interview as well as working on her designs for Nina and helping Elspeth prepare for her wedding.

She was determined to keep her career her main focus. Dropping everything to follow Lincoln around the globe was not going to build her career to the level she desired. If he'd been disappointed with her declining his invitation, he hadn't shown it. But then, why would he? He wasn't in love with her. The arrangement he had with her was temporary. Once their marriage was over he would move on with his playboy lifestyle as if nothing had changed.

Morag was already ensconced in the kitchen, an apron tied

around her waist and a wooden spoon in her hand. 'Lincoln told me to take a few more days off but I wanted to get back to work.' She stirred the mixture in the bowl in front of her and added gruffly, 'Thanks for helping me the other night.'

'I was worried about you. Are you feeling better now?'

'I'm fine. I just have to adjust my diet a bit.' Morag gave her a sheepish glance and added, 'No more cookies and chocolate.'

Elodie pulled out one of the bar stools next to the kitchen island and perched on it, wrapping her ankles around the legs. 'Gosh, I can't remember the last time I had a cookie or chocolate.'

Morag frowned. 'Is that because you're always dieting…because of modelling and all?'

'No, not really. It's because I never had them growing up. It was too risky having them in the house because of my twin's nut allergy.'

Morag met her gaze across the width of the bench. 'There's something I want to talk to you about…'

The hesitancy in the older woman's tone was unusual, not to mention her expression. Normally so brisk and forthright, and always wearing a frown, this time she had a worried look on her face.

'When you were looking for my insulin…' She swallowed convulsively and continued, 'I noticed the bottom drawer wasn't closed properly…that things were shifted around in there…'

'Why did you keep it?' Elodie decided to get straight to the point.

The older woman's cheeks developed a dull flush along her cheekbones. 'I tried to tell Lincoln I'd found it on the hall table, but he was so hungover after the wedding day and so angry…he wouldn't have your name mentioned. I was shocked when I saw it there. I didn't think you'd return it.'

'Because you had me pegged as a gold-digger?'

Morag's blush deepened. 'I know I should have tried to tell him a bit later, but I thought it best not to.'

'Why?'

'I thought if I told him you'd returned it he might consider asking you to come back to him.'

'But you didn't want him to do that, did you?'

Morag pressed her lips together and let go of the handle of the wooden spoon. 'I didn't think you loved him the way he deserved to be loved.' She swallowed again and met Elodie's gaze with an imploring one. 'Please don't tell him what I did. I can't lose this job. It's the only thing I have that brings me pleasure, a sense of purpose, a sense of being needed... I can't tell you how much *he* means to me. My own children don't speak to me now, because their father poisoned them against me. Lincoln is like a son to me. I know that sounds ridiculous, and sentimental, but I watched him grow up. Me and Rosemary, his adoptive mother, were at school together. He's the only connection I have with her now. I don't know his brother and sister the way I know him. I've known him all his life and I can't bear for him to think badly of me.'

Elodie jumped down from the stool and raked a hand through her hair. 'I'm sorry you've had such awful stuff happen to you. No woman deserves to be treated like that. And to lose contact with your children...well, that's heart-wrenching. But you're asking a lot of me to say nothing to Lincoln about this.'

'I know, and I won't really blame you if you choose to tell him. I haven't exactly been very welcoming to you.'

Elodie gave a long-winded sigh. 'I'm not going to tell him. Besides, he probably wouldn't believe me if I did.'

There was a pulsing silence.

'You do love him, don't you?' Morag's expression was

tortured with lines of guilt. 'You've always loved him...'
Her words trailed off in an agony of realisation.

Elodie stretched her lips into a humourless smile.
'More fool me. He doesn't love me back.'

'I know how that feels...loving someone who doesn't
love you the way you love them. You live in hope, wasting years of your life, and for what? To be rejected, cast
aside. But you have a second chance with Lincoln. He's
married you, after all, and—'

'Our marriage is a sham. We're only together to please
his dying biological mother—Nina. But I think you already suspected that.'

'But you're sleeping together?'

Elodie gave her a worldly look. 'It's what you might
call a marriage of convenience with benefits.'

Morag opened and closed her mouth, seemingly
speechless for a moment. 'I wish I could undo the past.
If I had my time over I would tell Lincoln about the ring
whether he wanted to listen or not.' Tears shone in her
eyes and she continued in a harrowed tone, 'I know it's
too much to ask you to forgive me...'

Elodie walked around to Morag's side of the bench and
wrapped her arms around her in a hug. 'It's in the past...
let's leave it there.'

How could she insist on the older woman revealing
her role in the disappearing engagement ring? As much
as she wanted Lincoln to know the truth, another part of
her understood the motivation behind Morag's seven-year
silence. After all, Elodie had her own secret—she loved
Lincoln and always had.

And there was no point revealing it now.

Lincoln came home a couple of days later and immediately noticed a different atmosphere in the house. His

housekeeper and Elodie seemed to have resolved their differences, for he found them cooking together in the kitchen. Elodie had a streak of flour on one cheek and her hands were busily kneading what looked like pizza dough. Morag was tearing leaves of fresh basil off a plant near the sink, and chatting to Elodie about a trip to Italy she had taken some years ago.

'Oh, hi, Lincoln.'

Elodie looked up with a smile that was so welcoming and bright something in his chest pinged.

'How was your Dublin trip?'

'Fine.' He stepped further into the room. 'Looks like you two are busy.'

'Elodie's teaching me how to make pizza from scratch,' Morag said. 'I've only ever used shop-bought bases. This is so much better.'

'Smells good so far.' Lincoln dropped a kiss to Elodie's lips, then dusted the flour off her face. 'How's the studio going?'

'Great,' Elodie said. 'I've employed two assistants and they're helping me organise things for my first show. It'll take a few months to get ready, but I'm hoping to have a collection together for spring next year.'

'I'll take over now, if you like,' Morag said. 'You two go and have a pre-dinner drink in the sitting room and I'll let you know when dinner's ready.'

'Thanks, Morag, you're a gem,' Lincoln said.

A minute or two later, Lincoln handed Elodie a glass of champagne in the sitting room. 'Here you go.'

'Lovely, thanks.' She smiled and took a sip, and then screwed up her nose and frowned.

'Is something wrong?'

She put the glass down on a nearby side table. 'I can't believe I'm saying this, but I seem to have lost my taste for champagne. I might just have a juice or mineral water instead.'

Lincoln got the juice for her and then sat beside on her the sofa, his body angled so he could look at her. She was dressed in casual clothes—a pair of black leggings and a grey sweater that had slid off one of her slim shoulders. Her hair was tied in a makeshift bun on top of her head and her face was free of make-up. He could have sat staring at her for hours.

'You seem to have affected a truce with Morag,' he said, to break the silence.

Elodie's gaze drifted away from his to look at her glass of juice. 'Yes, well…we've come to an understanding.'

'You looked very chummy out there. What brought about the change?'

She tucked one of her legs under her and brushed away a stray hair from her face. 'She thanked me for helping her the other night—not that I did much apart from panic.' She shrugged and briefly met his gaze, and added with a smile that didn't reach her eyes, 'I figure I only have to be nice for her for another few months, then I'll probably never see her again.'

Lincoln held her gaze for a beat or two. 'You do like reminding me of the time frame on our marriage.'

And for some reason he didn't like being reminded—even though he was the one who'd put the timeframe there in the first place. Almost three weeks had already passed…soon it would be a month, then two, then three, and before he knew it he would be facing not only the death of his biological mother but the end of his relationship with Elodie.

He didn't know which he was dreading the most.

Elodie gave one of her sugar-sweet smiles. 'I wouldn't

want either of us to get carried away because of all the fun we're having.'

He scooted closer to her on the sofa, reaching a hand to her face to stroke a lazy fingertip down the length of her cheek. 'I missed you.' His voice came out as rusty as a hinge on a centuries-old gate.

Something flickered in her gaze and the tip of her tongue slipped out to deposit a light sheen of moisture on her lips. 'I missed you too...' Her eyes lowered to his mouth and she snatched in a tiny breath.

Lincoln brought his mouth to hers, drawn to her with an almost unstoppable force. The softness of her lips beneath his sent a riot of sensations through his body. Heat, fire, throbbing lust. His kiss deepened, his blood thickened, his pulse quickened. His tongue met hers in a dance as old as time, a sexy salsa stirring his senses into manic overdrive.

He slid one of his hands along the side of her face, splaying his fingers against her scalp. Her lips responded to the pressure of his with equal passion and fervour, her soft moans of pleasure sending flames of heat through his body.

He lifted his mouth off hers, holding her face in his hands. 'How long have we got before dinner?'

Elodie stroked his jaw, her eyes shining with arousal, her lips curved in a sultry smile. 'How long do you need?'

'Not long.' Lincoln rose from the sofa and pulled her to her feet, settling his hands about her hips. 'We can save time by going to my study. I seem to remember you liked having fun in there...'

Her pupils flared and she nestled closer, the contact of her lower body sending a wave of powerful need through him that almost knocked him off his feet.

'Sounds like a plan.'

* * *

Elodie let Lincoln lead her to his study, a few doors down the long corridor. She went in before him, and once he was inside he closed the door and turned the key in the lock with a sharp click that sent a shiver racing down her spine.

She gave the room a sweeping glance, noting that it had also been redecorated, but stripped down rather than dressed up. It still had strong, masculine lines, with functional furniture—desk, chair and bookshelves and a modern lamp. There was a desktop computer, and a printer and scanner on a cabinet behind the desk. There were no items of sentimentality lying about, no photos or keepsakes. It was a reminder of the cool and clinical components to Lincoln's personality—the inbuilt traits that made it difficult for him to show, let alone feel, sentiment or emotion.

'New office furniture…'

Elodie trailed a hand along the top of his desk. A flood of memories rushed through her mind. Erotic memories of desk sex after one of their legendary arguments. Was he recalling those red-hot episodes? Remembering the explosive passion that had flared between them?

She glanced at him and added, 'I suppose this desk's been used heaps of times?'

Lincoln came towards her, his eyes blazing with incendiary heat. 'Not the way we're about to use it.'

His hands gripped her by the hips again, and he lifted her so she was seated on his desk. Elodie linked her arms around his neck, gazing into the bluey-green kaleidoscope of his eyes. 'You mean you haven't christened it with anyone else?'

'No.'

She didn't like to read too much into his answer, but it surprised her all the same that he hadn't brought any of his lovers into this room. 'Why not?'

His mouth twisted in a rueful grimace. 'Lots of reasons.'

'Give me one.'

His gaze dipped to her mouth and then moved back to her eyes. 'I always associated this room with you. That's why I changed it. I couldn't look at the old desk without thinking of all the times we'd made love on it.'

Elodie brushed her mouth against his. 'I'll let you in on a little secret…' Her voice was little more than a whisper. 'I've only ever had desk sex with you.'

He stepped between her thighs and brought his mouth closer to hers. 'Does it make me sound like an egotist to be pleased about that?'

'Maybe a little.'

He smiled and closed the distance between their mouths in a searing kiss that made the hairs on the back of her neck tingle at the roots. His tongue entered her mouth with a silken thrust that set her blood on fire. Molten heat erupted between her legs, the heart of her womanhood swelling, moistening, aching and pulsing with primal need. His tongue tangled with hers in a dance of lust that made her desire for him escalate to a heart-stopping level.

He left her mouth after a few breathless moments, trailing his lips down the side of her neck to her bare skin, where her sweater had slipped off her shoulder. His hands lifted her sweater and she raised her arms like a child for him to haul it over her head. He tossed it to the floor behind him, then his hands were going to her leggings. She lifted her bottom off the desk to help him remove them from her body, her heart racing, her pulse pounding, her breath catching.

He devoured her with his hungry eyes, his hands running over the globes of her lace-covered breasts with toe-curling expertise. 'I want you naked.' His tone was deep and husky.

'And so you shall have me…once we get things a little more even around here.'

Elodie began to undo the buttons on his business shirt, but she'd only got to the third one when he became impatient. With a grunt, he took over the job, stripping his shirt off and sending it in the same direction as her sweater. She slid her hands over his well-defined pectoral muscles, her blood ticking with excitement. She brought her mouth to his chest, licking with her tongue across each of his flat male nipples, then circling them in turn.

He drew in a ragged breath and placed his hands on the fastener at the back of her bra, deftly unclipping it. He lowered his mouth to her right breast, caressing the tightly budded nipple with his lips and tongue. Need throbbed in every cell of her body, the sensations he was evoking making her breath catch in her throat. He opened his mouth over her nipple and drew on the sensitised flesh, the sucking motion triggering a firestorm in her lower body. Then he moved to her other breast, teasing it into the same sensual raptures, the rasp of his tongue, the gentle graze of his teeth making her pant with longing.

Elodie worked blindly on the waistband of his trousers, desperate to get her hands on him, but he was too intent on pleasuring her. He pushed her back on the desk, pulling her knickers off her with one hand and tossing them to the floor. His mouth came down to her abdomen, his tongue tracing a light teasing circle around her belly button. Shivers coursed up and down her spine and a wave of tingling heat and tension found its way to her core.

His mouth moved down to the heart of her, his lips and tongue separating her folds, all too soon sending her into a freefall of mind-blowing, earth-shattering, dizzying release. She arched her spine, riding out the pulsating waves, unable to control her whimpering cries and panting breaths.

'Wow, oh, wow...' There were no words to describe the bliss still reverberating through her in delicious little aftershocks. But she finally sat upright and reached for him. 'My turn to render you speechless, I think. But we have to get you out of those trousers first.'

'That's easily fixed.'

Lincoln's gaze ran over her flushed features, his eyes smouldering, and he dropped his trousers and his underwear. He moved away briefly, to get a condom from the wallet in his trouser pocket, applying it and coming back to her.

She never got tired of looking at him naked. His lean, athletic build was wonderfully proportioned—toned muscles, broad shoulders, slim hips, long, strong legs.

Elodie slipped off the desk and pushed him down so his back was against it. She slithered down in front of him, caressing him with her hands first, enjoying the guttural sounds of his pleasure. Then she placed her mouth on him, using her lips and tongue to bring him to the point of no return. He shuddered and groaned and swore under her ministrations, his body finally going slack as the last wave of release flowed through him.

'You really know how to bring me to my knees...' His voice was rough around the edges, his breathing hectic. 'I'm not sure I can stand upright just yet.'

Elodie came up to stroke her hands over his muscular chest. 'My legs are still shaking too.'

He cupped one side of her face in his hand, his eyes holding hers with glittering intensity. 'We'd better not make Morag wait too long to serve dinner, but first I want to do this.'

He brought his mouth down to hers in a long, slow kiss that drugged her senses all over again. It was passionate, and yet surprisingly tender, a kiss that stirred her emotions and fuelled her hopes.

Was it crazy to hope he was becoming as invested in their relationship as she was? Was she a fool for hoping he was moving past the bitterness he had carried against for her the last seven years?

CHAPTER ELEVEN

A COUPLE OF days before they were due to attend Elspeth and Mack's wedding in the Highlands of Scotland, Lincoln informed Elodie over breakfast that they would have to travel separately, due to an urgent work issue that had cropped up.

Elodie put her cup of tea down and frowned. 'But what if you get held up? We're supposed to be there together. Won't it look odd if we're not?'

'I'll get there—don't worry.' He buttered his toast with a brisk scrape of his knife, the scratching sound loud in the silence. A frown was carved into his forehead, his eyes narrowed in concentration.

'Will you find it…triggering? I mean, being at a traditional wedding?'

He put his knife down with a little clatter against his plate. 'I've been to a few since—so, no, I won't be triggered.' He arched one dark brow and added, 'Will you?'

She bit her lip and picked up her cup again, cradling it in her hands. 'I'm trying not to think about it…'

'How's that working for you?'

'Not well. I feel sick already.'

It was true. She had woken up for the last three days with grumbling nausea, which she'd put down to the anxiety of attending a wedding so similar to her original one.

Lincoln sighed and reached for her hand across the table. 'What's worrying you specifically?'

She shrugged and lowered her cup to the table again. 'I don't want to spoil Elspeth and Mack's special day by drawing any attention to myself. You know what the press are like.'

'Is it because you'll be seeing Fraser MacDiarmid there?'

Elodie grimaced. 'That and other things.'

'What other things?'

She whooshed out a sigh. 'I'm sorry… I'm probably overthinking it all.'

He squeezed her hand, his concerned gaze focussed on hers. 'Sweetheart, talk to me. What is it about attending the wedding that worries you the most?'

Elodie blinked back the sting of sudden tears. Along with the nausea, her emotions were all over the place lately. 'I don't know…it's just the thought of getting ready with Elspeth and the other bridesmaids. It makes me… unsettled. I keep thinking about *our* wedding day—how I suppressed my doubts and fears all the way through the preparations. I sat there with Elspeth and the other girls, pretending to be the blissfully happy bride…'

She gulped and then continued.

'I didn't realise I was going to do a no-show until I was a block away from the church. And then I—I panicked. Like a full-on panic attack. I couldn't breathe, I was shaking, sweating, nauseous. I felt an overwhelming need to get away as quickly as I could. On one level I guess I knew the scandal and hurt it would cause, but right then and there I didn't care. I had to get away.'

Lincoln's hand was stroking hers in a soothing fashion. 'Listen to me.' His tone was as calming and stabilising as his touch. 'I'll be with you at Elspeth and Mack's wedding. I'll reschedule my meeting for next week so we can travel together. I'll help you get through it, every step of the way.'

Elodie met his gaze with her watery one. 'I'm sorry for what I did to you back then. I'm sorry I wasn't mature enough to recognise what I felt until it was too late.'

Lincoln gave a wry smile and squeezed her hand once more. 'It's in the past. We need to move on from it.'

But had he truly moved on? This six-month marriage deal was hardly what anyone could call a moving-on plan. He had once promised her so much more and she had thrown it away. He wasn't offering her a second chance. Their relationship was an interim thing to help comfort his biological mother in her final months of life.

And even though they were only a month into their marriage, Elodie could hear the clock ticking. Loudly.

'Oh, you look so beautiful,' Elodie said, standing in front of her twin the day of the wedding. 'And I don't think I've ever seen you look so happy. You're positively glowing.'

Elspeth grasped one of Elodie's hands in excitement. 'I'm so happy I could burst.' Then her expression sobered. 'But how are *you*? You don't seem yourself at all. And you haven't touched your glass of champagne.'

Elodie adjusted the right sleeve of her twin's wedding gown. 'I'm fine.' She gave a tight little smile. 'Just a little nervous.'

'Because of seeing Fraser? Don't be. He's done some work on himself and is quite pleasant to be around these days.'

'I'm glad to hear it but, no, it's not about him.'

Elspeth peered at her a little more closely. 'How are things with Lincoln?'

'Fine.'

'Just "fine"?'

Elodie drew in a skittering breath. Even the mention of his name was enough to get her heart racing. He had been so tender and attentive on their journey to Scotland, no one would ever think they were not the real deal, that their marriage was a temporary arrangement.

'He's wonderful.' She sighed and continued, 'So wonderful I keep having to remind myself we're only staying together another few months.'

'You want more?'

Elodie smoothed her hands down her own beautiful dress and sighed. 'Yes, well…haven't I always wanted more? More than he's prepared to give me, that is. Sometimes I think he's developing stronger feelings for me, but what if I'm wrong? It's not exactly something I can ask him. *Hey, honey, do you love me?* I'm not sure that's going to go down well, given the terms he insisted on for our marriage.'

Elspeth grasped both of Elodie's hands. 'I've always thought Lincoln has strong feelings for you. But I don't like to offer you false hope in case I'm wrong. All I can say is be patient with him. Some men take a while to recognise their own feelings.'

Would six months be long enough? Or would she end up bitterly disappointed in the end?

Elodie gave a rueful smile. 'I'd give you a hug, but I don't want to crush your dress.'

Elspeth pulled her into a big squishy hug regardless. 'Love you.'

'Love you back.' Elodie pulled away to look at her twin. 'Are you disappointed Dad isn't here to give you away?'

'Not really. My days of being disappointed by Dad are well and truly over. Besides, I have all I need in terms of love from Mack. And I really like Mum's partner, Jim. He's stable and reliable and so supportive of her.'

Elodie couldn't help thinking she was the only one in her family without the security of knowing her partner truly loved her.

But her twin was convinced Lincoln had done so once.

If so, could he do it again?

Lincoln wasn't part of the bridal party, so he took a seat along with the other guests in the local kirk. It being late autumn, the bridal couple had decided against a garden wedding at Mack's ancestral home, Crannochbrae, but the reception would be held there in the castle. It was also where Lincoln and Elodie were staying, along with other members of the bridal party and close family.

He hadn't seen much of Elodie since they'd arrived, as she was busy helping her twin prepare for her big day. But nothing could have prepared him for seeing her walk down the aisle as the first of the three bridesmaids. He stood along with the other guests, watching her take each step towards the front of the church.

He had said he wouldn't be triggered, but how could he not be? He remembered all too well the air of expectation that day seven years ago. And then the flicker of unease when the time had kept creeping past. He remembered the increasing murmurs of the congregation, the worried glances towards the back of the cathedral. The glances that had then settled on him, standing at the front with his groomsmen. He remembered the slow crawl of humiliation travelling over his skin when he'd considered the possibility that Elodie wasn't coming.

He recalled the moment when someone at the back of the cathedral had been passed a note, and how he'd come towards him, taking so long it had felt like a decade before he'd got to him. He'd taken the note and looked at it blindly, for endless seconds. It had been from the driver who was supposed to have delivered Elodie to the cathedral, informing him that she had bolted.

Lincoln pulled himself out of the past to look at Elodie coming towards him now. Dressed in a close-fitting cobalt blue satin dress that hugged every delicious curve of her body, her face beautifully made up, her hair in a sophisticated updo that highlighted her aristocratic features and swan-like neck, she was carrying a posy of fresh flowers with long flowing ribbons the same colour as her dress.

She glanced at him with a tremulous smile and he smiled back, sending her a wink for good measure. A light blush stained her cheeks and she continued walking up the aisle. He drank in the back view of her before the next bridesmaid came past. And then he watched as the bride came past, so uncannily like Elodie that it triggered him all over again.

The ceremony began and Lincoln listened to the words, watching the rituals and traditions with an uneasy sensation in his gut. Not because he didn't think they were genuine or worthwhile, but because his recent marriage ceremony to Elodie couldn't have been more different.

Was she feeling the same? Were the heartfelt words and vows and promises and the devoted looks the bridal couple were exchanging making her feel a little short-changed?

But he had been up-front with her about what he expected of their marriage. It was for six months and six months only. One month had already passed. They had five months to go and then it would be over. They would both be free to move on with their lives.

And hopefully, by then, he'd be able to go to any number of weddings and not be triggered at all.

Elodie smiled her way through the official photos, and continued to smile and chat to the others in the bridal party, but all she could think about was how sterile and clinical her wedding to Lincoln had been a month before. Watching Elspeth and Mack gaze into each other's eyes with such devotion had made her ache with envy. If only Lincoln loved her the way she loved him. Had *always* loved him. But her love now was a more mature love— a love that had grown up, letting her recognise her own failings in their previous relationship and how she had to be aware of not falling into old patterns of behaviour.

As she was on the bridal table, she wasn't able to be with Lincoln until the formal part of the reception was over. Then he came over to her with a smile, holding out his hand to her. 'Dance with me?'

Elodie took his hand and joined him on the dance floor in a slow waltz. 'Has it been absolutely dreadful for you on the table with all my rowdy cousins?' she asked.

'Not at all. I had a great vantage point from there to watch you all night.'

'I noticed you looking at me a few times.'

More than a few times. It seemed every time she'd looked his way he'd been looking at her. But then, she'd had trouble keeping her eyes from drifting his way too.

His eyes glinted. 'How could I not notice the most beautiful woman in the room?'

Elodie gave a twisted smile. 'I'm not sure Mack would agree with you on that.' She sighed and, focussing her gaze on the neat knot of his tie, added, 'It was a lovely service. I had trouble controlling the urge to cry.'

Lincoln tipped up her chin with his hand, meshing his

gaze with hers. 'Are you disappointed that our wedding last month was the complete opposite?'

She stripped her features of all emotion. 'Why would I be? We agreed on the terms.'

He studied her for a long beat. 'All the same, I could have made it a little less sterile.' There was a note of regret in his tone and a small frown pulled at his brow.

'But we don't have the same kind of relationship as Els and Mack.'

'Perhaps not.' He gave an on-off smile that didn't have time to reach his eyes. 'But then are any two relationships the same? Take us, for instance. Our first relationship was different from what we have now.'

'Do you think so?'

He turned her away from another couple who were getting a little close, his hold warm and protective. 'We talk more now. We don't argue as much. And making love with you is even more exciting and satisfying.'

'Even without the arguments?'

He smiled and brought her right hand up to his mouth. 'I do kind of miss those arguments.'

Elodie gave a sheepish smile. 'Yes, well…we both have strong wills and seem to clash on just about everything.' Her smile faded and she continued with a tiny frown, 'Makes me wonder why we got together in the first place. Our relationship was totally based on lust. I'm not sure it's the best foundation for a lasting union.'

The hand resting on the small of her back pressed her a little closer to the hot, hard heat of his body. 'It's a damn good starting point, though.' He lowered his head so his breath mingled intimately with hers. 'How soon can we go upstairs?'

Desire licked at her with searing tongues of flame. 'Not until the bride and groom leave.'

'How long will that be?' There was an impatient groan in his voice, and he lowered his mouth closer to her.

Elodie smiled against his lips. 'Too long. But I'm sure, knowing you, it will be well and truly worth the wait.'

And it was.

Elodie woke the following morning with a dizzying wave of nausea. Lincoln was still asleep beside her, one of his arms lying across her body.

She swallowed back the rising bile in her throat and gently eased out of his relaxed hold. She got to her feet and walked carefully to the en suite bathroom, her stomach churning, her mouth dry, her fingertips tingling as if her blood pressure was dropping. She made it to the toilet in time to release the contents of her stomach, but unfortunately there was no way to do so without making a noise.

Lincoln opened the bathroom door and rushed over to her. 'Sweetheart, are you okay?'

Elodie groaned and shook her head. 'Go away. I'll be fine in a minute.'

He pulled her hair back from her face, then reached for a facecloth and handed it to her. 'You must've had too much to drink last night.'

'I didn't drink at all… I—I think it's a stomach virus. I've been feeling a little off for a couple of days.'

'Why didn't you tell me?'

Elodie stayed hunched over the toilet, not quite confident that her stomach was settled enough for her to move. 'Please, just leave me to deal with this. I don't need an audience right now.'

Lincoln flushed the toilet and then crouched down beside her, his expression full of concern. 'I'm not leaving you. What if you pass out and knock yourself out or something?' He put a hand to her forehead. 'You don't seem to have a temperature, but you're clammy.' He lowered his hand from her face and straightened to get another face-cloth, this time rinsing it under the tap first. He crouched back down beside her and handed it to her. 'Here.'

'Thanks…' Elodie dabbed at her face, then handed it back to him. 'I think I'll be okay now.'

'Here, let me help you up.' Lincoln took her gently by the shoulders and guided her to a standing position. 'Do you feel up to having a shower?'

'Yes… I think so.'

'I'll stay with you.'

Elodie would have argued the point, but she was still feeling a little light-headed. Or maybe that was because he was naked and looking as gorgeously sexy as ever. She brushed her teeth and rinsed, relieved the bout of hideous nausea had passed.

Lincoln turned the shower on for her and helped her in.

'Aren't you going to join me?' she asked.

'Only to help you shower. Nothing else.'

He stepped under the spray of water with her, making sure not to take the bulk of the flow away from her. He shampooed her hair, gently massaging her scalp, then rinsed it and applied conditioner before repeating the massage. She was very conscious of his lean, athletic body so close to hers, wet and naked…and aroused.

'That feels divine…' She sighed and turned so she was facing him. Her hands settled on his slim hips and she moved closer to the jut of his erection. 'So does that…'

Lincoln placed his hands on her shoulders. 'I didn't get in the shower to have sex with you. You're not feeling well.'

'But I'm fine now.' Elodie pressed herself against him and he groaned. 'And you want me.'

'I can wait. I want to make sure you're feeling a hundred percent first.' He placed a soft-as-air kiss on the top of her damp shoulder.

Elodie stroked her hands down his chest, her heart skipping a beat at the tender look in his eyes. 'Thanks for making me feel better.'

He brushed her lips with his. 'Glad to be of help.' He turned off the shower and stepped out, picking up one of the bath sheets from the towel rail and holding it out for her. 'Come here and let me dry you.'

Elodie stepped into the warm folds of the towel and he proceeded to dry her. It was a thing he had never done, and it shifted something in their relationship. She had never allowed herself to be so vulnerable before. Seven years ago she would never have allowed him to see her hunched over a toilet bowl being sick, or bent double with period pain...

Period pain.

An invisible hammer swung against her heart, knocking it sideways in her chest. When was the last time she'd had a period?

She gave a jolt and Lincoln looked up from drying her feet.

'Sorry, was I too rough?'

Elodie stared down at him, kneeling at her feet, her mind whirling with dawning realisation. The nausea. The dizziness. The light-headedness. The sudden aversion to things she usually enjoyed, like champagne.

She swallowed and somehow got her voice to work. 'No...no... I was just getting a little cold.' She was, in fact, now shivering. Shivering with alarm. Panic. Despair.

How could she be pregnant? They had used condoms every time. Lincoln was pedantic about safety—it was something she admired about him. He would never intentionally put her or indeed any of his partners at risk.

Lincoln straightened and wrapped her in a fresh towel, warm from the towel rail. 'Go back to bed for a while. I can change our flights to London to a later time.'

'No, it's okay. I want to get back to work tomorrow.'

And get her hands on a pregnancy test as soon as possible.

CHAPTER TWELVE

LINCOLN WAS AWARE of Elodie's silence on the way back to London. She kept assuring him she was feeling fine, but he wasn't so sure. In the past, he would have been fooled by her assurances, but this time he wasn't. She still looked pale, and she was huddled into herself as if she was in pain.

He knew from experience that a stomach virus could knock you sideways, leaving you listless and wan for days... He put his arm around her on the way to the car once they had landed in London. 'I think we should get you to a doctor for a check-up, just to make sure you're okay.'

Elodie pulled out of his embrace with a jerk that caught him off-guard. 'Will you stop fussing? I told you I'm fine. I'm just tired from all the travelling.'

Her tone was sharp and impatient, but her expression didn't match. There was a nervous flicker in her eyes and she didn't seem to want to meet his gaze at all.

He decided against pressuring her. That was another thing he knew from experience—she didn't take kindly to being told what to do.

The journey was mostly silent on the way to his house, but a few blocks before they got home Elodie asked if he would mind stopping while she picked up something at the local pharmacy.

'What do you need?'

'Just…female stuff.' Her voice was little more than a mumble.

For a young woman who had spent years parading on catwalks in the skimpiest underwear and swimwear, Elodie could be surprising prudish about her monthly period.

Lincoln pulled into the next available parking space and turned off the engine. 'Do you want me to go in for you?'

She reared back, as if he had suggested he walk into the pharmacy buck naked. 'No. I'll go. I won't be long.'

She scurried out of the car before he could open the door for her and shut it behind her.

Lincoln waited on the footpath, holding the door open for her when she returned a couple of minutes later. She was carrying a paper bag in her hand and her head was down, her cheeks filled with more colour than he had seen in them for hours. She slipped into the seat and flashed him a *thank you* smile that didn't make the full distance to her eyes.

Lincoln resumed the driver's seat and continued on the journey home. He parked outside his house and turned off the engine. 'I guess I should be feeling relieved you need those.' He glanced at the package she was holding.

'What?' She looked at him blankly, her forehead still knitted with a frown.

'Tampons and pads.'

'Oh…right…yes…'

He flicked her another glance, but she was looking out of the side window. 'Elodie?'

'What?'

Her voice was little more than a croak, and she still didn't look his way. But he noticed how tight her grip was on the package she was holding—the paper bag was crackling as if she was crushing crisps.

'You don't have to be shy about having your period. I did grow up with a sister, you know.'

The paper bag went silent and she turned to look at him. 'I'm not having my period.'

There was a strange quality to her voice…an empty, hollow sound that sent a ghostly shiver across the back of his neck.

'This is a pregnancy test.'

Lincoln stared at her with his mouth open, his heart beating like a drum set on some weird staccato rhythm. He could barely think about having a baby without a wave of panic coursing through him. He was to be a *father*?

He hadn't considered the possibility for years. Seven years, in fact. He had once wanted a family like the one he had grown up in, but Elodie jilting him had made him reset his goals. When she hadn't shown up at the church that day, everything had changed for him. He hadn't been able to imagine wanting a family with anyone else. He had taught himself to be content with the thought of being an uncle to his siblings' children rather than long for a dream he had lost and couldn't get back.

But if Elodie was carrying his child…

'You think you might be *pregnant*?'

'I'm not sure…' She swallowed and continued, 'I've got some symptoms. I've had some bouts of nausea and I'm late.'

'How late?'

'A few days…almost a week.'

Lincoln looked at the package in her hands. 'We'd better go in and do the test. The sooner we know, the sooner we can plan what to do.'

He got out of the car and came around to her side, opening the door for her. She alighted from the car and looked up at him with a frown.

'What do you mean "plan"?'

He closed the door with a snap and took her by the elbow. 'A pregnancy would change everything. We'd have to shift the goalposts on our marriage. We'd have to take out the six-months clause and make it permanent.'

Elodie tugged out of his hold. 'Will you stop railroading me, for God's sake? I don't even know if I'm pregnant. We've been using condoms all the time.'

There was a beat or two of silence. Lincoln could hear his heart thumping and his stomach dropped. 'Is there a possibility it's someone else's?'

Her face blanched of colour and she pushed past him to go to the front door. Lincoln let out a curse and followed her. He opened the door and she stalked inside and made her way straight up the stairs.

'Elodie, you know I had to ask you that, right?' Even to his ears, his voice sounded hoarse.

She turned on the fourth stair to look at him. 'I know you did, but can we just wait until we see what the test says?'

'Sure.' He scraped a hand through his hair and sighed so heavily he was surprised the draught of his breath didn't knock over the hall table.

Elodie ran the rest of the way up the stairs to the nearest bathroom, closing and locking the door behind her. She stared at the package in her hand, her heart hammering as if she'd run up five flights of stairs instead of just one.

She ripped open the bag and the packaging and quickly read the instructions. She performed the test as outlined and waited for the result.

The first minute ticked by with agonising slowness, intensifying her distress.

If she was pregnant, Lincoln would want to stay married to her because of the baby—not because of her. Not because he loved *her*, but because he wanted his baby to have an active and involved father.

The second minute ticked past and her heart rate sped up.

She stared at the wand in her hand, not sure what she wanted to see.

The ambiguity of her feelings shocked her. She had thought she wasn't the maternal type; her biological clock hadn't made a sound—ever. But now, as she waited for the lines to appear, she thought about the possibility of a baby. Lincoln's baby.

The third minute passed, and then the fourth.

Elodie was trying to keep the wand steady enough to read it. The instructions had said to give the test a good window of time—five to ten minutes at least. She didn't know how to deal with the suspense. Everything depended on the results of the test.

Finally, ten minutes passed and she held the wand up to the light. *Negative.* She waited another minute, her heart so tight in her chest she could barely take a breath. A wave of disappointment ambushed her. She wasn't carrying Lincoln's baby. There was no pregnancy. No need to change the terms of their marriage.

No need for her to stay with him…unless he loved her.

Elodie put the packaging in the bin but kept the wand, knowing Lincoln would insist on seeing it for himself. She didn't have to call him upstairs for he was waiting outside the bathroom door, with an unreadable expression on his face.

'How did it go?' His voice held no trace of worry, anxiety or fear.

'It's negative.' She showed him the wand.

He peered at it, his brow furrowed. 'Are you sure?'

'I gave it more than ample time to develop. It's negative. I'm not pregnant.'

He met her gaze. 'Are you relieved or disappointed?'

'To be honest, I'm a bit of both.'

She went back into the bathroom and put the wand in the bin. She washed her hands and gave herself a quick glance in the mirror, but it was like looking at a different person from the one she'd been just ten minutes ago.

The before-the-pregnancy-test Elodie had not been the earth mother type. A baby was something other people had. It wasn't on her radar. Her business was her baby. Her design label was still in its infancy. It hadn't had time to develop and grow and become successful.

But the post-negative-pregnancy-test Elodie wanted to carry Lincoln's baby in her womb, to give birth to it with him by her side, to raise it with him in a household full of love. But wasn't that little more than a foolish dream?

Lincoln was still standing outside the bathroom when she came out again. 'I think we need to talk.'

Elodie gave him a stiff smile. 'Yes, we do.' She let out a long breath and met his gaze once more. 'Why did you offer to make our marriage permanent if I was pregnant?'

'Because it would have been the right thing to do. I want any child of mine to have my name, and to bring it up like I was brought up—in a loving home. Even if the baby hadn't been mine, I would still have married you to give it a loving home.'

'But ours wouldn't be a loving home, would it? I mean, we would love our child, but what about each other?'

Lincoln's throat moved up and down. 'You have feelings for me, don't you?'

'It's not my feelings I'm most worried about. It's yours.'

'You know I care about you.'

'But you're not in love with me. Not now, and not seven years ago. So we've basically come full circle.'

There was a thick beat of silence.

Lincoln set his jaw. 'What do you mean by that? We have an agreement. There's a lot riding on it. Nina, your label, the funds I've put up for you... We have five months left.'

'For me to do what? Make passionate love with you but never hear you say the words I most want to hear? I want someone to love me—not for how I look or how good I am in bed or whether I'm pregnant or not. *Me*.' She banged her hand against her chest for emphasis. 'Me, with all my faults and foibles. That's what I want from you. But you can't or won't give it to me.'

He scraped a hand through his hair, his eyes flicking away from hers before coming back with glittering intensity. 'Are you saying you're in love with me?'

'Don't look so surprised!' Elodie gave a cynical laugh that was nowhere in the vicinity of humour. 'You make it so damn hard *not* to fall in love with you. But it's not enough for me to stay with you. I'm not wasting another five months of my life waiting for you to feel something for me other than physical attraction. That makes you no different from thousands, probably millions of other men out there who feel the same way about me.'

She dropped her shoulders on a sigh and then went on.

'I get it—I really do. You have bonding issues that probably go way back to infancy. You were adopted—and, while it was a good adoption, you still carry the wound of being relinquished at birth, even if it's only on a subconscious level. You don't let people get close to you. You don't let them in. You don't show your vulnerability.'

Lincoln's features were set in stone. 'If you leave, the deal is off. I'll withdraw my financial support for your label.'

Elodie brushed past him to go back to the master bedroom and collect her things. 'Do it. See if I care. I'll find someone else.'

'Where are you going? Talk to me, for God's sake.'

She swung around to face him. 'Tell me what you're feeling right now.'

He frowned so hard his eyebrows met above the bridge of his nose. 'I'm angry you're running away again without talking this through. You're acting like a spoilt child.'

'I'm not being childish this time. Last time I was running away from myself more than I was running away from you. I couldn't even face up to the truth about myself back then, so how could I tell you? But I'm telling you now. I can't be with you because we don't want the same things out of life. You essentially want a six-month fling with me. Do you think I can't hear the clock ticking on our relationship? You put timelines on all your relationships because every woman you've cared about has left you. Your birth mother…your adoptive mother. And it's why you won't let your housekeeper go in spite of her appalling behaviour towards me in the past.'

'We can extend the time. I'm fine with that. We can keep it open and—'

'And what? A year on, two years or more, I'll still be waiting for you to fall in love with me. I'm not doing it, Lincoln. I want out. The pregnancy scare has jolted me into reality. *My* reality. Which is that I deserve to be loved for me. Just me.'

'Is this because I asked if the baby was mine?'

'No. You had an absolute right to ask that question under the circumstances. The press have made me out to be a female version of a playboy.' She sighed again, and added, 'I've spent years of my life pretending I don't care what people think of me, but deep down I do care. I've always cared. But I've buried those feelings so deep down they come out in other ways—such as in stupid and impulsive behaviour.'

'I don't want you to leave.' There was a raw quality to his voice. 'Stay a little longer. You might see things differently once you've got over the shock of thinking you were pregnant.'

Elodie went up to him and placed a hand on his lean jaw. 'Here's the thing that's shocking. A part of me wanted to be pregnant.'

He blinked a couple of times, his Adam's apple rising and falling. 'Then you can get pregnant. We'll stop using condoms and—'

She placed her finger over his lips, blocking the rest of his speech. 'No. Listen to me. I've worked so hard to form my own label. It's almost within my grasp and I can't let anything stop me now. If I have a baby with someone it will be in a couple of years, not now.' She lowered her hand from his face and stepped back with a sad smile. 'It's time for me to leave. I know you don't want things to end this way, but I think it's for the best. Please send my best wishes to Nina. I'll pop a letter in the post for her.'

'This is crazy, Elodie. You're not thinking clearly and—'

'It's not just about the pregnancy scare. Elspeth and Mack's wedding really got to me as well. I'm so envious of what they have together. I fooled myself into thinking we could be like them, but it's not possible. I see that now. And I saw it seven years ago.'

'I suppose I should be grateful for the luxury of watching you pack up and leave this time.' The stinging sarcasm in his tone was unmistakable.

'You can watch me if you like. But I'd like us to part on better terms.' She took another few steps towards the bedroom before stopping and turning around again. She took off her wedding and engagement rings and handed them to him. 'Here—just in case anything goes astray again.'

He didn't even glance at the rings. 'I don't want them.'

Elodie closed her fingers over the rings. 'I'll leave them on the hall table, like last time.'

But he had already turned and walked away, and she didn't know if he had heard her or not.

Even if Lincoln hadn't heard the sounds of Elodie leaving his house, he knew he would have sensed the exact moment she'd gone. The house was different without her. The energy, the atmosphere faded away to a bland nothingness.

He considered moving to another bedroom, so he didn't have to be reminded of her, or going to a hotel for a while. He didn't want to smell the lingering trace of her perfume or picture her lying in his bed with her red-gold hair spread all over the pillow. To be tortured by every memory of their month together living as man and wife.

To say he was blindsided was an understatement, but the pregnancy scare had thrown him right out of kilter. He still couldn't get his still spinning head wrapped around the negative result. He'd got himself so worked up, so focussed on doing the right thing by Elodie and the baby, it had taken him a while to realise there was no baby.

But it wasn't only the pregnancy scare that had thrown him. He hadn't been expecting her to walk out—not before their time was up. He was the one who was supposed to call time on their relationship, not her.

There was no way of keeping Elodie married to him unless he said the words she wanted to hear. His feelings for her were complex, and messy, and he didn't like thinking too deeply about them. They got him tied up in knots—gnarly knots that pulled on his organs to the point of pain. She made him feel out of control—not just in terms of passion but in terms of vulnerability.

To openly confess to loving someone you had to accept that they could hurt you, leave you, sabotage you... humiliate you. And hadn't Elodie done all that? He had spent the last seven years trying to block every thought of her from his mind. She fancied herself in love with him, but how could he be sure it wasn't just because of the financial help he had given her for her label? A gift of money had a way of triggering all sorts of strong feelings.

He walked past the hall table and saw her wedding and engagement rings lying there. He picked them up, staring at them for a long moment.

How could one woman wreak such havoc in his life? What gave her the power to make his gut churn at the thought of never seeing her again? Or, worse, seeing her with someone else? Someone else who would father her future baby. The baby she'd decided she wanted in the not too distant future.

He tossed the rings back on the table and turned away. Maybe a month in a hotel would be a good idea.

A hotel a long way from London.

Elodie didn't want to spoil her twin's honeymoon, so left it another week before she called her about her breakup with Lincoln.

Elspeth was sympathetic and understanding of Elodie's decision to leave, and offered whatever support she needed.

'Have you seen or talked to him since?'

'No. I think it's best not to. A clean break is better.'

'I guess so…' There was more than a speck of doubt in Elspeth's tone.

'I *know* so,' Elodie said with conviction. 'He's never really forgiven me for leaving him the first time. I'm annoyed at myself for even considering it might work between us. What was I thinking? I should've had better sense. He didn't love me before. He doesn't love me now. I have to accept he's never going to.'

And the sooner she got on with her life without him, the better.

Lincoln came back to his London house after a month of working in New York. Well, trying to work… He'd come down with the same stomach virus Elodie had had in Scotland and it had only intensified his misery.

Like the last time Elodie had left, he'd given his housekeeper strict instructions to remove every trace of her from the house while he was away. But he'd more or less given up trying not to think about her. She was in his thoughts day and night, torturing him with memories of her touch, her smile, her playfulness. And coming home made it even worse.

His house was so empty without her. His life was so empty without her.

His coping strategy in life was always to keep busy. He worked hard, played hard. He didn't have time for soft and fuzzy emotions. They didn't belong in his world of tough decision-making, wheeling and dealing and keeping an eye out for the next big challenge.

Elodie was the biggest challenge of his life and he had let her go.

He had lost her not once, but twice.

Lincoln wanted Elodie back and he hated himself for it.

He should have moved on by now. He should have moved on seven years ago. But he was stuck on her.

He would have to get unstuck soon, or he would be living the rest of his life as a monk. The thought of sleeping with anyone else made his stomach churn. He hadn't even looked at another woman while he was in New York. No one had turned his head or stopped his heart. The busiest city in the world hadn't held its usual appeal. He hadn't even enjoyed the deals he'd set up—in fact, the whole time he'd been bored. Empty and unfulfilled.

He wanted *her*. Only her.

Elodie was his nemesis—the one person who could make him feel things he had never wanted to feel for anyone. Was that love? Did he have this empty, aching feeling in his chest because he loved her and wanted her back so badly he couldn't think straight?

He still loved her.

Acknowledging the truth of those words was like suddenly remembering a language he had taught himself not to speak for years. But now he wanted to shout the words out loud.

I love her. I love her. I love her.

Morag appeared from the kitchen to greet him. 'How was your trip?'

'Awful.'

'I'm sorry…' Her gaze slipped away from his. 'Have you heard from Elodie?'

'No.'

Even hearing her name twisted a knife into his gut. What if she didn't believe him when he went to see her? He hadn't exactly given her a reason to harbour any hope that he might change his mind. The thing was, he *hadn't* changed his mind. His mind had finally revealed to him what he had been hiding from all these years.

He. Loved. Her.

'There's something I need to tell you about the last time Elodie left,' Morag said. 'I'm afraid you're not going to like hearing it.'

Lincoln frowned. 'Go on.'

Morag twisted her hands in front of her apron. 'She was telling the truth when she told you she left her engagement ring on the hall table. I found it.'

'Where is it now?'

Morag took something out of the pocket on the front of her apron and handed it to him. He stared at the ring box, his mind whirling. He hadn't believed Elodie about the ring. He had always thought she'd sold it and used the money to launch her career. He'd been so blind and prejudiced against her... Had he ever truly listened to her? Understood her? Believed in her?

He had kept her at arm's length, determined not to let her see how much he needed her, how much he loved her. How much it frightened and terrified him to love her, to openly admit it, to own it and say it out loud. He had always blamed Elodie for leaving him—but he had left first. In fact, he hadn't been there emotionally in the first place. Not totally, not unreservedly.

He looked back at his housekeeper. 'Why didn't you tell me she'd left it seven years ago?'

'I tried to, but you came back roaring drunk the night after she jilted you and you refused to have her name even mentioned in your presence. You told me to remove everything of hers from the house, just as you did this time.'

Lincoln could recall most of that conversation—most, but not all. Which wasn't something that made him particularly proud. 'Why didn't you tell me when I was in a better state of mind?'

'I thought about it that night, and the next day while you were sleeping off your hangover. I thought if I told you she'd left it behind you might go and find her, talk her into coming back to you.' Morag gulped back a broken sound. 'I didn't think she loved you, so I didn't tell you. But I was wrong. She did—she does. I think she always will.'

Lincoln's heart leapt right up to his throat. Could it be possible Elodie truly loved him? That it wasn't too late to undo the damage of his past mistakes and miscommunications? She had more to forgive of him than he ever had for her. Dared he hope she would find it in her heart to take him back?

'Does she know you have the ring?'

'She found it when she was looking for my insulin kit. She could've told you she'd found it that night, but she didn't. I think because she didn't want you to be hurt by my betrayal of your trust. And then, once I realised she knew, I begged her not to tell you. I shouldn't have asked her to do that for me. I'm worried it's contributed to your breakup.'

A rush of love and respect coursed through him for his beautiful Elodie. But she was no longer his—not unless he went to her and told her how he felt. How he had *always* felt.

'I need to see her. I was going anyway, so it has nothing to do with the ring.' He pocketed the ring and placed a hand on Morag's shoulder. 'You're not to blame for this. I am. I should've told her seven years ago what I felt for her.'

Morag's face lit up like a chandelier. 'You mean you love her?'

Lincoln smiled. 'You bet I do.'

Elodie was working late in her studio, doing some last touches on the collection of clothes she'd made for Nina. She had got Nina's measurements during a phone conversation with her, after she'd explained her reasons for leaving Lincoln. It had been a tough conversation to have—especially knowing of Nina's physical fragility—but Elodie had no longer been able to pretend. It was time to be honest about all things—most of all her feelings about the only man she had ever loved.

She was spreading out the last item of the collection on her work table when she caught sight of movement on the security camera covering the front door of the studio. She put the dress down and went closer to the security screen, her heart bouncing up and down in her chest like a yo-yo.

Lincoln was standing outside the studio, looking for a doorbell that didn't yet exist. His brow was furrowed and he kept reaching up to tug at his tie, as if it were choking him. He glanced up to the second floor, where she was working, but she wasn't near the window so he couldn't see her.

Elodie stepped away from the security camera and went over to the window. She unlocked it and opened it, bracing herself for an icy blast of the wintry night air. 'Lincoln?'

He looked up with relief flooding his features. 'I need to talk to you. Can I come up?'

His voice sounded rough around the edges, even from this height, and she could see the lines of strain and stress around his mouth.

'Sure. I'll unlock the front door.'

Elodie closed the window and went back over to the security panel, buzzed open the street door of the studio. The sound of Lincoln's firm tread coming up to her floor sent her heart thumping.

Was he here to pull the plug on her label? In spite of threatening to withdraw his support the night she'd left, he hadn't done any such thing. She hadn't been game to read too much into it, but she was grateful for the extra time to get her business up and running without having to seek another sponsor.

She was standing by her work table when he came in, looking windswept and tired and drained but as gorgeous to her as ever.

'I suppose you're here about the money?' She kept her voice calm and controlled. No mixing emotions and business, right? That was her motto, taken straight from his hard-nosed businessman's playbook.

Lincoln came over to her and took her hands in his. 'I have never said this to anyone before, so hear me out. I love you. I've missed you so much—not just this last month but for the past seven years. I've filled my life with work and activity, but the one thing that was missing was you. I'm sorry it's taken me so long to realise what was there all the time. My love for you.'

Elodie stared at him in shock, her heart beating so hard and fast it was making her dizzy. 'You're not just saying it? You really love me?'

'I'm not just saying it. I'm feeling it in every part of my body. I ache for you. I feel incomplete without you in my life. Nothing fills the emptiness you left behind. You're my centre, my anchor, my one true love, and I beg you to come back to me and be my wife. And one day even the mother of my children, if that's what you want.'

Elodie stared at him for a moment, struck dumb by his emotional openness. He had never shown her his heart, never opened it fully to her the way he was doing now. He had always kept a bit of himself back, and it had made it hard for her to believe he would ever toss away his armour and let her in.

She threw her arms around his neck and squealed for joy. 'Oh, Lincoln, darling, of course I will. I love you so much. I've been so sad about leaving you, but I convinced myself you could never allow yourself to love me. But hearing you say it…it's just so wonderful. There are no words to describe how I feel right now, knowing you love me.'

Lincoln framed her face with his hands and gazed into her eyes. 'You were right about the way I conduct my relationships. It struck a chord when you said the loss of my biological mother at birth and then the sudden death of my adoptive mother had made me shut down the possibility of loving someone in a romantic sense. The threat of losing that kind of love was too daunting, too terrifying. I realise now I rushed our first relationship. I didn't give you time or your own space for growth within it. No wonder you ran away. But I promise not to do it this time. We'll be true equals, working together on everything. I want you by my side for the rest of my life.'

Elodie rose up on tiptoe to kiss him. 'I want you by my side too. You are the only man I've ever loved. I truly was dreading going on with my life without you. I was considering a life of celibacy. I couldn't bear the thought of anyone else touching me.'

Lincoln gathered her close, hugging her so tightly it almost took her breath away. 'I'm the same. I spent a month in New York thinking only of you. I ached for you every night and every morning.' There was a catch in his voice and then he continued, 'I have another apology to make.' He released her a little so he could meet her gaze once more. 'I'm sorry I didn't believe you about the engagement ring.'

Elodie's eyes rounded to the size of baubles. 'Morag told you?'

He gave a grim nod. 'Yes—although I blame myself for the way I insisted on her removing everything of yours from the house. I even cut her off when she tried to tell me a couple of times, refusing to allow her to say your name in my presence. But the thing I find so touching is that you didn't betray what she'd done to me once you found out.'

'You're not going to fire her, are you?'

'Only if you want me to.'

'No, I don't. I think she got it wrong, but she did what she thought was best for you. She didn't realise I loved you back then. She thought I was a star-struck gold-digger. And her keeping the ring hidden from you more or less proved it to you.'

Lincoln gave a rueful twist of his mouth. 'The thing is, I think on some level I never believed you loved me. I'm ashamed to say I quite liked you being a little star-struck and infatuated with me. It fed my ego and allowed me to railroad you into marriage. But of course, that didn't go to plan. And I'm glad now that it didn't. I think we both needed time to let go of our baggage and come back to each other as fully mature adults who want to spend the rest of their lives together.'

Elodie smiled and tenderly stroked his jaw. 'I promise to always be little star-struck by you if you promise to be star-struck by me.'

'I'll let you in on a little secret—I've always been a little star-struck by you.'

And he covered her mouth in a kiss that left her in no doubt of his enduring love and adoration.

EPILOGUE

Eighteen months later...

ELODIE LOOKED AT Lincoln, talking to Nina in the garden of their London home. He was smiling at something his mother said, and Nina's face was shining with love and happiness and, yes, even good health.

Nina's cancer had gone into remission, and so far things were tracking well. It was a miracle—one they were all so very grateful for. Elodie had grown increasingly close to Lincoln's biological mother, and had found Nina's support during her rising career as a designer invaluable. Her first show had been a phenomenal success, and she was feeling more fulfilled than she had ever dreamed possible.

And speaking of miracles...

Elodie's gaze drifted to her twin Elspeth, sitting beside her devoted husband, Mack, each of them holding in their arms a cute-as-a-button baby girl—identical twins called Maisie and Mackenzie. The besotted love on the new parents' faces said it all, and no one could have been happier for them than Elodie—especially since she and Lincoln had their own special news to share.

Lincoln came over to her and slipped an arm around her waist. 'Shall we tell them now, my love?'

'Oh, my God, you're pregnant?' Elspeth cried out in

delighted joy. 'I just *knew* you were keeping a secret from me.'

Elodie's smile almost split her face in two. 'Yes—ten weeks. We wanted to wait until we were a little further along, but my tummy is already about to pop the zip on my jeans.'

Lincoln stroked a loving hand down the back of her head. 'We're expecting twins. Too early to know the sex.'

Nina didn't bother hiding the tracks of the tears pouring down her face. 'Oh, my darlings…you've made me the happiest person alive.'

Lincoln smiled down at Elodie, his expression so full of love it made her heart flutter. 'Our babies couldn't wish for a more beautiful and loving mother. And I couldn't wish for a more beautiful and loving wife.'

Elodie blinked back tears and grasped his hand, held it against her cheek. 'I love you.'

He bent down and placed a soft kiss to her lips. 'I love you too. Before, now and for ever.'

* * * * *

COMING SOON!

We really hope you enjoyed reading this book.
If you're looking for more romance, be sure to
head to the shops when new books are
available on

Thursday 23ʳᵈ December

MILLS & BOON

Coming next month

ONE SNOWBOUND NEW YEAR'S NIGHT
Dani Collins

Van slid the door open and stepped inside only to have Becca squeak and dance her feet, nearly dropping the groceries.

"You knew I was here," he insisted. "That's why I woke you, so you would know I was here and you wouldn't do that. I *live* here," he said for the millionth time, because she'd always been leaping and screaming when he came around a corner.

"Did you? I never noticed," she grumbled, setting the bag on the island and taking out the milk to put it in the fridge. "I was alone here so often, I forgot I was married."

"*I* noticed that," he shot back with equal sarcasm.

They glared at each other. The civility they'd conjured in those first minutes upstairs was completely abandoned—probably because the sexual awareness they'd reawakened was still hissing and weaving like a basket of cobras between them, threatening to strike again.

Becca looked away first, thrusting the eggs into the fridge along with the pair of rib eye steaks and the package of bacon.

She hated to be called cute and hated to be ogled, so Van tried not to do either, but *come on*. She was curvy and sleepy and wearing that cashmere like a second skin. She was shorter than average and had always exercised in a very haphazard fashion, but nature had gifted her with a delightfully feminine figure-eight symmetry. Her ample breasts were high and firm over a narrow waist, then her hips flared into a gorgeous, equally firm and round ass. Her fine hair was a warm brown with sun-kissed tints, her mouth wide, and her dark brown eyes positively soulful.

When she smiled, she had a pair of dimples that he suddenly realized he hadn't seen in far too long.

"I don't have to be here right now," she said, slipping the coffee into the cupboard. "If you're going skiing tomorrow, I can come back while you're out."

"We're ringing in the new year right here." He chucked his chin at the windows that climbed all the way to the peak of the vaulted ceiling. Beyond the glass, the frozen lake was impossible to see through the thick and steady flakes. A gray-blue dusk was closing in.

"You have four-wheel drive, don't you?" Her hair bobbled in its knot, starting to fall as she snapped her head around. She fixed her hair as she looked back at him, arms moving with the mysterious grace of a spider spinning her web. "How did you get here?"

"Weather reports don't apply to me," he replied with self-deprecation. "Gravity got me down the driveway and I won't get back up until I can start the quad and attach the plow blade." He scratched beneath his chin, noted her betrayed glare at the windows.

Believe me, sweetheart. I'm not any happier than you are.

He thought it, but immediately wondered if he was being completely honest with himself.

"How was the road?" She fetched her phone from her purse, distracting him as she sashayed back from where it hung under her coat. "I caught a rideshare to the top of the driveway and walked down. I can meet one at the top to get back to my hotel."

"Plows will be busy doing the main roads. And it's New Year's Eve," he reminded her.

"So what am I supposed to do? Stay here? All night? With *you*?"

"Happy New Year," he said with a mocking smile.

Continue reading
ONE SNOWBOUND NEW YEAR'S NIGHT
Dani Collins

Available next month
www.millsandboon.co.uk

MILLS & BOON
Desire

Indulge in secrets and scandal, intense drama and plenty of sizzling hot action with powerful and passionate heroes who have it all: wealth, status, good looks…everything but the right woman.

MILLS & BOON
MEDICAL
Pulse-Racing Passion

Set your pulse racing with dedicated, delectable doctors in the high-pressure world of medicine, where emotions run high and passion, comfort and love are the best medicine.

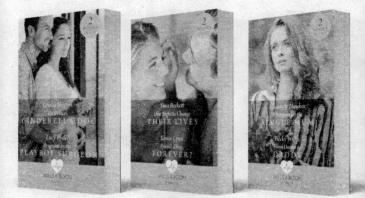